TRACKING TIME

Also by Leslie Glass
Stealing Time
Judging Time

LESLIE GLASS

TRACKING TIME

A DUTTON BOOK

DUTTON
Published by the Penguin Group
Penguin Putnam Inc., 375 Hudson Street, New York, New York 10014, U.S.A.
Penguin Books Ltd, 27 Wrights Lane, London W8 5TZ, England
Penguin Books Australia Ltd, Ringwood, Victoria, Australia
Penguin Books Canada Ltd, 10 Alcorn Avenue, Toronto, Ontario, Canada M4V 3B2
Penguin Books (N.Z.) Ltd, 182–190 Wairau Road, Auckland 10, New Zealand

Penguin Books Ltd, Registered Offices: Harmondsworth, Middlesex, England

First published by Dutton, a member of Penguin Putnam Inc.

First Printing, October, 2000
10 9 8 7 6 5 4 3 2 1

 REGISTERED TRADEMARK—MARCA REGISTRADA

LIBRARY OF CONGRESS CATALOGING-IN-PUBLICATION DATA
Glass, Leslie.
   Tracking time / Leslie Glass.
      p. cm.
   ISBN 0-525-94469-9 (alk. paper)
   1. Woo, April (Fictitious character)—Fiction.   2. Policewomen—Fiction.
3. Missing persons—Fiction.   4. Parent and child—Fiction.
5. Chinese American women—Fiction.   6. New York (N.Y.)—Fiction.   I. Title.
   PS3557.L34 T73 2000
   813'.54—dc21
                    00-031428

Printed in the United States of America
Set in Transitional 521

PUBLISHER'S NOTE
This book is a work of fiction. Names, characters, places, and incidents are either the product of the author's imagination or are used fictitiously, and any resemblance to actual persons, living or dead, business establishments, events, or locales is entirely coincidental.

This book is printed on acid-free paper. ∞

For Peter

Happy families are all alike. Every unhappy family is unhappy in its own way.

—Leo Tolstoy, *Anna Karenina*

ACKNOWLEDGMENTS

The inspiration for *Tracking Time* came from many sources. The impact of the recent spate of children killers has affected every community in America. As in no other time in our history, children and adolescents have become a source of suspicion, a threat to the nation from inside the family itself. *Tracking Time* is a story about the devastating effects of parents losing touch with the inner lives and needs of their children.

I am grateful to Detective Al Sheppard, formerly of Major Case Squad, NYPD, for his input and insights, to Precinct Commander Captain James O'Neill for hosting me as Commander for a Day at the Central Park Precinct, to Commissioner Howard Safir and the Police Foundation for all the good they do for New York City. Thanks also to Thomas Shelby, dog trainer to my own dogs, Peanut and Rocky, and a SAR officer in the Rockland County Sheriff's Department, who taught me so much about dogs and tracking that I had to write about it. Any errors about tracking, police procedure, and New York City geography are mine alone.

In the *Time* series, I try to present a realistic portrayal of the life of a psychoanalyst a hundred years after the birth of psychoanalysis, at a time when psychoanalytic theory is the basis for all interactive therapy in the mental health field, has radically impacted the way we think in every area of our society, and yet is no longer considered relevant to psychiatric training and is not taught in most medical schools. My appreciation this year goes to the Psychoanalytic Institutes around the country, who are encouraging their members to widen their outreach with programs to help a broader population of parents, children, and schools address the climate of aggression, alienation, and violence that's having such a deadly effect on young people today.

Greatest thanks to Dr. Peter Dunn, medical director of the New York Psychoanalytic Institute Treatment Center, who has been a wonderful teacher and guide in my research for this book and who read every draft. Any errors in psychopathology are his alone.

Thanks to Louise Burke, Nancy Yost, Audrey LaFehr, and all the good people at Dutton and NAL, who work so hard to edit, produce, and sell the books.

Last, each of us on this earth is on a perilous hero's journey. My special kudos this year go to Alex and Lindsey, Jonathan and Tom.

TRACKING TIME

ONE

J UST BEFORE TWILIGHT on a balmy September New York evening, Dr. Maslow Atkins set out for a jog in Central Park and never came back. He calculated that he had just the right amount of time to run south along the path closest to Central Park West to Fifty-ninth Street and back. Dr. Atkins was a man of regular habits. He timed himself on each outing, knew his speeds and his muscles. And the denizens who claimed the park as their own knew them, too.

Like many compulsive runners, Maslow felt edgy when deprived of his exercise. That day he'd watched a silvery morning turn to angry afternoon thunderstorms, and he'd been preoccupied by the threat of possibly having to run in the rain. The nagging irritation caused the slightest dulling of his senses and, unthinking, the young psychiatrist made a blunder in his work.

Maslow Atkins, M.D., five foot six inches tall, slender build, strong features muted only slightly by the perpetual beginnings of a beard, straight medium-brown hair just long enough on top to occasionally break free of its crest and fall forward to tickle his brow. Not large or classically handsome, Maslow was most notable for his eyes, which were, in turn, light brown, dark brown, and green, depending on his mood and the color of his shirts. His eyes were the most arresting aspect of his person, piercingly sharp in all his humors.

At thirty-two Maslow was a man not quite finished. He was a fully licensed psychiatrist, but not yet a father, not married, and not even fully certified to practice his chosen subspecialty of psychoanalysis. Throughout the years of his training he had kept his head down and worked hard. Coming and going from his building every morning in his suits and ties, and every evening in his running clothes, with the water bottle hanging on his hip, he looked like one of the thousands of afflu- ent people of his age who flocked to New York City from all over the country and the world to build a career, to make a name for them- selves, and probably not go home again.

He could have been a banker, a doctor, a lawyer, an advertising ex- ecutive, a money manager. In any case, he had the appearance of a se- rious professional on the rise. In fact, Maslow was a thoughtful person eager to do some good in life. And he was not from somewhere else. He was a New Yorker, born and bred just across the park on the East Side. Park Avenue, to be exact. He'd been a city brat and thought he knew all the angles. As a doctor, his guiding principle was the physician's oath: First, do no harm. And his personal rules about his own conduct were so strict that he would not take a drink even in a social situation lest it make him stupid or spin him out of control.

All through the moody afternoon, he'd brooded about his patient Allegra. Her name was lovely and light. The word conjured quicksilver in his mind. In music, *Allegro* meant fast. In Italian, happy. In Spanish, *Alegría* meant joy. Allegra, the petite raven-haired young woman of twenty, should have been as spirited and confident as she was beauti- ful. But she was not spirited and joyful. She was very troubled. Maslow felt an unusually deep connection with her and didn't know why. Some- times he thought she was copying his mannerisms. Her smile and the way she expressed things were oddly familiar. So were some of the stories she told, familiar even though she had not come from here. The way she crossed her legs and pursed her lips when she was angry were par- ticularly disturbing to him. But most disturbing of all, was the fact that sometimes she starved herself and sometimes she cut her own flesh.

In their session that day Allegra had told Maslow that in the first moments after she went to work on herself with a razor and watched the blood bubble up out of the cuts on her belly, she felt bliss. Then, nonchalantly, she'd lifted her blouse for him and showed the scars. The sight of so many even rows of red notches scored across her slender torso had made him queasier than anything he'd seen in medical school. She was his charge, his patient, and he was not working quickly enough to stop her. He was particularly chilled by the fact that whole rows of the red seams on her belly were recent, occurring without his knowledge after she'd started seeing him. A few were brand-new. The idea that she hurt herself after sessions with him disturbed him deeply.

That day after showing off her scars, she'd expressed confusion about sometimes caring about her father despite the horrific things he'd done to her. Maslow remarked that children loved their parents no matter what they did. She'd become enraged at him and had left his office in tears. Ever since, he'd been in a panic about what she might do to herself.

He was still worrying about it at seven o'clock when he returned home from work. He lived in a huge sixty-year-old co-op that took up a whole block on Central Park West.

"Some evening, huh, Doc." The heavyset evening doorman called Ben stood under the canopy, watching him approach.

"Sure is," Maslow agreed.

Ben stepped forward to open the heavy glass door for him.

"Thanks." Maslow waved, then crossed the cavernous lobby, newly decorated in mauve and cream. The elevator took him to the fifth floor, where his one-bedroom apartment faced the side street. Hurrying now, he peeled off his clothes, grabbed socks, Nike Airs, shorts, T-shirt from a shelf in the closet and pulled them on. In the kitchen he filled his water bottle from the tap and put into his fanny pack a couple of granola bars, his apartment keys, and the slender canister of pepper spray that looked like a pen. He didn't take his wallet. He didn't need money to run, and he certainly did not consider the problems of identification should something happen to him. He was a New Yorker and thought nothing could possibly happen to him. He was in and out of his apartment in less than six minutes.

In the lobby, Ben opened the front door for him again and scanned the sky. "I don't know," he said shaking his head. "Watch out for that rain. They say there's more to come."

"Not tonight," Maslow replied confidently. He picked up his feet and trotted across the street toward the park, his heart lifting at the prospect of an activity that always eased his distress.

Twilight was his favorite time of day in the park, and voices on the other side of the wall indicated he was not alone. Then, just before he entered the park, he saw his patient.

She jumped up from the bench and came over. "Hi."

"Hello, Allegra." He wanted to say no more. He wanted to slip by, but she wouldn't let him pass.

"I want to tell you something."

"Why don't you tell me in session tomorrow," he said gently.

"Fine," she replied angrily. "Whatever." Angry again, she took off down Central Park West.

He stopped for a moment to catch his breath and compose himself. Immediately to his left was the playground. To his right was Eighty-first Street. He crossed and entered the park, heading downtown. That evening it had an eerie quality, almost as if he were entering a land of remote rain forests and steamy, sun-basted jungles. At Seventy-ninth Street the canopies of huge old oaks arched over the sidewalk, high above the man-made arbor, which itself was densely covered with wisteria. Rain droplets clung to the leaves and glittered like diamonds in the last of the daylight that filtered through the layers of branches. The air was moist and smelled of earth. Maslow inhaled deeply, willing calm into his soul. He worked with very sick people in the hospital. There, staff was around him, and he knew how to protect himself. With patients in private practice it was different, and he didn't always know the right thing to do. He felt he'd handled this wrong and was glad that he would be able to consult with his supervisor in an hour to talk about Allegra, to get perspective and advice.

The sidewalk split. He took the route to the east and moved deeper into the park, heading toward the bridle path where he liked to run. The ground would be wet, but there wouldn't be any horses this late.

A high-pitched scream of surprise and pain stopped Maslow mid-stride. The cry came out of nowhere and was over in a second. Maslow spun around, searching for the source. He hadn't even picked up his pace yet. The bridle path was ahead of him just out of sight. Behind him, he could hear cars splashing through the puddles as they headed across the park to the East side. He knew he was up at the very northern tip of the rowboat lake, but it was still deep summer and the fully leafed trees hid the view on the other side of the railing that served as a barrier between the safe, paved path and the swampy slope that led down to the water's edge. In other seasons the lake and a footbridge were visible in the distance, appearing unexpectedly like some magical place in a fairy story. Today nothing could be seen through the mist.

The cry came again, this time a sustained wail.

Maslow leaned over the split-rail fence and peered into the curtain of dripping leaves. "Where are you? What's happened?"

"Someone's down here! She fell." An excited voice came from below him.

Maslow pushed some dripping branches aside. The fallen tree that spanned a small ravine in a clearing came into view. Long ago the log had been stripped of its bark and deeply carved with designs like a totem pole. Maslow had seen kids sitting on it many times and guessed that whoever had fallen had fallen from there.

For many people the first rules of New York City were, don't make eye contact with strangers and don't stop for anything. But Maslow was trained to move toward pain, not away from it. He climbed over the railing, pushed through the bushes, and stepped into the clearing. Down in the crevice beneath the carved log bridge he saw blue-jeaned legs skewed awkwardly from the body attached to them. The face was pressed down into the wet grass, but he had a chilling feeling that the crumpled body was Allegra's.

"I think she's dead," screamed the voice, now identifiable as male and filled with adrenaline.

"Hold on, I'm coming. Don't touch her, I'm coming," he cried. He scrambled over the carved log, lost his footing, and half-slid, half-plunged down the hill. The man at the bottom reached down to help him up, but the arm that snaked around his neck was surprisingly strong. It jerked him back. He staggered and lost his balance. He couldn't reach his mace or his cell phone, couldn't land a good kick to the person behind him. He panicked and started yelling, then the rock hit his head and he went down. After that, he didn't feel the branch hitting him, or the feet kicking him, or that he was lifted up, slung over someone's back, and hauled away like a large piece of garbage.

On Park Avenue, Central Park West, and in Long Island City, three sets of parents didn't know where their kids were.

TWO

A T A QUARTER PAST EIGHT, Detective Sergeant April Woo sat in the front seat of her unmarked gray Buick, irritably tapping her fingers on the dashboard. She noticed the light draining away, the sky deepening with the dark. The color right now would have been her absolute favorite blue if the rain hadn't left a slight fog clinging to the earth, muting the brightness.

It was Tuesday, a turn-around tour for her. She'd be home in her bed by two and back on the job tomorrow morning at eight. By four tomorrow afternoon, her week of four and two would be over. Thursday and Friday she had off. She was looking forward to spending the time with her boyfriend, Sergeant Mike Sanchez, lately of the Homicide Task Force, and she hoped nothing would come up to alter her plans. Woodrow Wilson Baum—a.k.a. Woody—the preppy-looking detective recently transferred from anticrime she'd chosen to train and to drive her, happened to be her biggest annoyance at the moment. She was trying to get him to think more and drive better, but like many men, Woody was dedicated to resisting anything he didn't want to do. Just now he'd ground the car to a stop without warning at Columbus Avenue and Eighty-fourth Street and dashed into the Cuban restaurant on the corner.

"I'll just run in for a sandwich. How about I get you some *buñuelos* and a coffee?"

Tempted, April didn't protest even though he was lying. She knew perfectly well he was trying to make time with the owner's daughter, Isobel, whom he'd met while chasing a purse snatcher a few weeks ago in Times Square. In fact, Woody had unceremoniously knocked the young woman down. Isobel Leon, twenty-five, slim, well-proportioned, luscious lips, long dark hair, a paralegal, had been on line to buy tickets for *Lion King* when he'd crashed into her. For Baum, who was a good-looking guy but hadn't a date in many months, it was a case of love at first smite.

It so happened that Isobel helped out at her father's restaurant at night, hence Baum's sudden interest in Cuban food. If the Columbia Café had been in Baum's precinct it would have been designated a "Corruption Prone Location." Cops were not allowed to frequent businesses in the precincts where they worked. As his supervisor, April was extremely cognizant of all department rules. Romance, though frowned upon in crime-related matters, was not exactly at issue here since they were not in prohibited territory. Still, he was lingering and she wanted to get back on the job.

Sergeant April Woo was the second-in-command in the detective squad of Midtown North, the precinct covering the west side of Manhattan, Forty-second Street to Fifty-ninth Street from the Hudson River to Fifth Avenue. It was a prestigious area encompassing the big office buildings and corporate headquarters on Sixth Avenue, the big hotels on Sixth and Seventh, the theater district and the Times Square area, Hell's Kitchen, Theater Row on West Forty-second Street, and Rockefeller Center. It was not a hot-button area in terms of violent crimes, but there was a fair amount of pickpocket activity and robberies in the stores. This area was one of the great magnets of New York, frequented by all the tourists who came to town. As such, it was a high-visibility precinct, carefully monitored. April was the only woman in the unit, foisted on her Puerto Rican boss as a political favor. The lieutenant disliked *La China Famosa* and was not so patiently waiting for an opportunity to disgrace and unload her.

Tonight April was sitting in an unmarked unit in her old precinct, the Two-O, acting as a detective supervisor covering the wider area called Manhattan North because a high-profile rape on a yacht anchored at the Seventy-ninth Street Boat Basin was occupying much of the detective squad from the Two-O as well as her own commanding officer, who'd taken a run uptown to join the party. On the Upper West Side, aside from the rape, there was quiet after the day's rainstorm.

April tuned out the background crackle on the police radio while she waited for Detective Baum to come out of the restaurant with his bribe of the crispy, sugar-dusted, honey-coated *buñuelos* and Cuban *café con leche*. Briefly, she brooded that she'd become so easy she could be turned for a piece of fried dough. Then she forgave herself because the evening tour had started on an upbeat note. She'd helped an old Chinese woman whose family inadvertently left her behind when they got off the bus. The woman could not speak a word of English. She did not know where she was staying or what the telephone number was. She'd been brought weeping into Midtown North, on Fifth-fourth Street between Eighth and Ninth Avenues, and there she had remained convulsed with tears on a folding chair for many hours until the tour changed and April—the only person in the precinct who could speak Chinese and deal with the situation—reunited the family in a New York–style happy ending.

A voice broke through the static with a radio run. April heard the 4th division radio dispatcher hit the alert button usually reserved for 1013s—officer needs assistance or other crimes of a serious nature.

"All units in the vicinity of the West Drive and West Seventy-seventh Street. Caller states someone is screaming in the area of the rowboat lake."

April checked her watch and leaned over to activate the siren to attract Woody's attention. Almost instantly he burst out of the restaurant and galloped across the sidewalk empty-handed.

"What do we got, boss? Suddenly hot to trot, he flung open the car door, leapt inside, slammed the door on his foot, yelped, gunned the engine. A nice show if his love happened to be watching from the window.

"Call for help in the park. Go in at Seven-seven," April ordered. She reattached her seat belt as Woody abruptly pulled out into the traffic on Columbus.

The driver of the BMW behind them braked sharply to avoid a collision. He leaned on his horn in fury and speeded up to catch them, maybe to have a shouting match, maybe to fight, maybe to take out a gun and shoot them. Clearly he had no idea they were cops.

"Christ, Woody," April muttered.

"Sorry, Sergeant," he said without contrition. He hit the siren to alert the BMW driver and the world in general to their status. Magic. The car behind them fell back suddenly. The cars ahead of them moved aside. April tensed as Baum played his favorite game. He had to run through all five lights to Seventy-seventh Street without stopping, no matter what color they were or what was going on with the traffic around them. His own personal rule was he could slow down when running a red light, but if he had to come to a complete stop to avoid an accident, the game was over and he lost.

April thought the game was puerile, but didn't fight the premise. In law enforcement, you did what you had to do. When a life was on the line, every second counted. Force of habit made her check her watch again. It would be noted how long it took officers to respond to the call. She didn't think of herself as competitive, but she wanted to be there first.

Traffic wasn't too bad. Baum was driving unusually aggressively, either to impress the honey who could no longer see him or to make up for the seven minutes he'd kept his supervisor waiting. April's verdict on him was still out. He was a wild card, but people couldn't hide their colors forever. The smart ones got ahead. The dumb ones got left behind. The squirrelly ones made trouble.

Baum was smart enough, but he was also squirrelly. He'd been in one of the rough and tumble anticrime units for several years and was having trouble coming in from the street. This kind of wild driving was an example. Baum sometimes went so far as to gently "nudge" the car ahead of him to get it to move over. He made other mistakes in judgment, too, which April tried to overlook on the grounds that he was green. They were all green in the beginning. Her motive for having him as her driver was that Lieutenant Iriarte, the CO of the unit, disliked the Jew almost as much as he disliked her. That kept Baum fiercely loyal to her, which was a refreshing change.

Woody was silent as he sped along the back side of the Museum of Natural History, made a gleeful left turn, and stormed the park without slowing down for the light at Central Park West. They entered the park, heading the wrong way on the drive. It was a good thing the lane was cleared for them.

Coming toward them at the same time, a blue-and-white 4X4 with two uniformed officers from the Central Park Precinct raced down the hill, and a female mounted officer cantered south on the bridle path from the Eighty-first Street entrance.

"Turn it off," April barked.

Woody turned off the siren, pulled onto the grass, and stopped. All seemed to be quiet in the area now. There were no bystanders to a fight, no sobbing victim sitting or lying on the ground, nobody screaming or calling for help. April and Baum got out. The officer in the 4X4 pulled up beside them but remained at the wheel. Daylight was nearly gone now. Only a few lights punched an eerie glow into the fog.

April lifted her department radio and spoke. "Midtown North Detectives Supervisor to Central. Units on the scene, Central. Will check and advise." Then she got out to investigate.

Central Park was eight hundred and forty-three acres of terrain that was unusually varied for a city park. It was both wild and cultivated, with broad shaded avenues for walking, playing fields south and east of where they were, the zoo across town at Fifth Avenue and Sixty-fifth Street. Tennis courts in the northwest, a five-mile running track that went up to Harlem, a bridle path, a rowboat lake in the lower west, a sailboat pond and Bethesda Fountain at Seventy-second Street. The notorious Ramble—thirty miles of unlighted, unpaved wooded paths, a hangout for adolescents smoking pot, gays looking for action, addicts looking for a hit or a mark, and the homeless—was not far away. Since the Giuliani administration strictly enforced zero tolerance on disorderly conduct and all the other quality-of-life values that were the new hallmark of New York City, there were not that many homeless. When dark came, the third tour of the Central Park Precinct, patrolling in cars, on scooters, horses, bicycles, chased them out.

"Hey, boss, it's probably some fag getting corn-holed in the bushes," the uniform in the 4X4 called out in a who-gives-a-shit tone. April heard and ignored the crude remark. Most likely he was right. Still, they didn't take any risks about people in trouble anywhere, and especially in the park. Every 911 call was thoroughly checked out.

The mounted officer joined the party. She slowed the panting horse to a walk, then reined in close to the Buick. The chestnut she was riding was a beautiful animal. It tossed its head and dropped a steaming load. "Anything?" the officer asked, unperturbed.

"Looks like whatever it was is over," April remarked. "But we'll check it out. Come on, Baum, let's take a walk."

She stepped off the pavement onto the part of the Ramble that skirted the water. Large boulders on either side formed a mini canyon. Between them, tall grasses still thick with their summer greenery rose over six feet high. In the cooling air there was no sound but the rustle of the grass and the leaves above. Baum pulled out his flashlight and shined it into the bushes and into the water as they walked along the shoreline. A family of ducks glided toward them, rippling the surface and almost taking her breath away with their beauty.

Then a sudden noise to her left lifted hairs on the back of April's neck. Reflexively, her hand brushed the 9mm Glock semiautomatic at her waist.

"Jesus, look at that." Baum shone his light on a rat the size of a lap-dog, scurrying across the rock.

All over the city April had seen plenty of those. "Maybe that was the cause of the trouble. Quite a specimen," she said with the cool of a connoisseur.

Farther on, the unmistakable sweet smell of marijuana smoke was trapped in a stagnant pocket of heavy air. The smokers were nowhere to be seen.

For ten minutes April and Woody walked around the area. If they'd found the smokers and they'd been kids, April would have given them a talking-to. She would have taken their names and called their parents. She often took young offenders into the station to give them a taste of the law. She liked to think that occasionally it did the job and scared them straight. But tonight nothing. No sign of the 911 caller, no sign of anyone in trouble. All they saw was the usual array of people minding their own business. And the rat. Finally the two detectives got back in their unit and drove away.

THREE

Dr. Maslow Atkins was due at Dr. Jason Frank's office for a supervisory session at eight-fifteen to discuss Allegra Caldera. As Jason waited for him, he couldn't help feeling just a touch manipulated by the younger doctor's urgent request for extra time that evening—not tomorrow or some other more convenient date. Jason did not get paid for supervising analytic candidates, nor for any of the teaching he did, but he rarely thought about that. His problem these days was stamina. He'd already been exhausted in the late afternoon when he agreed to extend his working day another half hour, and Jason wasn't taking fatigue as easily these days as he used to.

A year ago Jason Frank had reached his thirty-ninth birthday determined to devote his life to his patients, his teaching, his myriad speaking engagements, books, and articles, and whatever free moments he had left, to his actress wife, Emma Chapman. But now he was over forty and the birth of his daughter, April, had changed his priorities.

Tuesday was always Jason's longest day. Since seven A.M., he'd seen ten patients. The difference the baby made to his life was in what he did between and around them. Previously, he'd spent his fifteen minutes between patients opening his mail, returning phone calls, and fiddling with his clocks. Jason had an antique clock collection that measured time in a bunch of quirky and inventive ways and that required his constant attention. Other men loved cars, gadgets of all kinds, stereo equipment, big-screen TVs, sports. Jason was fascinated by time, the completely neutral force that worked for both good and evil. Without time there could be no change in the universe, no seasons or life cycles of any species, no growth of babies to adulthood. Time was many other things to humans, too. It was the good medicine that healed many wounds, and it was the poison that deepened others. Time's effect on a devastating blow to the ego could turn a person into a victim forever, or alternatively, a sadist, even a killer.

Mediating time's impact on the psyche was a big part of his job as a doctor. Jason's own preoccupation had been to create a diverse collection of mechanical clocks, all over a hundred years old, that accurately exhibited time's advance. His goal was to coax them to tick more or less together, neither gaining nor losing minutes as the day progressed. With a host of different movements, however, the clocks did not make uniformity of measurement an easy task.

Since the baby's arrival, Jason allowed many previously important activities to lapse, including the constant winding of his thirty-three clocks. For him, it could be said that although time was marching on, it was no longer measured by the sweep of a pendulum, but rather by the feeding times, the developmental milestones of his child. That day, during his lunch break, he'd run three miles (instead of his previous five) and spent the gained time with Emma and April, who was now nearly six months old and vocalizing freely for her besotted psychoanalyst father.

Jason's office was two rooms that he'd separated from his apartment years ago. Before the arrival of the baby, he'd rarely gone home during the day. Now he moved back and forth between the spaces almost on an hourly basis.

On Tuesday evening, after his last patient left, he picked up his messages. Two were cancellations for tomorrow and one was a request to speak in California in March. When he was finished rescheduling the appointments, he glanced at the row of clocks on the bookcase and realized that Maslow was late. He dialed home to tell Emma.

"Hi, sweetheart, when do you want to eat?" she asked when she heard his voice.

"I'm sorry, honey. I'm a little hung up here. You go ahead without me," he replied.

"I'll wait for you," she promised.

"I may be an hour."

"I'll wait."

"Up to you. How's the baby?"

"Sleeping." Emma yawned, and Jason's heart swelled.

"I love you," he murmured.

"Love you, too."

He hung up, sighing. He was tired, and anxious about a number of things, but life was good. All he needed was a nice dinner, a glass of wine. And to go to bed soon with his beautiful wife. The very last thing he wanted was to spend another half an hour or so dissecting Maslow's difficult patient session.

Four of Jason's own ten patient sessions that day had been painful. Marshal, a physician with AIDS, said he constantly fantasized flying to a splendid vacation spot to end his life there. Jason didn't think he meant it as a threat, but he was left with a nagging doubt. Daisy, a borderline personality he'd been struggling with for years, came in this morning claiming she'd been raped at a fraternity party on Long Island the previous weekend and now wanted to drop out of school for the fourth time. Then, Jason had visited Willis in the hospital where he was on suicide watch after his estranged wife got a court order to keep him away from her and the children. Last Friday Willis had attempted to gas himself with car exhaust in the family garage. The fourth case was Alicia, a former tennis prodigy managed by her father. Her father had given her a dog as a reward for her athletic talent when she was ten. He'd allowed her to pet and play with the animal only when she was playing well. In a rage, after Alicia lost a crucial juniors match just before her eleventh birthday, he'd given the dog to the ASPCA, where it was put to sleep. At the present time, Alicia was almost eighteen, weighed two hundred and thirty pounds, and for the very first time was seeking help, against her parents' clearly stated wishes.

Jason had no doubt that he would be brooding for some time about the things these patients had said to him and he had said to them. Still, having to address the therapeutic skills, or lack thereof, of the spectacularly insecure Maslow Atkins was a duty he would not dream of shirking. Psychotherapy was a skill that had to be rigorously taught, one by one, by master to beginner.

At a quarter to nine, Jason's mood changed from impatience to alarm. It happened like the audible click in many of his clocks when the second hand advanced to the half hour, just a beat before the peal of the chime. He experienced a cold shiver and felt something was wrong. Maslow was compulsive about time. He was always five minutes early. Jason knew how many minutes Maslow was early because he could hear the hinges on the door squeal each time someone came or went from his waiting room.

He frowned at the phone. As he did so, he realized that the two skeleton clocks on his desk, always four minutes apart, had both stopped at the same time. Spooky. Jason didn't like spooky. He wondered if Maslow could possibly have gone out to dinner and forgotten the appointment. He picked up the phone and dialed Maslow's number. It rang six times before the answering machine picked up.

Jason hung up without leaving a message and sighed again. He reached for the knot in his tie, pulled it loose, and stuffed it in his pocket. Uneasy, he wound and reset the two clocks on his desk. Then he dialed Maslow's number again, and this time he left a message. When a very compulsive person like Maslow wasn't where he was supposed to be and didn't call, something was wrong.

Jason had worked with the police often enough now to know how they thought about this kind of thing, how they acted when something turned up funny. Cops didn't wait overnight to see how a suspicious circumstance sorted itself out. They acted on the first shiver. Jason realized that in this particular situation he was thinking like a cop and fearing the worst. But he reminded himself that he wasn't a cop, so he left a note for Maslow on his office door and went home to Emma for dinner. The next morning the note was still there.

FOUR

O N WEDNESDAY MORNING April got up before dawn and dressed for a quick run. She put on a tank top and thin black sweat pants. Summer wasn't officially over for another week, but already the air offered its first taste of fall. When she trotted down the stairs of her second-floor apartment and opened the front door of the house she had been tricked into buying for her parents, she felt the first autumn chill bite into her cheeks, her bare arms and shoulders. All grogginess passed. She was fully awake now, reminded of her name on the thirty-year mortgage for a house in which she no longer wanted to live and could not escape without the benefit of riches she did not possess. Having agreed many years ago to support and live with her parents, April now felt she was in an unlucky and undesirable position for marriage. Without her salary to put in the wedding pot, she could not marry. The loss of face of having such a debt was so disgraceful to her that she could not even tell her lover her problem. It was a secret.

She sighed and started off on her favorite route in the Astoria, Queens, neighborhood where the Woos lived. It followed Hoyt Avenue under the approach to the Triborough Bridge. At five to six that morning, dense fog blurred the mammoth structure and paled the resolution of the lights necklaced above. At street level the house lights had a yellow cast. After nearly a decade as a cop, April had come to love the intimacy of night. Even more, she liked early morning, after the bad guys had gone to ground and before the commuters were out.

Now that she was spending nearly all of her precious off-duty hours with Mike, April's few solitary dawns had taken on almost a mythic importance to her. Just before the sun lightened the sky had been the time she used to jog every single day. When daylight arrived, she would return home, work with free weights, and finish her leg lifts. Hard exercise had always been part of her ritual. As a small-boned woman cop, she had to be extra tough both mentally and physically so no one could make the allegation stick that she wasn't up to the job.

Shivering slightly, April stepped out onto the street to scan the houses and cars of her neighbors. Always the cop, she carried her gun with her everywhere and looked for signs of trouble. At this hour the workers on graveyard shifts were not yet home, and workers on day shifts were just getting up. Astoria was no yuppie area. Around here people worked hard for a living, and not many jogged for exercise. Only once had a tough guy tried to bother her. He changed his mind when he saw the gun. Today nothing was out of the ordinary.

April's feet took off down the pavement. Until Mike had come into her life, she'd always been alone at dawn. She'd swallowed hot water with lemon, and eaten whatever her mother put in her refrigerator—cold rice, or sesame noodles, slices of drunken chicken, roast duck, or twice-cooked pork. Dry-fried beef with orange peel. Softshell crab, in season. Pickled vegetables. Things her father brought home at the end of the evening from the upscale midtown restaurant where he was a chef.

More yang than yin by her mother's calculation, April had lived thirty years in a strange isolation—her thoughts focused on getting ahead and her body prepped for the cop's job. But now, her life had changed. She was in love, and the deadly yin had moved in to weaken her resolve. Night and day she dreamed of her lover's anatomy—his legs and lips. His eyes and arms. The curve of his back and butt. His chest. His soul and manhood—*dulce, suave, siempre duro.* She loved him and she was afraid of loving him because of the many complications.

For starters, the prospect of a Mexican-Chinese union sent her old-style Chinese mother into a frenzy. An annoyance before Mike had come along, her mother was a nightmare now. Skinny Dragon hated everyone who wasn't Chinese. She absolutely despised all foreigner ghosts with complete democracy. Independent of her mother's bias, of course, April wasn't entirely open-minded on the subject of cultural mythologies herself.

For example, Mike had many girlfriends before he met her. Most of them had been just a few dates; but some had lasted longer and of those, several kept calling him to check if he was still off the market. Occasionally April would hear him on the phone, being nice, talking longer than a truly committed man should talk. Skinny Dragon liked to tell her that all Spanish ghosts were cheaters, and this one was sure to break her heart in the end. How could she not worry constantly about that? This morning, though, the endorphins kicked in and April's spirits soared into the stratosphere, all financial and fidelity concerns forgotten.

Forty-five minutes later, just as she was getting out of the shower, the phone rang. She grabbed a towel and ran into the bedroom to pick up. "Sergeant Woo."

"Hey, April. It's Jason. Sorry to bother you at home."

"Jason, my friend. How's that gorgeous baby of yours?" April toweled herself dry and grabbed some underwear from the top drawer of the dresser. Her bedroom was about the size of a postage stamp. From where she stood, she had a good view of the chaos in her closet—summer clothes and winter clothes, mostly slacks, jackets, and calf-length skirts—were all stuffed together in such bulging disarray that the door hadn't closed for years. She contemplated her huge wardrobe with dismay, thinking she didn't have a single thing to wear.

"She's a doll," Jason was saying.

"I'd love to see her. What is she, six months now?" April combed the tangles out of her wet hair with her fingers.

"Five and a half. Why don't you come over? Emma would love to see you. She's not shooting her new film until the beginning of November."

"Wow. Where does this one take place?" April couldn't help being impressed that she personally knew a movie star.

"Oh, here in New York, of course. Emma doesn't want to leave our daughter till she's twenty. I didn't wake you, did I?"

"No, Jason. You didn't wake me. What's up?" The alarm button had gone off at the sound of his voice. Jason was an important doctor, a busy man, who wouldn't call her just to make small talk.

"A psychoanalytic candidate I'm supervising, a young psychiatrist, didn't turn up for a meeting last night. He didn't answer his phone this morning, and he didn't call in. I'm concerned."

"Any particular reason?"

"He's just very conscientious, very obsessive. If he had a medical emergency, he wouldn't forget to call and cancel."

"Hold on." April padded into the other room for her notebook, took it out of her shoulder bag, and came back. "Okay, give me the info."

Jason gave her the pertinent information. Maslow Atkins was the man's name. His address was in her old precinct, the Two-O. The right thing to do would be to call one of the detectives from her old squad to take care of it. She told Jason she'd let him know who'd be looking into it.

"Thanks," he said. But he sounded disappointed that she wasn't taking care of it herself.

The suite of small, windowless, detective squad rooms on the second floor of Midtown North was just waking up at eight o'clock when April came in to work. No one was in the holding cell, and Lieutenant Iriarte was holding court in his office. Like every unit commander, he had his favorites. In his case they were the unlikely trio of Creaker, Skye, and Hagedorn. Skye was tall and brawny, of Irish–Native American extraction, so he said. He had a broken nose, blue marbles for eyes, and a number of scary-looking scars on his shaved head. Creaker was a short bodybuilder with a boxer's blunt face and arms so thick no jacket sleeves were wide enough to hide the muscles. Hagedorn, the computer expert and Iriarte's absolute favorite, was big and soft, and had a pale pudding of a face, and limp, discouraged-looking, mouse-brown hair. These two yangs and a yin, by April's estimation, were among the least evolved humans on earth. But they were not as bad as the detectives she'd worked with in the Two-O—always watching the surgery channel on TV. And she had to admit that Hagedorn was a first-rate hacker who'd helped her out with background checks on the computer more than once.

Iriarte was a small, good-looking Puerto Rican, a really snappy dresser with a matchstick mustache suspended exactly midway between his nose and upper lip, and strong family values. At the moment he was wearing a gray suit with a slight lavender tinge, a yellow shirt, and a black tie. He gestured through the glass wall of his office for April to join them. She did.

"Hey, Woo, what's up?" he asked, acting real nice.

"Not much. Some little stuff. It was pretty quiet last night. What about your rape victim?"

"She's still in the hospital, guy beat her up pretty bad. Turns out she's a hooker. Her pimp thought she was dealing on the side, followed her on board, locked up her customer in the stateroom, then raped her and knocked her around. The suspect says the three of them were friends, were partying, and the other guy got out of hand. The DA's not even considering rape charges, and the customer doesn't want his wife to know, so the scum may get lucky and walk away." Iriarte shook his head. His three ugly henchmen shook theirs in unison. Disgusting what went down.

He finished his narrative and glanced down at the short stack of sixty-ones, the complaints that had come in during the night. Down to business, he called in the other five detectives on duty, went over pending cases and assigned the new ones. When he was finished with that, April returned to her office and dialed the number of Maslow Atkins, Jason's young shrink. She didn't expect him to answer, but it was worth a try.

She listened to the voice on his answering machine, soft and regretful that he wasn't available to take the call. Something about his tone stuck a chord in April. She was a cop who worked on instinct, always assumed the worst. The bottom line was Jason Frank was a fancy doctor, but he was also her friend. They'd worked on many cases together, and he always helped her when she asked him.

The correct procedure was for Jason, or some relative, to fill out a missing person complaint in the precinct where the person lived. April always went by the book, but today she swerved off the straight and narrow. All she did was decide to check out this missing person herself. As a boss herself now, she often acted on the saying "Better to rumble like rocks than tinkle like jade." But no independent action in policing goes unpunished.

FIVE

THE GIRL WHO called herself Allegra Caldera did not kill herself Tuesday night after the terrible incident with Maslow Atkins. She thought about killing herself. She *wanted* to kill herself. She longed to throw herself on the subway tracks in front of an oncoming train. The pressure to end her miserable life was tremendous. When her train rolled in, she didn't throw herself in front of it. But when she got home at midnight, the urge to cut herself became unbearable.

She considered filling the tub with hot water, then cutting her wrists and watching her blood pulse out in the bath. If she drank a bottle of vodka, she'd be high and wouldn't even know she'd died. The problem was it wasn't so easy to kill herself. Especially since her mother and father were home. They went to bed early at night and didn't hear her come in, but they would definitely wake up if she turned on the water. Also she had a paper on Hawthorne due in American Lit.

Like a lush on the wagon, she brooded and longed for the knife, but in the end she kept away from that, too. She promised herself she wouldn't even look at it. She holed up in her room and took a Dex to write the paper. The paper was about people who hurt other people, who did bad things because they couldn't help it. It centered around the selfishness of men in all ages and how women were destroyed by them. She knew a lot about that and enjoyed writing it.

In the early Wednesday morning hours, she was wired and overtired. And like many, many early mornings in the last six years, she had the powerful desire to cross the hall and stick a kitchen knife into her parents' chests a dozen, maybe two dozen times. She wanted to stab them, hack away at them. She thought a lot about Lizzie Borden, what Lizzie might have been feeling a hundred years ago on that hot day in Fall River, Massachusetts, after a heavy lunch, with no air conditioning in the sweltering upstairs rooms, and the smell of garbage wafting everywhere through the house. She imagined everyone sweating in their beds, snoring—maybe as loudly as her father with the deviated septum did.

Allegra wished she had the guts to explode on the scene, like Lizzie Borden, and destroy the people who hurt her. She wished she could splatter their guts everywhere. She lusted for their blood and feared her rage. After she finished writing her scathing paper she took a few Valiums to calm down and sleep. Then in the morning she couldn't even get out of bed.

She decided not to go to her American Lit class at Hunter College in Manhattan to hand it in, after all. The novel they were studying was one of her least favorites—*The Scarlet Letter.* She hated that smug novel about adultery among the Puritans, and she loathed the grad student teaching assistant who taught it and whose comments about her work were so stupid and vicious. She already knew what the TA would say about her paper on *The Scarlet Letter.* Allegra was always in trouble with the TA, an arrogant little twit who'd graduated from Harvard and thought he was so smart.

But she was in trouble in general. Her father and mother wanted her to be a professional like them so she would always have a way of supporting herself. She knew that meant they didn't want to take care of her. They wanted her to graduate so they could be done with her, and she didn't know what the hell to do with her life. She was hopeless; she knew she could never do what they did. She didn't know what kind of job she could do.

At six-thirty, right on schedule, her mother stood by her bed with a cup of coffee in her hand. The five-foot-five, size-four, hundred-and-fifteen-pound, blond-haired, amethyst-eyed Puerto Rican beauty was trying to get her daughter's attention. As usual, she was full of questions, and her lovely face was set with anger and concern in equal measure.

"Honey, I worried about you. Where were you last night?" she complained and queried at the same time with not a hint of Spanish in her voice. She was born here, but had a brain from another planet. Allegra had complete contempt for her.

"I had a date." Allegra turned over.

"You had a date in the middle of the week?" Her mother pursed her pink lips. "What kind of date?"

"Shouldn't you be at work, Mom?"

"No." She checked the clock on Allegra's desk. "I have five minutes for my daughter. What kind of date?"

Allegra turned over again and sat up. She had a heart-shaped face, short, light brown hair, her father's dark eyes, a splattering of freckles across her nose and cheeks. Her mother and everyone else thought she was pretty, but with a drop-dead gorgeous mother like hers, how could she believe it?

"Here, take your coffee."

Allegra knew her mother's motherly smile was a fake.

"Thanks. Just put it down," Allegra said.

Grace studied her. "You don't look very happy for a girl who's had a date. He isn't married, is he?" She set the cup down on the night table, frowning. "Drink the coffee."

Allegra hated her. Under the sheet, she pulled her nightgown down. "What's in it?"

"Just milk. Drink up."

Allegra turned her head to examine it. "Looks like cream to me," she said. She'd rather die than drink cream.

"Would I give you cream? I wouldn't give you cream. It's milk. You need it for your bones. I love you so much, sweetheart. Tell me about your date. How old is he? What's he do? Is he cute?"

"He's very cute." And he hates me, she didn't say. "Go to work, Mom."

"Not until I know who you had a date with. I never hear anything about your life anymore," she complained. "How do I know what you're up to?"

Allegra stared at the coffee and said nothing.

"You missed dinner last night. What date could be worth hurting your father?"

"What?"

"We both missed you last night, but he was really hurt."

Allegra made a disgusted noise. "He's always hurt."

"There was no date, was there? You just stayed out to avoid your father." Her pretty little mother shook her head sadly.

Allegra felt bad for her misguided mother. "You're wrong. I had a date," she said.

"Who was it?"

"None of your business."

"How can you talk to me like that?" Grace took her hand off her perfectly formed hip and left the room, shaking her head. "I know there's no man," she murmured. "You just want to hurt us, that's all."

"There is a man. There is," Allegra said softly.

As soon as her mother was gone, Allegra poured the cream-spiked coffee down the sink. Then she hung around all morning thinking about *The Scarlet Letter*. She brooded about why people did what they did. Why did Emma Bovary and Anna Karenina have to commit suicide because of their love affairs? Why fall for a jerk in the first place? Why not kill the men who hurt them? Why kill themselves? Where was the *sense* in the thing? She couldn't figure life out at all.

After her mother left for work, she lay there dreaming about Maslow Atkins. She wanted to go on *CNN*, on *60 Minutes*, on *Sally Jesse* or the *Springer Show* and tell the truth about her "doctor." She wanted to tell the whole world about the fraud he was and the fraud she was, too. She knew it would make a good story.

SIX

D AVID OWEN WAS in an excited condition around seven when his mother, Janice Owen, came into his room without knocking and screamed at him for a while. She continued screaming as she left to get in the shower. He pulled the covers over his head to block out the noise. Jesus Christ. He wished she were a bug he could squash.

There was no sign of his dad, who worked on Wall Street lawyering people to death twenty hours a day. David wondered if he'd worked all night again and hadn't come home at all. It was hard to know. His father was always gone by the time David hauled himself out of bed, which he did his best to avoid every morning. Only rarely did he succeed in staying in bed. Not even throwing up worked with his mother anymore. Now he had to have a *fever* of 101 to get her attention.

Jesus Christ. Same shit every morning. David hated school. *Hated it*. He heard the kids call him a loser. Did they think he was deaf? They said it practically to his face. He hated it. He'd rather be dead than go there. The work was too hard for him, and he just couldn't manage being cool.

He watched the other boys being easy with each other. They knew how to make friends and hang out. He just couldn't do it. He didn't know how to act or what to say. He had friends from camp, but no one at school ever came up to shake his hand when he arrived in the morning the way the "in" kids did with each other. No one called him at night. No one invited him to their parties. Mostly they ignored him. But sometimes he heard them refer to him as a loser. It made him nuts.

Every school morning David hid out under the covers as long as he could, playing with himself, moaning, and trying to avoid being taken to school by his mother. If he was lucky and managed to be really late, she'd leave him. But that didn't happen too often, either. Janice Owen liked taking her son to school in her limo. It made her feel she was being a good mother. David was certain she did it just to torture him because he was too old for that. Everybody else came on their own. On the subway or whatever. Only the little kids came with their mothers in the car service. But his mother just loved getting him in that car—he, unshowered and hastily pulled together, she in a suit with her hair styled and sprayed and her makeup on, wearing jewelry, talking so fast the words swam together like a school of fish. She called the big swing north up to his school in the navy blue Lincoln Town Car—on her way to the bank that was more than thirty blocks south—their quality time together.

This Wednesday morning, when he felt elated and close to happy for the first time in his life, she came into his room three times. First in her robe, then in her skirt and silk blouse with her hair still wet. Then dressed to kill, strapping on her watch. By then, she was yelling like a maniac that if he didn't go with her, he wasn't getting the Beamer when he finished Driver's Ed and his private Saturday morning driving lessons. That made him get up, throw on his clothes, and leave his building on Park and Sixty-fifth Street and jump in the limo with his mom just like always.

As soon as Janice was in the car she got happy. She yammered on about the bank's second merger with another bank in three years and her chances, this time, of being promoted or fired and her contingency plans in either case.

"If I get promoted and you get a 3-0 average, we'll go to the south of France this summer. And if Dad can't go, Dad can't go." She gave him one of her high-wattage, brave smiles. "What do you say?"

David yawned.

His mother's smile broke up. "I thought those pills were supposed to wake you up. Are you taking your *pills*?" she demanded.

"I'm awake," he grumbled. He was taking the Ritalin, but he'd stopped taking the Zoloft on the second day. It made him feel funny.

"Did you take your *pill*?" Sharp look from the hyper mom.

"I took the pill," he assured her.

"What time did you get home last night?" Questions, questions, every day the same questions.

David looked at his mother and saw an evil person, someone who took pleasure in torturing him just because he wasn't like her. Her disappointment in him had squared her off. When David had been a little boy, his mother had been a pretty, smily woman, giggling all the time. Now she was hard and cruel as a mirror, twenty pounds too fat, dressed to the nines, and all business. She fixed him with her steely eyes, hammering him into the corner with all her questions. And she never answered any of his. *Does Dad have a girlfriend? Do you have a boyfriend? Are you getting your face lifted? When can I stop going to that asshole shrink?*

"Early," he lied. He never even saw her last night. When did *she* get in? He was pissed at her for lying to him, but he gave her a sincere look because he was going to flunk math and get a C in biology, and he wanted that Beamer bad. He knew she'd give it to him.

The limo sped up Park Avenue, and he peered hungrily out the window as they passed Brandy's building at Seventy-fifth Street. Brandy had told him she'd give him a call as soon as her mother let her out. They'd be together by noon, going over their triumphs. *Now* he was cool.

"Good, I'm glad you slept well. You need your rest." Janice's eyes softened. She was satisfied, snapped open her briefcase, and started flipping through a pile of papers. Then her cell phone rang and she answered it. She became engrossed in her conversation and didn't even notice that David got out at a red light two blocks shy of school. She was happy with their exchange and had no idea he was playing hooky.

SEVEN

Woody was at his desk talking on the phone, chewing a bite of bagel, when April came out of her office at half past eight. She could tell by the way he had his feet up on the desk and was making decorative little piles of crumbs with the end of his pen that it was a personal call. She caught his eye and wiggled her fingers at him just the way her boss did to her when he wanted her to jump.

His brow furrowed. "Now?" he mouthed at her.

"Now," she said loud enough for the three ugly henchmen to exchange glances.

Woody said something she couldn't hear and hung up. "What's up, boss?" he asked.

"A shrink didn't show up for an appointment last night. We're going to check it out."

Woody processed that bit of information as he got to his feet. April knew he was thinking the lieutenant hadn't mentioned any missing person complaint. She didn't enlighten him as they left the squad room, trotted down the stairs, said hey to some uniforms hovering around the front door, and went outside to their unmarked unit. Not until they were in the car did she give him Maslow Atkins's Upper West Side address, which just happened to be outside of their precinct.

"Who is this guy?" Woody asked.

"Young shrink in training with Jason Frank."

"I hate those head-shrinker quacks," he remarked.

April would have rebuked him for his idiocy, but her cell phone bur-bled. She rummaged through her shoulder bag, disrupting the clutter of tissues, rubber gloves (for not contaminating evidence at crime scenes), notebooks, her telephone and address book that contained every source she'd ever used, second gun, lipsticks, hairbrush, wallet, badge, aspirin, all the essentials she needed to function. The phone was at the bottom.

She grabbed it and flipped it open, but before she could speak, Woody stopped abruptly at a light, flinging her against her seat belt.

"Jesus!" she erupted.

"*Estas enojada conmigo, querida?*" Mike replied anxiously.

April scowled at Woody and spoke softly to Mike. "Why would I be angry, *mi amore? Te quiero mucho.*"

"I have no idea; I'm such a wonderful guy."

Uh-huh. "Did you get into trouble last night?" she asked sweetly, guessing he had a guilty conscience about something.

"No trouble, I promise." The soft sweet voice was working to soothe.

"I'll bet," she murmured.

"Well, maybe just a *little*. The bar fight, the hooker brawl, and the trip to ER." He was teasing, but she didn't exactly laugh along. An evening out with his old partner might include any or all of the above.

"Talk to you later. Something's doing," she told him. Then she glanced at Woody and sighed, wondering what was up with Mike. She wasn't a detective for nothing.

Woody accelerated through Columbus Circle and shot up Central Park West. She ignored his high-speed race past the Museum of Nat-ural History. He slowed down just enough at Eighty-second Street to do a gut-wrenching U-turn. He just missed a speeding limo coming at them from the north, braked hard in front of Maslow's building's en-trance, and gave April a big grin. Something was up with him, too. Men had a primitive way of communicating.

She'd warned him, but Woody wasn't settling down after his rough-'em-up years. Now, she didn't want to give him the satisfaction of chewing him out. She wasn't his mother. She got out and slammed the car door.

The doorman came running out and screamed at them. "No parking here!" His accent was thick. He was a Russian. Alex Yelsin, his tag read. Alex looked about forty, had a big fleshy face, angry red-rimmed eyes. His belly strained the buttons of his uniform jacket.

"Police." April's hand reached into her purse and instantly connected with her badge. She pulled it out and showed it to him. "I'm Sergeant Woo," she told him.

Alex glanced at the badge, unimpressed. Then his angry eyes looked her over as if he didn't believe a Chinese could be a cop. She was used to it. She pointed to the curb in front of the building. There was no yellow line there. Anyway, they were cops and could park anywhere they wanted. If they got a summons, they had recourse.

The guy was still unimpressed. "Something wrong?" he asked.

Woody came around the side of the car. April introduced him. "This is Detective Baum. We're looking for a tenant by the name of Maslow Atkins."

"So?" Alex challenged them.

"Have you seen him?"

"See him every day."

"Did you see him today?" Baum asked.

"Today?" He looked at Woody, scratched the side of his nose. "No, not today."

"Would you ring him, please."

They trooped inside to the cavernous lobby. Yuppies with their briefcases and workout bags trooped out around them as Alex tried the intercom. April reached into her purse and turned her phone off.

When Yelsin rang, there was no answer from Maslow's apartment on the intercom.

"We need to check out Dr. Atkins's apartment," April told him.

Alex shook his head. "Oh, oh, oh. You'll have to talk to the super."

"Fine."

They hiked across the lobby to the building office, where more Russians were sitting at desks eating highly caloric bakery goods. An obese woman in a black pantsuit with intense magenta hair, magenta nail polish, and matching lipstick was the manager. Her name was Regina. She didn't want to help out.

"It's a lot of trouble for me to do it," she complained.

April shrugged. *Too bad.*

With pursed lips, Regina collected the key, and they went up in the elevator. On Maslow's floor they followed her down a long hall and around the corner. As they neared his door, a strong aroma of bacon lingered from someone's breakfast. Homey touches of everyday life like this always gave April a bad feeling. Once she'd smelled toast outside the apartment of a man who hadn't shown up for work. The toast had given her the false hope that the man they were looking for was just taking a day off. But when she and Mike, who'd been her supervisor at the time, had gone inside, they'd found the man stone cold with a plastic bag over his head.

Now she didn't want to open Maslow's door and find him in his bedroom with his throat cut, hanging from the chandelier, or lying on his bed, dead from pills. He was someone's son, friend, colleague, maybe boyfriend. Her heartbeat accelerated as Regina fumbled with the locks. She didn't realize she was holding her breath until the door was open and she had a clear sight line into the living room.

Regina started to go in first, but April shook her head. "Please stay here for a moment."

"This is my building," she protested. "I have to know what's going on in here."

"You'll know soon enough," April told her, then nodded at Woody. The two of them went in, leaving Regina muttering angrily in Russian just inside the door.

The lights were on, as if Maslow were home. But the place had the dead silence of emptiness. April's gaze swept the unexceptional living room. White walls, bare except for three large photographs, beige wall-to-wall carpet. Blue sofa, two red club chairs, a simple desk with one drawer. Laptop computer on top. Desk chair with wheels. Above the desk a bookshelf full of medical and psychiatric texts. Another pile of books neatly stacked under the desk. Phone with message light blinking.

April moved into the bedroom and exhaled. The bed was made, and on it no dead body was waiting for her. There was no body in the bathroom, either. The towels were carefully folded on the towel rack. Hairbrush on the sink with light brown hair in it. She looked in the medicine cabinet. The large quantity of prescription medicines indicated that Atkins either had health problems or was something of a hypochondriac. None of the drug names were familiar to her.

Back in the bedroom, she found his plastic hospital ID and his wallet under the gray suit, white shirt, and blue-and-red striped tie he must have tossed on the bed before he went out. April looked through the wallet quickly. Stuffed in the billfold compartment were two foil-wrapped condoms that looked as if they'd been mashed in there a long time. She put them back before Woody could see them and make a smart remark. On the floor were black loafers and discarded black socks. It looked as if the doctor had come home, changed, and gone out without his identification. She frowned and moved on. The air conditioner was off. It was hot in the apartment, and a powerful smell of rotting Chinese food emanated from the kitchen. April checked the refrigerator. Diet Coke was the only food group represented. In the garbage were white containers with the gluey leftovers from a Chinese meal that must have been eaten several days ago.

Back in the living room, Woody hit the play button on the answering machine. By now Regina was in the apartment. All three of them listened to the messages. Two were from Jason, asking him to call right away no matter what time he came in. Two were from the same girl. The first time she said, "I'm—um—really sorry for walking out. You upset me. Please call."

The next few calls were hang-ups.

The last call was the same girl voice again. "I don't *want* to explore it in the next session. I need you to talk to me *now* so I don't do something."

Woody gave April a look. Girl threats were not his favorite thing. April jerked her head. "Let's go."

"Disgusting." Regina was sniffing around the garbage.

"Please leave it for now." April said.

"Are you finished here?"

"Not quite. I want to talk to the doorman who was on duty last night."

"That's a lot of trouble for me."

April gave her a little smile. "You can give me his number at home."

"I don't have to do that. He's on the day shift today."

"Fine. Let's go talk to him, and no one else in here until further notice, okay?" April left it to Woody to close up. She was upset by the wallet with Maslow's ID on the bed. This was a sticky situation. As far as she knew no sixty-one had been filed. The missing doc was not her case, not her jurisdiction, but he had become her problem. She had a bad feeling about it and knew she'd have major explaining to do if further investigation of his work, his life, his patients, and the contents of his computer became necessary.

EIGHT

IT TURNED OUT that Ben, the four-to-eleven-P.M. doorman last night, was filling in on the back elevator today. April and Woody talked to him as they rode up to the fourteenth floor with a Federal Express driver delivering a package.

"Dr. Atkins came in at seven," Ben told them importantly as the manually operated elevator jerked its way up. "These guys are cops," he told the FedEx driver.

"No kidding," the man replied without interest.

The elevator stopped. Ben heaved the doors open, the driver got out, went through the door out into the main hallway, and disappeared. The elevator bell rang, but Ben didn't close the doors.

"At seven," Woody prompted.

"Yeah, I remember everything. I have a memory for details. Ask me anything. It rained pretty bad in the afternoon. I had to take the mats out to cover the carpets. Thems are new carpets, and it's a big lobby out there, I have to put down two sets. Takes twenty minutes to get them all placed just right. So I place the mats. Then at five, all them damn dogs have to go out. Let me tell you, those dogs make a mess when it rains."

April took out her notebook and began writing in it. She had a lot of things on her mind now and let Woody do the talking.

"How about telling us about Dr. Atkins," he said.

"I was telling you." Ben gave Woody a dirty look, then leaned his shaggy white head April's way. April's nose twitched. The man smelled of sweat and stale beer. She hated beery breath on people who supplied information.

The elevator bell rang. Ben ignored it.

"The rain stopped at five-fifteen. By six-thirty I was thinking about taking the mats up. But I was starving. I thought I better wait to see if we were going to get some more. I went out on break for a sandwich. I go to that deli around the corner on Columbus. There's two, but I don't like the Korean one."

"Stick to the facts. We don't need a novel," Woody grumbled.

The bell rang a third time. The FedEx driver returned minus his package. Ben closed the doors and got the elevator moving again. He was in a bad mood now. "Cops. Who knows what they're after."

April didn't comment. The FedEx driver didn't comment. Ben stopped on ten. Two uniformed maids speaking Spanish got on with four bulging bags of laundry. "*Hola*," they said to Ben, then continued a lively conversation as the elevator went down to the main floor. There, the FedEx driver took off without looking back.

"Nobody gives a shit," Ben complained.

The maids kept up a heated argument as the elevator continued down to the basement. When the doors opened, they hoisted the bags . off the elevator still going at it. April felt a pang of sisterhood. The topic was lying, cheating *hombres*.

The bell rang a few more times. Several floor numbers popped up. Ben closed the doors.

"All we got here so far is a time frame. Let's finish up," Woody said.

Ben gave him another dirty look and spoke to April. "You take this down. I don't want no trouble later. Here's the fucking time frame. I just came back from my break. I had a cup of coffee. I ate the sandwich. It was bologna on rye, four pickles."

All the people waiting for the elevator upstairs leaned on their bells at once, but April didn't care. After the elevator man started treating her like a secretary, April lost her patience.

"Just take us up to the lobby and leave the door closed until we're finished," she told him.

Ben took the elevator up without a word, then went on as if there had been no interruption. "I ain't had time to drink the coffee when

Dr. Atkins comes down the street. If you don't let me get these calls, I'm going to lose my job," he whined.

"What time?" Woody asked.

"Seven, I already told you it was just seven. I opened the front door for him. He went upstairs. I drank my coffee. A few minutes later he came out in shorts and took off."

The bells sounded like a swarm of angry bees.

"Then what?"

Ben shrugged. "That's it."

"What time did Dr. Atkins come back?"

Ben scratched his cheek. "He didn't come back."

"Are you sure?" Woody asked.

"Of course I'm sure. No one gets in here unless I let them in."

The swarm got angrier.

"Can I do something about this?" Ben was getting desperate.

April shook her head. "What about when you go to the bathroom?" she asked.

"The door's locked. They have to wait. Just like now." He licked his lips.

"So Dr. Atkins went out in his shorts. Did you see where he went?" Now Woody.

"Of course I did. I watched him. He went across the street to the park. A girl was waiting for him. They spoke. They went into the park together. He didn't come back."

"What did the girl look like?"

"Real pretty. Black hair. Pink sweater. Tight pants. Looked like she might be a hooker." Ben smiled for the first time. "But you know girls these days. She might have been a debutante." He smirked some more. April glanced at Woody.

"Did you ever see her before?" he asked.

"Maybe." The phone in the elevator rang. Ben picked up and said, "No problem, I'll be right there."

April shook her head. *No, you won't.* "Did you ever see this girl go up to Dr. Atkins's apartment?"

"Not that I know of."

"How about a name?"

"Nope."

"Okay, that's it. You can let us out now."

The elevator doors slid open. April and Woody crossed the lobby and went outside. At a little after ten, a full sun beat down. The chilly morning had become a brilliant day, summer all over again.

"The park?" Woody said.

April hesitated. Last night they'd been on a radio run when they'd gone into the park. Now was different. The park was not like any other precinct. It was almost another country. When she'd been in the Two-O, every time a detective or officer from another house stepped foot in the park, they'd had to notify the captain of the Park Precinct that they were working there. It was an ownership thing, a protocol thing.

But, for the second time that day, she strayed off the straight and narrow. She nodded at Woody. He grinned, knowing they were in the wrong as they left their unit in front of Atkins's building and crossed Central Park West, heading to the place where the doorman said he'd last seen Maslow Atkins with a black-haired woman in a pink sweater. Possibly the girl on the phone, April thought.

By all appearances the doctor had gone out to run in the park, met a girl, maybe changed his mind about Jason—or forgot about him— and gone to her place for the night. That was a nice clean possibility. A nastier one would be, he'd been mugged. The mugger wouldn't have gotten much of anything, though; Maslow had left his wallet at home. April made a quick connection with the 911 she and Woody had responded to last night. She frowned, thinking about it. They had to call the local emergency rooms and the other precincts to see if anybody had anything on it. She and Woody had reached the entrance to the park and went in.

Above April, the sun filtered through the trees, dappling the light and warming her face. The temperature must be up to seventy-eight already, and the heat felt good. *Please let Maslow Atkins not be a mystery,* she prayed. Anything but a mystery. Cops hated mysteries.

She unbuttoned her light jacket and inhaled. After the rain of yesterday, the park smelled fresh and green. Nannies and mothers wheeled strollers piled high with park toys toward the playground. She prayed some more to the Chinese gods. *Please, ghosts and dragons that make so much trouble for humans, back off, let me find Jason's friend alive and well.* She and Woody moved deeper into the park. Automatically, their two pairs of feet took them downtown, toward Seventy-seventh Street, where they'd seen the rat. They followed the route that skirted the rowboat lake. At Eightieth Street, they were north of the water. At Seventy-ninth Street a steep hill, almost deep enough to qualify as a ravine, led down to a wide shoreline, swampy and so thick with fallen trees and high grasses that the ground was completely obscured. If someone had been thrown down there, the body might stay hidden there until the corpse decomposed and began to stink. That wouldn't take too long in this mild weather. April shivered suddenly in the heat. They could see the water now, skirted east, scanning the base of the boulders and the spaces between rock and bushes.

This was the famous Frederick Law Olmsted triumph, the park he designed more than a hundred years ago that was still so wild in places that if one ignored the skyline at its perimeter, a city person could imagine the country. Just over a mile to the south, Midtown North waited for their return. The park ended at Fifty-ninth Street, where her own precinct boundary began, and the stunning city skyline spread out on the southern horizon. They were looking for signs of a disturbance, but they didn't see any.

They were silent as they retraced their steps to the place near Seventy-seventh Street, where they'd entered the park last night. The tire prints of the 4X4 and hoof prints of the mounted officer's horse were still there embedded in the grass, telling the story of their convocation. April slid down the bank to the water's edge, wetting her feet in the marshy ground.

"Damn."

"Something?" Woody asked, sticking to dry ground.

Stuck on a branch, the tail of a condom snaked gently with the current. Next to it, nestled in the mud, was a brown beer bottle bottom, showing the jagged edges of a broken neck. Half the label turned out giving the name, New Amsterdam. At a couple of dollars a bottle, it would hardly be the first choice of a vagrant.

"Just my new shoes."

"Whatchu looking for, Detective Woo?"

April was startled by the sound of a gravelly voice. "Who's there?" she called.

A balding man dressed in khaki pants and a blue parka who smelled of human waste crawled out of a space between two boulders. April recognized him immediately from the old days when she'd worked the Two-O.

"Pee Wee, what are you doing here? I thought you'd cleaned up your act and joined the Doe people."

"I tried it, didn't like them blue suits. All those rules."

He looked drunk and dazed, not fit for any kind of structure, certainly not the Doe Fund that put homeless men to work cleaning the streets, gave them food, a salary, and a place to live, but also required them to wear bright blue jumpsuits, not so different from the ones worn by prison inmates.

"And my people out here missed me too much. I help out here, keep the peace, you know that, Detective." Pee Wee tried to focus his swimming eyes. "Ain't seen you around for a while. You been on vacation or something?"

"I've been promoted. I'm a sergeant now, and I don't work in this area."

"Whatchu doin' here, then?"

"Got a 911 call last night, Pee Wee; know anything about it?"

"Yeah, I saw you," he said, nodding.

"You saw me?" She gave him a surprised look.

"Yeah and him, and 'nother cop on a horse, and two in a jeep."

"No kidding." Now Woody was interested.

"Yeah. A guy got whacked. Too bad." Pee Wee shook his head. "One of those running guys. You here about that?"

"Where?" The news was like a punch in the belly. April's blood beat in her temple.

Pee Wee scratched his whiskers. "I'm real hungry," he said.

"I'll get you some breakfast. Where's the dead guy?"

Pee Wee looked down at them from where he stood higher up on the lake bank. He scratched his beard some more. "I don't know. Dincha see him?"

"Where?" Woody demanded. "Where?"

"Right here, I don't know." Pee Wee's voice slurred.

"What kind of bullshit is this?" Woody barked.

Pee Wee looked hurt. "Do I do bullshit, Detective? The detective here knows me. I keep the peace, I'm the one stops the fights, don't I? I tell you what's up, don't I?"

"It's sergeant now," April said automatically. "Why didn't you say something when you saw us here last night?"

He stood there, shaking his head as if he had a palsy.

"Looks like you're an accessory."

"No way." Pee Wee a.k.a. John Jasper James, an ex-sergeant in the U.S. Army and a Vietnam veteran, protested. "I didn't have nothing to do with it. I thought I saw a guy go down. Maybe I'm wrong. Who's gonna believe an old drunk's story anyway?"

April could have called the detective squad commander of the Park Precinct to come and get Pee Wee James and take him in for questioning. She might have been instantly off the hook in the case and gone quietly on with her day. Any sane detective would have done that. But April wanted to clear up the mystery herself. Whatever mishap to Maslow Atkins occurred, it happened on her watch. And the missing man was Jason's student.

This time April swerved off the straight and narrow and sealed her fate in the matter. She decided to take Pee Wee James into her own house for questioning, then make arrangements to get some uniforms and search dogs out to look for a body. She was on another commander's turf. She thought about calling Mike to discuss the matter before she went any further, but she was in a hurry and figured her notifications could wait.

NINE

MASLOW'S FIRST AWARENESS was the pain behind his eyes. His head swam, and so did the room. He was lying flat on his back, drenched. His fingers were in a puddle. He moved three fingers, as if over piano keys, and figured out they were in water. He didn't know how his fingers could be in water, too. And the back of his neck. What the—? The world was dark.

His head hurt, he was blind and confused.

"Chloe, open the door." His voice came out a croak. He was a seven-year-old locked in the linen closet the day the pipe from the bathroom cracked open.

The family had been on Cape Cod. Outside a storm was raging. It was one of those terrible northeasters that rocked the coast for days, scaring him to death because it always seemed as if the rain would never end. His twin sister, Chloe, had been the one to discover the drying racks in the linen closet during a game of hide and seek.

On the day of the storm, he'd gone in there to hide. He'd climbed up on one of the racks. Chloe had come by and closed the door hard, locking him in the closet. Then a pipe cracked open, splashing water on his face. The space was so tight he couldn't even get down off the rack to open the door. Now, over twenty years later, he whispered, "Chloe, come back."

Maslow's head throbbed. He didn't know why Chloe had locked him in the closet. She *knew* he didn't like hide and seek.

"Chloe." He struggled to move and found that he was stuck.

He was terrified and wished he could be more like his sister. She could stay still for fifteen minutes or more. In the middle of a game she could leave her hiding place and find a new one, sneaking like a cat. Chloe wasn't afraid of anything.

"Please don't leave me here, Chloe. I don't want to live without you," he whimpered.

Chloe could sneak up on him anytime she wanted to. "*Boo!*" She scared him to death.

"Chloe?"

The smell was like the flats where they used to dig for clams at low tide on the Cape. It smelled like the house the day it was opened for the first time in the summer. Once they found a dead bird in the fireplace. The lady who came to clean told them that a downdraft of the wind must have caught the bird and dragged it down the chimney where it couldn't get out. The idea of the bird trapped in the fireplace, beating itself to death against the bricks, upset the twins, and they had taken the small desiccated corpse outside for a proper burial in the sand.

Mold and rot were the odors in his nose, like the space under the house where Chloe and he once hid to escape their second sailing lesson. He'd been eight and a terrible swimmer. The instructor had made them all capsize their little boats and tumble into the freezing choppy bay with all their clothes on. Maslow had panicked in the cold water even though the life jacket kept him bobbing on the surface.

When his father came up for the weekend, Maslow told him he didn't like sailing and didn't want to go out again. His father got so angry he hit him. Hit him really hard. After that Maslow started wetting his bed again.

One morning his mother wrapped him in the wet sheet at breakfast and told him she'd send him to day camp just like that if he ever did it again. So he and Chloe hid under the porch. All morning they heard their parents fighting and looking for them. He'd always hated hide and seek.

He lost consciousness thinking he was a bad boy hiding from life with his sister. Hours later, he woke up again. He still thought he was on the Cape even though the house had been sold soon after Chloe died.

"Close the window, Chloe, it's raining on the bed." Maslow moved his lips. He felt like shit.

A roar came and shook the earth. He couldn't get away from the sound. It came again and again. His mouth was crusted with dirt. Dirt was in his mouth, too. His mind wandered around his life. At one point he was telling the pretty blond doctor taking care of his sister that he'd rather die than Chloe.

He still dreamed about the way the doctor ruffled his hair, and said, "You're a fine child, we don't want to lose you."

He tried to explain that he was the boy, he should be the one. Boys were always picked first.

But she shook her head. "We can't make the change. It doesn't work like that."

Why not? They were twins? They had the same blood. Wasn't he supposed to get whatever she got?

"You're the lucky one. It's not your fault. You just didn't get it."

But would he get it later?

"No," the doctor said. "No. You won't ever get it."

But how could he *know* that? He wandered on through his life. He lost consciousness again. The next time he heard his own gasping breath he thought he was drunk at a loft party in Soho.

Ninth grade.

The cool kids had gotten a couple of kegs of beer, marijuana, and some pills he later found out were Ecstasy. About seventy-five kids were there. His friend George had invited him. When Maslow told him he wasn't allowed to go to loft parties, George told him not to worry, it wasn't a real loft party. George had this car service. He said they could leave anytime they wanted. Maslow's father was away on a business trip, as usual, and his mother hadn't cared about anything for a long time. So he went in George's limo.

George got them in the door. Then he gave Maslow some beer. Maslow took it even though he was nervous. It looked like a loft party to *him*. He drank some beer and started talking to this girl, Gloria. The beer made him feel less nervous. Gloria was very pretty. She asked him how old he was.

He thought his answer over very carefully. Gloria looked pretty old to him, maybe as old as eighteen. She was wearing a tight dress, really short. He was afraid if he said sixteen, she might think he was too young.

"Seventeen," he said.

She made a face. "I'm only fifteen. You're too old for me." She was dancing alone to the music.

Quickly, he changed his tune. "I was just kidding. I'm really only sixteen." He felt stupid; he couldn't even dance with her.

"Why lie about something like that?" She walked away.

He had another beer, and the beer made him feel it didn't matter. After a while he had two more. Then George passed him a bong and he had a few puffs. He'd seen bongs in the Village, but this was the first time he'd had one in his hand. He puffed and the pot smoke nearly took his head off.

That was how he felt lying in a puddle unable to move now. He had no idea where he was or how he got there. There was dirt all over him. It hurt to breathe. It hurt to be awake and remember his dead sister, about whom he did not think much anymore. It was very dark, the roar came and went, and the smell was like death.

TEN

ALMOST AS SOON as Jason had finished talking with April, he was sorry about involving the police in the Maslow situation before looking into it a little further himself. As the morning progressed, several explanations occurred to him. Maslow was on staff at Manhattan East, a psychiatric hospital. An emergency there—a suicide, or some other crisis, could easily have kept him busy all night. Maslow might well have been on call last night. Jason forgot to mention that to April, and later felt a little ashamed of himself for using a police detective as his own private investigator.

Jason's anxiety about what he'd done was transmitted to his first three patients. He was supposed to maintain the highest level of interest in the most detailed of accounts of his patients' daily lives. As soon as his attention wavered, and the precious empathic bond was severed, his patients always retaliated. He understood this, but he was human and these comments often got to him despite all he knew.

That morning, between nine and eleven, Jason took three direct hits from nuclear warheads. From his eight o'clock—a young woman who had a great job and many suitors but felt numb and hopeless inside—he learned that he was a cold and selfish man who used to be good-looking and well groomed but was now a depressing slug who would never have the love of anybody worthwhile. Like herself.

"You remind me so much of a man I went out with, Tony Ramero, who was a premature ejaculator," she said.

Jason's eight-forty-five patient, a bazillionaire who kept trying to pay Jason with his Centurion American Express card for the free air miles, was scornful of Jason's tendency to buy four identical blue and red ties for twenty-eight dollars from vendors on the street. "You're some cheap bastard. I bet you never go to a decent restaurant," he charged.

Jason did go to decent restaurants and liked his ties. He didn't reply as he wanted to: *We all have our money issues.*

At quarter to ten Jason called April Woo to tell her about Maslow's hospital job. She wasn't there. The thought that she might be looking for a man who was at work made him feel really guilty. He went next door to say hello to Emma and the other April. He played with his beautiful baby for a few minutes. She gurgled her baby secrets, drooling into his ear, then spit up on his shoulder when he kissed her good-bye. Jason's ten o'clock patient remarked that he smelled of throw-up *again*, then announced that he was sick and tired of Jason's hangovers.

"You look like shit. Circles under your eyes, shirt coming out of your pants. A spot on your shirt. You're a *mess*. You should see somebody about this." This from a guy who made daily cocktails out of every prescription upper and downer known to man and considered a drug-free day one when all he did was smoke pot from morning to night.

April Woo called just when he was on his way out to teach a class on transference to psychiatric residents at the medical school. He was in his office bathroom with the water on, scrubbing the spit-up out of his shirt. After drenching himself trying to get the water off in time to catch the phone, he launched into his apology.

"Thanks for returning my call. I'm really sorry about bothering you with the Atkins thing. I've been thinking about it, and I forgot to tell you he may have been on call last night. If you haven't gotten to it yet—"

"I'm on it now."

April's deadpan voice jolted him. "What's up?"

"It appears that your student, Atkins, went home around seven, changed his clothes, then went out for a jog. The doorman in his building says he met a young girl and they went into the park together. He didn't come back to his apartment last night."

"Hmmm." Jason dabbed at his wet shirt with a towel.

"Did he have a girlfriend, Jason? Maybe he had a change of clothes at her place."

"Ah, I don't know."

"Family?"

"I don't know much about his private life."

"I thought you were his supervisor," she said accusingly.

"I am."

"How do you supervise them if you don't know what their counter-transference issues are?"

"Jesus, April, how do you know about that?" Jason was stunned by the insight.

"I'm a supervisor myself, Jason. You think you own psychology?"

"Ah, this is different. Analytic candidates don't talk to their supervisors about their private lives. They talk to their *training analysts* about their private lives. They talk to me about their patients' lives."

"Uh-huh, so this missing candidate of yours has two psychoanalysts, one for himself and one for his patient? Who's in charge of the two of them? Anybody know the whole story?"

"No, it's complicated. His own analyst keeps to strict confidential-ity—" Jason broke off, knowing it must sound a little strange.

"So, what did you talk about with this guy, anything useful?" April herself sounded strange.

"Where are you?"

"In the park."

"What are you doing there?"

"It's complicated. What did you talk about with him, Jason? I have to know what was going on in his life. I need the basic facts," April said. "Everything he did in the last twenty-four hours and the rest of his life."

"April, you're scaring me to death," Jason said. "What happened?"

"We had a 911 of trouble in the area last night. We're thinking your friend might have been mugged. We have a vagrant who says he wit-nessed an assault on a jogger. There was no sign of him last night, though."

"Have you checked the hospitals?"

"We've started checking ERs, nothing yet."

"You checked his home?"

"First thing. His wallet, telephone and appointment books were there. A big wad of cash. Does he have an office?"

"Yes." Jason was silent for a second, thinking fast. "Is this inebriated person homeless, April?"

"Yes."

"Does he know more than he's saying?" Jason glanced at his watch. Shit, he was going to be late for his class. He wondered if he should cancel.

"It's possible."

"What about the bum being the mugger—?"

"It's a possibility."

Neutral. That damn neutral voice. Jason was really rattled.

"Look, I'm on my way to teach; what can I do to help?"

"This shouldn't be my case, Jason. Know what I mean? So I'm short-handed here, and out of my territory."

"I'm sorry about that." The clocks were ticking. Jason was late. Shit. "What do you need?" he asked.

"Well, you know how shrinks hate to talk to cops about their patients. Maybe you could talk to Maslow's doctor, get me some background on him. Parents, friends, other relatives, habits, sexual preference. State of mind." Her voice started to break up.

"April, are you on a cell phone? April?"

The voice came back. "Yeah."

"People don't just disappear."

"No, of course they don't. So help me out here."

"Of course. What's your next step?"

"I'm calling in the K-9 unit."

"WHAT?" Dogs? Was she nuts?

"You can't be too careful." The voice broke up again.

"Oh, Jesus, April—"

Silence.

"April, talk to me."

"Kkkkkkk."

The phone went dead. Shit! Jason didn't have time to wait for her to call back. He stuck his beeper on his belt and left his office, wondering what Maslow had wanted to tell him about Allegra before he disappeared.

ELEVEN

T HE NOSE OF A COP is used to unpleasant things. But it turned out to be quite a chore for Woody to install the vile-smelling John Jasper James, a.k.a. Pee Wee, into the backseat and drive downtown to Midtown North in the close confines of the Buick. Woody opened the front windows all the way and leaned into the wind, but he still kept his right hand clamped over his nostrils. April noted the acute sensitivity without sympathy. She was wondering when Jason would have some information for her, and she was beginning to doubt her judgment about this action. Lieutenant Iriarte was going to freak out.

"When do I get something to eat?" Pee Wee demanded as they cruised down Ninth Avenue.

"As soon as you give us a story we can work with," Woody told him. Woody loved this. He was used to making waves.

Pee Wee snorted.

"You happen to notice how bad this guy needs a bath?" Woody asked conversationally. "He's stinking up the unit something criminal."

"How'm I gonna take a bath, where I live, huh? It's not me, anyway. This outfit wasn't new when I got it."

"Where'd you get it from, a corpse?" Woody turned left on Fifty-fourth Street, passed a parking place close to Ninth, then cursed when there wasn't a space any closer to the station house.

"Stop here. I'm going up. You park and escort John James here up-stairs. Thanks." April got out and slammed the door. This door-slamming was an American, not a Chinese, thing to do. Now that she was a sergeant, American self-expression was coming a little easier to her.

She smiled when Woody muttered, "Fuck." Now he had to take the flak when he came into the squad room with the odoriferous bum. She hurried inside.

"Your boss is looking for you," barked Pete Mongers, the lieutenant on the desk.

"Thanks." April took the stairs two at a time. When she opened the squad room door, something was up. Seven extravagantly dressed—looked like South Americans—were all yelling in Spanish at once. Iri-arte was using his smoothest manner to soothe their ruffled feathers. Then he saw April and his placating expression changed.

"Where have you been?" He snapped at her as if she were the one to blame for everything.

A woman with big red hair and a tight yellow suit, who'd been yakking a mile a minute in haughty Spanish, raised her voice even higher and blocked April's advance with her curvy body. She screamed at Iriarte that she needed her matter attended to *pronto!*

Even April got it. Iriarte gave the woman a quick formal bow, assur-ing her that he was attending very seriously. Then he turned to April and jerked his head at his office. April was momentarily blinded by flashes of sparkly light from the boulder-sized diamond rings on the fingers of both the men and the women.

"Move." Her boss gestured angrily at her again, but before she could navigate around two gesticulating women in pink and red, Woody marched in with John James. Simultaneously, the agitated Spanish-speakers recoiled from his stench.

The unctuous lieutenant was galvanized into action. He led the Latino crowd into his office himself, came out, and spoke to Hagedorn. Hagedorn's Spanish left something to be desired, but he was the only one in the squad room at the moment other than April who knew how to talk to nice people. Hagedorn went into the office. Iriarte shut the door on them, then advanced on April and her malodorous trouble-maker.

"What the hell are you up to? I've been trying to rouse you for two hours."

"I tried to reach you. But something came up."

"I don't give a shit. You know where these people come from? One of them got mugged on Fifty-seventh Street. Who the fuck is this?" he pointed at Pee Wee.

"This is John James. He hangs out in Central Park. I know him from the Two-O."

"Oh yeah, he one of their street crime boys?" Iriarte took time out for a joke. Ha ha.

Woody, who was a little sensitive about his past, looked the other way.

"I help out, don't I, Sergeant?" Pee Wee looked hurt.

"Yeah, sure you do," April told him.

"What do you think you're up to, Woo? I have something important for you to do here." Iriarte's Spanish contingent was keeping his temper in check, but only just.

"You gonna give me something to eat?" Pee Wee whined.

"Later," Woody told him.

"What'd you bring him in here for? Get him out of here," Iriarte growled.

Woody glanced at April. She nodded toward the door and mouthed, *Wait for me.* When the two of them were out of sight, she spoke.

"I know it's unusual, sir, but I need to keep him here for a few minutes. He's a witness in the Atkins case."

Iriarte's fingers traveled nervously to the gray silk square in his jacket pocket. "What are you talking about?"

"Woody and I are following up a 911 from last night."

"*What are you talking about?*" His irritation escalated.

"That call for help last night didn't turn up anything, but there's a report of a missing person. I'm checking it out."

Iriarte's eyes narrowed with suspicion. "What report?"

"We were covering the area last night, sir."

"What report? I have no report!"

"It's a missing doctor, sir."

"Are you hard of hearing or something? This is not your case."

"I'd just like to clear it up since Woody and I checked out the missing doctor's apartment, made a preliminary search of the area, and requested more help."

"What! Why don't I know about this?" Iriarte started to scream.

"I called in, sir. You weren't available." April lied with a straight face. Now she was floundering, looking for a lifesaver. There wasn't one.

"I don't have any message of this. We have a mugging here. You have no business working out of the area. Who knows about this? Are you crazy, bringing some park bum in here?"

"It wouldn't look bad if we broke the case, sir. And I'd like to find the doc; he's a student of Jason Frank."

Iriarte smacked his forehead. "A fucking headshrinker case? Is that what this is? *Ay Dios!* That fucking Frank again. What are you, crazy?" He screamed some more.

Shouting erupted from the lieutenant's office. He turned to her. "Get rid of this. I'll give you an hour."

"Thank you, sir."

A few minutes later, April had John James sitting in a room downstairs, tapping his foot and waiting impatiently for a feed.

"Pee Wee, how would you like a nice shower and some clean clothes?" she asked sweetly.

"I'm fine. I can take care of myself," he said, glancing sullenly at Woody.

"Doesn't look to me like you're doing too good a job of it."

"I have new clothes on order," he quipped.

"A comedian," Woody responded.

"Detective Baum is right. We don't have time for a comedy routine. What's going on with you?"

"Like I told you. About a year ago, I got recruited from those Doe people." Pee Wee licked his lips.

"Recruited?" April gave him a surprised look.

"They come around looking for people, you know how it is—"

"That's not the way I hear it. I hear you have to get cleaned up and apply, isn't that what you did?"

"Nah, some lady recruited me. I know what I'm talking about," he insisted.

"Maybe you got in some kind of trouble back then. You want to tell me about that?"

"I didn't do nothing. You know I don't get in no trouble anymore. I'm an old man."

"I can check it out, Pee Wee."

He shifted uncomfortably. "I was part of a *program*. I didn't like it, that's all. Now I have other people take care of me."

"Doesn't look like that to me. Who are these people?"

"I'm down good," he insisted.

April shook her head. "Okay, says you. We'll get back to that. Tell me about last night. Did you make that 911 call?"

"Yeah, right." Woody interjected.

April gave him a warm smile. "Never underestimate, Detective. John James here used to be one of our best people. Always knew what was happening in the area. If there was trouble, he'd be the one to make a call, isn't that right, Pee Wee?"

"Used to be a lotta trouble. Those gay boys and the wildings—they were bad. Once those monsters from uptown set a friend of mine on fire. Behind the museum . . ." Pee Wee's dirty hands trembled. "You got a cigarette for Pee Wee?"

April shook her head. "You'll have to wait. Detective Baum here has asthma."

Woody blew air out of his nose. *Yeah, right.*

"So what happened last night? You make that call or what?"

"No. There were two faggots out there. One of them must have made the call. Had to be a cell phone, didn't it? The nearest call box is practically in the Bronx," he muttered.

Not true. There was one close by, on a tree. "Come on, Pee Wee, I haven't got time for this. What happened?" April demanded.

"I don't know. Two faggots were doing each other in the bushes beside the lake. I fucking hate that. I told them to get away from my place, but they were too into it, didn't give a damn. Live and let live, I say. So I took off for a while. When I came back one of them was laying there. Looked dead to me." Pee Wee rattled his foot. The soles of his old sneakers flapped. He had no socks, and his feet were black. April didn't believe a word he was saying.

"How did you know he was dead?" she asked.

"I seen a lotta dead people in my time."

"You see a girl in a pink sweater?" Woody asked.

Pee Wee shook his head. "A girl? I didn't see no girl. Just the two faggots. Then the body. I turned away for two seconds and then there warn't no body."

"This is a hell of a story. You're drunk, Pee Wee." April glanced at Woody.

Woody got the idea. "Maybe he rolled the guy himself. What do you think, boss?"

"Sounds very plausible to me. You have a little accident and mug somebody, Pee Wee?"

"No way," he protested. "I don't do that. I'm an old man."

"Okay, what do you say I give you a nice reward then? You tell me what really happened out there—where our missing p is—and I'll get you new clothes, food—"

"And lodging for the rest of my life. I know where this is going, but I ain't taking no fall." Pee Wee lost his cool. "I ain't *done* nothing. I just saw the two faggots, that's all. Maybe I got it wrong. Maybe the guy was just taking a rest. Maybe he got up and walked away."

"Jeeesus fucking Christ!" Woody muttered.

"See what happens when you try to tell the truth?" Pee Wee complained.

A quick knock. The door opened and a uniform stuck her head in. "Here's that sandwich, Sergeant," she said. "And Officer Slocum from K-9 is up on Seven-seven and wants to know if you're coming up."

"Tell him I'll be there in ten minutes." April was already on her feet. She turned back to John James. "What's the matter?"

"You got me all upset. I pissed my pants."

Disgusted, Woody removed himself from the area. April was already at the door. Young Officer Marcie was going to have to deal with this. Amazing how the people who didn't freak out over the human frailties were usually the females.

"Look, you sober up, have a sandwich and some coffee. Officer Marcie here will set you up with some clothes. You're going to get yourself showered and we're going to talk again later when you're sober, okay?"

"I'll help you out, but I ain't staying here. I know my rights." Pee Wee didn't look in the least ashamed about his accident.

"You listen to me, Pee Wee. Together, we're going to get this story right, that's the only right you need to think about, got it?" April left the room and beckoned to the uniform. They conferred outside.

"Marcie, I want you to bag and label every article of his clothes. Get him cleaned up—and run a warrant check on him for me—oh, and hold him down here, will you?" she added.

"Yes, ma'am." Officer Marcie had no problem with the command.

April wanted to point that out to the squeamish Woody Baum, but what was the point? She shouldered her heavy purse and headed out. "Come on, Woody, you lucky devil, we're going to the dogs."

She stopped at the precinct door. Jason Frank had taught her that one of the perks of being a high-class woman was having men open doors for her. She turned her flat-affect face to Woody and waited to see what he would do.

Thrilled to escape the housekeeping duties, Woody opened the door for her with a little bow. "After you, boss."

For a moment she almost liked him.

TWELVE

APRIL TRAVELED TO the Park Precinct, a hundred-year-old renovated stable on the Eighty-fifth Street transverse, to inform the CO there that within the hour, a K-9 unit would be doing a search for a missing person around the area of the rowboat lake. Luckily Captain Reginald, whom April didn't know, was out in the field when she arrived. So was Sergeant Mackle, CO of the detective unit. Because neither of them were there, she didn't have to embellish her story with any lies about what she was doing on the case. She ended up speaking with the second whip, Captain Rains, a tall, heavyset man with a lush crew cut who looked unhappy with the news that a man had gone missing in the park last night. This would make big trouble for the park, the jewel in the New York City crown, and hence for the precinct dedicated to maintaining its security.

"I'll inform Captain Reginald immediately," Captain Rains told her.

"Thank you, sir."

Ten minutes later, April and Woody met up with Officer Sidney Slocum outside Maslow's building not far away on Eighty-second Street. Slocum was the opposite of Mackle; short, skinny, freckled, entirely bald, with a ginger-colored mustache so extravagant it made Mike's merely luxuriant one look puny. He was wearing an orange Search and Rescue jumpsuit, and if he was lucky, he weighed a hundred and twenty after a big meal. His dog was a huge German shepherd with a flat collar and leather leash that looked as if it weighed as much as its trainer. The two had come in a blue-and-white, and two other patrol cars were parked nearby. So far so good. No shouts from Iriarte. No challenges to her authority yet. April was still hopeful that she'd be able to pull off the operation without a hitch. She was dreaming.

She got out of the gray Buick, which still smelled pretty bad from Pee Wee, and approached the dog trainer.

"I'm Sid Slocum. Sergeant Woo, I presume. You in charge here?" he asked.

April nodded. Instantly, the dog growled and lunged at her, setting the tone for their relationship. April jumped back and assumed a kick-boxing stance.

"Don't worry about Freda, she's a sweetheart," Slocum assured her, hiding a smile under his mustache.

April didn't think it was so funny. "Yeah, well tell her I'm carrying. This is Detective Woody Baum." April jerked her chin at Woody, who approached with caution.

The dog, however, seemed to like *him*. She strained at the leash for the chance to shed all over Woody's navy jacket and lap at his hand. "Hi, guy." Woody wiped the slime on the shepherd's head and looked pleased by the manly exchange. April thought the drooling, growling hulk wasn't even a close second to Dim Sum—the six pounds of adorable, smart-as-a whip apricot poodle that was the Woo family pet. It didn't have much judgment if it preferred Woody to her. She had her doubts about its finding Maslow. So much time had passed that it was probably too late for this kind of hunt.

"Is this all the backup you have?" she asked to cover her anxiety.

"Yep. Four uniforms, the three of us, and Freda. It's a pretty small area. We're not talking about the Jersey Wetlands here. If your man is here, we'll find him." Another smile. Slocum was full of confidence. Then his expression changed when an ABC news van cruised by and the driver stuck his head out of the driver's window.

"I heard something big's up in the park. Missing jogger. You here about that?" The man's eyes looked red and his long gray hair was gathered up in a ponytail.

"You're misinformed," April told him, frowning.

He *heard*? How did he hear? She hadn't used the police radio, hadn't told anyone but Iriarte. She had a really paranoid thought. How bad did Iriarte want to mess her up? She frowned as the van moved half a block down CPW, did a U-turn, and parked in a bus stop to wait for the story to emerge.

"Jesus," Slocum swore, then pointed at one of the uniforms. "Get that asshole out of there. We have to close off the area. No cars, no people. It confuses the dog."

April's beeper went off. Lieutenant Iriarte's number flashed on the screen. She pulled out her cell phone and dialed the squad room. A minute later he came on screaming, "Where are you, Woo? I got the PC on the phone. He wants to know how come no one briefed him on this? Your missing person case is on the fucking news!"

April eyed the ABC truck. "No kidding?" she said.

"You don't have much of a life expectancy, Sergeant. Give me your location, I'm coming up there."

"Yes, sir." She gave the entrance to the park as Maslow's Place Last Seen, then hung up and checked her watch. It was two on the button. Her boss would be there in fifteen, twenty minutes. Her heart was racing. Her palms were wet. Her head felt light. The PC himself was going to ream her. Her mother's dream would come true. The whole world would see her cease being a cop. She'd be disgraced on the evening news, on the morning news. She'd lose her boyfriend, the man she worshipped and adored. Why? Why had she done this? Then she remembered Maslow was still missing and the minutes were ticking by.

"Come on, Officer, let's get started," she said.

"Call me Sid. Good girl, good girl. We're going to work. Yeah, yeah. You hot, old thing? Good, good, good." Slocum pumped the dog. She responded by practically taking his arm off in her eagerness to get going. He turned to April. "We need to get a feel for this guy. He live here? I want to start at ground zero."

"Uh-huh." The dog growled at her, and April stepped back uneasily.

"Wow, this is an unusual reaction for Freda. She always loves everybody."

"Uh-huh." April didn't believe it.

They crossed Central Park West and went through the routine with Regina again to get into Maslow's apartment. This time she kept a respectful distance as Sid unleashed the dog and let her run around the apartment, root into the armpit of Maslow's jacket that he'd left on the sofa. She leapt up onto the bed, dove into the pillows. Then, finished with that, she raced into the kitchen, where the rotting Chinese leftovers drove her into a frenzy.

Slocum glanced at the stereo, computer, medical texts. "What is this guy, a medical student?"

"Doctor. A psychiatrist."

"Jeeze. Hear that, Freda, this guy's a headshrinker." The dog raced back into the bedroom, nosed into the pants on the bed, and came up with the wad of bills and the wallet.

"How do you like that? I didn't even tell her to fetch. Good *girl*, Freda, but put it down. You don't get a tip unless you find the guy alive." The dog dropped the money. A bunch of twenties and fifties fanned out, looking to April like several weeks' pay.

"Interesting," she murmured. "Woody, bag that and the wallet so they don't disappear, will you?"

Woody stepped forward to comply. The dog growled when he reached for the money.

"Interesting," April said again. Freda had an interest in cash. So did April. She wondered why Maslow had so much on hand.

"Guess he wasn't heading off for a night on the town. Anything in the hamper? I need something only he touched."

"Nothing there, I checked."

"Was he depressed? Did he have any illness we didn't know about? What about his medications?" Slocum asked.

They went into the bathroom. Sid checked out the medicine cabinet. "Hey, look at all this. This guy has asthma, allergies, psoriasis, migraines. You name it. Today must have been laundry day."

"Maybe he has a maid. We can check that out." April glanced at her watch. "You have enough now. Let's get the show on the road."

Slocum swore at the neat apartment and empty hamper. He debated between the suit jacket flung on the sofa and the T-shirt and socks lying on the floor in the bedroom. He chose the T-shirt, approached it with a plastic bag, slid the thing inside without touching it himself.

"Freda, come, baby. We're going to work." He held out the bag for the dog to sniff. Freda leaped around for a while, trying to get into the bag. Then she lunged at April's crotch without warning.

April let out a yelp. Sniff, sniff, sniff, slobber, slobber, slobber. The dog nosed her privates while Slocum and Woody yucked it up. Then, Freda lost interest in April and moved on. She shoved her muzzle into Woody's crotch, smacking her jaws at the delights she found there, causing manly consternation and more macho jokes. Freda sure knew what she was doing. She then dived back into the bag for more of Maslow. Sid reattached the leash.

"Go find," he said.

The dog went for the door, knocking the hovering Regina out of the way and nearly off her feet. Freda panted at the elevator, sniffed it all over when it arrived, and they got inside. Down in the lobby she sniffed the rug, stopped, headed for the door. Sniffed the brass struts holding up the canopy, peed on one of them, then dragged Sid right to the corner and across the street to the park.

THIRTEEN

M ASLOW HEARD THE SOUND of a barking dog and opened his eyes. He saw very little. He tried to move. But his whole body was stiff and aching. A hammer pounded in his head. The light now was gray, the smell of pond scum was overwhelming. He knew for sure it was pond scum when a bullfrog hopped over his face with a wet splat, spiking his heart with terror. Other creatures were alive in here, too. He could hear their movements around him. Things that he knew would start eating him as soon as he died.

Now he heard a dog and prayed that someone had come looking for him. He didn't want to die.

"Here, I'm here." When he opened his mouth to scream, all that came out was a soft moan. He couldn't seem to get his voice up to full volume.

He tried to move his fingers and his mouth, but pain was all he felt. He didn't know how long he had been here. He was aware that he'd felt sicker before, that he'd fallen asleep. He'd awakened, then dozed some more.

Maslow was irritated by his weakness. He couldn't seem to rally enough energy to get himself going. Through a haze that felt like a bad drunk, Maslow knew he was not dead. Chloe was not talking to him. Nor was he trapped on the drying rack in the linen closet in the Cape Cod house that was long gone from his life. He knew his fantasy that

Chloe was still alive and ten years old in Massachusetts was only a fantasy.

He was not a child and not a sixteen-year-old, drunk for the first time. He was not twenty-five and knocked out on the street after trying to help someone in a bar fight. He was not an intern in ER. He was way past all that. He was a psychiatrist now, a candidate at the Psychoanalytic Institute. He remembered his class on personality disorders the night before. He remembered his session at his Central Park West office with Allegra and how upset she'd been because he'd told her it was normal for a child to have loving feelings for a father, even if the father abused her. But that was about it.

He couldn't remember anything after coming home and getting ready for his jog. If he had not gone for the jog, he could be dreaming. But the creatures crawling on him were no dream. He was not where he was supposed to be. He was in terrible pain. He couldn't move at all. Something had happened to him. And if he didn't do something about it soon, he might well die.

His brain worked slowly. He was a doctor. He should be able to figure out what was wrong with him. He heard the barking of a dog and other noises he couldn't identify. The persistent roar troubled him. He knew he should be familiar with the sound. He struggled to remember what it was. A roar just like it occurred every few minutes night and day all year around. What was it?

Roar, vibration, then quiet for a while. He should be able to identify it, get some clue to where he was. He tried to distract himself from his fear of the dark and the creatures scurrying around there. He was in a hole. Definitely a hole. His breath caught in his throat. A hole of some kind.

He heard people shouting. He didn't know if the shouting was real, or just the sounds of people in his memory. His voice wouldn't work to call back to them. Was he paralyzed? It hit him suddenly that the roar was the subway under Central Park West. He was underground. Yes, in a hole close enough to hear the subway.

But he could breathe, so there must be air coming in from somewhere. It was dark, but not always totally dark. He knew he had to get up, get out of there, but he couldn't seem to get going. His hips and legs wouldn't move. He didn't know why. Suddenly he was eye to eye with a rat. His heart almost stopped with terror. The rat scurried over him, and he couldn't do a thing about it. The sound of the barking dog faded. He closed his eyes and prayed. *Come back. Please, God, come back.*

FOURTEEN

WHEN THE PHONE RANG at quarter to twelve on Wednesday morning Cheryl Fabman was writhing around on her stunning sea foam silk sheets in the bedroom of her fabulous new Park Avenue apartment. Simultaneously, she was trying to find a comfortable position and assign an appropriate name to her multiple miseries. First on her list: Her doctor, Morris Strong, the most prestigious plastic surgeon in New York—for whom she'd had to wait nearly a year just for a consultation—had assured her that a "slight discomfort" after the liposuction and lip-enhancing procedures was the worst she could expect.

At his urging she'd had the hip, thigh, abdomen, and butt sculpting by liposuction as well as the lip procedure on the same day. A full five days later she was not experiencing mere discomfort, nor even simple pain. Her body was now perfectly shaped and encased in Lycra, but she was in agony. Total and complete agony. She did not blame God or herself for the pain. She blamed Dr. Strong for lying to her. Next, she blamed her ex-husband for being a jerk and going through with the divorce after she very nicely said she'd have him back. After that came her decorator for being late, her lawyer for not doing better on her behalf, and her fifteen-year-old daughter for not loving her nearly as much as she should.

Because of her stupid lawyer and stingy husband, Cheryl's apartment was only six rooms on Park Avenue and Seventy-fifth Street instead of ten rooms on Fifth Avenue below Seventy-second Street. Because of her decorator's tardiness, the smell of paint was still very intense and made her sneeze frequently. In her postsurgical condition, Cheryl's every sneeze threatened the inside of her plump new lips and made them feel as if they might burst free from their fan of stitches and split open like ripe plums. It was not unlike sex after childbirth.

Which brought her to her daughter, Brandy, who should have hurried home right after school yesterday to take care of her, order soup for her from the deli, and complain about her father. Brandy was a disappointment on all fronts, particularly on the father front. She did not complain about him at all. Cheryl found this stoicism abnormal, not to mention unsatisfying to herself. Not only that, Aston Gluckselig, the love of her life at the moment, was way over fifty, was heavy, and didn't have as much hair or height as her ex-husband, Seymour. Aston's balding head came to her forehead when she wasn't wearing heels, and to her chin when she was. On the good side, he was a very prominent man, extremely well known among the UN crowd. He was a lawyer. He made millions of dollars, and he loved her. The only thing that stood in the way of their marrying was that he was waiting for his aged mother to die and his last child to graduate from college before breaking the news to his second wife that he was divorcing her for another woman. Luckily Aston's mother was ninety-eight.

Cheryl did not blame herself for fucking him in the private swimming pool in the garden of his house at the exclusive Round Hill Club in Jamaica the first night they met. The pool was surrounded by flowering oleander and had seemed quite hidden, but in fact happened to be only a few feet from the bedroom where her then husband, Seymour, turned out not to be sleeping and, worse, not at all blissfully ignorant of what was going on. In spite of Cheryl's certainty in her heart of hearts about her husband's own *years* of cheating, he faked a huge heartbreak thing and made a big stink, threatening to kill them both. His lawyers advised him to choose divorce as an alternative action. She offered to forgive him, to no avail. Now he had whores all over the place, and she hated his fucking guts for being such a hypocrite.

The phone stopped ringing, and Brandy stood by the bedroom door peering in.

"Mom, is it okay if I go to school now?" she asked.

"Brandy, thank God you're up." Cheryl groaned and removed the frozen gel pack from her aching lips.

"I've been up for hours. Can I go to school now? They called. I said I was on my way."

"I didn't hear the phone ring. Come into the light where I can see you." Cheryl didn't feel at all well.

"There is no light." Brandy hit the light switch, turning it on.

Cheryl yelped. "Shit, are you trying to kill me?"

Silence from the kid. That really hurt.

"I'm bad, baby. Really bad," Cheryl said, hoping for love.

"You aren't going to die, are you?" Brandy said sullenly. "If you die, you know Dad will get me."

"No, of course I'm not going to die. I just hurt all over. The prick doctor lied to me. He told me this would be a piece of cake. And I still feel like shit."

"You want something to eat, or another painkiller before I go?" Brandy studied her mother. "You don't look great." Brandy reached out to touch her. "Maybe something's wrong with the surgery. Should I call the doctor or something?"

Cheryl squinted into the bright light, then jerked away, squealing, "Don't touch me. I'm all right." Then, angrily, "Where were you last night?"

"With Dad, doing my homework. Remember, Tuesday's my night with *him*."

Cheryl didn't remember anything like that. "I've been lying here in agony, worried to death about you all night. Don't you remember you were supposed to come home and take care of me yesterday?"

"I thought you had a nurse taking care of you," Brandy replied.

Cheryl had sent her away two days ago. She changed the subject. "How is your father?"

"Fine." Brandy rolled her eyes to the ceiling.

"You didn't tell him about the surgery, did you?"

"He wouldn't be interested." Brandy studied her nails, a horrible color, almost black.

"Are you sure you didn't tell him?" Cheryl demanded suspiciously.

"He doesn't *care*, Mom. You could have a boob job the size of California and he wouldn't give a shit." The voice of a heartless adolescent.

Cheryl groaned. So much for the family she'd given her entire life for. Her bastard of a husband leaves her for twenty-year-old whores, and her daughter twists the knife.

"Was the bitch there?"

"Which one?" Brandy giggled.

"Jesus, how many are there?"

"Just kidding. She wasn't there. I told you it was our night."

Cheryl closed her eyes against the hurtful fantasy of her daughter and ex-husband in an intimate tête-à-tête in the dining room of the Central Park West apartment twice the size of hers that she knew cost over four *million* dollars exclusive of the lavish, but utterly tasteless, furnishings. Brandy had reported that he'd bought only the most expensive modern Italian furniture, everything shiny and slick, the sofas and chairs in those weird shapes. And there were *no* antique accessories like she had. Absolutely none. He'd left their entire life, their whole history behind. There was nothing soft even in Brandy's room there. Not a plant, not a pillow. Nothing. He'd scattered the money freely on nothing at all. Cheryl was sure he'd fucked the decorator, fucked the woman from the carpet company. He'd fucked the paraprofessional in his divorce lawyer's office, then the divorce lawyer, even though she was older than Cheryl herself. The man was a fucking maniac. Talk about childish revenge.

All of her miseries stabbed at Cheryl's gut. Something bothered her about Brandy's report of last night. Cheryl wanted to call her on it. She wondered if the kid was now lying, too. Brandy lied about everything. She gave her child a sharp look. There was nothing wrong with Cheryl's eyes. "Jesus, what the hell is *that*?"

"What?" Brandy said.

"That outfit is bad, Bran."

Brandy was wearing a pink fuzzy sweater the size of a hanky. She had a small frame and breasts large enough to nourish all the children in a well-populated state. The breasts stretched the sweater way out of shape and hiked it high up on her midriff. Her jeans hung low on pudgy hips and were pegged tight down to surprisingly coltish ankles. Cheryl groaned some more.

The daughter she'd prayed would come out more like her than her father looked like a refugee from a road show production of *Grease*.

Here they were in a new millennium, with beauty aids more advanced than at any other time in history. And of all the daughters in America, she, Cheryl Fabman, had to have the only one who wouldn't do a single thing to fix herself up. Brandy's short brown hair was, well, brown, flat on top, flat on the sides. Her chubby cheeks showed no sign of bones anywhere. Her eyelids were pale and virtually lashless—her eyes pitifully small for the brilliant blue that was the only thing Cheryl could claim as hers. And worst of all were the breasts—the breasts! The least Brandy could do was camouflage the freaking breasts just a little. The sight of her daughter looking like such a poor imitation of a tart was so disturbing it was almost enough to distract Cheryl from herself. Her daughter was a disaster, a complete disaster. She couldn't *bear* it.

"What?" Brandy's lips were stuck together in a pout.

"Trust me on this. The outfit makes you look fat. What are you eating? I told you *no fats*. No *sugar*, Brandy. What's in your mouth?"

"Nothing."

Cheryl sat up a little. "*Something's* in your mouth. What is it?"

"Nothing's in my mouth. I have a class, Mom. I gotta go."

"I thought today was One World Day." Cheryl's lips hurt or she would have had a lot more to say.

"It is, but I can't skip the whole thing. Do you want me to take it as a sick day?"

"No, if you have to go, then go. But come back at five. I want to see you for dinner."

"You can't eat anything," Brandy reminded her.

"Neither can you. We'll have soup together." Cheryl shook her head. "What did your dad give you for dinner last night?"

"He took me to the Posthouse for a steak."

Cheryl closed her eyes. Their old hangout. "You didn't eat the French fries, did you?" she demanded.

"Just a few. Not all of them." Brandy broke free of the door. "Bye, Mom. Don't die on me. Promise?"

"Put on a sweater or a jacket, anything to cover up those boobs," Cheryl replied.

FIFTEEN

DAVID HUNG OUT on Lexington Avenue, waiting for Brandy to get away from her mother and call him. It took all morning. He had eggs, bacon, and hash browns for breakfast in a coffee shop on Eighty-sixth Street, then moved on and had a second breakfast of pancakes and sausage with lots of syrup in another coffee shop on Seventy-ninth. The food hardly calmed him at all as he waited and waited. Brandy didn't try to reach him until almost one. They met up on Madison, crossed Fifth Avenue, and started walked west through the park. They were going to Seymour Fabman's apartment to celebrate their first killing.

As he walked, David was thinking about how good it felt to hit a man and bash his head in. It was more exciting to think about that than to worry about his payment. Brandy promised to do it with him on her father's sofa, the one in the window overlooking Central Park. He was a little worried about it since she'd told him she'd had sex many times before, and he'd never done it even once. He snorted. But he was a dangerous man now. No one could claim he was a loser anymore.

"How's your mom?" he asked, thinking Brandy looked just unbelievable in the fuzzy sweater. And was now his slave forever.

She clicked her exciting tongue pierce against her teeth. "You wouldn't believe what they did to her lip. Ugh, it's so gross. No one will ever kiss her now."

"Why?"

Brandy rolled back her top lip to show him where the doctor had made incisions to plump up her mother's deficient lip. The view of the pink wet flesh on the inside of Brandy's mouth almost made David nuts with excitement. He wanted to grab her on the spot, kiss her, and feel that metal pierce with his own tongue. She hadn't let him kiss her in the week and a half since she'd had it done because she was afraid of infection. Today was the day. She'd promised.

She let go of her mouth, made a little skip away from him, and grinned at the bump in his pants, daring him to come and get her. This rendered him speechless with joy and pain. Should he grab her? Shouldn't he grab her? He hated it when she shrugged away from him. He wasn't sure what she expected him to do. He felt the power had shifted last night, and now he had to be the boss. He struggled with his confusion about it.

"Any trouble with your mother?" she asked.

"Nah, what about you?" he asked, biding his time on the boss thing.

Brandy shook her head. They walked in silence for a while, knapsacks on their backs. As they neared the West Side, almost by tacit agreement they swerved north, away from the corpse in the cave. David's excitement about the promised sex gnawed at his ulcer. He chewed a Maalox.

"Are you *sure* your dad won't be there?" He concentrated on the parent who could bust them for skipping school. That would be a royal pain given the circumstances.

"Of course I'm freaking sure. He goes to work, doesn't he?"

"Yeah, but last night, you said he wouldn't be there, and there he was la—" David snorted again. Seymour Fabman had been naked on the sofa, lapping at his girlfriend's crotch. David giggled. Brandy had run like a rabbit when she saw her father going down on a girl who looked as young as they were.

Brandy turned the color of her sweater. "Shut up," she warned.

"Well, he *was*. Did he see us?"

"He didn't call my mom," she said vaguely.

They came out of the park at Eighty-sixth Street and David stopped short. "Jesus! Already?" He was pumped now.

News vans were lined up along Central Park West just outside police barricades. Emergency vehicles and police cars blocked the Avenue even to buses. Cops were swarming all over the place, trying to get the traffic north of Eighty-fourth Street out of gridlock.

"Wow. Wow, look at that."

They headed toward the blue police barricade, then past it, right down the emptied middle of the street. A lot of other people had the same idea. No one stopped them. At Seventy-ninth Street Brandy walked up to a cop, who wasn't doing anything. It was a girl cop, bulging in her uniform. Her hair was straggling out of a ponytail, and she stood by the park wall, looking over at the activity inside.

"What's going on?" Brandy asked.

She looked them over and shrugged. "Someone's missing. They're looking for him."

"No kidding," Brandy said excitedly.

"You kids better watch yourselves."

David wondered what she meant by that. They moved on, didn't speak to anyone else. At Brandy's father's building, they stopped. The doorman was glued to the canopy in front.

"Is my dad at home?" Brandy asked him.

"Nope. He went out at eight this morning, same as usual."

"Anyone else there?"

He shook his head.

Brandy and David went upstairs to the twelfth-floor apartment with the great view of the park. "This is cool," he said in the elevator.

"Yeah. I hope they find him soon," Brandy agreed. They got out and walked quickly down the hall. In the apartment, the music was off now and the place was cleaned up. They went straight through to the big windows facing the park in the living room. Right away they saw the man with the orange SAR jumpsuit being dragged along by a shepherd with one of those orange necklaces that glowed in the dark. The two were out by the edge of the lake. Nearby, some cops were beating the bushes and bending over to pick things up.

Brandy disappeared into the kitchen.

David's chest burned with the excitement. His gut, too. He was afraid his dick wouldn't work and wondered why it was easier to smash someone's head in than have sex. He hoped that Brandy wasn't in the mood.

SIXTEEN

BEFORE HIS CLASS Jason ran over to Maslow's office to leave a note on his door telling his patients he wouldn't be in that day and to call Dr. Frank. He also had some information on Maslow Atkins—his number at work, his parents' home number, his father's office number. He knew Maslow's analyst, an M.D. called Bernie Zeiss. Bernie and Jason served on several committees together at the Institute. Jason thought of Bernie as a plodding, rule-following prig of the old school who obstructed every attempt at modernizing the field of psychoanalysis. The last thing he wanted to do was talk to the man about sensitive issues that involved confidentiality. To get anywhere with Bernie he was going to have to lie. If he lied, he might get in trouble. He decided to risk it.

After teaching his psychiatric residents at the hospital, which was about a half mile north of his Riverside Drive apartment, Jason walked home. Several taxis slowed as they neared him, but for once he didn't flag them down. He needed a few minutes to rethink the situation, and even more, he needed a break outside in the fresh air. As he walked, he was grateful for the caress on his face of the light breeze off the Hudson River and the familiar view of the New Jersey skyline. On this Wednesday in early September the trees on the Palisades were green, and there were still sailboats scooting around on the water. He had the terrible foreboding that big trouble was coming. Without realizing it, he picked up his pace. He was jogging by the time he turned the corner on his block. A large blank-faced doorman he hadn't seen before

opened the heavy wrought-iron and glass doors of his prewar building
and stood in his path.

"Can I help you?" he asked, indicating the sign that said all visitors
had to be announced.

"It's okay. I'm Dr. Frank. I live here."

"Oh, okay. I'm George."

"Hi, George."

Jason didn't have time for more pleasantries. He had twenty minutes
before his next patient and a lot to do. He nodded and rushed to the elevator, which was visible in an old-fashioned cage, was over eighty years
old, and broke down all the time. Jason could see its bottom all the way
at the top of the building. The stairway circled the cage. Jason took it
two steps at a time. His stomach rumbled as he ran up the five flights,
but he didn't want to think about the comfort of food.

In his office, his phone told him he had nine messages. His answering machine drove him nuts. Many people left extremely long messages about absolutely nothing. Sometimes it took fifteen minutes to
get through them. He skipped through this group quickly. His stomach
rumbled. There was no message from Maslow, but he hadn't expected
one. He punched out the number of Manhattan East, where Maslow
worked as a staff psychiatrist thirty hours a week. It took a while to locate Dr. Ira Kiln, who had employed him there.

"Oh, Maslow is turning out very well. He's an excellent doctor," Dr.
Kiln assured Jason when he finally got him on the phone.

"Yes, I know—"

"And a wonderful young man—very caring and easy to work with."
Dr. Kiln went on at some length, frustrating Jason's effort to inform
him that he was not calling for a reference.

"I know he's a first-year psychoanalytic candidate at your Institute.
He talks about you often, and—"

"Did you happen to see him last night?"

Dr. Kiln stopped short. "No, Maslow doesn't come in on Tuesdays.
What's this about?"

"Thank you so much. I really appreciate your help."

"What's this about?" Dr. Kiln asked again.

"Oh, nothing. I'm just trying to locate him, and I didn't have his
schedule."

Jason sighed and called Bernie. Naturally, Bernie's machine picked up. Jason told Bernie's voice mail he needed to talk to him about a matter of extreme urgency, gave his number, and hung up. He checked his watch. He had seven minutes left. He dialed Maslow's parents' home number. A woman answered on the second ring.

"Hello, this is Dr. Jason Frank. I'm one of your son's teachers at the Institute," Jason began.

"How do you do, Dr. Frank." The woman had a soft, hesitant voice.

"Is this Mrs. Atkins?" Jason asked.

"Yes."

"I'm trying to locate Maslow—"

"My husband isn't here right now. You can reach him in his office some time after noon."

"I'm sure you can help me. Do you know where Maslow is?"

"No idea, he travels a great deal for his company. His secretary will know. She has his schedule."

"We're having a little miscommunication. I'm not talking about your husband. I'm talking about your son, *Maslow.* Do you know where I might find *him*?"

"He's very busy, too."

"I know he is. That may be the reason I'm having difficulty locating him. When did you speak to him last?"

"Let's see, what day is it?"

"Wednesday."

"I think we spoke with him last Sunday—or maybe it was the Sunday before . . ." The soft voice trailed off.

"You didn't talk to him last night or this morning by any chance?"

"Oh no, he never calls when he's traveling."

"Maslow is out of town?" Jason was puzzled.

"Really? Where is he?" Mrs. Atkins asked.

Jason chewed on his lip. The woman was on another planet. He spoke patiently. "As far as I know Maslow is right here in the city, and I'm trying to reach him, not his father."

"Well, his father is more likely to know where he is than I am. No one tells me anything. Do you want his number at the office?"

Jason had Jerome Atkins's number at work but he said, "Yes, thank you," and wrote it down a second time.

The clock on his desk told him he had four minutes left. Jason noticed that the two numbers he had for Jerome Atkins were different. He figured one must be the company number and the other his private line. Jason dialed the one his wife gave him.

"Mr. Atkins's office."

"Yes, this is Dr. Jason Frank calling. I'm a colleague of Mr. Atkins's son, Maslow, and I need to talk to him. Is Mr. Atkins available?" Jason shifted his gaze from the clock on his desk to the six valuable skeleton clocks on his bookcase. He watched their pendulums swing back and forth, ticking off the precious seconds until his next patient was due. He shook his foot with impatience.

"No, Mr. Atkins is out to lunch. Can I give him the message?"

"Yes. Would you tell him Dr. Frank called, and it's a matter of some urgency." Jason gave her the number and hung up.

His phone rang. He grabbed it on the first ring.

"Jason, this is Bernie Zeiss."

"Oh, Bernie, thanks for getting back to me so soon."

"What's up?"

"Look, to make a long story short, Maslow Atkins is missing and I need some information about him."

"Oh, I'm a nonreporting analyst at the Institute. You know I can't tell you anything without talking first with the head of the educational committee—"

"Bernie, just listen for a second. I know it's highly unusual to call an analyst about a patient, but Maslow is a student of the Institute, he's part of our family, and he may be in trouble. We have to—"

"Well, I can put in a call to Ted right away. He'll put the question to the committee, and I'll get back to you tonight after the scientific meeting."

"Bernie, this isn't the program committee where we argue over whether we're going to accept a paper no one will come to hear. A man's life may be at stake here. There's not time to check with Ted Tushy. You understand?"

"What do you have to do with this, Jason?" Bernie asked, suddenly suspicious.

"The police are looking for Maslow. If you don't talk to me, Bernie, you'll have to talk with them." Jason tried to be patient.

"Jason? What has happened?"

"I don't have time to go into it. There are police and tracking dogs searching for Maslow in Central Park. I need information right now."

"Well, what do you need to know?" Bernie said hesitantly.

"Was Maslow involved in anything illegal?"

"What? No, no. Of course not!" Bernie sounded shocked. He recovered quickly. "Maslow was a very fine young man. Obsessional with marked sexual inhibitions. We were making very fine progress."

Jason's stomach growled.

"He spent an excessive amount of time studying and exercising, a good boy. He was terrified of his sexuality. But we were making good progress. Excellent progress." Bernie clicked his tongue, thinking about it. "You know, last week he had a date, his first in a year. He met a girl in the Institute library, a graduate student at Columbia. A fine girl. It didn't go as well as I'd hoped. Unfortunately, her specialty is the representation of the Virgin Mary in the iconography of the Roman Catholic Church. For Maslow, it was as if she herself were a Madonna. He tended to view women as either asexual idealized madonnas or as whores."

That got Jason's attention. "Was there a whore?"

"He did have this analytic patient, the borderline hysteric you were supervising him on. He was troubled by the treatment. He saw her as a wounded bird to be rescued. She was obsessed with him. He thought he saw her on the street, following him. I wasn't concerned about his competence. I felt his anxiety was induced by her intense transference. You were very helpful to him, but of course he felt he couldn't be completely honest about it with you. He was worried that his feelings for his patient were not appropriate and were making her worse. She's a self-mutilator and he feared suicide. My own view is that Maslow had a patient who was trying to get him to enact the overly intimate relationship she had with her father, and it made him nuts as he tried to resist."

It made sense. Jason knew that Maslow's patient had been abused by her father and figured out that she was trying to embroil her young analyst in some kind of reenactment.

"Working, working, run, run, run. That was Maslow. He wanted to keep his feelings at bay," Bernie was saying. "But around this patient, he had uncanny experiences."

"What kind?"

"He thought he saw her on the street. He heard her call his name or thought he saw her. She told him stories that had eerie resemblances to things in his own life. Things that no one else knew. He wondered if she was doing research on him, if she followed him. I told him we've all had experiences where a patient has seemingly supernatural intuitive knowledge. Freud himself believed in telepathy. It doesn't mean that the patient is doing research. Maslow was having difficulty accepting that such feelings are natural for him to have with such an ill patient."

Jason noted that for someone who had been so reticent about confidentiality, Bernie was now spilling out information at a rate of more density that he had in thirty years of Institute meetings, and also that he was talking about Maslow in the past tense. Bernie couldn't be stopped. Now he was Sherlock Holmes.

"But you know, last week he looked up, saw this Virgin Mary girl across the table in the library. They started talking and he asked her out for dinner. It started out well. They were both bright, intellectual, attractive, and the conversation was easy. He asked her about her work. She had documented antifemale bias in the depiction of the Madonna in the church of San Paolo de Tey. Maslow was impressed. She asked him about his work. She was very interested in the concept of penis envy, and it gave him a chance to expound. Then she turned on him, told him that psychoanalysis is phallocentric and a central tenet of the male hegemony. In other words, the date didn't go well. I'm worried about this Virgin Mary girl. She had a lot of anger about this. She could be a latent psychopath who went after him."

"Unlikely," Jason said.

"Well, she hated psychoanalysis—you never know."

"What about homosexuality?" Jason asked.

"Oh, for him just admitting he had feelings for a girl was difficult enough. To help him get in touch with his unconscious homosexuality would have taken another twelve years." Bernie chuckled. "No, he liked girls."

Then his voice changed. "I've got to go. Now I'm going to need you to sign a release for this, Jason. You are to tell nobody. You understand, nobody! I broke analytic confidentiality for you. You have to sign a release."

"Yes, of course," Jason said, thinking Bernie should be so lucky. His stomach rumbled some more. Now he was really concerned. Forget the Virgin Mary, it was that patient contacting Maslow out of his office they had to worry about. They could have underestimated her pathology. Instead of a garden-variety hysteric, she could be a psychotic stalker. And they missed it. He was appalled. They'd been encouraging this boy like a lamb to keep treating the patient in analysis while he became more and more anxious. They missed it, both analyst and supervisor. They'd failed Maslow.

Jason knew he had to talk to this girl right away, but also that he had to go through the Institute to do it. Could he lie to Miss Vialo in the education office to get the patient's chart? His many clocks told him he had three minutes to his next patient, not enough time to start the process.

Jason's patient who was due now came from a midtown office and was often late. His stomach growled louder, demanding fuel. He'd settle for a soda. Did he dare take a chance on running home for a minute to grab one? He didn't have a door leading directly from his inner office to his apartment. If he wanted to go home, he had to go out into the hall, dash to his front door, unlock it, and duck into the apartment, adrenaline racing with the fear of getting caught. If he were seen going next door, of course, his patient would know where he lived. It was bad enough when they caught sight of Emma. She was a movie star, and her appearance in the hall got them all excited. They wanted to know what she was like and if he knew her. It made him want to move to another planet.

Jason debated quickly: to slip out or not to slip out. Thirst won. The buzzer hadn't rung yet so he strode out into his waiting room. Then, stealthily, he opened the door to the hall. Empty. Good. Heart beating, he sprinted to his front door, opened it, fell in, and slammed it just as the elevator stopped on his floor. Inside the apartment the mail was still stacked on the hall table. In the kitchen Emma waved at him from her stool by the phone. Sounded like she was talking to her agent. Jason kissed her on the forehead, grabbed a diet ginger ale, and poked his head out the door. Damn. In the hallway, the thirty-two-year-old investment banker waiting there had an angry look on his face.

Jason gave the man a weak smile and broke his no food rule. "Hi, want a soda?"

Jergen Walsh put his index finger to his chin. "Do you have a Sprite?"

What did he think it was, a restaurant? "Sorry, no." Jason let him into the waiting room, then excused himself. He dashed into his office, closed the door, checked his machine to see if Jerome Atkins or Maslow Atkins had called. They hadn't. He went back to the waiting room door, opened it. "Please come in."

The young man came into the office, looked around suspiciously, then pointed at a plant in the corner. "What's that doing here?" he demanded.

"Is it a problem?" Jason asked. It was a very pretty geranium plant that Emma had given him.

"It's full of spores. I'm very allergic."

Jason was exhausted. He needed to call the Institute and talk to Miss Vialo. He didn't have time for psychosis. He took the time anyway. Not to deal with Jergen would have made him much worse. No matter what, Jason didn't want to fail anyone else today.

SEVENTEEN

BY FOUR O'CLOCK on Wednesday afternoon the missing jogger was the major breaking news story in New York City and NYPD's priority case. Nothing except bomb scares and murdered children upset New Yorkers more than the possibility of disappearing without a trace. The Mayor and the PC instantly became the center of the media frenzy, stepping up to the microphones demanding results and promising to spare no expense to get to the bottom of the disappearance.

As a result, dozens of people had been deployed to clear the park. Detectives were swarming the area. Emergency vehicles blocked Central Park West all afternoon. For hours cops, TV crews, bystanders, everybody who knew about the case had been waiting for a dog to come up with something.

By four in the afternoon, nothing had been found. Freda was still repeating the same game: bounding up and down the edge of the lake, then turning suddenly toward the interior of the park only to gallop back, plunge into the tall grass and disappear. When she came out of the grass, she circled and circled like the poodle Dim Sum did when she was getting ready to do her business.

The spot that kept her interested was near where April and Woody had come up with the broken beer bottle that morning. April had examined the mucky spot herself. They'd found a sneaker that had been there for ages, the floating condom, a button, a crushed Coke can, a piece of filthy waxed paper, cigarette butts, and other small bits of garbage. The ground itself was undisturbed. No chance a body was hidden or buried there.

"Why does she keep going back there?" April called to Slocum, who stood on a boulder watching the dog like a parent who doesn't want his child to know how irritated he is.

"Something," he called back, noncommittal. "She's onto something."

April heard the excitement in Slocum's voice, then, "Shit!" when Freda finally resolved her lengthy afternoon activities by taking a huge dump in the bull's-eye of her area of interest.

"Must have been some animal there. Maybe a squirrel or something," he explained.

Exhausted, April let herself collapse for a moment on an obliging rock. A few blocks to the north, Woody had been working for hours asking different people the same questions. A dozen other detectives were doing the same thing in different spots. A lot of information about people's comings and goings had to be processed.

Except for what they'd gotten from Maslow's doorman and Pee Wee James, however, no one else admitted to having seen Maslow last night. Didn't mean anything. Sometimes people didn't know they'd seen anything relevant for weeks. For now, though, the search was slowing down. They were giving up. Maslow may have come in here, but he wasn't here now. April checked her watch. Lieutenant Iriarte had long ago come and gone. He'd told her to stay with it until her tour was over, then take her days off as usual.

Now her tour was over, she had two days off in front of her, and the last thing she wanted to do was take them. She was frustrated and didn't trust Woody, Slocum, or the damn dog, Freda, to do their jobs right. She didn't want to go home. She wanted to stay right there and work round the clock until she found the missing man. She stood there scowling angrily at the dog. What kind of tracker could follow a scent from a man's apartment down to the sidewalk, find the place where they knew he'd come into the park, then not be able to find the place where he'd exited?

If he'd walked to another entrance, wouldn't the dog have been able to follow him there? If someone had carried him out, wouldn't the dog be able to isolate the smells? Giving the sniffer some credit, April did consider the possibility that if Maslow had been assaulted and slightly injured, he might have been disoriented. He might have hailed a taxi right on the park drive and been driven away. But the dog didn't lead them to the drive and then stop. So where did Maslow go?

April was discouraged. A whole day gone and she still didn't know what was up. She didn't have a good feeling about any of it. She decided to check out Maslow's office, get a list of his patients, start digging. There was no way she was going home. Her cell phone rang. She dug it out of her pocket. It was Mike.

"Hey," she said.

"Hey, *querida*, I'm seeing your little butt on the news right now. You hit the big time with this one." Mike's voice sounded amused.

"My butt?" April was horrified. Publicity was the last thing she needed.

"Yeah, the cameraman must like you. You and the dog are all over the place, wagging your little tails."

"Great." She watched Slocum extricate a plastic bag from his pocket and pick up the doggy do that represented the only product of the dog's workday. And hers.

"What's happening?"

"Not much. The only whisper we have on the missing p is from a drunk who says he saw a gay guy beaten to death last night."

"Is your guy gay?"

"Possibly. I don't have background on him yet."

"What about a body?"

"Nothing so far." April watched Slocum offer Freda more scent of Maslow, saw the dog obligingly sniff into the plastic bag with Maslow's scent in it, saw the dog sneeze. Her dog Dim Sum sneezed whenever she was angry.

"I'd say the dog has had it," she added.

"Uh-huh. What else?"

"Well, our witness happens to be Park Patrol, remember him?"

"Oh yeah, Pee Wee something. Used to hang out by the lake."

"That's the one. He was so drunk this morning he peed in his pants. I've got him in a room at Midtown North. He should be relatively sober by now."

"May not do much good."

"I was thinking about Maslow taking off in a cab. He left a big wad of cash at home. But maybe he had more with him. It's just that he went out in jogging clothes. He wouldn't exactly leave town like that, or go to a restaurant, but I'll check out cabs."

"What me to join you?"

"Join me in what way? Without a body, there's no homicide, *chico*. This isn't your turf."

"Not yours, either. They're giving this to Special Case," Mike said.

April was silent, remembering Iriarte.

"I'll meet you at Midtown North in an hour. We'll talk about it then," Mike said gently.

"I can't do it in an hour, Mike. I have to check out Maslow's office, and talk to Jason—"

"You're off it, *querida*. Trust me on this, will you?"

"Kkkkk." April made the sound of static and terminated the call. Uncharacteristic independence was taking her for a ride. To April's mother, dragons, ghosts of unknown ancestors from China that disappeared long before April was born in New York City, and poor harmony were responsible for everything that went wrong in life. April wondered which was making trouble for her now.

From her rock, she watched two detectives she knew were from the Special Case Unit saunter over to Slocum. Slocum greeted them like old friends, then called the romping dog and clipped on her leash. Together, the K-9 team headed away from her. April knew that the dog and trainer's fifteen minutes of fame were over. She wondered if the dog, like herself, felt the anguish of loss of face and defeat.

D ON'T BE MAD at me. You know I can't take it." David leaned down close to Brandy as they left her father's building. She jerked away from him, her eyes on the crowd that had gathered on the street outside the park.

"I'm not mad at you, David," she said coldly. "You just tried to rape me. Without my consent, I might add."

"I didn't." He put a hand on her shoulder. "Please, I don't want you to be mad at me."

"I said I'm not mad." Brandy shrugged off the hand. She was thinking about her father's stash in the old cookie jar that her grandmother had bought for her when she was a little girl. The cookie jar was one of the few things he'd salvaged from the marriage. The pot was first-class and there was a lot of it.

Brandy never saw him put the stash in the cookie jar because she never saw him do much of anything these days. She hadn't spent one single night in the room he'd had decorated for her over the summer. He was really pissed at her. *Really pissed.* He hadn't come to see her at camp. He'd told her he had business meetings that weekend. And after she got back he kept breaking dates on her. They'd only been together once, not that she cared that much. He'd been a drag ever since the divorce. The one time they had dinner, he'd raised the subject of the pot. They'd been in a restaurant. He'd ordered a bottle of wine and let her have a glass. Brandy lost herself in the memory of that evening with her father.

"How's your mom?" he'd asked, busy looking around at other people, not at her.

"Great. She's lost about ten pounds, and she's getting her face lifted as soon as the apartment is finished," she'd told him.

He turned to look at her for the first time, his eyes popping with surprise. "Really?"

She nodded. "Do you think she's going to marry Aston?"

His lips went together in a thin tight line, his jaws worked, and she heard the noise he made whenever he was upset. His teeth grinding metal. "Whatever makes her happy," he said. But he didn't look like he meant it.

"Do you have a girlfriend, Dad?"

Seymour Fabman lifted his chin and glanced over at the waitress, a girl with a great body and short black hair. "Nah, would I do that to you, baby? You're my girl." But he wasn't looking at her when he said it. Then, he'd raised the other subject, the thing that was on his mind. The pot.

"Hey Bran, I want to know the truth about something."

"Sure, Dad." She finished her glass of wine. He poured her more, then added some water from the Evian bottle.

"You ever try any drugs?"

She gave him that wide-eyed innocent look she was always perfecting in the mirror. "Me? What kind of drugs do you mean, antidepressants like Mom takes?"

"Your mother takes antidepressants?" That was another new one for him. "Really?" He almost fell off the chair. Brandy loved freaking her parents out.

"Yeah, something like that; it makes her calm down."

His face screwed up some more. "I guess your mom isn't doing so well." Then he flashed her a mean smile. "No, I was talking about other kinds of pills, the kind you use to get high, and pot—alcohol, that kind of thing. You ever do it?"

Brandy giggled. "Where would I get something like that, Dad?"

"Maybe your mother," he said slyly.

"Nah, Mom doesn't do that."

"I guess her thing is men," he said bitterly.

"Aston's terrible, Daddy. I hate it there. Can I come and live with you?" She couldn't help herself. The suggestion just came out. A trial balloon to see what he would do.

"What's wrong with him?" Seymour lifted his chin again, the way he did when he was all dressed up, checking himself out in the mirror, and thinking he looked pretty good.

"He's, like, disgusting and Mom is all over him. Dad, do you use those kinds of drugs?" She flapped her eyelashes at him, knowing exactly what was on his mind. The pot in the cookie jar. He was concerned that either his source was shorting him, or she was coming over and stealing it. It wasn't a hard one. But parents were dumb and Brandy was a very good liar. She stole things all the time, and he never knew they were missing.

"I have some friends who do," he said smoothly. "You know what happened? Somebody left stuff at my place, and some of it was missing later. Do you know anything about that?" He didn't exactly ask if she came over on her own when he wasn't there. He'd know for sure if he asked the doorman. If he didn't ask, it wasn't her fault. He was probably afraid to ask. So fucking passive.

"You never invite me over, Dad. Maybe the maid took it."

That got him thinking and shut him up. But that was three weeks ago, the last time she'd seen him until yesterday. And he'd lied to her. He had gotten a girlfriend to replace her. She couldn't believe her eyes last night. Her dad going down on some blond bimbo almost as young as they were. Really gross. And now David wanted to try it.

Returning to the present Brandy hopped off the sidewalk into the street. "Wow, this is wild," she said about the news vans all around them. "I hope they find him soon. Maybe we should help them look."

Still on the subject of his feelings about her rape contention, David followed her like a big shambling dog. "You know I'm not supposed to get upset."

"Who says?" Brandy muttered, disgusted with him.

"My doctor. Look at me, Brandy, it's just because I love you. You made me like that. You tease me, then I want to be inside you. It's not my fault. You promised."

"So what. Maybe you didn't get the job done. Maybe he's not really dead."

"Oh, Jesus!"

"Well, how do you know? How many dead people have you ever seen?"

"I saw my grandfather."

"In a coffin? That doesn't count. Maybe we should try another one. The first one happened too fast."

"Shut up, Brandy!"

A vaguely familiar-looking woman wheeling a grocery cart full of plastic bags looked inquiringly at Brandy. Brandy gave her the finger.

"You promised after *one*, Brandy. You got your *one*," he said angrily. "You're not coming through."

"But I didn't promise *today*," Brandy snapped.

"What do you think I cut school for, huh? Why do you think I did *that*?" He tugged on the edge of her fuzzy sweater. She tugged back. He punched her lightly in the arm. She recoiled.

"Ow! Don't piss me off. You hate school. You wanted to see what would happen. It has nothing to do with me." She was getting really annoyed at him, wasn't sure she wanted to fuck him at all. She rubbed her arm, oblivious to the people looking at them.

"Fuck you, Brandy. This whole thing was your idea. If my mom found out, I'd never get the Beamer."

"You'd go to fucking jail," she muttered under her breath, skirting a bunch of people who had stopped to gab in the middle of the blocked-off street.

"What for?" he whined.

"What fucking for? I'm only fifteen," she reminded him.

"Hey! I'm not supposed to get upset. My ulcer will start bleeding, and I'll have to go to the hospital again. I don't want to get mad at you, okay?" His face was red and his hand was bunched into a fist. He looked a little scary.

"Okay, okay, don't be upset," Brandy placated him.

"You do this to me. This is *your* fault. You wiggle around, and I can't help myself."

"I don't wiggle." She shut out his whining, then cheered up as they headed north. "Look at this. The whole world is watching that asshole dog running around the park. He's got to be one shit tracker. Isn't this great?" she said excitedly.

"Yeah, it's pretty good," David had to admit.

"We should do this again. Really." Near the park entrance, they merged with the crowd of bystanders and media gathered outside the park wall. One video team was set up and doing an interview with a woman in a leather jacket. Brandy thought she recognized the interviewer and admired the cut of the jacket.

"My mom would look great in that," she remarked.

"Yeeah, right. Your mom."

Brandy walked around the video camera to get a better look. She was distracted by a man talking into a tape recorder. He pulled a cigarette pack out of his pocket, extracted a cigarette, and lit up with a Zippo. Brandy knew from the Zippo, the rich smoke, and distinctive blue wrapper that the man was French and the cigarette was an unfiltered Gauloise. She considered asking him for one in his native language and blowing him away with her French.

"You're too cocky. You're going to get us in trouble." David took her arm roughly and trapped it against his side. Once again she dodged him, pulling hard to get away.

"Don't be such a dick."

"Hey, kids! What—are you blind or something? That's a police line." A big cop swung around suddenly, waving his night stick at Brandy as she casually stepped between two police barriers with a pair of cops at each end.

"What's the problem?" She stopped immediately, cocked her head to one side, and flashed him one of her bright innocent smiles that always brought male attention down to her chest level.

"What's the matter with you? Don't you know when you see one of those you don't go there?" The cop sounded angry. He was big and heavy but looked pretty young. Brandy pegged him right away as someone who hated kids. She also noticed that his blue eyes slid down to her chest before turning to David.

"Where do you think you're going?" he demanded.

Brandy piped up. "What's happening? I live up there." She pointed toward her dad's pink building down in the next block. "We saw all the activity and wondered what was going on. Is that a crime?" she smiled some more, clicking her tongue pierce against her teeth. The cop's interest excited her.

He looked at David and asked the question again. "Where do you think you're going?"

David shifted his feet, moving closer to Brandy. "If you're looking for someone maybe we can help you," he offered timidly. If she could be daring, he could be daring. He smiled at her to show he had balls.

"You want to help us?" The tall cop poked the short cop next to him with the nightstick. The two had been talking, watched the crowd. Now they had something to focus on. They grinned.

"Yeah, maybe we could, like, help out," Brandy said.

"That's very nice of you. Do you guys hang around here a lot?" The short cop joined the conversation. He seemed nicer than the first one.

Brandy jutted a hip in his direction. "Uh-huh."

"No kidding." He smiled in a friendly sort of way.

"I bet we know everything that goes on here," Brandy bragged, basking in the cop's smile.

"No kidding." The tall cop aped the short cop.

"Well, we do." Brandy thought he was mocking her and plunged into motor-mouth mode. "I see a lot from that window. David and I both do. Just like in that old movie, the one my dad likes because the wife gets offed—you know which one I mean. Hitchcock, very *noir.* The guy sees a murder from the window, and it turns out . . ."

"Hitchcock?"

"He was a filmmaker," Brandy explained. "He really revolutionized the whole suspense thing in moviemaking, but you're from that time so I bet you already know that."

"Oh yeah, you think I'm that old?" The cop looked over at the pink brick building she indicated, then at the trees in the park, very leafy and green. "Did you see something from your window you'd like to tell us about?"

David chose this moment to intervene. "We sss-ssaw a tracking dog, and we're good at finding things."

"Yeah, what are you looking for?" Brandy asked.

"Nice sweater," the second cop said. He was short, had a crew cut. "What color would you say that sweater is?"

"Pink," Brandy piped up quickly, pleased that he'd noticed.

"Pink. It's really nice."

"Thanks. Pink is really in this season."

"Why don't you come along with me. There are some people you can talk to, how about that?"

"Why can't I talk to you right here?" Brandy gave him a big smile. David gave her a little punch. Maybe they were getting too daring.

"Because, I'm not in charge of the investigation." The big cop was serious now. He wasn't looking at her right. Brandy didn't like that.

"Whatever," she muttered. "Do I get to see the dog?"

"Maybe when it's done working."

Brandy bounced on the soles of her expensive Nike Airs. "Cool," she said. She felt up now, way up, and starved to death from the pot. She didn't care that David was getting anxious, and she had no idea that her eyes gave her away.

NINETEEN

AFTER THE SPECIAL CASE detectives took off and Slocum left with the dog, April went in search of Woody, who had been busy asking questions and photographing people on the scene with disposable cameras all afternoon. The cameras were a surprising new initiative on his part. She walked north and found him under a tree near Eightieth Street talking to a boy and a girl. The girl, she realized with a jolt, was wearing a pink sweater.

Right away April pegged the two of them as private school kids. She saw their rank in the way they stood. Even from way off down the path she could tell the girl was holding court, aware of the power of her little body. Her voice carried a long distance.

"I love dogs. I bet you don't know anything about dogs. I know everything about dogs." She was excited, was bouncing on the balls of her feet. "You should see me work with that dog," she said.

"Sure." Woody caught April's eye. Relief was evident in his face as she strolled over.

"Hey, Sergeant, I've got a present for you. A real find. A tracking expert with a sense of style. Nice sweater, huh." He rolled his eyes at April as the girl turned to her.

"Yes, I'm an expert." The girl bounced some more, the boy couldn't take his eyes off her.

Woody raked at his crew cut with one hand and introduced the kids with the other. "This is Sergeant Woo." He turned to April. "What we have here is Brandy Fabman. She lives right over there." Woody pointed out the pink brick building, then checked his notes for the exact address. April spoke before he could recite it.

"Hi, Brandy." She gave the girl a warm smile.

Woody pointed at the boy. "This is David Owen. He lives on Park Avenue, but he hangs out here a lot. Brandy goes to All Saints, she's a tenth-grader. David's at Madison Prep; he's in the eleventh grade. These two have been going to camp together since they were nine. How about that?" He went on without taking a breath. He took a picture of them. Brandy gave him a big smile. David put a hand in front of his face.

"Brandy's mom and dad just got divorced, and last Friday her mom had everything done. Everything! It's hard to imagine, isn't it? David's mom is a banker at York Bank, his father's a lawyer at Debevoise Plomptom. They want to help us out," he finished. "Isn't that nice?"

"Hi, David." April gave him a smile, too, but he didn't return it. She could see the girl was high. She smelled beer, guessed they'd been drinking, maybe smoking pot, too.

"You're a cop? I bet it's cool to be a cop. Nice outfit," Brandy commented. There was nothing nervous about her.

"Thanks." April appraised the fuzzy pink sweater. At least two sizes too small. "Yours is hot, too. Angora?"

"How'd you know that?" Brandy gave her a wide-eyed stare.

"I'm a cop. I know everything." April smiled again. "What's up with you guys?"

"Could I see your gun? I've never seen a gun up close." Brandy kept on bouncing. She was wired, no doubt about it.

"Nope."

"Okay." Brandy spun around, changing the subject abruptly. "Hey, where'd the dog go? Did it find what you were looking for?"

"What are we looking for?" April asked.

"David and I know all about search dogs. I'll bet you're looking for a dead body."

"We're looking for a man who disappeared last night. Do you know anything about it?"

The girl spun back to Woody with surprising grace and gave him a hurt look. "Why wouldn't he tell us that?"

"He must have had his reasons." April glanced at Woody. He shrugged.

"You cops are spooky," Brandy giggled.

"Thank you," April said. "How come you know so much about dogs?"

"That dog that was here was a real dork. I bet I could fake it out easy." Brandy stopped bouncing, moved off the sidewalk, and drew a line in the dirt with her toe, challenging.

"No kidding. How would you do that?" Woody asked.

Brandy shrugged.

"I bet you couldn't. Freda's pretty well trained," April told her.

"Is that its name? Freda? I had a great aunt Freda. She looked just like that dog." Brandy laughed. So did David.

Kids acting out. April was half amused. The other half thought they should be whipped. "So, how can you help us?" she demanded. "Where were you in the park last night?"

"In the park? In the park?" Brandy frowned at David. "Didn't it rain? Yeah, it rained last night. Nope, we weren't here. We did our homework and watched a movie."

"Where did you watch the movie?" Woody asked.

"My dad's," Brandy said loftily.

"What was on?"

Brandy smiled. "Who is this guy that's missing?" She drew another line next to the first one. Both cops watched her.

"He's a doctor," April told her slowly.

"What kind of doctor?"

"A psychiatrist."

"Eeew. David goes to a shrink. He *hates* him, don't you David?"

David's face went red. "I do not."

She punched his arm. "Yes, you do. You go every Thursday at five. His name is Frog. Frog, right?" Brandy started hopping on one foot. "Your shrink's name is Frog, isn't that crazy?"

"Clog." David said, looking miserable. "His name is Clog."

"How do you spell that?" Woody asked.

"I don't know." The kid was alarmed. "Brandy!" he said. "We gotta go."

April checked her watch. Smiling, she made a small motion of her head at Woody. *Separate these kids.* "God, I'm tired. Come on, Brandy, let's sit down for a minute." She headed for an empty bench, talking as she walked.

The girl followed her at a skip. "Can I see your gun? Please. I won't shoot it or anything."

Back on the gun. April ignored the request. "You know, I'm thinking about yesterday. It rained in the afternoon. It didn't rain at night. Maybe you went out for a while in the evening and forgot about it. You look like you enjoy a good party, drink some beer, smoke a little pot. What else?" April's tone was neutral.

"Oh no, no, no. You got the wrong person. My dad doesn't let me out at night." Brandy shook fingers decorated with black nail polish at her. "I don't do anything like that. Don't you know how bad that stuff is for you?"

"Do you live at your dad's?" April asked.

Brandy hesitated for a beat. "I live mostly with my mom. She just had surgery, though. She's kind of out of it." Finally, Brandy threw herself down on the bench, keeping a worried eye on David. "What's that guy asking him?"

"Same thing I'm asking you—what you did and what you saw in the park last night. What you do for entertainment, that kind of thing."

"Nothing. I told you, we weren't in the park last night, and I don't do drugs. My parents would kill me."

"Oh come on, everybody does it. I know what it's like."

Brandy gave her a sharp look and a little shake of the head. "Don't get me in trouble."

"Why would I get you in trouble? You look like a nice girl to me."

"Ha," Brandy said, but she was pleased.

"Anybody with half a brain could guess what a pretty girl like you would be doing in the park with your boyfriend."

Brandy blushed and swung her legs. "He's not my boyfriend."

"He looks like he's crazy about you."

"Doesn't mean he's my boyfriend. And I wasn't in the park," Brandy added.

"That's not what the officers over there said you told them."

"Look, we were in my dad's apartment. We saw the SAR dog. We came down because we wanted to play with the dog, that's all. I know how to work with dogs. I could give you some tips."

"What kind of tips?"

Brandy shrugged. "I know about dogs, that's all."

"How do you know about dogs?"

"I'm a dog trainer."

"No kidding. Who did you train with?"

"John Zumech—ever heard of him?"

April was stunned. She'd not only heard of Zumech, she'd worked with him. She looked at the kid with sudden interest. Maybe Brandy wasn't a complete flake. The girl yawned, and April caught sight of the tongue pierce. Okay, what was she seeing? A girl whose parents were just divorced; her mother was taking care of her own business, having her face lifted. The kid was acting out with alcohol and pot. But a lot of kids did. Right now Brandy looked wistful.

"Brandy, I can see you've taken something. If I took you into the station and searched you, would I find anything on you I shouldn't?"

Brandy laughed uneasily. "You're a cop. I bet you like to hurt people. Are you going to arrest me and beat me up? That would be so cool. My mom and dad would have your *ass*."

April's face didn't change. "Brandy, I'm with the good guys. I don't hurt people. I help them."

"Well, if you want to help that guy, you should try another dog. This one doesn't know shit."

April tended to agree with her. "Okay, it's getting late. I'm going to let you go home now. But I'm going to talk with Sergeant Zumech about your dog-training skills, and also your parents."

"Wow, do you know Sergeant Zumech?"

"Yes, I do."

"You know Peachy?" Brandy was stunned.

Peachy was Zumech's Doberman. "Yes, I know Peachy," April told her.

"Wow. My mom calls this kind of coincidence synchronicity."

"No kidding, your mom must be a smart lady."

Moodily, Brandy stared at David and Woody. "Not really."

April smiled in spite of herself. No daughter thought her mother was smart.

"He took my picture, why?"

"We're looking for a girl in a pink sweater, fits your description."

"Wow." Brandy frowned. "I saw a girl in a pink sweater yesterday. I saw her today, too. Real thin, long black hair, is that the one you're looking for?"

"Might be. If you see her again, will you give me a call?"

"Sure, I will, sure. I love to help."

April and Brandy exchanged phone numbers.

Then she met up with Woody.

"Anything?" she asked.

"They're high, but I don't think they know anything. Want to bust them?"

"It's an option for later. Right now I want to check Maslow's office," April told him. "It's up on Eight-nine and CPW. Let's go."

They hurried out of the park. The show was over. Central Park West was moving. The barricades were down, the media circus had moved somewhere else, and the park was open to the public again.

TWENTY

AS THE LIGHT FADED to black, Maslow moved his arm for the first time and realized that he was not bound. Where he was lying, flat on his back, was damp and rocky, but the puddles he'd felt around him before were gone now. His mouth was dry and he was starving. He inhaled deeply, trying to get control of the weakness, the dizziness and pain in his head. He was like the old man with a brain tumor he'd seen in the hospital just a few days ago. Every exchange, every moment had taken ages. Ten minutes to raise his arm, to pick up a foot, answer a question. "Give me a minute," he'd say. Maslow was like that now.

He told himself in a few minutes he would explore his prison. When he was ready. Now he would try to think. He could trace the events of his last day. He remembered waking up and worrying about the date he'd had with Vivian last week, how much he'd liked her. He remembered how upset he'd been that they'd argued. He'd been worrying about it for a week, obsessing about whether he should call her back. After a week, he wondered if it was too late to call her. Would she be insulted that it had taken him so long? He wasn't sure he liked her anymore. But then, she called him and left a message. The message was she'd left her pen somewhere. It was a blue pen, a gift from her mother. She asked if he remembered it, if he'd seen it. He hadn't seen it, didn't remember it. He wondered if the call was just an excuse to talk to him. For two days he'd played the message over and over trying to figure it out. Did she like him, did he like her? What should he do about it in either case?

That day he'd had classes, had lunch, saw two psychiatric patients, and had his session with Allegra in his office—the one that upset her so much. He'd called Jason, gone home, and changed for jogging. He remembered the rain. It had been raining all afternoon. When he came out of his building, he'd seen Allegra. She was sitting on a bench outside the park. In that moment when she came up to him and didn't let him pass her by, he knew she really had been following him for some time.

That was all he remembered. Nothing after that. He'd been with Allegra and now he was here. He had an ache in his throat, as if he'd been punched there and lost his voice. His chest hurt, and it was hard to breathe. Maybe a collapsed lung, maybe cracked ribs. He couldn't tell. He realized he was shivering. He knew he had to get moving, drink, and eat something. He put his hand out and felt a crumbling surface, like the beach at low tide, inches from his face. At his sides the space widened a little, but only a little. Even if he were able to sit up, there was no room to do it.

Panicked, he felt for his chest and stomach. It was then that he realized the fanny pack he'd taken with him when he left home was still on him. Lying on his back, moaning with terror, he groped around in it for his cell phone. With the phone he could call someone and get out of there. He found the phone, felt the talk button, pushed it, and heard a beep. He moved it up his chest and raised it to his face. There was no flashing light to indicate how much life the battery had left. That's how he knew he'd been in his grave longer than eighteen hours. He didn't know how much longer he could last.

TWENTY-ONE

J ASON DEBATED BYPASSING the hierarchy at the Institute and just calling Miss Vialo in the education office for Allegra's chart. In the end, he knew there would be nothing but trouble and accepted the fact that before calling Allegra, he had to go through Ted Tushy, the chairman of the Educational Committee, to explain the reason for such an unorthodox action. He left a message for Ted in his office, and Ted called him back less than an hour later. All day Jason had been screening his calls, which made his patients entirely paranoid and nuts. It was exhausting dealing with their edginess along with everything else.

When Ted called him back, Jason was with a patient, but finally they connected. "What's the crisis?" Ted asked.

"Maslow Atkins is missing. It's possible he's been treating a psychopath. I need to reach her."

"We can't have a violation of patient confidentiality." Ted was as dogmatic on the subject as Bernie had been. A colleague's life was at stake. They didn't get it.

"You're absolutely right," Jason told him solemnly. "That's why I want to protect the process, Ted. As the supervisor of this case, now that the analyst is missing, I'm the person clinically responsible for the patient. All I want to do is call her and arrange for a consultation to discuss the situation."

The last thing Jason wanted to do was tell Ted he was going to investigate the patient. Jason could feel Ted sweating all over the phone. He thought it would be overkill to point out that if the patient had killed the analyst, it would do even more harm to psychoanalysis and the Institute. Ted intuited the thought.

"God, we've been trying to get publicity for analysis for years," Ted muttered. "This is a hell of a way to get it."

"My thoughts exactly."

"The last thing we want to do is endanger our good name."

"Absolutely right. Or our candidates," Jason added.

"It's so hard to get good candidates these days," Ted said sadly. "Did you talk to Maslow's analyst?"

"Yes, I did. Even in this situation Bernie remained the jerk he always was. I had to squeeze information out of him with a vise, and even then I didn't get much at all."

"I see," Ted said, clearly pleased the psychoanalytic process was safe in Bernie's hands.

"Look, I've got to run now and meet with Maslow's parents. I'll check with the patient very carefully, and keep you apprized of the situation at every step," Jason said.

"Good, good. Keep me apprized. Keep me apprized."

Jason said that he would. That was at four in the afternoon.

At six, when Jason rang the bell of Jerome and Adina Atkins's Ninetieth Street and Park Avenue apartment, he was a very unhappy man. He'd gone through hell with Miss Vialo to get Allegra's personal information only to find out that no such person lived at the number the Institute had for her. Further investigation revealed that no residence existed at the address the patient had given. Nor was any Allegra Caldera listed in the phone book or registered at the university she said she attended. Allegra had invented herself.

This confirmed Jason's fear of a failure in the Institute's screening process. They thought they were careful. Prospective analysands had to write biographies. They were interviewed three times by a senior analyst. Each case was then considered by a whole committee. Allegra's case had been reviewed by no less than ten experienced people. The young analysts were supervised every step of the way. Now it was clear that a major slipup had occurred and a young woman had fooled them all. She could be anybody, capable of anything, and Maslow could have known, even unconsciously, that he was in danger.

When Jason arrived at the Atkinses' door, he had the feeling that he was on the fault line of an earthquake. As a psychiatrist, he'd always had a healthy respect for madness. He knew that as carefully as people cultivated facades of civility, their rage and potential for aggression were barely under the surface. But he, unlike Maslow, was experienced and knew how to handle it.

As he stood at the door, his head pounding and his throat dry, he prayed that Maslow had not been lured into disaster by a troubled person who should never have been assigned to his care. The door opened before he could bring himself to ring the bell.

"You're Dr. Frank? Come in. He's waiting for you in the living room." Mrs. Atkins had short, tightly permed brown hair that was gray at the roots, soft pale skin that drooped sadly under pale blue eyes, and several double chins. Her features were gathered together in a face that had never been lovely. She looked at least seventy.

"Maslow?" For a second Jason felt a rush of elation.

"No, no, his father."

"You're Mrs. Atkins?"

"Yes." She turned away without shaking his hand.

Jason followed her on a black-and-white checkerboard marble floor through a foyer with gilded chairs and tables lined up like soldiers along smoke-mirrored walls. At the living-room door, she waved her hand and left him.

"I'd like to talk with you both," Jason said before she managed her escape.

"No need." She turned back to him, lifting her shoulders helplessly.

"On the contrary, we can't do without our mothers." Jason smiled and waited at the door.

"What's that?" From his armchair Jerome Atkins, a small, dapper, bald-headed man wearing a red bow tie and lightweight herringbone business suit, flashed them a look of supreme irritation.

Adina dropped her head as if to duck a blow and took a seat in a fragile chair as close to the door as she could get. She was a woman ready to obey whoever she deemed the highest authority.

Jason crossed the white carpet quickly. Jerome Atkins stood, held out his hand, then sat down abruptly without shaking Jason's.

"This thing is all over the news. People have called me. What do you want from me?" He had the face of a desperate man.

"Maslow's disappearance is on the news?" Jason was astounded.

"They have a pack of dogs. They're searching the park." Jerome glanced at his wife. "She's suffered enough. She doesn't need to hear this."

Adina stood up to leave.

Jason shook his head. "Please stay, I want to talk to you both."

Jerome looked away from his wife. "What happened? The police won't tell me anything."

"I don't think they know yet. Has anyone from the police talked to you about it?"

"No, no, I've called them. They're calling me back. Let me tell you, this is a terrible blow." Beads of perspiration dotted the man's forehead. "I'm sure he's dead. If he were alive, I'd know it." He said this with no emotion.

Jason was surprised by how many people associated with Maslow were ready to accept that with no evidence to support it. "Well, I don't want to jump to that conclusion. That's the reason I'm here. I want to talk to you a little about your son's life to see if there's someplace he might have gone, some reasonable explanation for his disappearance."

"No," Jerome said sharply. "Let's not go into it. We know what happened. You don't have to sugarcoat the truth for us."

What truth? Jason shook his head. "Nothing has been established—"

Jerome Atkins cut him off angrily. "They can't even find his body— this is a disgrace." He glanced at his wife. The couple sat so far from each other in the cavernous wood-paneled Park Avenue living room, he had to turn his whole body to get a view of her.

Jason sat between them. He, too, had to shift positions to see her. As he did, he took in the rose-colored drapes on huge windows, the multitude of small pink sofas and gold chairs. Mrs. Atkins had taken a brocade pillow onto her lap and was busy twisting one of its gold tassels in her hand. Her face was pale, shut down. Jason suspected that she was in shock, a hurricane on a distant horizon.

"Are you all right? I could arrange for you to have some medicine—" he asked.

"He's not the first one," she said, shaking her head.

"First what?"

Mrs. Atkins played with the fringe. "Maslow had a twin sister."

"I didn't know that," Jason murmured.

"That's not exactly relevant to anything, is it?" Jerome said nastily, turning back to Jason. "She died over twenty years ago. No point in talking about it." He raised a hand to his forehead, realized it was wet, pulled out a handkerchief.

"She was a beautiful child, a perfect child—blond, blue eyes— smart. Very smart. And Chloe had a wonderful nature. She never complained, no matter what. Never a word. Her name was Chloe. Isn't that a pretty name?"

"Beautiful name." Jason could hardly breathe through the layers of pain in the room.

"She died when she was eleven. Leukemia."

"Adina, it was twenty years ago," Jerome said sharply, dabbing at his forehead.

"I'm sure you know, doctor, that over eighty percent of children who have leukemia now survive," she lectured him.

"She's probably the reason Maslow became a doctor," Jason said softly.

"Too late for us," she said bitterly.

"Were the twins close?" Jason asked.

"Of course. Maslow adored Chloe. Everyone did. She was a magical person, her daddy's dream girl." Mrs. Atkins gave her husband a smug smile.

"He didn't come about Chloe, he came about the boy."

"Chloe was an angel. He's always been a heartache," his mother said.

Jerome Atkins covered his eyes.

"Really?" This was news to Jason.

"Yes, Chloe was an absolute angel. Always smiling, no matter how sick she was."

"I was asking about Maslow."

"What's there to say about it?" Atkins broke in angrily. "A young man with a bright future couldn't think about anything else but being a damned shrink. Doesn't that tell you all you need to know?"

Jason had heard a similar view expounded by his own father, who'd wanted him to be a heart surgeon. "Is that a bad thing in your book?" he asked, feeling the sting of rejection all over again.

"The boy probably provoked his attacker," Atkins speculated coldly.

Jason's distress escalated. "Why do you say that?"

"It wouldn't be the first time. He was interested in crazy people, wasn't he? He talked to the wrong people all the time. It can get you in trouble in this city."

"Chloe was no trouble at all. She was an angel," Adina said.

Jason repressed the urge to muzzle her. "Did something happen to Maslow recently?"

"Oh, the kid hasn't lived with us for years. He used to get into bar fights, street fights regularly. He'd come home with a black eye or a bloody nose. What a waste!" Jerome Atkins waved his hand impatiently. "The city is to blame for this. These people shouldn't be out on the street."

"What about his friends? Maybe they can tell us more."

"What more do you need? He was a misguided young man. All he talked about was work. He didn't have friends."

"What about girlfriends?"

Atkins snorted. Clearly he didn't think much of his son in that department either. Jason turned to Mrs. Atkins. She looked like a person having an out-of-body experience, maybe on a visit to an angel in heaven.

Jason felt like shaking these two people. The mother couldn't talk about anything but her dead daughter. The father could only think of his disappointment in Maslow's decision to become a psychiatrist. In the absence of any evidence whatsoever, his father spoke of his son as if he were dead. But so had Maslow's analyst. Jason was also saddened by the fact that neither parent had called their son by his name. Speaking of him the way they had was a kind of soul murder. If this were a homicide, that alone would be a reason for the police to suspect them. But Jason wasn't a cop.

It seemed that he alone was praying that Maslow Atkins was alive and well and for some unknown reason playing hooky from his life. Jason left the apartment knowing no more about Maslow's present life than he had before his visit. But it was certainly no mystery why the young man had defied his parents to become a doctor of the mind.

TWENTY-TWO

APRIL WAS IN A HURRY. She had three things on her to-do list before meeting Mike. She wanted to search Maslow's office, locate his appointment book and list of patients, and listen to the messages on his answering machine. After that she needed to run over to Jason's apartment on Riverside Drive and spend half an hour reviewing everything he knew about the missing man. She also had to question Pee Wee James again now that he'd had time to sober up.

Between worrying about keeping Mike waiting and not being able to clear the case in the next ten minutes, April was feeling a lot of stress. By the time Woody double-parked on the block between Eighty-ninth and Ninetieth Streets, a deep ache had traveled down her spine from the base of her head to the space between her shoulder blades and was now gathering momentum, jabbing sharply at her lower back as well. She was feeling so much muscle distress she didn't have the energy to complain about Woody's traffic violation. If he got a summons, he'd have to deal with it. Tough. Before he had a chance to kill the engine, she was already out of the car, trying to stretch her screaming muscles into a semblance of quiet.

Something was wrong with those kids. She couldn't get them out of her mind. Brandy's mugging for Woody's camera, David's being freaked out by it. Both of them stoned, knowing Zumech, and worse, being in the right place at the right time during a police investigation. There were too many matches for comfort, but they didn't seem to have any connection to Maslow. They didn't even know who he was or what was going on. She shrugged them onto the back burner of her thoughts. They were troubled losers. Kids like that made her sad about the state of the world.

Maslow's office was in an ordinary Central Park West building, one of those massive, well-kept, sixteen-story brick structures with rich canopies and doormen in matching uniforms that were inhabited mostly by wealthy, educated Caucasians unlike herself. It was just like the building where he lived and much nicer than anyplace she'd ever resided. The doorman was a good-looking Hispanic in a neat navy uniform. April nodded at him, and he didn't stop her and Woody when he saw where they were headed. She wondered if she looked as if she needed a shrink and smiled at the thought.

The first door on the right just inside the lobby had Maslow's name on it and two others listed above it. A note on the door told Maslow's patients to contact Dr. Jason Frank. Woody went first, checking the door before ringing the bell. They were both surprised when the handle turned and the door opened on a waiting room in the minimalist style— a square room with cracking beige paint, a few shabby chairs, a sofa of indeterminate color, and three coffee tables littered with well-thumbed *Life* magazines. Most surprising of all was the ultra-thin girl sitting on the sofa, looking forlorn and playing with her long black hair.

The girl glanced up eagerly when the door opened, saw that it was not the person she was anticipating, then looked down and inspected her watch. April copied the action. Woody did the same. All three watches read five-thirty.

"Are you waiting for Dr. Atkins?" April asked.

The girl nodded.

"Didn't you see the note on the door?"

"Yes."

"Did you call Dr. Frank?"

"No, should I?"

"Dr. Atkins isn't coming in today."

"He'll come in for me," she said.

"What makes you think so?"

"He's very late, but I'm sure he's coming. He promised." The girl frowned.

"Is he often late?"

"Late? He's never late. I'm a little worried, but I know he won't let me down. Are you two his next appointment?"

"Any particular reason for worry?" Woody jumped in without any invitation from his boss.

The girl tilted her head to one side. "Oh, you know New York. Elevators get stuck. Cranes fall over. My grandfather was hit by a bus once." She lifted a shoulder. "His whole side was black-and-blue for weeks. He died of a blood clot, though."

Woody looked as if he might pass out with delight over this account. His humor was a little off as always. "What's your name?" he asked.

"Allegra Caldera," she said easily.

April couldn't believe her ears.

"Hi, Allegra, I'm Detective Baum. This is Sergeant Woo," Woody introduced them, clearly smitten again.

"Police?" the girl said excitedly.

"Yes. We're from the police." April showed off her gold shield, guessing this was the girl they were looking for.

"Police?" Allegra said again, puzzled this time, as if the word had a funny taste. April noticed that her fingernails were badly bitten, and her sharp collarbone showed clearly through the thin fabric of her white blouse. She was a schoolgirl, pretty, starving, and not very old. Her eyes showed alarm, but she didn't seem to be afraid of them.

"Yes, we're looking for Dr. Atkins."

"He didn't do anything wrong, did he?" *This* appeared to be the girl's worry. She jumped off the sofa.

"No, of course not. But he's missing." April noted the flushed face and girl's puzzlement. *She,* at least, did not appear to be stoned.

"He is?"

"Didn't you see all the activity? This section of Central Park has been closed all afternoon. It made a mess of the whole West Side." This from Woody, suddenly a conversationalist.

Allegra shook her head. "No, I got off the subway at Ninety-sixth Street and walked over."

"Where were you coming from?" Woody's voice was funny. The idiot had the dazed look of someone who'd fallen down a flight of stairs.

He was talking, but he wasn't all here. Pretty girls had a devastating effect on him.

Allegra saw it, too. "The Bronx. I live in Riverdale. Why are you asking me these questions?"

"We're tracing Dr. Atkins's actions yesterday to see if we can figure out where he might be."

"Well, he *must* be here." Allegra ran over to one of the three doors off the waiting room and knocked. "Dr. Atkins," she cried. "Dr. Atkins! Open the door!"

April gave Woody a look as he pulled out his camera. They had a situation. The girl thought Maslow was inside the office, and they hadn't searched here first. Were they both out of their minds? How could they have missed this? If Maslow was inside the office, he was probably dead. Maybe he was a suicide. Maybe he'd had a heart attack. It happened. Sweat rolled down her sides. Or he could have been murdered here. Jesus, if she'd called out the whole city on this, and the man was dead in his office, her entire career, indeed her whole life, was over. She was an idiot, an unbelievable idiot.

The girl was weeping. "Oh God, I'm really sorry."

Another click in April's mind. This was the voice on Maslow's answering machine.

"Listen, Allegra, calm down. Tell me what you know about this," she said.

"I will, I will, but please, check in there first. I'm so scared."

"Sure." Good plan. April snapped her fingers at Woody. *Get a grip.*

"Boss?" he said blankly.

"Take Allegra out in the hall."

"Are you going to break into his office?" she cried, blocking the door.

"No. I'm just going to open the door."

"That's breaking in. Isn't that against the law?" Allegra demanded.

"We're the law," April told her. "This is what we do. Go out in the hall."

"Oh my God, don't touch anything. He's a doctor. Everything in there is confidential."

The hair rose on April's neck. What was she seeing? What was coming out of this kid? What was going on here? "Sit down," she ordered Allegra. "And don't move."

"Boss?" Woody queried, eager to do the break-in.

"I'll do it." April would have used her precious Mastercard, on which there was a balance due of eight hundred and thirty-two dollars because of two pairs of really pretty shoes, a suit for herself, and the recent colorful shirts and ties she'd bought her lover. But using the card would not have negated the debt.

Instead, from her purse she pulled the thin flexible strip locksmiths use when people lock themselves out. It was one of the necessities she kept with her at all times.

Both Woody and the girl watched as she slid the strip between the door and the lock and popped the door open. They all held their breath as April went into the still, empty room. Then her phone rang and she answered it.

TWENTY-THREE

LIEUTENANT MIKE SANCHEZ was having a bad day. He had a hangover and the guilts on two fronts about the love of his life, April Woo. First thing was April had messed up big time on this Maslow Atkins case and wasn't backing off to save her ass as she should. Out of kindness and concern for her future, he felt he had to be straight with her.

On another front, he wasn't looking so good himself. He'd made his own little blunder and had to confess, because keeping secrets from the girl he intended to marry was not his style. It all started last night when he went up to the Bronx to have dinner with his mother, Maria. She still lived on Broadway and 236th Street in the Bronx in the apartment where he'd grown up. After dinner, he'd gone down to the Van Cortlandt Bar and Grill to meet up with his old partner, Devon, for a few beers. Tuesday had been a hot and steamy night, the air conditioner was working overtime, and he hadn't been there for thirty seconds when Carla Diverso came over.

"Where have you been hiding yourself?" she asked. "I was about to give up on you."

"No kidding. What's up?" He didn't want to get involved with her, but he didn't want to be mean either. The kid's life was nothing but trouble.

"You never talk to me on the phone anymore. I've been hanging around for weeks, hoping you'd stop by," she complained, then gave him a big smile to soften him up.

"Okay, so talk."

While he waited for Devon to show up he'd let Carla tell him her troubles, which turned out to be legion. She wanted him to be her "friend." Of course he knew what that meant. It got later and later, and Devon never showed up at all. Mike had a few too many beers and explained that he couldn't be anybody's friend, he was going to marry April.

"That's great. I'll help you choose a ring," Carla told him excitedly. "I'll go with you tomorrow."

He had no idea why, but it had seemed like a good idea at the time. Carla ended up spending the night at his place, but all they'd done was talk about April the whole time. Now he felt like a great jackass for letting Carla worm into his life, even for ten minutes, let alone a whole night. He'd intended to tell April the whole story this morning. Then the jogger thing came up.

April was in trouble with everyone. She was late. And he was getting impatient. He rang her on the cell phone to see what was keeping her. She picked up right away.

"*Querida*, where the hell are you?" he demanded.

"Uh, Maslow's office. Any news?"

"No. What about you?"

"I'm just finishing up."

"Well, finish fast. I need to talk to you," he said.

"I'm on my way," she said.

He felt a little better. If he got her a really nice ring, maybe she wouldn't be so upset about losing the case.

TWENTY-FOUR

ARMED WITH ALLEGRA'S ADDRESS, phone number, and a promise to talk again tomorrow, April and Woody made a big mistake. They believed it would be a piece of cake to call her in again for further questioning tomorrow, and they let her go. Then, they collected Maslow's appointment book, patient lists, and speckled patient notebooks, and drove to Jason Frank's Riverside Drive building. She'd promised Mike she was on her way and left Woody downstairs in the car.

"I'll just be five minutes," she told him.

Upstairs in Jason's apartment, Emma opened the door with baby April in her arms. Before April had a chance to say hello or admire the baby, the phone rang.

"Excuse me." Without warning, Emma handed over the baby and went to answer it. April had seen babies in her time. At family gatherings they were always the center of attention. For a decade Skinny Dragon had been using other people's adorable babies to beat April over the head with the lack of her own. April had come to look on them as triple trouble because of the woes they brought her.

Jason and Emma's baby had blue eyes. Not much reddish hair, chubby cheeks, and a rosebud mouth. She was actually pretty cute. She studied April with a serious expression for a few moments, then broke into a huge grin, revealing the beginnings of a tooth in several places. "Aaaa," she said.

"Hi, yourself." April couldn't help being impressed.

The baby drooled down her chin. A long string of saliva descended from her mouth and landed on April's sleeve. April thought this was better than a dog nosing her crotch, but only just.

"Hi," she said again and bobbed the cute bundle up and down a few times. The baby giggled. April felt this was going pretty well. In the intense pleasure of the moment, she forgot that Mike and Woody were waiting for her.

She gathered the courage to move into the living room, where some of Jason's many clocks started chiming the hour of seven at ten to. The clock was ticking on her case and on her life, but she had spent an hour with Allegra in Maslow's waiting room and eliminated her as a suspect. She was now so late she figured she could take another minute or two to imagine what it would be like to be a mother.

She sat in one of the big comfy chairs at the end of the sofa and settled the baby on her lap. April Frank didn't seem to mind this, either. She leaned forward and started to gnaw on April's jacket collar. "Uh, uh, uh." The baby sounded like Skinny Dragon, concentrating on some important, slanderous gossip that could ruin a person's life.

April tried a little conversation. "Tastes great, huh?"

Emma stood in the entry arch watching them. "You two look very cute together. You should try motherhood, April."

Just what April had been considering herself. She jumped as if burned by the idea. "Uh-*uh*." She handed the baby back as fast as ever she could. "Great for you, maybe."

"Don't you think she's cute?"

"She's more than cute, she's gorgeous, and probably smart, too." Still, April couldn't help thinking of motherhood as the fatal disease that would turn her into the crone her mother was. Naturally, she didn't believe that the burden of her debts or the fact that Skinny Dragon hated the man she loved and anything whatever to do with her fears.

"She loves all the toys and rattles you gave her. They're just right for her now. Jason told you, didn't he?" Emma looked very good in a pale yellow sweat suit. Beautiful blond hair, lovely body that didn't look an ounce fatter. Her face was sweet and calm. Motherhood was agreeing with her.

"Yes, he told me. You look great, Emma," April said admiringly.

"Thanks, I'm happy."

More clocks started chiming. For a while it got pretty loud in the room. Seven o'clock came and went. The two women talked for a few minutes about work and babies. April had a sad feeling that she did not have family pleasures like this. She never had a moment to relax, play with a baby, and have girl talk with a woman her own age who wasn't on the job. She was always in a hurry. Someone was always yelling at her. Even now she was supposed to be off duty and couldn't even think of taking a day off. Something had come up. A person was missing, and she wouldn't rest until she found him.

"I'll be right back." Emma dropped the baby on April's lap a second time and disappeared into the kitchen. This time the drooling infant went for her watch. April forced herself to remain where she was and let the sweet baby gum that until Jason arrived five minutes later looking horrible.

When he said, "How's my little sweetheart," neither woman had the slightest doubt which of the three of them he meant. He kissed his wife and his daughter, then hugged April distractedly. But his face was pale, and the pleasantries didn't last long.

"We have a very serious situation here, potentially very dangerous." He glanced at his wife, then at April. He sat on the sofa and rubbed his face with his hands.

"You know, at our Institute we offer analysis for very low fees—three or four years of intensive treatment with highly trained candidates, like Maslow Atkins, who are already practicing M.D.'s or Ph.D.'s. The patients are often students or academics who hear about the program through one of the universities."

The baby started to whimper. Emma got up and immediately took her into the kitchen. Jason glanced at them adoringly then watched them leave the room before he went on. "We have a process for screening, and Maslow's patient, the one he wanted to see me about last night before he disappeared, passed muster by a lot of people, including me."

April nodded.

"But I did some checking today. I found out the girl is not enrolled at the university she said she attended. She does not live where she said she lived, and her name is false, too. We don't know who she is, or where she lives, or why she faked her identity to get into the program." He got up and started pacing the living room.

Something clicked. "Is the girl you're talking about five-four, about a hundred pounds, black hair, brown eyes, anorexic, very pretty?"

"How did you know?" Jason was surprised.

"Woody and I interviewed her only a few minutes ago. She was waiting for Maslow in his office. She was also the last person seen with him last night."

An expression of intense relief settled on Jason's features. "Good. Where is she now? I need to talk to her right away."

April shook her head, feeling a little queasy. She didn't want to say she didn't know where the girl was. "She didn't seem dangerous to us. She seemed like a kid who had a crush on her doctor," was what she said.

"April, in the fifty-year history of the Institute, nothing like this has ever occurred. If something's happened to my supervisee because of an error in selecting a patient, it's my fault. It happened on my watch."

April shook her head again. "I don't think this girl has anything to do with Maslow's disappearance. I interviewed her myself. She didn't even know he was gone."

"You have to understand the elaborate hoax she pulled off. She lied to all of us." Jason was pacing again in his agitation.

April felt bad for him. She could see how a dangerous mental patient, violent and on the loose, could be a hot-button item for him. Like a convict who breaks parole with a repeat crime, the psychiatric patient who becomes violent while under treatment cast suspicion on the whole field. April thought she was pretty good with her takes on people, and that wasn't the girl she'd just seen. Or was the little white ghost playing tricks on her, too?

"Well, this is just my intuition. I may be wrong. In any case, we have to investigate other avenues as well. What about Maslow's other patients, his friends, parents?" she asked.

"Well, his parents are a sad pair. They don't seem to know their son very well. They were no help." Jason gave April an enigmatic smile. "Let's get back to Allegra. What did she tell you?"

"She told me Maslow annoyed her during their session yesterday, so she walked out. She saw him going into the park later and wanted to apologize. But he wouldn't let her. He walked away from her and that was the last she saw him. She hung around for a while, but when he didn't come back she went home to Riverdale on the subway."

"And you believed her?" Jason shook his head. "This girl is a good liar. Clearly she's very intelligent, a self-mutilator. Maslow was upset about her. I need to talk to her myself. You'll have to find her."

April's face went deadpan with the order. She intended to find her. "I'd like her file, Jason. Are you sure she hurts herself?"

"Oh yeah, she's a cutter; she uses razor blades. She was examined by a doctor; her injuries are genuine."

"Does she cut other people?"

He sank into an armchair, ready to lecture. "It's very rare for someone who hurts herself to attack others. For her, cutting brings relief from tension and misery. People who do it feel better when they see their blood trickling out. Then they feel ashamed of themselves later."

April had to get out of there. "Why are you so concerned?"

"I told you, the girl was lying about her identity, as well as a lot of other things. She's highly motivated and highly organized. It's not beyond the realm of possibility that she cut herself just to get into the program. Who knows what she wanted to achieve and how Maslow fits into the picture. Certainly she gained Maslow's sympathy around the issue of her self-destructiveness, as well as her lack of a safe and protective father. She claimed she was raped from the age of five or six by her own father. It's clear Maslow was attracted to her, cared for her a great deal, and was very troubled by her. He would have been better defended against someone whose angry feelings and aggressive acts were outwardly directed," Jason mused. "And of course he was worried about suicide."

"Patients lie," April murmured. She was scared silly that she'd missed something.

"Patients lie all the time, but psychiatrists are not supposed to get duped."

April pointed to her watch. "Look, Jason, I have to go."

"Well, find her, will you? And thank you, really. Do I count on you too much?" For a second he looked concerned about it, but only for a second.

April smiled. "No. Of course not. And I love the baby. Emma looks terrific. What a great mother she is. I'm happy for both of you."

Jason got up and gave her a hug. "Anytime you want some help getting there yourself give me a call."

"*Moi*, consult a headshrinker?" April laughed nervously. "I wouldn't have a thing to say."

"Everybody has a story, April. And again, I can't tell you how much I appreciate this."

Downstairs, Woody was standing by the car muttering to himself for being kept waiting so long. He was really upset when she told him they'd let a suspect go.

TWENTY-FIVE

A T MIDTOWN NORTH, John (Pee Wee) James was not in the inter-view room where April had left him, but she wasn't surprised not to find him there. Detectives used the rooms twenty-four hours a day. She started searching for him. She now believed he was the only one who knew what happened to Maslow Atkins. But Pee Wee wasn't in the holding cell in the squad room or any of the cells downstairs, either. Deeply distressed, she ran around the precinct looking for him. It wasn't until Woody asked at the front desk that she found out John James had been released soon after noon, eight hours ago.

April panicked. Who had questioned him? Who had sent him on his way? Where was the paperwork? Her brain whirled. He was their only lead, and by now he'd be drunk and out of it again. She headed to the stairs that led up to the detective unit.

"You can't trust anybody. We'll have to go out and find him," she complained to Woody.

"He wasn't in the park all afternoon. Maybe he's taken off." Woody made a point of tapping his watch. "I want to get these photos developed."

"Forget the photos. Just because we didn't see him doesn't mean he wasn't hiding out somewhere. He hates to leave the park. Shit!" She charged up the stairs with her head down.

"Hey, *querida.*" Mike was standing at the top of the stairs looking relieved.

"Mike!" The sight of him made her heart soar. In one second she went from cold rage to meltdown. He had that sweet look on his handsome face that she found irresistible. He was wearing one of the blue shirts she'd given him and a very pretty tomato red tie.

"How long have you been here?" she asked, putting on a stern expression to cover her soft feelings.

"Five or ten years. Where have you been?"

"Working. Pee Wee's been released, and I wanted to talk to him when he was sober. Now I have to go out and find him. I'm sorry."

Mike shook his head. "Let's go eat."

"Sounds great," Woody said. "I have a date, can I bring her?"

"*You* have a date?" Mike was incredulous.

"Yeah, I have a date." Woody tugged at his tie.

"I'm sorry, Mike, I can't. I have to work." April didn't want to admit yet that she'd lost two suspects in one day.

"The case can wait. We're having dinner."

April's scalp prickled with alarm. That wasn't like him. "What do you mean?" she asked slowly. The case *couldn't* wait. She was aware that they'd become a tableau on the stairs. Mike blocked her way to her office in the squad room. She had to explain. It couldn't wait a *minute.*

"Have a good evening." Taking charge, Mike dismissed Woody.

"Thanks, boss . . ." Woody made a quick about-face on the stairs and took off before April could revoke the order.

She was stunned. "What do you think you're doing?" Mike didn't have the right to dismiss one of her detectives, causing her to lose face in front of one of her people. Her face burned with the mortification of disrespect from her own boyfriend.

"Let it go. You must be hungry." He took a step down, but she didn't move.

It felt as if solid ground were turning to sand under her feet. Her cheeks were on fire. "I can't let this go, Mike. I have a missing person and now the only witness we have is missing, too."

"Well, it's not your show." He moved down two more steps and put his arms around her.

"What?" She'd never expected this kind of response from him. She was stung by his show of power and intended to move out of the way, but she was puzzled. She loved the sweet and spicy way he smelled, the way he looked in his new colors. She loved the warmth of his little secret smile that meant he loved her, and she was rooted to the spot. The man she knew could never hurt her.

"It's okay. We'll sort it out." He hugged her in her precinct where love was off limits, and she was too distracted to move. Any other man, any other time in her working life, and she would have sent him flying down the stairs. Now, in the middle of all her worries and his causing her to lose face with Woody, her only ally in the squad, she let the electricity of love flow through her. Less than an hour ago she'd been thinking of having his baby. Now she let him divert her from her job. All her values were breaking down at once.

"Yo quiero, te amo," he said softly.

He liked her, he loved her, that was nice. Then her bewilderment ceased. "What do you mean it's not my show?"

"Don't take it personally." He'd suddenly become elaborately casual. He took her arm and tried to move her gracefully down the stairs. "I love you. How about dinner?"

"I don't want dinner. I caught this case. I want to keep it," she insisted.

He shrugged as if the thing were out of his hands. "Major Case has it now. The PC calls it. I don't call it. Let it go." The winning smile cajoled her. Let it go, he was saying. Be a good sport. She was being manipulated by her boyfriend and didn't want to be a good sport. She wanted to have a temper tantrum.

He took her arm and turned her around. This was trouble. She knew if she got into a shoving match with a lieutenant on the stairs, she might be able to inflict some damage; but a crowd of uniforms would gather, everyone would be amused. And he would win in the end.

"What do you feel like eating? I'll buy you the dinner of your dreams." Mike gave her another ingratiating smile. They got to the bottom step. He had her moving toward the door.

Conflicting emotions kept her quiet. Wasn't she supposed to have some choice in this? They were leaving the precinct. He was supposed to love her. If he loved her, why was he doing this? Mike's ancient red Camaro was parked across the street.

"Okay, querida, fill me in," he said as they got into the car.

More outrage filled her. He started grilling her before she'd even attached her seat belt. Her cheeks burned some more at the disrespect for her *car*, too. She didn't want to leave her car there on Fifty-fourth Street. She wanted to go home on her own, *later*. Now, she wanted to go back upstairs to her office and check with the parents of those kids, check with the parents of Maslow Atkins, check this patient list, try to locate Allegra.

Mike looked serious as he gunned the engine and headed east. Where the hell had *he* been all day? He hadn't done anything useful. What was with him? She studied his profile and sighed. Even when he was humiliating her she thought he was cute. That was a bad sign.

She gathered, without his even telling her, that *he'd* been the one assigned, and the case was now his. He was the big gun, after all. And she was just a water pistol. She shook her head to cool down. How he managed to do these things she had no idea. The heat slowly receded from her face. She was used to working with him. She trusted his judgment. Maybe he could help her. Old habits die hard.

She collected her thoughts and slowly began to tell him about Jason's call from Maslow, about Maslow's concern for his patient, about his meeting a dark-haired girl outside the park, his not returning home after his evening jog—if he ever actually planned to take one. She described her search of Maslow's apartment, finding his wallet and the cash, the voice on the answering machine. She told him about Officer Slocum's search of the area with the dog, Freda, and how she'd called the K-9 unit because Pee Wee insisted he'd seen a dead man. Some of it he'd heard before. She told him about all the people she'd interviewed, including the two kids at the end of the day. She told him about Allegra.

As she told the story, she had the strong suspicion that the 911 call she'd investigated last night might actually have had nothing to do with Maslow. It now seemed more likely that his mystery patient whom she let go was a skillful psychopath who had somehow killed or kidnapped her shrink.

When she finished talking, Mike told her that a check of ERs had turned up nothing. "But he's a doctor. If he's gay and met with some mishap during a sexual encounter, he might well have called a friend to treat him privately. I keep wondering if it's a gay thing," he added.

"Pee Wee James may have seen him in a homosexual encounter. Jason told me Maslow was a rigid, careful kind of guy. The call for a meeting may have felt like a flare to Jason. But something makes me think Maslow wouldn't bother him just because he had a bad patient session. The second thing is that Pee Wee kept saying he had people taking care of him. Who could be taking care of him? Maybe the whole thing is some kind of set-up. Maybe Maslow wanted to disappear. Why do I have the feeling he's still alive?"

April thought of the soft voice on the answering machine again. She fell silent as they entered the Midtown Tunnel. He was heading home to Queens. That meant she'd have to come into the city with him tomorrow to get her car. Good. She'd worm her way back on the job. She knew how to handle Mike. She added to her list of things to do. Call John Zumech, the tracker. Develop the photos Woody had taken of Allegra. Someone out there knew who she was. Locate Pee Wee. She had her agenda and calmed down. Mike would rub her back. They'd make love and erase jurisdictional lines.

The moon over Forest Hills was just a sliver short of full. Mike parked in his covered space in his building's lot and they went upstairs. From the elevator April smelled roasting chicken from Mike's apartment. She was puzzled. When did he have time to go to the grocery store, purchase a chicken, put it in the oven? She glanced at him. Under his lush mustache his mouth tightened.

"What's going on?" April asked.

"Nothing," he said, but he didn't look happy. He inserted his key, opened his door, marched into his apartment, then stopped short, his eyes rolling up in his head.

"Jesus." He whistled softly. "Jesus, what the hell are you trying to do to me?"

Lying on Mike's sofa wearing the nightie Mike had bought April only three weeks ago was a girl with an absolutely stunning body. Nightie, color peach. Legs, long and brown. Hair, long and curly, dyed blond. Lips, big and red. Eyes, brown and surprised by the reaction she was getting from Mike. She was wearing no panties. April's first thought was: Where are my matching panties with the white lace?

"Oh my God, it's *April!*" the girl cried, jumping up. She wasn't a bit alarmed. "Oh my *God*, I've heard so much about you. Mike thinks the world of you." She crossed the living room to give April a hug. She was barefoot, tall. Looked about fifteen.

Mike intercepted her. "What are you doing here, Carla?" He took her by the arm. Speechless, April watched him.

"You promised me money for that dress, and then you left without giving it to me." Mike quick-stepped her toward the bedroom. "Put on some clothes and get out of here."

She turned her head to look at April. "Wow, April is so pretty. Just like you said, Mike."

"I never promised you money for a dress." Mike kept talking as he shoved her into the bedroom.

"How can I go to that party with my boyfriend with nothing to wear?" she complained.

"Carla, out!" Mike said.

"You said I could stay *as long as I wanted*," she wailed.

"I never said that."

"You did, you *said*—whatever I need, you'd see to it."

"You're going home now."

"I told you I can't. My parents would kill me," she squealed.

"Carla, you told me if I let you stay one night, you'd be out of here by ten."

"But, Mike, I have *nothing* to wear. I need some clothes. Come on, Mike, be a pal. Don't be mad. I made you guys dinner, didn't I?"

The voices faded when Mike closed the bedroom door. Then, Carla's voice, sulky but resigned. "*Okay, okay,* I'll go if you give me a hundred dollars. . . . Oh, come *on*, Mike, you know I wouldn't have told my dad. He'd kill you."

Those were the last words April heard. She was out the front door, and taking the stairs because she didn't want to wait in the hall for the elevator. She took the stairs at a fast clip, her cell phone out. If she'd been another kind of girl, she might have stayed to hear his explanation and chew him out. But she wasn't in the mood. He'd let the girl spend the night. He hadn't told her. He'd stolen her case. Her back hurt like hell. She'd deal with all this tomorrow.

Her heart was an angry drumbeat in her chest. Her hands were sweaty and shaking. She realized she was mad enough to have shot them both. In one evening she could have given up her career and had a baby, or killed for love. She'd never wanted to be at risk for passion like that. She punched in the number of the nearest precinct, where an old school friend was Desk Sergeant. Only in this was she lucky today. Laura was on duty and answered herself.

"Laura, it's April Woo. Listen, could you send a unit for me? I'm on a case at the Garden Towers, know where that is? Yeah, that's right. My car won't start. . . . No, no, I don't need a tow truck. Just a lift." She gave the address and hung up. Great, now she was lying. But lying for love was a step up from killing for it.

By the time she got downstairs, a blue-and-white was pulling up in front of the building. Sometimes it paid to be a cop. She dove into the unit and gave her home address to the driver. Whatever Mike was doing to get Carla out of his place, he didn't do it in time.

She fumed all the way home to Astoria. More luck, bad this time, was Skinny Dragon Mother waiting at the door as she got out of the car.

"Spanish call tlee time. Something long?" she cried out into the street. Clearly, she hoped so.

TWENTY-SIX

A FTER THE DOG SEARCH and their encounter with the cops, David
and Brandy were still a little high. David wanted Brandy to come
to his place, so they took a taxi to the East Side apartment where his
parents never were and the maid they called his nanny had already
gone. The place was like a museum after closing, dead and deathly
quiet. Not even the phone ever rang there. David took Brandy into his
room.

"Want to see something to get you in the mood?" he asked.

"The mood for what?" Brandy bounced on his bed, knowing what
this did to him.

"You promised, Bran, don't let me down again, okay?" he said angrily. He opened his laptop and turned it on.

She laughed. "Fine, let's see a movie." She knew he could show
movies on the computer.

"This is better than a movie." He clicked a few buttons and brought
a picture up on the screen that blew her away.

"Wow." She studied it with her thumb in her mouth. At first, like
with her dad last night, she couldn't figure out what the two people
were doing. Then she got it. "Holy shit!"

He clicked to the next one, then the next, and the next, running
them quickly to show off his collection.

"Wait a minute, will you? Wow." She didn't know which interested
her more, the spread legs and pussies of the old women, the young girls

licking each other's teeny breasts, or the mature women with tits as impressive as hers in a threesome with a man whose cock was bigger than anything she'd ever thought existed in real life. She clicked her tongue pierce against her teeth and slapped at David's grabby hands when he swiveled around in his chair to get to her.

"Jesus. Is that thing real?" She hung over his shoulder, mesmerized. The picture showed a kid, maybe sixteen, seventeen, with his cock sticking straight up. It looked like a mushroom on a thick stem, huge, much bigger than David's. The boy's chest and belly and *thing* took up nearly the whole space except for the little girl with blond hair, about five, on the lower right of the screen looking at it with her mouth open and her little tongue showing. The title was "Little Sister 1."

David laughed. "Of course it's real. Want to see more?"

"Little sister 2" showed the blond girl lying on her back with her finger stuck in her little hairless pussy and a different boy with a different-shaped penis hovering over her.

This made Brandy uneasy. "Do they do it?"

"Nah. In this series she just does blow jobs." David clicked and the picture disappeared, then clicked on a file called "Mom and Pop." In that one, a woman who looked a lot like Brandy's mother was on her hands and knees in a black bra with the nipples cut out. She had big tits. A guy as gorgeous as Brad Pitt with another huge cock was fucking her from behind. This one was a video, and Brandy could see the thing going in and out. She'd never seen anything like it. She wondered if he was doing it in her *ass* and noticed that the man was not wearing a condom. This made her uneasy, too.

David was all turned on by the pictures and her breathing on his neck. He swiveled the chair around and pulled her over so that she was standing between his legs. It annoyed her at first, but then he reached under her angora sweater, squeezed her breasts, and started breathing so hard she thought he'd have a stroke. She giggled and rubbed against him, undecided how far she'd go. He wasn't a very good kisser, but his cock was up there, and she almost felt like it. Almost.

"Oh, Bran," he moaned, pulling her over to his bed, a queen. A nice big bed with a bedspread that Brandy recognized as a Ralph Lauren. She liked the fifty-three-inch TV, too, but was not interested in it at the moment.

The laptop was on the desk. The same scene played over and over on the computer. David got on top of her, but Brandy kept her head turned away from his sucking kisses. She focused on the screen, where the cock kept going in and out. She liked watching it. David moved on top of her, trying to figure out what to do next, and she felt his cock trying to bulldoze through his clothes. His weight was crushing her.

"Daavvvid!" she complained.

"You promised."

"Show me another one."

Grumbling, he got off her. He was all rumpled and red in the face. He sat at his desk and clicked on another file for her. She jumped up to see it better. This one showed a young boy with an older woman sitting on him. David returned to the bed and pulled her between his legs again, rubbing against her frantically. Then suddenly he stopped. Brandy was disgusted. He hadn't even started and he'd come in his pants. So much for that.

He got very subdued and showed her the "Daddy" series to remind her of what she'd seen her own daddy do last night. Then they drank some of his father's New Amsterdam beer. After that he felt better and wanted to try sex again. He knew his mother wasn't coming home for hours. But Brandy had another idea. If he was such a good driver, why didn't they take his parents' Mercedes out of the garage and go for a ride.

"Fine," he said. He was pretty high on Brandy at the moment. He'd drive to the end of the earth if she asked him to.

They went downstairs to the garage in the building and took the Mercedes out. The attendant knew David and didn't question them. David was not nervous at all. He'd driven the car before with his driving instructor, but never at night. This time, as soon as he got in and adjusted the seat, he felt great right away. They headed out to Long Island, filled the tank at a gas station in Queens, got some junk food to eat, and he was thoughtful enough to use cash so his parents wouldn't find out. They were out for a few hours driving around, and David didn't hit a single thing even though it was night. He could read maps and everything.

Brandy crashed into a dark mood when he told her they had to go home. She wanted to stay on the road forever. They had money, credit cards. "Why not split?"

David snorted. He was angry at her getting him all messed up again. He had long since sobered up, and by ten-thirty he was thinking about all the cops she'd talked to in the park and given their names. That was an irresponsible thing to do, considering that bum who'd seen them there. He was worried about that bum.

"Come on," Brandy whined. "It's early. Don't be such a dork."

"Look, Bran, my mom will be home soon. And I have stuff to do."

She blew air through closed lips. "What stuff?"

"I'm not sure. Who knows, he may have been breathing. Maybe I should make sure he's dead." He didn't mention the bum, didn't want to scare her.

"So what if he's alive? He'll die soon. How long could he live without food?"

"It was your dumb idea that they try another dog tracker. If they get Zumech and Peachy out there, for sure they'll find him tomorrow. When they do, he better be dead."

"It's your own stupid fault. You should have made *sure* he was dead before we left. I thought you were so OCD."

"What's that?"

"Obsessive compulsive. You know." She twirled her finger around her bangs.

"Shut up, you idiot. I'm ADD."

She snorted. "Crazy is crazy."

"You don't know what you're talking about," David raged.

"You're so fucking crazy, David. What difference does it make?"

"Don't call me crazy!" David said menacingly. Sometimes she got so flaky he wanted to squeeze her neck to shut that damn blabbing mouth of hers.

"Well, what do you want to do about it, asshole?"

"I want to talk to Zumech."

"What for?"

"Just do," David said vaguely.

Brandy shrugged. "Whatever."

He was silent as he drove to Zumech's place. He wasn't sure why he wanted to see him. He just knew that was where he needed to go. It was on the south shore of Long Island, not far away. In less than ten minutes they were cruising past his house. There was no sign of him.

No sign of Peachy in the dog run. The lights were on in the house, but no one came to the door when they rang the bell. He had an idea. He tried the side door of the garage. It was open. Zumech's car was there, but it was locked. The garage had a weird smell. David poked around for a few minutes, looking for the source. When he found it, Brandy realized what he was doing. They gave each other the high five because now they really could fake out any tracker alive.

In great spirits, they drove back into the city across the bridge, and the car was back in the garage long before midnight.

"See you," David said when they got outside.

"What are you talking about?"

"You're going home now."

"No, I'm coming with you."

"Uh-uh. You take too many risks. I have to do this myself." The truth was he was getting tired of her and wanted to fix the situation himself. It was serious now. He had to do this thing his own way.

"You're not treating me right!" she said accusingly. She looked really mad.

His cheek twitched at the unfair accusation. It was the kind of thing his mother said to his father. He relented.

"Oh, all right. Just do what I say and keep quiet."

A dog walker in a sweat suit jogged by with a golden retriever on a retractable leash. David hailed a cab, shaking his head at having given in. It made him feel like a loser. She got in with him, all cheerful again, and they took a cab to the West Side.

They entered the park in their usual place, walked north, watching for homos, the homeless, and the place where the lights ended and the Ramble began. Across the water, near the spot where the tracking dog had lost the missing man's scent, was the same girl who'd been hanging around last night. She was sitting alone on a bench under the light where the police call box was.

Brandy shuddered. "That girl has a death wish," she said.

At least she didn't turn to look at them as they turned east and went deeper into the park. David didn't hear the remark. He was thinking about the bum who always bothered them, who'd seen them last night and happened to be a piece of scum no one in the world would miss. He was excited by his plan to rid the earth of a troublesome cancer.

TWENTY-SEVEN

PEE WEE JAMES had no watch and didn't look at the clock in the precinct when he was released by the police. All he knew was that the sun was high in a sky so blue it hurt his eyes. He looked down at his feet as he shuffled out onto the sidewalk. He was trying to figure things out. He had no actual memory of how long he had been at the station or what he had told the Chinese cop or the other guy—maybe it was two guys—who talked to him before letting him go.

He was sure he hadn't told them anything about the game with the two kids—a twenty a day for a long time. Pee Wee wanted a dog, and that was enough to take care of a dog for sure. He thought about that twenty a lot. He was torn between getting the twenty from the kids, or dealing separately with the guy in the cave. If he helped the guy, maybe he'd get a bigger reward, enough to go down south where it was warmer.

Pee Wee wondered if the man was still there. Those kids were so high they didn't even think to gag him, didn't tie him up. He'd watched the whole thing and knew if the jogger came to, he might be able to crawl out. Pee Wee had slept in that cave out of the rain himself, more than once. In AA they always said it was important to have a goal. Pee Wee James had a goal. He was going to check to see if the guy was still there, make sure he was okay.

Central Park was a strange place. The paths were black at night, and not even Captain Reginald knew everything. The boss of the park traveled off-road in his Jeep three, four times a day, making the rounds. When he saw Pee Wee in the playgrounds, looking through the garbage cans for the leftovers the nannies left behind, the captain always moved him along. But not even the captain knew he didn't leave the park to sleep somewhere else as he was supposed to.

And no one knew about the cave that used to be a runoff for water from the rowboat lake a hundred years ago when the park was built and the lake was higher, covering everything that was now swamp. It had been several hundred feet larger at this end, and at least six feet higher. But Pee Wee was a historian. He knew about the iron gate over the cave and the foliage that covered it.

When he left the police station, he made his way to Eighth Avenue. During the morning, he'd eaten two sandwiches and drunk several cups of coffee. He'd washed up in the public men's room of the precinct, and all in all he was pretty pleased with himself—happy with his new clothes, the pair of sneaks that fit him pretty well, the socks, khaki pants, black T-shirt, and white sweatshirt with a green palm tree on it and "Florida" spread wide across the front. Best of all, he'd gotten a quilted maroon jacket that looked waterproof and would prove useful when the season changed. But he had a mother of a hangover, was not entirely clear about what was going on. He was getting the shakes, too.

The weather was warm and dry. Pee wee was not surprised that no one from the cops offered to drive him back to his home in the park. In fact, the plainclothes officer who let him go gave him five dollars and discouraged him from returning there. He was used to it. Words had no impact on him. Cops had been accusing him of everything under the sun for decades now, and they were always wrong. He'd heard it all a hundred times, but he was one of the good guys.

In the last fifteen years he'd lost his job, his wife, his home, his children, and everything else that had kept him going since his war days. He'd been in police custody more times than he could count. For several years, he'd lived in flophouses and a mission down on the Bowery. After that he'd scrounged around the Port Authority bus station over on the West Side, sleeping intermittently in shelters and on the street. He didn't like the shelters. Too many bad people, too much AIDS, too many rules. After ten years, he'd drifted back down to Alphabet City on the Lower East Side.

In each location, he'd cycled through his days getting drunk, being drunk, sleeping it off, begging, drinking more. From time to time he was disorderly and bellicose. When he was sober and when he was drunk, he saw himself as a helper, the only one who'd pull a knife on a raper or mediate a brawl. He'd been a killer of Cong in 'Nam, knew how to fight. And like then, he was still one of the good guys, misunderstood and a little down on his luck.

In his war days and the early years afterward, Pee Wee had gone through periods where he'd do weed and alcohol, cocaine, and whatever substances were popular on the street. But that was back when he was trying to keep up with life. After he lost his home, he went for the cheapest thing. He'd become a pure old wino, too broke and disorganized for anything else. He'd long since completed his descent.

Now he was thinking about the five in his hands and the twenty on the come. For several hours he wandered around the Disneyland of the new Times Square, looking for haunts that no longer existed. He bought some Thunderbird with the five the cop had given him, drank it, then walked north toward the park. He didn't get very far and lost track of time early on.

By nine at night he was dozing pleasantly among acquaintances on the corner of Ninth and Fifty-seventh Street. There, a wide, three-foot brick garden wall provided good seating and a place to sleep it off. In winter in the wide open space of the almost park someone always made a fire in an old oil drum. In summer, spring, and fall there were farmers markets. In all seasons there was a gathering of homeless right across the street from the D'Agostino supermarket.

Pee Wee was roused from a comfortable drunk by a fight going on around him. Guys were arguing, yelling. He was lying on the brick wall when one of them wanted his space, or something. One minute he was sleeping and the next he was picked up. He was punched, knocked down, and his head smashed hard into the pavement. It happened in a few seconds, and he went out cold for a while. When he woke up there were cops standing around. One of them was trying to wake him up.

"Hey, fellow, you okay?"

"Course, ah'm okay. Whadya think?" Cops were talking the way cops always talked. Through bleary eyes, Pee Wee saw people standing around. A girl cop stood over him, big as a trailer in her uniform. An even bigger guy was talking to another cop.

"This gentleman here says you hit him," the woman said.

"Hit a cop, are you crazy?" Pee Wee had no idea what was going on.

"No, no, you and your pals here were fighting."

"Not me, no." Pee Wee realized he was flat on his back.

"He says you took his sandwich. He tried to get it back and you slugged him."

Pee Wee had no memory of any such thing. That was a ridiculous, an outrageous accusation. He sat up and began the struggle to get to his feet.

"Hey, wait a minute. Looks like you got quite a crack on the head there." The cop tried to restrain him.

"Nahh, thash crazy." Pee Wee didn't like being restrained. He brushed the hands away and stumbled to his feet. The cops were having a conference, a regular convention there with a crowd around him. Everybody was pretty quiet now. It almost made him laugh.

Yeah, now he remembered. Two guys were fighting, but not him. Yelling. He had nothing to do with it. He took off, dizzy and a little disoriented, a common enough condition for him. The convention was over. Nobody stopped him. He walked north on Ninth, then east on Sixtieth, didn't want to run into Lincoln Center. He felt pretty good, almost high as he headed slowly toward the park. It took him more than two hours to go a mile to the place where he lived between two boulders by the lake. He kept his possessions there, including several quilts, and a tarp that he pulled over his head when it rained or snowed. People were talking to him in his head. Different stories were playing there from different times in his life. Over the years the social workers and church people had encouraged him to have goals. He'd gone to AA at more than one point in his life.

"You have to have goals to maintain sober living," they all said.

He had goals, Plenty of them. And could maintain sober living anytime he wanted. In fact, he was sober a lot of the time. Almost all the time. His goal was he wanted a dog to help him beg, to protect him, and to keep him warm in winter. That was his first goal. He had others.

He hit the park. He remembered the cops there looking for some-body. He couldn't remember who. Then after a while he remembered. He couldn't remember when the cops had been there. He forgot he was looking for the girl and the kids with the twenties. The park was quiet now. Even the birds had settled down for the night. Inside the park, he stumbled along the path toward his place. He saw a large rat and some guys in an unmarked car who might be cops. Where was the kid with the money? The cops drove by and were gone. Pee Wee stopped behind a leafy shrub to take a piss, still thinking about getting another twenty.

He remembered the guy in the cave. Pee Wee was a responsible member of society. He didn't want the guy to be hungry or uncomfort-able. He'd take him some water from the lake, give him a blanket. What the hell. He felt a little dizzy and sat down in the dirt for a mo-ment. He forgot what he was doing, blacked out. Sometime later, he got up and stumbled on, the twenty back in his mind. He knew he had to do something, but he'd forgotten what.

TWENTY-EIGHT

W ITH EACH RUMBLE of the subway a fine dusting of sand loosened from the crumbling rock above Maslow's face and rained down on him. It felt as if the earth itself were alive and trying to entomb him. When Maslow became fully aware of it, the feeling had returned to his hands and arms in stinging tingles. But his legs were still numb.

Dirt was in his eyes and mouth. "Oh God!" He raised his hand and smacked it on the ceiling only inches from his face. It jumped to the right and hit a wall of gravel. Panic-stricken, he felt around him and discovered another wall to his left. Whimpering, he realized that he was buried alive. The only thing between him and death was a thin pocket of foul air.

"Oh God, save me," he whispered. He closed his flooding eyes and saw nothing. He was alone in his grave. All he heard was the pounding of his heart and the rasp of his breath, louder than any thunder he'd ever known. He struggled to breathe, and terror became the animal that consumed him.

If he could have moved his legs, he would have thrashed in agony. If he could have yelled, he would have shrieked his protest. But he could not move, could not utter more than soft moans. He was able to raise his wrist to his face but could not see well enough to read the dial of his watch. Nor could he estimate the time that had passed by the condition of his body.

He felt weak. He felt sick. He felt cold, then hot. He'd been hungry earlier, but was not so hungry now. As a doctor, he knew that loss of appetite always occurred after the first day of fasting but returned with a fierce vengeance very soon thereafter. He also knew a healthy person could live in moderate temperatures without food or water for a long time. Earthquake victims trapped in the rubble had been known to live four, five, even six days. But Maslow was no victim of a natural disaster.

His whole situation seemed to come directly from his own childhood dreams. To be paralyzed and unable to escape an enemy. To be trapped in the dark, cold and hungry. To be all alone with his terror. Everything that was happening to him now had been common features of his own private nightmares. Except for one thing, to have a patient capture and kill him. That scenario had never occurred to him.

Maslow felt as if he had been dreaming all his life. *Wake up.* A patient had done this to him, and he could not let her win. Slowly Maslow organized his thoughts. He had made a promise to help his patients. In return they were supposed to respect his body and space. They didn't always, but on psychiatric wards he had never found it terrifying to deal with persons acting on orders from Venus to rape him, to get his sperm and plant it inside themselves just for a while so they could take it back and propagate the moon. Once a highly educated young man who had reminded Maslow of himself had become upset in the hospital and suddenly erupted in a rage. He picked Maslow up, and threw him across the room. Maslow grabbed a chair and held the man off like a matador until a male nurse arrived to subdue him.

He'd felt like a jerk for not being more careful then. Now he felt like a monumental fool. He had no chair, no weapon, nothing. He could hardly breathe let alone sit up. Maslow was furious at himself. How could he have let this happen?

As he lay on his back, buried, terrified that he would die, he kept thinking, *If I were a more experienced doctor this wouldn't have happened.* He blamed himself for everything. It was obvious to him that Allegra had a psychotic transference and wanted to possess him. His memory of the day stopped at meeting her outside the park. He was certain that somehow she had overpowered and gotten him here, but he had no idea how she might have accomplished that. Allegra was a small girl. She might have been able to surprise and knock him down but not move him. He would not have come in here on his own. *He was packed into the ground.* She could not have done that alone.

Some hours after his discovery of the fanny pack, he realized he still had the granola bars and the water bottle. He lifted the bottle to his lips and wet his mouth. The taste of the water made him think that maybe Allegra never intended to kill him. His hands were not bound. He had air and water and food. Maybe this was a test of some kind.

An analyst never stops analyzing. Slowly Maslow relived all of his sessions with Allegra, trying to find a clue in something she said that would help release him. So many times the humor or sadness in her remarks had resonated in him. He had felt as close to her as he had felt with anyone in his life. During the months they were together in therapy, he'd thought of her almost as if she were his friend, his sister.

But some of the things she'd said never rang true. Something was wrong with her stories. He'd ignored his suspicions and believed her at the time, but now he saw what the clever young woman had done with him. She had given him a sense of ease. He'd felt comfortable with her and that feeling of comfort had eroded the boundaries between them. His own trust of her had encouraged the violation. He was a stupid jerk, a giant sap for trusting and believing a borderline patient.

And now he was in a hostage situation with no one to help him get out. If he could talk with her now, he would tell her she was a good girl, that he understood and cared for her, that everything she'd done he could explain to her and others. He'd tell her that he would protect her and she'd be all right. And he'd ask her to tell him all that she wanted from their relationship. He'd assure her that he would give it to her as soon as he got home and had a bath.

Don't ruin your life with this, Allegra, don't go a single step further. I'll give you whatever you want. He played it through in his mind. Maybe she'd show up.

He took two tiny bites of granola bar and chewed them down to nothing before wetting his tongue with the water from his bottle. He consulted frequently with his body, praying for feeling to return to his legs. If he could move his legs, he could crawl out. He heard the rumble of the subway and the wind blowing in the trees. He heard honking horns. It was not hopeless. He was not on Mars or Venus. His city was all around him. Someone would find him. He prayed that someone would find him soon. He did not want to think about dying there.

TWENTY-NINE

ALLEGRA CALDERA WAS ASHAMED of herself for not telling the detectives her secret. She should have told them everything she knew the minute they said Maslow was missing. The whole city knew he was missing—everybody except her. This was all her fault. The whole thing. She could not forgive herself for continuing the lie.

After the police locked her out of his office, she walked downtown, back to the building where he lived. There, she wandered back and forth, waiting for him to return. When it started getting dark, she marched back uptown and hung around his office some more. She knew she was the most pathetic creature on earth.

She kept thinking that wherever she looked for him she had a ninety percent chance of missing him. By eight o'clock she was on Eighty-second Street again, standing by the park entrance where she had seen him last. He'd looked very small in his shorts and white T-shirt, really slim, about the same size as her father. Her father had his disappearances, too. She should have gotten used to them, but she never did.

When she was so dizzy with hunger that she could hardly stand up, she went to the coffee bar on Columbus and had a cup of espresso, no sugar. For her it was dinner. Finally at ten o'clock she entered the park once again.

Allegra thought she must have walked miles going nowhere at all before she finally sank down on the bench and let her grief out in great heaving sobs. She couldn't lose the only person in the world she really loved. She couldn't lose him before he knew her.

The Chinese cop had given Allegra her home number. Allegra still had it with her. The call box was right there, right near where she was sitting. It was painted dark green and had a plaque that read "Gift of Central Park Conservancy" on it. She thought of calling the police on the phone. The detective had seemed very nice, understanding. Allegra wondered if she should call her and explain everything.

But what could she say? If she hadn't spooked Maslow, he wouldn't have had to avoid her. He wouldn't have had to run away. He would just have jogged right back out of the park as he was supposed to. She didn't understand why he hadn't just jogged back. He was angry at her, but he would never run away.

She didn't understand him at all. He was so rigid, just like her father. He hadn't let her explain last night. But the truth was Maslow never let her explain. He just never let her. No matter how hard she tried, he wouldn't let her take her story where it needed to go.

It made her sick to think that he was in the dark about so many things. And now he might never know her. Allegra sat there for a long time struggling with emotions that were too big to hold inside her. She loved her mother, loved her so much right at that moment. She wished she could go home and tell her mother everything. But her mother would be so angry. Her mother believed intelligent people should solve their own problems. Her father felt even stronger about it. He was almost a maniac about it. They both believed that psychiatrists were the very last resort, only for people who were *really* crazy. Allegra wasn't really crazy. Ordinary people like them could get over anything. Her mother wanted Allegra to just *get over it*, just get on with her life. She'd be furious, just furious at what Allegra had done to get relief. So many lies her parents and she had told, and for what, so that she could expose them all in the end? No, she couldn't tell her mother.

There was another reason Allegra could not leave her bench and return home to her real identity. She was afraid to go on the subway. She couldn't go down those stairs and face the train tonight. Now she had even more reason to kill herself.

Allegra was in a state of extreme agitation when she saw the shadows of the two kids slinking into the park. Boy and girl. The boy, very big. The girl, little, like her. She frowned in the dark. She'd seen them last night. They'd come out of the park while she was waiting for Maslow to return. They'd been a mess. She remembered their wet sneakers, squishing as they walked past her. Again, she thought of calling the detective. Maybe they had seen Maslow. But she didn't call the police, and she was too tired to follow their fast pace. She moved to another bench and waited for them to come back.

THIRTY

JANICE OWEN got home from work at eleven. The apartment was dark. She picked up the phone. There were no messages, not even from her husband, Bill. In the kitchen was a note left for David by Alvera, the housekeeper they'd had since David was two. The note read, "I waited to six, Can't wait no more. Pills came"—arrow to the re- fill of David's antidepressant, Zoloft, from the drugstore on the counter—"Your dinner in fridge, microwave five minutes. It's your fa- vorite, chili. Alvera."

Janice was annoyed. She had to be a damn detective to find out what was going on with everybody. She read the note, furious on two counts. Alvera was supposed to stay until David got *home* so David wouldn't have to eat *alone* every night. As a devoted mother, Janice took a lot of care to make sure she had these things covered. She didn't like it when her carefully arranged schedule didn't work out according to plan. Now she finds out Alvera had left early *again*, and probably had counted on David to cover for her. The fact that the note was still sitting there meant either David had come home and left again be- cause no one was home, or David had *not* come home and eaten his dinner and he'd lied when they'd talked on the phone. She'd spoken to him at seven during the cocktail hour before her business dinner. He'd told her then he was on his way home. But who knew with him.

These last few years David had been a huge pain in the neck. He wasn't "flourishing," so said the idiots at his fancy school. They'd wanted to kick him out. She and Bill had vigorously opposed hurting David in that way, so they'd had dozens of meetings with counselors, and testers, and psychiatrists to get David back on track. They wanted and expected and *needed* a kid who "flourished" just the way they had. The kid was loved and cared for. There was no reason for him not to do well.

She was most gratified to find out that the important tests, the intelligence ones, showed that David was smart, not stupid. He just didn't concentrate well. He was depressed. They'd gotten him one of the best psychiatrists, referred by the counselor at school, an expert on Attention Deficit Disorders. The psychiatrist prescribed medications; the school had been appeased by David's test scores and granted him a stay of execution. After all her hard work promoting David's cause to the school, plus their investment of thousands of dollars in fees for tests and consultations, diagnosis, medication, and treatment, Janice had been confident they'd finally gotten *everything* worked out last spring. He'd done well at camp.

But now in only the second week of school David was starting to slip already. She was very *angry* at him for letting her down. She couldn't bear the idea of starting the year like this and having him get behind again. She didn't need this.

Before she'd gotten home, Janice had felt successful. She'd left the office early to have a forty-minute massage, a facial, and her hair blow-dried for the event that evening. At the dinner, she'd been complimented on her new red-and-black Escada suit that her sales consultant at the Fifty-seventh Street store had advised her to take even though Janice had been afraid the standout color was something of a risk. Elaine of Escada, who was well informed on these matters, had insisted that combinations of red, gray, and black were going to be the power colors this season. The whole of last year had been gray, gray, gray, completely unrelieved, and it had been a horrible, difficult year all around. The color of spring and summer had been pink, pink, pink everywhere. She didn't wear pink. Since Janice was afraid she'd lose her job in the new merger, she'd taken the plunge for red. Yesterday her boss and associates had like the suit, so she felt hopeful if *they* didn't get fired, she wouldn't get fired. At dinner, she'd enjoyed the wine and the food.

But now she was upset again. She did not want to be upset with her wonderful courageous David—who had a problem flourishing because of his ADD, which made her feel guilty because she had no idea where it came from since she and Bill were so *very* focused—so she played detective and looked in the fridge for the chili. She knew if he'd eaten it that he had come home after speaking to her. She hoped this was the case. Unfortunately, the chili was still there, wrapped in plastic wrap, sprinkled with cheese and onions the way he liked it. David was a big eater, despite the terrible pain he had from the *awful* Ritalin all the doctors bar none said he had to take to concentrate on his schoolwork. If David had come home, he would have eaten the chili. Janice wandered into her son's room, her pleasure in the wonderful evening draining away with every passing minute. "Jesus!"

There was clutter everywhere. Toys from when David was ten. Pennants from camp. Books, papers, used and unused athletic equipment. Even though Alvera cleaned it up and changed the sheets every week, it smelled horrible. Stale, sweaty boy smell and who knew what else. It occurred to her that she should search his room for signs of drug use. All the ads about kids said she ought to be thinking about this, and she knew other mothers who probed and pried *constantly*. But David said the idea of drugs disgusted him, and that was good enough for her.

The room tugged at Janice's heart. She resisted the urge to snoop. The kid had problems studying, that was all; it wasn't his fault. He was brave about it, terribly brave, she knew. The other boys teased him because he was big. He was in a hard school and struggling to stay there—and as it turned out he *deserved* to be there. He was no dummy. The kid surprised them all with his psychological testing. The kid was actually *smart*. He could do the work if he wanted to. He could be a star.

By eleven David was supposed to be, if not *in* bed, at least in his room and *ready* for bed. Still, Janice didn't want to jump to conclusions. Maybe she had misunderstood him. Maybe he had a good excuse. She went back into the kitchen and sat on the stool in the kitchen, played with Alvera's note, and called David on his cell phone. The phone rang three times before the answering function picked up.

"Hey, it's David. I'm not here right now. Leave a message."

This upset Janice even more. How could he not be there right now? He had the thing in his *pocket*. Janice screamed into the phone. "David! Call me right *now*. You know the rules. It's a *school* night! I'm supposed to know where you *are*." She slammed down the receiver.

Then she realized she hadn't told him where she was, so she called again. "*David!* I'm at home."

She hung up a second time and marched into her room to undress. It was a hard, masculine room, everything in colors of beige and brown because Bill didn't like anything girly. She wasn't surprised that *Bill* wasn't home. He worked even longer hours than she did and was often out of town. This upset her, too. Despite the comforting massage, tension crept back into her neck and shoulders. She wished Bill were there to consult about David.

When they were together the couple talked about David and his problems endlessly. Usually he was in the other room because neither of them actually spent any leisure time with him. It was difficult when he was so sullen. So their family outings consisted of dinner together Saturday nights at one of the better restaurants and that was *it*. Although *that* was a lot of fun. The three of them recorded and rated every meal in a journal, carefully listing what they'd eaten and drunk and how much they liked or were disappointed by the restaurant.

David remembered every single thing about every restaurant from the time he was three. She could call him up any time of the day and ask him about something they'd done years ago, and he could tell her without having to look it up in the journal. Sometimes she'd be in a meeting and she'd call him with the question just to impress her friends.

They didn't do anything else but eat for entertainment. Bill was focused on his legal cases; he wasn't athletic, wasn't interested in the theater or movies or having a country house. If they planned a vacation, it was always with the caveat that he might have to cancel at the last minute. Even by Janice's standards he was a workaholic. She was angry with him for not being as good a father as she was a mother, but she would have liked his advice tonight.

Finally she poured herself another drink and turned on the news. On the news she heard a story about a missing man in Central Park. This alarmed her further because she knew that David played there with that *really nasty* girlfriend of his whom she wished would fall off a cliff and die. She waited for her son and husband to come home from wherever they went to escape her. She had another drink and fell asleep.

THIRTY-ONE

GO TO BED, MOM, everything's fine." Wearily, April closed the front door of the house and climbed the stairs to her two-room apartment. Dim Sum joyously yapped at her feet and her mother followed close behind.

"That big rie, *ni*. I see you on TV, small news tlee time." Skinny Dragon Mother began to wheeze. For almost ten years, since she'd stopped working, she'd gotten no exercise. Leisure time hadn't been good for her.

"What's long with boyflen?" Even though the front door was closed and Skinny didn't have to show off her English for the neighbors, she screamed in English anyway.

"Go to bed, Ma." April's nose told her that her mother had had a big day. She'd walked three blocks to the beauty parlor. The chemicals that curled her two inches of naturally straight gray hair into a fine frizz and dyed it black and shiny as shoe polish smelled like a combination of ammonia and artificial raspberry jam. She relented.

"You look great, Ma. Did you get your hair done today?"

"No!" Skinny slammed the door as hard as she could. "Don't cly," she ordered. "Get betta boyflen. One two tlee."

"What makes you think something's wrong?"

"Call tlee time."

"I told you. Everything's fine." April threw her purse on the hot pink tufted sofa from Little Italy that she'd bought both as a great luxury and a rebellion from the hard Chinese chairs in the living room. The effort of not thinking about Carla's long tanned legs made her head feel as heavy as a brick.

Skinny Dragon Mother flashed one of her powerful silent messages that only an idiot wouldn't understand. Message 403 was a bit of detective work worthy of any squad in the city: *Everything couldn't be fine. Worm daughter slept at home last night and night before. Came home tonight again. Tomorrow day off. If everything so fine, why no boyfriend for three days?* Skinny was so excited by the prospect of April's failure at love with a Spanish ghost, she'd stopped the wheezing for the moment. Her renewed health didn't help April's morale one bit.

"One two tlee," she repeated, about getting a new boyfriend.

April didn't miss much, either. Usually the dragon—real name Sai Yuan Woo—was happy to show off her brightly colored, look-like-silk blouses that didn't match the patterns of her slacks and jackets. This was her attempt at scaling the peaks of high American style. But tonight she'd dressed down; she was wearing her peasant outfit. Black peasant pants, shapeless black cotton jacket, black canvas shoes with the rubber band across the top. She must have changed when Mike called those three times trying to reach her. Whenever the dragon dressed this way, she wanted to hide her true motives and true self. Her goal was to appear humble and simple to the daughter she wanted to control, and nothing special to the gods who ruled the heavens and earth so they wouldn't confuse her prosperity in Astoria, Queens, USA, with happiness and cause her harm. Whenever Sai became a peasant, ten kinds of bad luck for April were on the way. The outfit was as lethal as a voodoo hex.

The phone rang, the dog started barking. April stood there, certain that pins were sticking in the real her. The ringing phone caused her mother—way overbalanced at the moment with aggressive male yang—to grab her arm and roughly shake her. Skinny was several inches shy of five feet and weighed about three and a half pounds, but she spun April around with no trouble. The phone rang a few more times. April ignored it.

"Maybe boss," Skinny screamed.

"It's not my boss."

"How know, *ni?* Maybe lose job." Sai punched April's arm. She didn't want worm daughter to lose job until she had a rich Chinese husband. When she wasn't calling April worm daughter, she called her *ni*, which was just plain old you.

"Okay, okay." The screaming that passed for love in the Woo household propelled April into the bedroom just in case Maslow had been found in the last hour and she'd missed it. But they both knew the caller was the Spanish threat to the Han dynasty.

"Sergeant Woo," she said into the receiver.

"*Querida,* why are you acting like this? Are you crazy? Carla is nothing to me. She's just a mixed-up girl I helped once. I told her all about you. She has the highest opinion of you. You're overreacting. You know what girls are like. This is nothing." Mike blabbered into the phone.

"*Mi amor,* I know what girls are like. *La puta* was wearing my nightgown, demanding money from you."

"What's this *puta?*" Skinny Dragon screamed.

"Ma!" April put a finger to her lips.

"I can explain it," Mike insisted.

"Well, explain some other time. Stealing my case and cheating on me in one day is more than I can swallow."

"*Bu hao waiguoren, guole,*" the Dragon muttered happily. Looked to her like the Han dynasty was safe for another day.

"That's not fair," Mike protested.

"Fair has nothing to do with it." The teenager was in his apartment. She was scantily clad and she was not his sister. Mike didn't have a sister. And she wasn't his cousin because she didn't speak Spanish. April knew Carla was one of those girls on the phone that Mike talked to longer than he should. He was certainly guilty of letting her spend the night. And he was guilty of not saying a thing about it this morning.

Skinny picked up a pillow from April's pathetic single bed and started whacking it with gusto. She was having the time of her life. "New boyflen, one, two, tlee," was her new chant.

"April, I don't want to end the evening like this. I made a mistake. I had a couple of beers and let her crash at my place. She slept on the sofa. I swear I didn't touch her," Mike insisted. "I never promised her any money or any clothes. Trust me on this."

Oh, now he'd been drunk. It was sounding worse and worse. "Thank you for sharing that. I happen to know that men will do anything when they're drunk," she said softly. "What do you think they invented alcohol for? I love you, but don't call me back tonight, okay? I just need to calm down." April hung up. She didn't want to fight with her mother listening.

Skinny finished punching the pillow and patted her new hairdo. "You hunglee. I got good dinna. Happy famree clab, Oh Oh soup, flied lice, ramb and scarrions." Skinny reeled off the menu.

Her mother's cycle of batter then feed filled April with a deep sadness. Why would her mother be glad to see her lose face? Her cheeks burned yet another time and tears that she would never in a million years let escape prickled painfully behind her eyes. Why couldn't she have a sweet and sympathetic mother? The phone started to ring again. She decided not to answer it. Skinny's silence as she trotted down the stairs for food from her kitchen spoke loudly. Triumph had never been sweeter.

THIRTY-TWO

MORE THAN ANYTHING in the world April wanted to sleep, but the ghosts and goblins intervened with a review of the Chinese facts of life to punish her for falling in love. Fact: All men were *bu hao* (no good) ghosts; they always reverted to their true selves in the end. Fact: The only worthwhile constants in life were the struggle for money and position, or: getting ahead. Everything else (like pleasure) was a waste of time. Fact: There was no way men could be in harmony with all that yang pushing and shoving them in all the wrong directions. Didn't matter what you called it. Yang or testosterone; same thing. Fact: Of all the ghosts (kinds of people in the world) the very worst ones were the Spanish ghosts. Fact: Mike Sanchez was a Spanish ghost.

Around and around these facts went. Did she really believe this? Not a whisper. Was the belief system deeply ingrained in her? Definitely. Skinny Dragon brought her food on a tray, just like the restaurant person she used to be. Her father, who'd cooked the food himself earlier in the evening and brought it home on the subway just for her, hid out in his room smoking and drinking scotch, a silent presence who nevertheless let his views be known. April didn't want the food but was not able to resist her mother's attempts to cheer her up.

"*Ni*, you know how much best quality food like this cost at Shun Lee Dragon?" she scolded in Chinese, then resorted to English. "Fifty dolla!"

April smelled the delicate aromas of soft-shelled crab bathed in sweet ginger sauce, the spicy lamb and scallions, the fried rice with just a touch of oyster sauce for flavor; and she thought: more like a hundred and fifty dollars. She played with the chopsticks, wishing she hadn't been so hard on Mike on the phone.

"Hey, no good worm, *ni ting* (listen you). Too much trouble, bring home on subway. Just for *bu hao* daughter. Eat."

"Oh, Ma, I can't eat. I had a bad day."

"Had good day. Lose bad yellow ghost. Now find China ghost. No cry," she commanded in Chinese.

"You don't know anything, Ma." Mike is a good man. Just too trusting.

"I know Spanish *gui, bu hao*."

April sighed. The daughter was no good—nothing better than a worm. The Spanish ghost was no good. By Skinny's estimation nobody was any good. The dragon tapped her head to show her knowledge lay beneath the awful dyed hair.

"Don't call him Spanish. His name if Mike. He's a good man." With a soft heart that sometimes got him in trouble. But April didn't want to debate the matter with her mother.

"Eat," Skinny demanded. "You feel better."

April knew her mother meant well. She started eating to shut her up. As she ate, she was reminded what a good cook her father was. The crab was still crunchy and delicious even after the trip on the subway, only a few stops to Astoria, not that far. She chewed on a yummy crab leg, weighing her options. She'd put in a number of years with Mike. He'd been her supervisor, but had acted more like a partner, teaching her how to think and how to operate with different kinds of people. Before she'd worked the Two-O, she hadn't personally known anybody who lived in buildings with staff to open the doors and announce visitors and take out the garbage and fix the toilets when they didn't work. She'd never known that apartments could be bigger than houses, or known people who wore suits and coats that cost more than she earned in a month. She'd never had a sip of white wine in her entire life until she'd had it with Jason and Emma just before baby April was born. She'd never had sangria or a margarita until she had it with Mike last winter. Her heart did a little dance as she thought of how giddy she got when she had only a little bit to drink and how funny Mike thought she was when she lost her inhibitions. She didn't like to think how he'd been with Carla when he lost his.

He was the opposite of her in every way. She was reserved, nervous about everything, and quiet. He was expressive, not worried about much of anything, and occasionally wild. She had no doubt that he would come over and make a scene. He'd come in the middle of the night. He'd insist on being let in. She'd feel like shooting him dead but wouldn't do it because killing a cop was a big no-no for career development. He'd be sweet and cajole her into letting him in. He'd tell her how much he loved her. April knew just how the scenario would go. She'd let him in to show her mother who was boss and, even more important, to prevent Mike from losing face with her family. And whatever he said, she'd go with the flow. She'd already lost face by running away from an unpleasant scene. That had been weak. Now she had to restore her face and his by listening to what he had to say.

While she waited for Mike to turn up, she went to bed. But neither Mike nor sleep came. She started brooding about Maslow and the mistakes she'd made in the case. She wished she could start all over again. After a few minutes, she got up and went into the living room for her important address book that contained the names of all the sources she'd ever used. John Zumech was the very last name in her book. She dialed his number. It was way after midnight, and he took four rings to pick up.

"Zumech," he said in a deep gravelly voice.

"Hi, John, it's April Woo. I'm sorry to call so late."

"It's okay. I wasn't sleeping."

"How's that dog of yours?" April came into the subject sideways.

"Peachy's great. What's up?"

"How are you, John?"

"I'm great, too. How about you?"

"I have a teeny problem."

"You need me?"

"I do. In normal circumstances I wouldn't be calling so late. Missing p. Last seen heading into Central Park in jogging shorts."

"You know I'm not going out at night on a cold lead."

"Oh yeah, I know."

"You got a missing doctor. I saw you on TV. What can I do that my friends in K-9 can't?"

"Yes, well, you always told me that Sid Slocum was an idiot."

"Did I say that?" John laughed.

"Yeah, you always told me you gotta trust your dog. Slocum didn't seem to get what his dog was doing."

"What was she doing?"

"Looking for a place to take a dump. How do I know? I'm no tracker. Anyway, I met some friends of yours. They suggested Slocum was an idiot, too."

"Really, who?"

"Couple of kids. Brandy Fabman and David Owen."

"No kidding, I used to know those two pretty well. They're camp friends of my daughter. What are they up to?"

"Guess what, they turned up this afternoon and talked their way into the park. Seems they saw the search from the girl's apartment and wanted to offer some advice on tracking."

John made a honking laugh. "Those kids! Ha ha. City rats. I never saw kids so turned on to tracking. I did some exhibitions up at their camp two years ago. They were so excited they came out to visit us during the winter. A couple of weekends, they came out for a day, helped me do some training." He chuckled some more.

"One time I took them out to the beach at Montauk. God, you wouldn't believe how much those kids were into it. How are they?"

"Well, they're into something else now."

"Oh, yeah?" Zumech's voice became a shade less hearty.

"They were high as kites, John."

His tone sobered. "That's too bad. They were good kids. Are you sure, April?"

"Yeah, John, I'm sure."

He was silent for a moment. "Well, what can I do for you?"

"I'd like you to try again, with Peachy."

Long silence. "Why?"

"The missing man is a friend of a friend. I'm afraid we might have overlooked something."

"What could you overlook? I saw clips of people mucking around in the rowboat lake. It's not very deep. If he was in there, you'd have found him. We're not talking great wilderness tract here. If he were somewhere in the bushes, any dog, even Slocum's, would have found him."

"I know, that's what Sid said, but I want to try again anyway."

"Ridiculous. The scent's been scattered by now. Hundreds of people have contaminated that area. You know the facts of life on tracking, April. A good dog can do a lot if you get going in a few hours, up to ten. But this guy went missing—when?"

Facts. April didn't want to hear any more facts of life tonight. "Last night. That's not so long."

"April, this is a *city*. Millions of people."

"So what?"

"There's nothing left of your guy for Peachy to smell."

"Unless he's dead," April argued.

John sighed. "What makes you think he's dead?"

"It's just a possibility, is all. We have a mental patient on the loose. Come on, help me out." She was exaggerating about Allegra, but it worked.

"A mental patient?" John whistled. "I didn't hear anything about that."

"It's not out yet." April didn't want to say more.

"You have anything with his scent on it?" he asked. She could hear him getting interested.

"Hers."

"Hers? A girl mental patient?"

"Yeah, and we don't have her scent. What are you doing tomorrow?"

John sighed again. "Fine, I'll give it a try. But no cars, no busses, no media, no people on CPW. Can you swing that?"

"Of course," she told him. A big lie since she was off duty and off the case. They set a time and a meeting place. Then, for the fifth time, she called the number Allegra had given her. Again no answer, just as Jason had predicted. Thank God for Woody's camera. They'd make up a wanted poster of the girl and circulate it tomorrow. They'd put it on TV if they had to. She had a family, people who knew her. They'd find her. April fell asleep waiting for Mike, but he never came.

THIRTY-THREE

PEE WEE SMELLED CORPSE SMELL. He'd known that smell all his life. He knew it from the flood that took his brother and his dog when he was nine, and the tornado that flattened the barn and killed all the animals he'd tended. He knew it from 'Nam. He must have killed fifty people there. And he'd killed one or two more defending his territory since. Accidents.

He was sitting on the ground with his head in his hands, wondering what it was that he'd forgotten to do. Oh, that smell was strong. He shook himself, like a dog shaking off the hurt. Then he saw the girl and stumbled toward her. He'd lost track of time and thought it was the cop from the fight a while ago when everybody was yelling at him.

"Don't follow me," he raved angrily at the girl. "Why are you following me. I didn't hit nobody." We waved his arm, shooing her away. The scene spun out of control. Ants the size of fat caterpillars marched across his face. Other insects swarmed in front of his eyes, blurring his vision. A spider monkey swung down from the tree next to him and poked him in the chest, almost knocking him over.

"You're drunk, get away," the girl said.

The scene spun back into focus. Pee Wee remembered this wasn't the cop, this was the one who promised to give him that twenty to keep the secret about the guy they pushed into the cave. This one was here to give him that twenty so he could have a dog.

"I wan my tweny. Member my tweny?" he said hopefully.

"I said, get lost." She waved a tree branch at him.

The leaves on it looked like snakes, shaking their heads at him. Not so funny. He lumbered toward her. She smelled like a corpse. For a second he was back in 'Nam with the smell of the dead all around him.

The boy came up. He started talking to the girl. He told the girl to go for a walk. She wouldn't go away. He gave her a shake but she wouldn't leave.

"Don't do that . . . nice girl," Pee Wee mumbled.

"You scumbag!" The boy hissed at Pee Wee. He let go of the girl and came toward him.

"You gonna gimme that tweny?" Pee Wee said

"Yeah, sure I'll give it to you. Come over here."

Pee Wee moved toward him. The girl shook the branch at him, confusing him.

The boy told the girl to go away. She said she didn't want to. They started arguing. Pee Wee became confused again. He wanted to break up the fight. He put his hand up to protect the girl.

Suddenly the boy punched him. He fell to the ground groaning. "Wha—?"

He must have gone out for a moment. The next thing he felt was someone rolling him over. He saw blood on the sidewalk. He thought he was in the police station, having a shower. He didn't know what was happening. His sequences were all off. He felt drunk, but not good drunk. He pulled himself to his feet. The girl with the snakes was saying something. She wanted a trophy. He struggled to figure out what she was talking about.

The boy was trying to shut her up. He put his hand on her mouth. Pee Wee lunged to save the girl.

The girl shook the tree branch, hitting him with it. "Get out of here, you're drunk."

"Oh, no, ah'm not drunk. Yur drunk," he said angrily.

The big guy was coming after him, threatening him with a broken bottle. "No, you don't. No, no, no."

"No one needs scum like you."

The words galvanized Pee Wee. Nobody called him scum and lived to tell about it. "I'm fucking kill *you*," he cried at the tree branch full of snakes.

The girl swung at him with the branch. He plunged into the fight, grappling with three or four of them. He was fighting a whole army. A big guy came at him. Pee Wee felt all blurry and confused with all the screaming and yelling in his head and the smell of the dead. He thought he was in the war again. Hot liquid ran down into his eyes. It was blood. He was hit. He went down. Then, a second later he was up again, swinging. His hands were shaking. He fell over before he connected.

The big guy grabbed his hand to help him up. Pee Wee lunged at the girl. She hit him with the tree again. Then the guy was punching him hard. The last thing he saw was a knife.

"Whaaa?" He was confused by the knife.

He was caught between the guy hitting him, the tree branch with snakes, and the knife in his face. His vision failed and he went down. His eyes furred over for the last time. He never knew that the knife was there to cut off his finger.

THIRTY-FOUR

DEEPEST DARK NOW, and the panic was back. Coarse sand crusted Maslow's mouth and eyes. He was afraid that soon he would be covered with dirt. He scrabbled away at the gravel on either side of him. Dirt fell on him from above. His tongue worked constantly trying to clear his mouth and he had to restrain himself from using all his water to rinse it clean. He was terrified that the bank of packed sand over his head would fall, and he wouldn't make it through the night.

He could feel his hips, but his legs didn't seem to be part of him, and he didn't have the energy to shift toward his feet. He prayed for someone to come. As he listened to the muted city night sounds, he slipped into the far past and was assaulted by childhood memories again. A ferrous smell of disintegrating iron, the source of which he could not see, reminded him of the corrosion that had so irritated his father in the garden chairs and the grates over the basement wells at the house in Massachusetts.

The first whiff of rust made him think he must be under a grate with the fresh air and freedom above him. But he knew that could not be. He had not fallen down into something. He was stretched out straight, lying on a bed of pebbles and sand. Both air and sound were coming in from the direction of his feet It was possible that his legs were pinned, and that was the reason he could not move them. His explorations with his hands indicated that his upper body at least was wedged in under a shelf of caked sand and crumbling stone. Some

large rock might be above that, but he could not feel the dimensions of
it. He was in a hollowed-out shallow place, like a grave. He could not
have fallen in such a way.

The air was cooling now, and the earth around him deeply chilled.
The skin on his arms, his face, and his hands was so cold, in fact, that
he wondered why he was not dead already. He was underground,
buried alive. He made himself think of far colder places than this
where people had survived horror. There was no heat in concentration
camps. There had been no heat in the trenches in World War I. Soldiers in every war throughout history had survived worse conditions
than this. Prisoners in the frozen gulags survived. Who else? Naked
slaves in the holds of sailing ships crossing the ocean—starving, freezing, and seasick. Maslow made lists of survivors in his head. He
thought of himself in a war, his enemy someone he'd trusted and tried
to help. He thought of Chloe, only eleven years old, her whole body
black-and-blue before she finally died. Her death was an atrocity. He'd
survived that.

Coming from the direction of his feet, Maslow smelled night and
rusting iron and thought of his passion as a boy for how things worked.
He'd wondered at the way rust consumed shiny paint, gnawing the
color and strong metal away from the inside and crumbling it into reddish brown dust. Every year, before Chloe died and the house was sold,
he'd helped sand the rust off those garden chairs and paint them a
deep green, only to see the patches of decay revived over the winter by
the salty sea air.

He smelled something else—the chlorophyll in leaves, wet earth,
and water. The smells reminded him of the sweet, fresh air of outdoor
nights when Chloe and he used to catch fireflies and put them in a jar.
Then, they'd sat side by side on the beach, watching the fireflies blink
on and off and studying the stars. He'd never felt such companionship
with anyone else since. Near death, he felt very close to Chloe now.
The granola bar he clutched in his hand was the same as the ones they
used to eat together as their snack in the afternoons. The granola bar
had attracted an animal that scampered back and forth across his feet.

The first time the animal jumped on his shoe Maslow felt the
weight of it and pins and needles in his feet. He grunted with terror
and beat on his chest and hips with the fanny pack. The animal scam-

pered away. But now it was back, scratching around in the dark. Maslow knew that as soon as he fell asleep, it would invade like a marauding army. It would chew its way into his fanny pack and eat his only food. If he was unconscious, it would eat him. In the slums rats gnawed on babies in their cribs. He'd seen the bites during his rotation in the ER. People had survived that, too. He hoped it wasn't a rat.

He could hear himself moaning and praying to God to save him. He dreamed of his old daddy, the one who used to sleep at home when he was little. He dreamed of his mommy before they lost Chloe, the mommy he had before her smile died. He'd never been her favorite. She used to call him "Maslow the nose" because he could always tell when she'd changed perfumes, or ingredients in food. If an herb or spice was left out, he'd identify it. She seemed to like that about him. He had one real skill. But that was it.

His father had a big nose that he despised. Maslow didn't like thinking his own nose would grow as prominent as the one his father disliked so much. He'd been hurt by his mother's nickname. But she told him his nose was a good thing. "Noses" were paid big money in perfume companies, at wineries, and all places where the palate counted.

"You have a palate, Maslow. If all else fails, you can smell for a living." And she'd laughed, but not really in a mean way.

The laughter and the name had hurt Maslow anyway. He'd wondered where one could smell for a living in America. Later he found out the nose played a role in the history of psychoanalysis. It was first thought by Freud and his best friend, Wilhem Fleiss, that sniffing cocaine could cure hysteria.

Maslow was exercising his fingers and arms, and letting his mind wander around his sister's death, his mother's decline, his father's withdrawal from their lives. He heard the swish of someone walking through grass, the crunch of feet on stones. His heart started pounding loud as thunder again. Someone was coming. No one was calling his name, so it must be Allegra returning for him as he'd prayed she would.

He closed his eyes. "Allegra?"

"Allegra." His cry was only a whisper.

Nothing.

"Don't go."

After a pause, he heard the harsh sound of metal grinding against stone. That ferrous smell. Then a worse smell. The smell of the lab, the autopsy room. Powerful. A sharp pinpoint of light stabbed at him from his feet in. He shut his eyes against it.

"Hey." It was a girl voice. Sharp as a knife, but not familiar at all.

"Allegra, help me," he said weakly.

"Jesus Christ, he's got fucking food!" Boy voice.

"And water!" Girl voice.

"Where did it come from? Hey, you!"

Someone kicked his feet, and the feet exploded with stabbing needles. Another kick, and tears poured out of his eyes.

The girl screamed, "Ahhhh. Did you see that?"

"Turn on the flashlight. I can't see a fucking thing."

"It's a rat."

"Jesus. Will you shut up." Someone crouched down and shone a powerful light on Maslow's wet, sand-crusted face.

"Help me."

"Look at that. He's alive!" Boy voice.

"Shit, now he's seen us."

Maslow couldn't believe it. They sounded like kids, little kids. He held out his hand to the person at his feet. "I can't see a thing. Help me out."

Sound of revulsion. "Don't touch him. He's disgusting."

Maslow was lying on his back, helpless as the two examined him from far enough away so that he could not grab them. He didn't want to debate the matter. "I promise no one will know," he said softly. "Just let me out."

"Kill him, David, and let's get out of here." Another kick and explosion of pain.

"No. Don't do that," Maslow ordered sharply. He was not going to let two kids murder him as if he were nothing but a kitten or a bird they'd caught.

"What's the matter with you, do it!" the girl said impatiently. "I want to go home now. It's creepy here."

No sound from the boy.

"Here, take my knife. Stab him in the throat."

Maslow's breath came faster. The threat of the knife made him hyperventilate. "Don't even think that. You'll go to jail for the rest of your lives."

The girl blew air through her mouth.

"I don't know who you are or why you did this. Doesn't matter why. Just pull me out and take off. I won't tell anyone."

"Uh-uh, too late. Go ahead, David, kill him. Two will make you a serial killer."

"Shut up, Brandy."

"Help me. Nothing will happen to you. I give my word."

"Jesus. He has a *phone*! And food and water." The girl reached in and grabbed them. "Fuck it, I'll do it myself."

"What's going on?" A shout. "Dr. Atkins!"

"Holy shit, who's that?"

"Jesus, it's that girl, spying on us."

The flashlight went off.

"Go out and get her, David."

"Shhh."

"Dr. Atkins!" Maslow knew that voice. It was Allegra's.

Two of them were in here, and she was out there. What the hell was going on? Maslow held his breath, not knowing what was going on.

"Get help," he called.

Silence. Maybe she was leaving.

He called out again. "Allegra, get help."

"Maslow?" Puzzled voice. "What's going on?"

Then she came inside. And the two kids turned their attention to her.

THIRTY-FIVE

I N APRIL'S FIRST SECONDS of consciousness, she was hit with a blinding
headache and didn't know where she was. Then she turned her head
and saw the white ruffled curtains in the small windows of her bedroom and groaned. Her legs explored the confines of her narrow bed,
and she remembered a few things. She was not in Mike's apartment in
Forest Hills in a bed as big as a playground, where the kitchen, living
room, and bathroom were bigger, newer, and higher than hers; there
was air conditioning that cooled the whole place, and a terrace where
she and Mike had sat many times over the summer, drinking beer, kiss-
ing and fondling each other, and watching the lights of Manhattan in
the distance.

The headache escalated as she remembered Skinny Dragon Mother
insisting that the man she loved was a *she* (snake). She remembered
telling Zumech a search in the park would be no problem. She remembered her little slipup of losing Jason's mental patient without a
name. She dragged herself out of bed to face the day.

Like millions of American-born Asians, April believed that she was
100 percent American, with no foreign accent and none of her
mother's ridiculous superstitions or prejudices about the nature of
people, character, or luck. And yet, she had no doubt that something
was in the air. Call it the stars, the ghosts, the dragons, the yang that
was the force of irritable, risky male action. Didn't matter, something
was weird. Events were spinning out of control.

The missing shrink had a patient who wasn't the person anyone thought she was—and who was also a good enough liar to fool everyone, even April. Mike's judgment had failed over Carla. In the boys and girls department, it was pretty clear that the girls were winning.

Now April was losing her harmony, too. Whenever it came to Jason Frank, she couldn't let go. She just couldn't let go. She just couldn't. In Asian thinking, good luck (lots of money) and long life were the most important things to have. Getting face and saving it were the most important things to do.

In the face department, April suffered humiliations everywhere she turned. On the job she was bossed around by people stupider than her. She was doubted and snubbed by the civilians she served, by the males she outranked and the males who outranked her. At home she was constantly humiliated and berated by her mother, who wanted for April only what she wanted for herself. She wanted her only child, and a daughter at that, to be rich, idle, the wife of a Chinese businessman or doctor, with many babies and a big house she could fill with anything she wanted. A TV the length of the room. A big car. Big one. Maybe two. She wanted that important married daughter to spend more time caring for her, listening to her problems, buying her gifts, and making her happy in all the little ways that daughters should.

April was angry with her mother for failings of her own, like not learning how to drive and change lightbulbs, speak better English, read the labels on cans and bottles, work for the community as other Chinese matrons did. But when April weakened she felt sorry for her mother. Skinny was not educated, was not a college graduate as she was. April had gone for six years at night to get her degree from John Jay College of Criminal Justice, and she did not consider herself by any means finished in the education department. She felt sorry that her mother worried and suffered so much over so many wrongheaded ideas. April had no doubt that Skinny suffered a great deal, and she knew at the same time she had to both set limits and social-work her mother to ease that suffering just a little. Call that filial duty.

Same thing as a cop, she had to toe the party line. She had to hold her head up and keep it down at the same time. She had to know how to work the system. And although she had risen from beat cop to detective sergeant, second whip of the Midtown North detective unit, most of the time she felt she was still treading water, getting nowhere.

Jason Frank was the only highly educated white man who trusted and believed in her. He didn't know her mother or father or bosses and how much they disrespected her for one thing or another. To Jason, she was not just an Asian cop with a yellow ghost boyfriend. She was the hero who'd literally walked through fire to save his wife, and she had the scars to prove it. To him she was the only one in the department who could get things done. Jason and Emma had elevated her to a place of esteem where she'd never resided before. Their daughter was named after her. There was no honor greater than that.

April could not lose face by letting Jason down. Could not do it. Today, she did not go out jogging, do her leg and arm exercises or her abdominal crunches. Instead, she stood under the shower and let cold water bombard her throbbing head. She drank two cups of hot water with lemon juice, swallowed two aspirin, and dressed carefully in a lavender blouse, a cinnamon suit with a short skirt and a long jacket to cover the Glock at her waist. She finished the outfit with an iris print silk scarf that mixed both colors. She let her hair dry straight, didn't care how she looked. She was in a no-nonsense mood. She was going to get into trouble, maybe even ruin her career.

The honking began at six-forty-five when she was dressed and almost ready to start the walk to the subway because she'd left her car in the city. Even before the noise brought her to the window, she knew the horn was that of Mike's aging red Camaro, and the racket it made would wake her mother and father. She didn't want them making a scene so she grabbed her purse and ran downstairs. When Mike saw her coming, he got out of the car.

April's headache disappeared, and instantly she was on super alert because Mike looked the way he did when he was about to trick a dumb suspect into giving up the story that would put him behind bars for life. She shook her head as the lover of many women spread his arms to give her a big hug as if right now that had to be the thing she desired most on earth.

"Mira, mi amor. Yo soy tuyo. Todo, todo tuyo. Tu es mi vida, todo. Soy tuyo." Today Mike was wearing another bright blue shirt, the color they called

French blue, which practically broke your eyeballs. April had bought this one herself, too, as well as the bubble-gum pink tie he was wearing with it. She smelled his powerful sweet and spicy aftershave that drove women nuts and made men like her father think he was gay. He was saying that he was hers, that she was his whole life, and she was moved by the pleasant sound of a man pleading in Spanish.

In the boys and girls department, however, she knew she must never let him get the upper hand, so she walked around him and got into the car, where she firmly closed the door before he could give her that hug.

"*Querida*, what is this?" he said, looking hurt.

"Thanks for coming to give me a ride," she said, gazing straight ahead out the window.

"Of course I would give you a ride. What did you think?" His tone was soft. He stood at the car window, looking like a lamb. "You're not mad at me, are you?" He looked at her with his melting love look. She could feel it burn through the window. He didn't even mention last night. He was going to bluff his way through it. Men!

"Let's go," she said, all business.

"Of course, of course. Where are we going first?" Soft, soft voice. He moved around the car, got in, started the engine, gunned it, and pulled out into the street. If he was worried about the missing jogger the whole city was looking for, he didn't show it. That pissed her off, too.

She did not answer.

"*Querida*, I get the feeling you're mad at me," he said.

"I am."

He countered with indignation. "You left in a hurry last night. You didn't have a car. What did you do, fly?"

"Yeah, I flew."

"I should be mad at *you*. You didn't return my calls. What kind of behavior is this from someone I adore with all my heart?"

She said nothing as he threaded through Astoria streets.

"*Querida*. How about breakfast?"

"No way."

"Let's talk about this."

"Go ahead, talk."

"I met this girl before you came to the Two-O."

"What was she, twelve then?"

"No, she was over sixteen. She was a kid in trouble. She'd run away from her parents. She'd been abused. She was on the street."

"La-la-la-la." April started humming to block out the confession she feared was coming.

"*Querida*, don't make me mad," Mike said softly.

"Call me Sergeant, we're on the job."

"Oh Jesus, you're my girlfriend. We're a couple. Couples work things out."

"La-la-la-la-la." April sang some more.

He laughed. "Oh, come on. I was kind of proud of having a girl like that think she was in love with me. Gorgeous girl like that. Old guy like me. I thought it would give me points with you, make you like me more."

"Are you crazy?"

"Look, I saw her in a bar. The girl was in trouble, she had no place to stay. I told her she could stay at my place."

"How drunk did you have to be to make that offer?"

"I wasn't drunk, just a little too trusting." His mustache twitched.

April shook her head. "Doesn't play. You gave her my nightgown."

He took his hands off the wheel and braked again. "No! I would not do that. She slept on the sofa with all her clothes on. She must have put it on after I left. The only mistake I made was trusting her to leave in the morning."

"You're a cop. Cops don't leave street people in their homes while they go off to work. Who do you think you're kidding?"

"Do you think I'd have taken you there if I'd known she'd be there *nuda*? *Escucha*, I never did it with her. Trust me on that one."

She chewed on that for a moment, tempted to believe him. The man was *muy stupido*. And, if it worked out between them, she would have the pleasure of throwing this incident in his face whenever they fought for the rest of their lives.

He braked for a red light at Van Dam. "Do you want to help me with my case? I'd welcome your support," he said magnanimously, moving right along now that he'd won his argument.

"Oh yeah, what about the other little matter? You dismissed my detective last night."

"There was nothing more to do. It was time for you both to go home." He kept his reasoning tone. The light changed. The morning traffic crawled to the bridge.

"You undermined my authority. You made me lose face." April said. Frankly, she wasn't going to let it go.

"It wasn't intentional. It was a bad day. I'm sorry I caused you distress. Very sorry."

"How did you worm your way into this case?" she demanded.

He gave her a little smile, a little shrug. "I have my ways." He changed the subject. "Tonight will be good for you, I promise."

"Oh yeah?" She doubted that very much. So much for getting any substantive information from him.

"Yeah."

It was a boy-girl kind of conversation, steeped in nuance and not much on content. The informational flow was always going the other way. She hated that. The traffic crawled off the bridge into Manhattan. The sun was climbing up the sky behind them. Time was marching on, and they had to hurry with it.

THIRTY-SIX

Janice Owen did not remember going to bed or Bill's coming in during the night. The sound of the shower made it rain in her dream. Her baby was getting wet. He was tucked tightly in the stroller, but she'd lost her umbrella. It was a strange-looking baby; something was wrong with his head. She hurried to get out of the rain, pushing the stroller and running in bare feet. A dwarf was following her. He wanted to take the baby from her. Janice struggled out of the dream, heard the shower, and realized her husband was home.

She dragged herself out of bed, padded into the kitchen for coffee, and turned on the news. The dream left a residue of unease she needed to shake. The morning news reported that the man who'd been missing the night before was still missing. Today the Central Park story was expanded with reports of a number of recent assaults there as well as the two homicides in the last year, which included a woman raped and strangled in the Ramble and a man whose cause of death had never been established.

The bad dream, her husband ignoring her in the shower, and the unpleasant Central Park story caused Janice to storm into David's room, where he was curled up on his bed, sleeping like a baby. And stinking to high heaven, she might add. Unbelievable smell! She opened the window of his room, then stormed back into the bathroom, where Bill was humming away in the shower.

"Bill, where the fuck were you last night?" she screamed, sliding open the shower door.

Bill had shampoo on his blond hair. His body was covered with soap. The warm water was pelting down making stripes in the soap. He had a full erection, was singing and dreamily soaping his cock when the first bomb of Pearl Harbor struck him. "Huh?" he croaked in surprise.

The still-prominent erection reminded Janice that she and Bill hadn't had sex in months and months. This enraged her, too. How *dare* he get a hard-on at a time like this.

"Do you know what's going on in your own city? Do you know where your son is at night? Do you know any fucking *thing* at all?"

Indignantly, Bill turned his back on her and let the water cascade down.

"Was *your son* here when you got home?"

"What's with you? Of course he was."

"Do you *know* for a *fact* he was?" Janice stood there in a filmy nightie, her eyes still gummy with sleep, holding a coffee cup like a cross against the devil. The man was avoiding her. He didn't *care*.

He grabbed a towel and got out of the shower, brushing past her almost roughly.

"Bill!"

"What?"

"You almost knocked me over," she cried.

"You're dreaming. Are you drinking too much again?"

"I *never* drink." Indignantly, she followed him into the bedroom, where he tried to close himself in the closet.

"Don't try to avoid me. We have to talk." She opened the door. He turned his back on her again. Water from the shower dripped down his back, stabbing her in the heart. He toweled his back and his butt.

"I'm late. Maybe tonight," he muttered.

"Not tonight. Now!" she insisted. Bill was still a good-looking man. She knew how many women were attracted to him.

He groaned hugely, stabbing her again. "Janice, give me a break."

The groan broke her. Give him a *break*? "All you get is breaks. You're never around. You're always out with that tart. The least you can do is give your son *five* minutes of your precious time." It was out of the bag. She retreated a step, shocked that she'd said it.

"Where did you get that idea? There's no tart in my life." He turned to look at her for the first time, shocked to hear her talk like that.

"Oh yeah, I forgot. You call that ugly bitch your associate. You're out with her *every* night. You come home at three, four in the morning. Do you think I'm *stupid*?" Once her deepest fear was out in the open, Janice kept screaming.

"We call that *work*, Janice," he said angrily, his face mottled with the blood rushing to the surface, showing it all.

"*Right*. Give *me* that kind of work," she said bitterly.

"You're crazy." He turned his back on her a third time, pulled on a pair of shorts, then the Loro Piana navy blue nail-head cashmere trousers of a Bergdorf Goodman suit. He grabbed a shirt from a hanger, not even looking at it first. He was in a big hurry.

The deep blush, the nail-head suit, and the great big hurry were more than Janice could bear. She had a headache and a hangover. She swerved to the subject most likely to move him.

"Bill, I can't take all the responsibility of David myself. I've done all the parenting here. You have to participate. This is his *junior* year. His whole college career, maybe his whole life, depends on his knuckling under now."

"Knuckling is an incorrect image. You don't want him to knuckle under, you want him to *settle down* and *work*."

"Fine. You're his father, you talk to him."

"What do you suggest that I say?"

"Well, he's breaking the house rules again," she said, furious at both of them. Bill also was breaking the house rules, but one thing at a time. "Tell him you know about it. You're going to dock him his allowance and ground him if he doesn't knuckle under and live up to his potential."

Bill finished tying a new tie, a stunning Ferragamo with love-birds on it so vivid you could almost hear them coo. Janice had never seen it before.

"Where did you get that?" she demanded.

"Do you like it? Peggy gave it to me."

Janice paled. Peggy was giving him inappropriate gifts now? Love-birds? "I think it sucks a big one," she said.

Bill came out of the closet with a small tight smile on his smug face. He was gleaming all over—face pink and healthy, newly scrubbed and shaved, fancy suit, lovely new tie. He brushed by his wife, who was still holding the coffee cup, her thickening body showing clearly through the nightgown.

He marched into his son's room. David's head was under the covers.

"Good morning, David. Say hello to your father."

"You two are fighting again. You woke me up," came the angry response.

"David. Your mother and I love you very much. We're both very proud of you. Now listen to me. I want you to come home after school and get on the stick, you hear me? You're a wonderful, bright, brave boy, and you deserve all the good things life has to offer. We're proud of your efforts and we want you to try harder. Not for us, for yourself."

He turned back to his wife with an expression that said, *There, I spoke with him. Satisfied?*

No, she wasn't. There was one thing he hadn't mentioned. "And keep out of the park," she added. "I don't want you in that park. It's not *safe*. Your breakfast will be ready in four minutes. Meet me in the kitchen." Without looking at Bill she went back into the bathroom for her turn in the shower. She knew he'd be gone by the time she came out.

In the bedroom David was muttering, "Fuck you both."

THIRTY-SEVEN

CHERYL FABMAN awoke feeling human for the first time since her surgery. She shoved her feet into satin mules and gently moved herself from her green satin bed to her white carpeted floor, then into the bathroom to pee and take her first good look at herself. All the bathroom surfaces were marble except for the large mirrored inserts in the walls. All her mirrors told her she didn't look bad at all. A nice side effect to the week in bed was that all signs of fatigue and irritation over her present predicament were gone from her eyes.

Cheryl could not help admiring her lips, which were very impressive now despite a bit of swelling that would probably not completely disappear for another week or two. The inside of her mouth felt funny, but so what? She hiked up her nightgown to her waist and twirled in front of the mirror a few times, taking in from several angles her still Lycra-encased hips and thighs. She had been thin before. With nearly two pounds of pure fat removed from vital spots she was even thinner. But she was most proud of the lips; they definitely looked movie-star plump.

As Cheryl studied herself, she reconsidered the skills of her doctor. At the time of the consult, Morris Strong had suggested a few other little things she might do. Botox shots for the vertical frown-lines between her eyebrows were out of the question because it contained active botulism and paralyzed the nerves or something. He'd also suggested she do her eyes, of course. She was forty-three. She thought she'd wait on the eyes to see how the lips went.

Dr. Strong had informed her that in California they were doing full face-lifts at forty-two and it was better to start young. She pulled at the creases just beginning to tug at the corners of her mouth. He'd told her she could look twenty if she wanted to. But why bother? The Bastard, Seymour, was forty-two, a year younger than her and fat as a pig. Aston was fifty and looked sixty, another fat pig. She was forty-three and looked *maybe* twenty-eight. She was still a stunning woman. She could probably do better than either of them without any more work done.

She twirled some more. Nice butt. Really. Despite the Vicodin she'd taken last night, her eyes were clear. She saw that her hair needed freshening up, though. The yellow was too strong, maybe she'd go a little less brassy for the fall. She finished her assessment and padded into her daughter's room.

Brandy was still asleep. The air conditioner was humming away. It was freezing in her room and Brandy was buried deep under the covers. Cheryl checked the clock. Seven-thirty.

"Bran, honey. Wake up. Did you sleep through your alarm?"

There was no movement under the covers.

"Hey, kid, wake up and smell the flowers. Today's a school day."

Cheryl didn't want to lose her good feeling. She was through being an invalid. Where did it get her, anyway? No one cared how she felt. She'd be up and out of there today, ready to start a new life with new hips and new lips. Brandy had a mirror on her bedroom door. Cheryl looked pretty good in that one, too. She primped a little, fluffing her hair.

"Brandy, are you okay? Don't you want to see how good I turned out?" Cheryl frowned at her daughter's mess.

"Uh-huh."

Cheryl didn't like the mess, or the way that uh-huh sounded. "Honey, what's the matter? You don't sound very enthusiastic. Don't you know what time it is?"

"Uh-huh."

"You've got to get going or you'll be late for school. You promised me you'd take your studies seriously this year."

"Uh-huh."

A third uh-huh. What was going *on?* "Brandy, I'm losing my patience. Get up and clean this mess up. It stinks in here. And get ready for school. Where were you last night, anyway? I waited for you for hours."

This got her talking.

"With Dad. I got home at ten. You were out cold." The covers moved, but Brandy's head did not appear.

"That's not *true.*" Cheryl was stung. Maybe she'd had a Vicodin or two for the pain. But she was up practically all night thinking about her daughter, she was sure of it. "That's a lie, you know I never take pills," she said.

"Oh, come on, you were so fucking wasted you wouldn't know if an atom bomb hit."

"Jesus Christ! How dare you talk to me like that! I'm your loving mother. Don't you forget that," Cheryl exploded. "Look at your clothes. They're disgusting. What do you do, spend your time in a sewer? I know what you were up to, you little slut! You weren't with your father any more than I was."

"Well, at least *I* can see him any time I want. He hates *you* so much he wouldn't see you if you were dying of cancer."

Cheryl's breath made a noise that was meant to be a growl but came out like a sob. The pain of it all got her voice going. "I'm going to give him a little call about this. Look at your clothes. I've never seen anything so disgusting in my life. If this is his idea of parenting, I have a little surprise for him."

Brandy was out of her bed like a shot. She was wearing a pair of her father's boxer shorts and a T-shirt. "Don't touch my stuff," she cried. She looked horrible. Dark circles around her eyes. The pudgy teenager's body from hell. Cheryl freaked just looking at her. Brandy was a spawn of the devil, protecting a pile of filthy clothes and dirty sneakers. This child was never going to be a debutante, never going to be pretty, never going to turn out to be anything at all. She was hanging out in the park, God only knew *what* she was doing. Cheryl didn't know how she was unlucky enough to have an impossible kid like this.

"I'm your mother. I *will* touch your stuff," she screamed. "It's my job to see that you're taken care of. And I will not have you turn out a *slut* and a nothing. You little bitch! What are you hiding, *pot?*"

"Oh, come off it, you and that creepy friend of yours smoke pot all the time. So does Dad."

"*Dad* smokes *pot*? Are you crazy?" Cheryl was shocked, and screamed some more. Her ex-husband was an absolute uptight and boring square, a Republican, who never thought about anything but business and had ridiculous views about everything. They'd had no fun at all for years, and he'd never once smoked pot with *her*. *Not once*. She couldn't believe it.

"He's got a cookie jar full of it, smokes it all the time," Brandy said.

Cheryl's eyes popped. "I'll kill you. I'll fucking *kill* you if you smoke that pot with your father. I'll put him away. You're a nothing. You're going to be a God damn good-for-nothing, just like him. And watch me. I'll send him to jail. I will."

Brandy whined, "I feel bad. Mommy, get me some coffee. I'll go to school. I'll clean up. I'll do it, okay."

"You *better* do it." Cheryl softened immediately, thinking she'd order out for the coffee. "What kind do you want? Cappuccino? Mochaccino?"

"Look, don't hassle Dad. I was just mad at you for giving me grief all the time. I lied about the pot."

"You lied about the pot?" Cheryl said, suddenly sorry that she'd exploded like that. She always overreacted.

"You know I don't do that stuff." Brandy stood there guarding her filthy clothes. "I'll take care of this, okay?"

"I'll get that coffee for you, but hurry up." Cheryl didn't ask her daughter why her clothes were such a mess. Kids were hell, everybody knew that.

"I'd like a Danish, too," Brandy said.

Cheryl went into the bedroom for a robe and to call the deli. While she was dialing, Brandy ran out into the back hall and dropped her clothes and shoes down the garbage chute. They went down with a satisfying whoosh and disappeared forever.

THIRTY-EIGHT

J OHN ZUMECH WAS SIX FEET TALL with a medium build, no discernible fat on his body, long legs, and a salt-and-pepper crew cut of the kind that had been reviled since the Vietnam War by those not in the armed services but was recently making a comeback. He had a nose that had seen too much fighting action, a thin mouth with a small scar in the shape of a C that curved down toward his chin from one corner, a cleft in his chin, stormy gray eyes that were not exactly challenging but took a person on with full intensity. Women liked him. And even if he had not been wearing the orange SAR vest, no one would mistake him for anything but a military man.

As promised, he was waiting inside the park where April and Woody had responded to a call for help on Tuesday night. He was wearing hiking boots and was playing with a flat leather leash. His red Jeep Cherokee, as always in such situations, was packed with search and rescue equipment. He'd parked it on the grass. Because the day had already warmed to a hot Indian summer eighty-two degrees in Central Park, the windows were all partially open. The huge head with sharp pointed ears of the Doberman pinscher called Peachy was stuck out a back window, and she whined like a frustrated child.

As Mike and April pulled up alongside the Jeep, the dog's whine got louder. Mike cut the engine quickly. The dog flung herself at the door as if there were a chance she could propel herself through it. The vehicle shook with her efforts. Her agitated moans made an eerie sound and raised the hairs on the back of April's neck. She glanced at Mike. If he was on edge, he didn't show it.

John slapped the leash against his palm and immediately started complaining to April. "The two of you stink. You know, perfume like that will knock a dog's whiffer out for hours."

April greeted him through the open passenger window. "Hi, John, thanks for coming. This is Lieutenant Mike Sanchez. He's in charge." She didn't bother to apologize about the smell. Hers was just soap and Mike had no idea this was coming down today.

John plopped a Yankees cap on his head and leaned down to window level. "Hey, Mike. This isn't going to work. Look at that—dogs, people. Cars. Buses." He straightened up and pointed out the people lying out on the grass, walking on the paths, the traffic over the wall on CPW. The area hadn't been cleared as he'd requested. He looked disgusted. He leaned back in and raved on.

"A, April here promised a different scenario, and B, Peachy is the best dog in the world, but she couldn't do anything with this even if you'd cleared the area as promised. I knew this was a mistake. Not only that, you guys aren't playing by the rules. I stopped over at the CP Precinct. Courtesy thing. The CO over there had no idea we were working here today. What's up with you?" This last he directed to April.

Mike confirmed John's reading of the situation by giving his neck a little exercise, making a manly connection to John that April read perfectly. Oh my God, she thought. Mike had no actual intention of supporting for her operation. Peachy was pacing the backseat of the Jeep now, as well as whining. Mike got out of the Camaro, hiking at his belt. he was going to abort on her.

April unhooked her own seat belt, but stayed where she was to watch the scene play out. John was understandably upset. It was against procedure to work in any precinct without full knowledge and support of the CO there. In addition, John had a bit of a chip on his shoulder because so many people, including the PC, had no faith in the dogs. He hated to be made a fool of. And this was pretty bad. Not only that, John hated the prospect of Peachy's failing at a task no animal could possibly be expected to fulfill.

Mike's agenda, on the other hand, was not entirely clear to April yet. His smile was in place, but that was all. Unlike other cops April knew,

Mike had a smoothness about him; the man could calm an erupting volcano. Since he'd become a lieutenant last spring, Mike's leadership qualities had a new authority. He was the man in charge, the Alpha male here. He still hadn't told her what his position on the case was or where he was going with it. But he was acting like a boss. That meant he didn't care if he made an enemy of John, and even April herself had to be careful. Like any PD boss, he could turn on her and crush her like a bug. She'd seen it happen a thousand times with the dumb uniforms who thought they could get away with having boyfriends on the job. The only one happy with the situation was the dog. Peachy bayed and scratched at the door, desperate to work.

"Hey, John. I've heard a lot of good things about you." Mike approached the dog trainer with his hand out. "And this is the famous Peachy who found that banker, right?"

John's tense smile eased up and he shook Mike's hand. "Yeah, Peachy's the one. Our most famous case. Back in '92. This guy Randolph was buried alive in a Queens cemetery. An angry employee did it to get even with him. You read about it in the paper, right? What you don't know was that Peachy located him through his airhole. His scent came right up through that hole."

"Smart dog," Mike said. "Sorry about the precinct slipup. We didn't want to keep you waiting. Is someone on the way?"

Smart Mike, April thought.

"No way, Peachy can't do anything with this. Too many people. Too many cars. And you know, a repeat of yesterday . . ." John shrugged, clearly softened by the praise. The dog was going crazy. April kept her mouth shut.

Mike pointed at the dog. "She always like this?"

"Peachy? No, she's an extremely well-trained dog. She'll sit on the seat until I give her clean scent of the missing p and tell her to 'go find.'" John went over to the window. "What's with you, honey lamb?"

Peachy was nuts trying to get out of that car.

Goose bumps rose on April's arms. Something was up. The dog knew it right away. "She wants out, John. She wants to find him." Finally April got out of the car herself.

John laughed. "She doesn't know who *he* is, sweetheart. She can't find if she doesn't have a scent of your guy." He tried soothing the dog.

Peachy whimpered and pawed John through the window. "Hey, that hurts."

"What does she want?"

John shrugged. "Beats me. Humans have maybe five million olfactory cells in their noses. A Doberman, like Peachy, has one hundred fifty to *two hundred* million cells. She can smell a ball thrown by a kid two days ago, squirrel pee in the grass, a parrot on somebody's shoulder half a mile away—you name it. Young dogs can go wild in an environment like this. With scent particles of literally everything falling all over the place, they're bombarded with stimuli we can't even imagine." John was showing off for Mike.

"That's very interesting. I had no idea." Mike patted the dog's head. He appeared to have all the time in the world. "And they can search for a lot of other things, right?"

"Of course. Lots of things."

"A cadaver?" April approached the trainer and the dog in the car with extreme caution. "Hey, Peachy." She wasn't exactly afraid of it, but wanted to stay out of slobbering range.

"Sure."

"Or something else that's out of place on a scene?" April's eyes were on the dog, who was yelping and carrying on. People were starting to drift over for a look. Pretty soon the Central Park Precinct officers would be on their case. It had been stupid to neglect them. But it was clear she wasn't in harmony, wasn't doing anything right.

John frowned at his barking pride and joy. "Quiet," he commanded.

The noise stopped. Peachy tensed, shivering all over, at attention.

"Why don't you let her out," April suggested. "She's a tracking dog. Let her do her thing."

"She's acting crazy, like a puppy." John opened the car door. "Maybe she has business to do."

"Yeah, and maybe she knows something that we don't." April looked over at Mike. Their eyes locked, and he gave her a smile. Her stomach did a little flip. The dog wouldn't let them pursue the subject further.

As soon as the car door was open a crack, the Doberman threw herself against it and leaped out like an Olympic athlete. April was shocked. Peachy seemed bigger than the last time she'd seen her. She jumped on John, almost knocking the six-footer over. With her two front legs on his shoulders, she was as tall as he was.

"Off," he commanded.

Instantly, the two front legs went down. At the same time the dog raised her muzzle to take in huge snoutfuls of the air above her head. Then she grabbed the leash out of John's hand and pushed it at his arm, shoving him hard.

"The kid wants to work. Let's go," April said, pleased that at least the dog supported her.

Suddenly John's mood changed. "Whatever you say. I'm good to go." His jaw tightened as he clipped on Peachy's leash. "Down," he commanded. Peachy dropped to her stomach. He went to the car and returned in a few seconds with a bottle of Evian and a bowl. He filled the bowl with the water. "Okay," he told the dog.

On command the dog got up and slurped at the contents of the bowl. "They work better when they're hydrated," he explained. When the bowl was empty, John gave Peachy a large dog biscuit. Peachy crunched it down in one bite. Then she stood at attention, looking at him expectantly and growling at the back of her throat.

"Good girl. What a good baby. Want to go to work? Huh? How about it? Let's go work. Yeah, baby." The C scar by the side of John's mouth cavorted with his enthusiasm. His color was up and April could see him zoning with the dog.

Finally, he turned to April and Mike. "I want you two to stay here; you have a radio, right?"

Mike shook his head. "I don't want to use the radio. You have a cell?"

John nodded.

"Okay, we'll keep you in view, but if the dog takes off, use the cell to contact us. I'm calling in to let the captain know we've decided to work the area."

"Fine. Whatever you say. Good girl. Good girl. Peachy, just one more second and we're out of here." He was careful to keep Mike with the stronger scent away.

Mike gave John his number. John punched it into the phone memory. "Technology," he muttered. "And Mike, one warning. This is not a bomb dog. This is not a drugs dog. This is a people dog."

"Meaning?"

"She expects to find live people here in the city, in the park. She doesn't expect to find a dead person. I suspect she either smells a dead person or a dead animal. There are two schools of thought on whether they can tell the difference. In any case, that's why she's acting like this. She may smell your man, and he's dead. I'm just preparing you, okay?"

"Oh, let's not be too pessimistic," Mike replied. "She could also be turned on by delicious smells at the zoo." He gave April a triumphant little smile.

April hadn't thought of that. The zoo was a mile away across the park at Fifth and Sixty-fifth Street. Penguins and polar bears and who knew what else.

John shook his head at Mike. "Not a chance. Okay, Peachy. Go find for Daddy." Peachy took off, nose high in the air.

Not more than five minutes later, a hundred yards from where they'd been, under a thin layer of fresh leaves, the dog located a drib- ble of something that looked like intestines. Mike and April saw her stop and bark happily. They ran to the spot as John was praising her, be- fore he even moved in to see what she'd found.

Looked like insides, stank like hell. What got them interested was that there was nothing else. No body, either human or otherwise. It was a weird find. If animals had been at something, they wouldn't eat the bones and leave the tissue. Mike used his radio to call in the find. If the tissue turned out to be human, they'd have a homicide on their hands.

THIRTY-NINE

ALLEGRA WAS ON HER STOMACH with one foot caught under the gate, a sock in her mouth, and her bleeding, broken nose flattened into the sand. Her ankle and wrists throbbed, but breathing was her real problem. The sand under her face was warm and wet. When she tried to inhale through her nose, she made a gurgling sound, like mucus in a bad cold. Each breath drew a trickle of blood down her throat because there was no way out of her mouth. She knew that iron taste. She was drowning in her own blood. She yanked at her foot. If she could have ripped it or bitten it off like an animal in a trap, she would have done it.

She was petrified. She could breathe through the sock and the bloody nose but only when she was calm. When panic overcame her, she made noises—stifled half sobs, inarticulate and incomprehensible. No words could escape to express her agony. Why—? What had she done to make this happen? The sock deep in her mouth triggered her gag reflex. All these years she'd wanted to die, and now she was dying and didn't want to. Not like this.

"Fucking bitch!"

She was kicking like hell and gagging on the sock when the boy swung the gate back crushing her ankle and shooting a rocket of pain up her leg. She could hear the thud of rocks thrown against the gate. A gate to nowhere. And she heard the soft voice of Maslow Atkins calling out. "Stop! Wait!"

She wasn't sure what happened. What happened to her? She'd

been dozing on the bench, thinking of her mother, when suddenly she'd been startled by the voices. She smelled pot smoke. Two of them, the same two kids were back. One was crying, the other laughing. They were high, manic. Allegra knew the signs. Happysadcrazymad.

The two were in the dark, but carried the kind of flashlight that made a tiny point of illumination to shine on a keyhole or a theater program. It looked like a star bouncing along the ground. All she did was follow the star through the high wet grass, up a sloping bank, and into the bushes. She hardly knew what she was doing. She never expected to find Dr. Atkins. She'd been completely astounded to hear his voice. He was pleading. She'd never heard him beg. She didn't think. She just went to get him.

And then it happened so fast she didn't know which one of them tripped her and smashed her head against the ground, which one of them pulled her shoes off and used the laces to tie her hands behind her back. She was like a doll mangled by fighting children. They'd left her, just like that. She was a dead doll. She'd never get up again.

Allegra lifted her head to breathe, crying in the dark. "Agghhhmm-mmm—"

After a while, her neck ached so badly she had to let it rest. Her head dropped and her face fell in the dirt. She tried to spit the sock out, but each time she raised her tongue her throat closed up.

"Allegra. Allegra, listen to me. Move over here. Allegra. Come on, we can help each other. Come, please."

She heard him and struggled to obey, tried to roll over; but her foot was pinned. Her hands were tied. She bucked her hips and twisted her wrists against the laces, cutting off circulation in her hands and painfully wrenching her shoulders. What was wrong with him? Why couldn't he just move over to her? Why was he letting her suffer this way?

"Allegra—"

"Argggh." She was dying. She could feel herself dying, and a moan was the best she could do. It was exactly the way she'd felt in treatment with him, too. She'd never been able to find the right words, the open sesame words, for him to help her get out of the dungeon.

Allegra hadn't had anything to eat in three days, just some water and the coffee. She felt dizzy from the pain in her nose and the drip of blood down her throat. She was dehydrated. Something happened with electrolytes when you didn't drink enough. She'd passed out a few times from hunger when she was dieting, so usually she was pretty careful. She was beginning to hallucinate. She could hear her mother calling for her.

"Dylan, Dylan. Come home."

She imagined Dr. Atkins calling to her, too. "Allegra. Shhh. Don't cry. I'll save you."

Hours passed and her panicked moans got softer.

FORTY

GRACE RODRIGUEZ came into the office at eight on the button. She was wearing a black suit and was ready for war. She walked into the office that she still shared after all these years with a young associate—this latest one a fat boyish twenty-nine-year-old who was constantly eating on the sly throughout the day whenever he thought she wasn't looking, though how he thought she'd fail to notice when she was only a few feet away in a very small room she couldn't begin to imagine.

This morning Craig Hewlett's space was utterly crumbless, so it was clear he hadn't arrived yet. Grace's heart pounded as she put her purse in the top drawer of her desk and purposefully started the long trek around the building to her boss's office. Even though it was the worst day of Jerry Atkins's life, she was going to have it out with him anyway.

The prosperous accounting firm of Haight-Atkins was contained on one whole floor of a large Third Avenue office building. The walls were a mind-numbing pewter throughout. The floors were covered with industrial-quality ashen carpeting that was shampooed only once a year in the spring. Grace's own space had no amenities, not even a chair for visitors. Jerry's office, where the clients went for their meetings, had to be luxurious, however. His furniture was cherry wood, the chairs and sofas were cushy, the colors turquoise and rose like those used in resorts in the Caribbean. This disparity in their stations, however, did not always rankle Grace.

Usually her self-awareness didn't extend to hurt and bitter, and when she was troubled, she would hide behind cheerful, reassuring smiles like malignant cells sometimes hid in otherwise benign tumors. Her life was carefully structured to shield her from hurt; she thought she was above it, able to roll with whatever punches came her way. But today her daughter was missing.

Historically, Grace was alone with Dylan on Wednesday, Thursday, and Saturday nights. And for many years they had been joyful evenings. In recent years, however, her times with Dylan had become ever more painful and difficult. Dylan was twenty years old and still living at home, doing her own thing, coming and going just as she pleased. But she'd become rude and disrespectful, uncommunicative. Grace went over the list of her grievances. In addition, she looked as if she didn't eat anything. She'd promise to come home for dinner, and then didn't come home. When she did come home, she played with her food but didn't swallow very much. Since the summer her bad behaviors had escalated, and last night Dylan hadn't come home at all.

To get to Jerry's office on the outermost tier of the building, Grace had to come out from an inside bank of offices where she worked in a cubicle, then travel all the way around the building on the hallway where privileged partners had offices with big windows and views of the East River and Queens, or the great Manhattan skyline north and south, or Third Avenue looking west. When Grace reached the place where she could see actual natural light shining in from the windows of offices whose doors were open, she felt like a rat coming out of a maze.

She could hardly breathe, her heart pounded with such anger at the mess she and her daughter had become. In the last few months during spring and summer Dylan started acting really weird. Grace had done some soul-searching as she wrestled with herself over what to do about it.

All she'd wanted was a child, a baby girl to love as her mother hadn't loved her. On her walk around the building, she went over her story in her mind. She'd had her baby, and for a long time she'd thought Dylan was enough. When Dylan was a little girl, Grace had enjoyed every minute they were alone. They'd made cookies and played house, done puzzles, learned the ABC's, then math, then social studies, then whatever. She'd thought it was pure joy to have a child. When she was very little, Dylan had spent her days with a nice grandmotherly type who lived in the building. When she was two, Grace took her to all-day school programs. She went to a nearby public school. By middle school Dylan was independent, was coming home on her own, did her homework, and waited patiently for her mom to come home. A good girl.

Grace had always known that Dylan would be her responsibility alone. That had been the deal, and she'd always been perfectly content with it. Their nights together they'd had the independence she thought she valued so highly. She was a mother, protected but free. True, she was not a partner in the firm and had no real job security. Haight had no women partners in the firm. Another excuse of Jerry's for not making *her* a partner despite her many years of service was the fact that she did not have her MBA, and he refused to give her the time off or the money to get one. Still, she liked her job well enough, and had never thought about moving to another. Jerry gave her a few hundred extra in cash every week. He helped her buy a lovely condo, and she had the little girl she'd always wanted.

That had been the story she told herself. But now too many things had changed. The little girl was now a big girl, a big problem Grace could no longer ignore, and one she couldn't manage by herself. Grace turned the corner and entered Jerome Atkins's office without knocking. It was early for him to be there, but he hated his wife so much that in a crisis she knew he'd be sitting at his desk staring out the big windows of his corner office, which was high enough to offer a southwest span of magnificent open city views. Pointing in his direction on his desk was the same photo that had been there since the day she met him when she was interviewing for her first full-time job at twenty-two. The photo was of his wife, his son, Maslow, and his daughter, Chloe, who was alive then, but had been dead now for more than twenty years.

"Oh, it's you," he said, shaking his head when he saw her. "Terrible thing about Maslow. I'm sick to death about it."

At the time of Jerome's sixtieth birthday party two years ago, Grace hadn't been invited to the celebration party so the magnitude of the milestone had been lost on her. Now with his eyes sunk deep in purple hollows and his face drained of color, she was shocked to realize that her Jerry, the man she'd loved and trusted for twenty-three years, was an old man.

"Sweetheart, I'm so worried. How are you doing—?" His look stopped her. "I guess that's a stupid question," she finished lamely.

"Don't call me sweetheart here," he said automatically.

"Evelyn isn't in yet," Grace murmured, crumbling like a cookie as always. Evelyn didn't suspect anything. No one did. He had her tucked away in Long Island City, where no one they knew ever went. He liked her beauty, liked playing house.

"What do you want?" He was wearing a custom suit as black as hers.

"I want to talk to you," she said softly. "About Dylan."

He shook his head. "I've had dozens of calls. News cameras were at my apartment this morning. I had to go out the service entrance. You wouldn't believe what's going on."

"I need to talk to you, Jerry."

"I'm waiting to hear from the police. A ransom call could come in at any time." He spoke as though to a child.

"We have another serious problem, Jerry," she said softly.

"Well, I don't have time to hear your complaints. You can tell me tomorrow. If I can make it. With all this I don't know if I can make it tomorrow." He made a little hand gesture that she was supposed to take as a dismissal. Time for her to trot back into her cage. She was his toy, nothing more.

Instead of leaving, she moved to the door, closed it, returned to a soft turquoise chair, and sat down. "Jerry, your daughter didn't come home last night."

"Dylan? Why not?" He looked surprised.

"My guess is that she's upset about her brother."

"You're not making any sense." His tone was flat. He was walling up.

"I am making perfect sense. Your daughter wanted to know your son; you didn't want her to know him. It weighed on her something terrible. Now he's missing. How can you be absolutely certain the two have nothing to do with each other?"

"I'm sure."

"What if she told him, and he killed himself?" Grace's heart pounded. She didn't like the look on his face—blank, flat, cold. Like the times she'd wanted to be a partner and he'd argued it would look bad, like all the times he'd fought her on raises, like the time Dylan wanted to go to a private university and he'd refused to pay for it. He was out to lunch on this, too.

"She's loyal. She loves me. She wouldn't do that to me," he said.

"Are you implying I'm not loyal?" A tear came to Grace's eye. After everything she'd sacrificed for him?

"You want to expose me, bankrupt me, ruin my life after all I've done for you?" he said, gaining energy with the prospect of such a huge betrayal.

"I get the feeling you don't care about your son." She'd always supported herself. He'd never even supported her. She stared at him, stunned by a new disturbing thought. He didn't care about her, that she'd guessed. But he didn't care about his precious son, his legitimate child, either.

"Maybe he let me down," he said. More tragedy king.

"Your perfect son let you down?" She shook her head, amazed to hear this. Her Jerry was a cold man, an iceberg.

"You're in a strange mood this morning," he remarked. "What's the matter with you?"

"How did Maslow let you down?"

"Look, forget I said that."

"I get the feeling you don't care whether he lives or dies."

"I'm under a lot of stress. I didn't mean it." He pointedly checked his watch, then made the hand motion again to dismiss her. She didn't budge.

"I've accepted your demands for secrecy all these years, Jerry—"

"Well, of course you did. You're the woman I love. You're everything to me."

"That's why you support your wife's credit card bills and go on vacations with her instead of me?"

"But I don't like it. I'd much rather be with you."

"Men don't go on vacations with women they can't bear to be in the same room with."

"You're twisting my words again. Look, it's eight-thirty. I have to—"

"What about the press? What about *our* baby?"

"Don't threaten me," he said angrily. "I won't take it. Not today."

"I'm trying to get through to you, Jerry. Dylan has been following Maslow."

"How do you know?" He swiveled back and forth in his chair.

"I know. She told me she was going to meet him."

"When?" More swiveling.

"I don't know. Months ago. I didn't think anything about it. She's been upset ever since you wouldn't let her go to Swarthmore."

He made an angry noise. "For Christ's sake, that was three years ago, and City College was good enough for me, wasn't it?"

"Maybe for you, but not for Maslow."

"Maslow was different," he said harshly.

Grace sighed. "That's exactly what Dylan thinks. Your legitimate son is better than she is."

"Go away, Grace, I'm disgusted with you. If you loved me you wouldn't hurt me this way now."

"You hurt your daughter. You hurt me. And now Maslow. You only care about your precious reputation, your precious business. What about the rest of us? I can't let this go on, Jerry. I can't." She shook her head sadly. "I can't. Not now."

"All right, I know. I know. I don't know what comes over me. Of course you're important. You're everything to me. I'll tell." He shook his head with great conviction. "I'm going to do it. You'll see."

"You have to call the police today."

"No! Not today. It would kill my wife."

"You should have thought about that earlier. Now it's too late. You have to help them find Maslow. You have to tell them everything you know about him and about Dylan so that they can find him."

"If you're so certain she knows something, why don't you ask Dylan yourself. No, I'll ask her," he said, resolving the issue to his satisfaction.

"She didn't come *home*. You're making me repeat myself." Jerry was so rigid, Grace felt she, too, was going crazy. He was like a brick wall that could withstand any pressure. He'd tell lie after lie, would do anything to squirm away. It was as if she were seeing him for the first time. An old selfish man, capable of killing any of them rather than be exposed for the self-serving bastard he was.

He sighed hugely. "I'll take care of it. Trust me."

"I can't trust you," she said softly. "I'll tell the police about Dylan myself."

"You don't mean that, sweetheart. She's your baby. You don't want to hurt her, expose her to all kinds of questions and ridicule, do you? Really?"

"I mean it." Grace's eyes flooded. "The children have to come first this time."

"Okay." His facade cracked, and he caved in the way he had over the raises but not anything else. "Okay, there is somebody I can tell. Not the police. But somebody who can help. Okay? Are you satisfied now?"

"I'll be satisfied when both your children are safe." Grace got up and walked out of the office without another word.

Evelyn was at her desk with that smug smile on her face. "Raise time again, Grace?" she said as Grace passed her on the way out.

FORTY-ONE

When baby April opened her eyes with Thursday's dawn, her daddy was standing watch over her crib, wearing a T-shirt and purple briefs. Today, she didn't even have to look around for him or whimper for attention. He'd been awake, worrying for hours. He was actually waiting for her to wake up and keep him company.

"Hey, little sweetheart," Jason cooed at her.

"Aa aa." She smiled and reached up her arms.

Not quite Dada, but close enough. He picked her up, hugged and kissed her a little, changed her diaper, gave her a bottle, played with her for a few minutes, then went into the bedroom.

"Hi," Emma murmured.

Jason sat on the bed, kissed Emma for a while, then put April down beside her sleepy mother. Bolstered by the love of his family, he began his day. He had a seven A.M. patient, an eight o'clock patient, a nine o'clock patient, and a dozen messages, including calls from Ted Tushy, Bernie Zeiss, Miss Vialo, and three other prominent members of the Institute. They might all have innocent reasons for calling late last night, and again before he was even in the office this morning, but Jason thought it was more likely that he was in trouble. Last night he'd gone to the Institute in search of Maslow's and Allegra's files. Several events were going on when he got there. Dr. Cone's second Wednesday of the month discussion group, two committee meetings, and a supervisory group were enough activity to cover his unauthorized visits to the education office for Allegra's file and to the boardroom where, due to overcrowding at the Institute, some of the personnel and candidate files were kept.

He collected them with no trouble and left, thinking it was likely to be more difficult to obtain a list of all the patients with whom Maslow had come into contact at Manhattan East. After he got home and studied the files without learning very much that was new, he rolled around all night wondering if there was any possibility that Allegra could have been a patient and seen Maslow at Manhattan East. Allegra wasn't her real name, and it was possible that Maslow didn't know her personally from there, but she might have seen or known *him* and been attracted to him for some reason or another of her own. Maybe she'd seen him treat a patient there with kindness.

It was very common for patients to contact each other when they were "out," why not a doctor? In any case, it was Maslow himself who had proposed Allegra to the Institute program. The file said what Jason already knew, that she'd come to him as a patient. What the file didn't say was *how* she'd come to him. Who had referred her?

Now it was clear his visit to the Institute had been noted, and there were people who wanted an explanation. He didn't call anyone back. Instead he watched his caller ID box. At eight-forty-five and eight-forty-nine he had hang-ups that the magic screen told him were from Jerome Atkins's private line. At nine-fifteen, the phone rang again from the same number. Jason picked up again and this time, Jerome Atkins spoke.

"Dr. Frank," he said formally.

"Yes."

"This is Mr. Atkins."

"Yes." Jason was in a session and couldn't reveal too much. He gave his one-word answers with his eyes on his patient, who, unluckily enough, happened to be the paranoid investment banker, Jergen Walsh, who had scheduled two extra sessions this week to work out the Sprite incident of yesterday (why had Jason insisted on offering him a soda when Jason knew Jergen only liked Sprite? Why had he been denied the Sprite, etc.?) Jergen's session this morning had already been interrupted by a ringing phone twice. He was audibly grinding his teeth.

"I need to talk with you," Jerome Atkins said.

"Of course. That would be fine."

"I will come to your office." The man's voice was authoritarian. Yesterday, he'd insisted that Jason come to his home.

"Fine." Jason's appointment book was open, secured by a rubber band on his schedule for that day. Last evening when he'd left his office for the night, he'd had a fully booked eleven hours of patients. Since then, on his office phone, he'd received a miraculous two cancellations in a row, starting at nine-thirty. Throughout his session with Jergen he'd been debating canceling the rest of the morning to continue his background check of Maslow. "When did you have in mind?"

"I'll be there in twenty minutes," Atkins said. "Where are you located?"

"Fine. I'll see you then."

"Very good." Jerome sounded pleased. The dumb luck of two cancellations allowed him to think Jason had nothing else in the world to do but receive him.

Nonetheless Jason was pleased himself. He gave his Riverside Drive address and hung up. Immediately, Jergen turned on him. How dare he take a call on *his* time? This was the price Jason would have to pay. He braced in his chair for the attack. It came right on schedule.

Jerome Atkins arrived thirty-five minutes later, after Jergen had verbalized all his violent fantasies about Jason and left feeling better. Jason used his few free moments between the two appointments to run through his messages again. There was still nothing from anyone he wanted to talk to. When the doorbell announced Atkins, he buzzed him in, then quickly dialed the cell phone number that April had given him last night so he could stop trying to reach her through the frustrating precinct phone system.

"Sergeant Woo." She picked up after the first ring.

"April, this is Jason. Anything new?"

"I can't say on the phone." April's voice had the flat tone that meant something was up.

Jason's heart rate spiked. "Can we meet, then?" he asked.

"I'm working now, give me a call later."

"That will be difficult." He had patients. He needed to schedule his day. The phone made some noise and she was gone with no further comment. This alarmed Jason even more. With Maslow's father there, however, he didn't have time to call her back.

He hurried from his desk to his waiting room, where Jerome Atkins stood examining the display of three antique clocks on a table along with some fairly recent issues of nonthreatening magazines for activities that attracted Jason but he knew nothing about, like *Yachting* and *Field and Stream* and *The Book of Everything*, a tome that amused some people and irritated others because it didn't have anywhere near "everything" in it.

Atkins wore a black suit, a white shirt, and an unexpectedly jaunty black-and-white polka-dot bow tie. The outfit made him look pale and gave something of a mixed message about his state of mind. When Jason opened the door, Atkins raised an accusing finger to the brass bull with a clock on its back. "This clock is broken," he announced angrily, demonstrating that he was a man who had his own view of things.

"Good morning, Mr. Atkins, please come in," Jason replied.

Atkins hesitated, glancing around at the stylish wooden chairs and bench that were not very comfortable, the lovely Persian rug, the flowers that Jason had set out on Monday. He scowled at the clock that wasn't broken at all. It wasn't ticking because Jason had forgotten to wind it. Then slowly Atkins moved forward into Jason's office, where he was met with more upsetting obstacles.

"Where am I supposed to sit?" he demanded.

"Wherever you feel comfortable," Jason replied.

There was a swiveling leather chair in front of the desk, an armchair beside the desk, an analytic couch next to that. Several other small armchairs were grouped against the wall for those occasions when Jason met with a couple or several members of a family. The obstacle for Maslow's father seemed to be the analytic couch. After some moments of tense deliberation, he sat in the armchair.

Jason sat in his desk chair. "Thank you for coming," he said gently. "This must be very difficult for you."

"Don't misunderstand. I'm not here for comfort. I hate psychiatrists."

Jason gave him a sad smile. "But we can be very helpful at times."

"You think so because you get paid for it. But I don't think so. Let's get one thing straight. I'm not here for help, so don't expect to bill me." Atkins's face was brittle. He was a man who liked to fight.

Jason did not react. He was used to people's being defensive about his specialty. "If you hate psychiatrists so much, your son must be a disappointment to you."

"He was very stubborn," Atkins said tersely.

Again that "was." Jason pressed his lips together and made no reply.

"You have no idea how difficult this is."

But Jason did. Only a second ago he had acknowledged the difficulty. "What can I do for you?" he asked.

"I want to be clear about this. I don't need a psychiatrist personally. I'm here for my son."

"I appreciate that."

"It's a very complicated situation. I'm concerned about him—what happened to him, I mean." Atkins pulled a snowy handkerchief out of his trouser pocket and dabbed delicately at his top lip, then replaced it.

Jason nodded. "Of course you are. Do you have something to tell me about it?"

"I don't want the police to know about this. I need your word as a doctor and a gentleman that you won't reveal what I'm about to tell you to anyone. Because if you can't guarantee confidentiality, I can't tell you anything."

Jason didn't answer. He was struck with the disturbing idea that Atkins might have harmed his own child.

"It is my firm belief that this has nothing to do with Maslow's disappearance, that's the reason I must insist on confidentiality." Atkins said pompously.

"Mr. Atkins, I can see your point, of course. Uh-huh-huh-huh." Jason reached for the nearly empty cup of cold coffee on his desk to cover a sudden choking cough.

"Good," Atkins said.

Jason raised a hand. "Please let me finish. I certainly respect your wish for confidentiality, but . . ."

"This is a requirement, not a wish."

"Let me tell you the problem here. Confidentiality does not apply in certain situations. In criminal cases if a person is going to be arrested, I have an obligation to—"

Atkins flushed a deep red and interrupted again. "This is not *criminal*. It's a *family* matter."

"I see. Does what you have to tell me regard Maslow's welfare?"

"I just told you I do not believe so."

"I may have to be the judge of that."

"You're a stubborn and arrogant young man. I'm only asking that you keep my private confidences. I'm not asking for the cover-up of any crime."

Jason hadn't been called "young man" in many years. He suppressed a smile. "If you want to tie my hands, I'm not sure what I can do for you."

"I'm not tying your hands," Atkins insisted.

"Then let me ask you again. What have you come to me for? How can I help you?" Jason glanced at his clock. His time was being wasted. He hated that.

Atkins shook his head angrily, then abruptly changed his tone. "You have met my wife," he said softly.

"Yes, she seems like a fine woman," Jason said.

"She and I have nothing in common."

"I see."

"I've had a—friend—for many years. A lovely woman." Atkins looked down at his manicured nails, then couldn't resist adding, "A younger woman, of course, very pretty, not like my wife, not materialistic at all, and very sweet. When the friendship began, I never intended anything personal—" Pause. Nose swipe. Out with the handkerchief. Dab at the lips. Back into the pocket with the handkerchief. Jerome's right eye twitched.

"She was the one who wanted a sexual relationship. I didn't even think of it. But—" He sighed and spread out his hands. "Sometimes things happen. My child was sick. My wife was distraught. She never recovered, of course, you could see that." Atkins glanced at Jason for a doctor's confirmation of that.

"Well, the fact is, *Adina* has never been the same since Chloe died. We've had no relations since then."

"The loss of a child is a catastrophe," Jason murmured. "Has she been treated for depression?"

Another long pause. Jerome's answer was a sniff. "My friend had a child."

"Your girlfriend?"

"Yes."

"What is her name?"

"How did you know it was a girl?"

"Your girlfriend's name?"

Atkins swallowed. "Her name is Grace. She has a daughter."

"I see. What is your daughter's name?"

Atkins shook his head, pursed his lips. "Her name is Dylan, Dylan Rodriguez."

"Dylan Rodriguez. How old is Dylan?"

Atkins's eyes filled with tears. "She's twenty."

Jason realized that he had been holding his breath. He exhaled. "You have a twenty-year-old daughter?"

"She's Grace's daughter."

The clock on Jason's desk ticked off thirty seconds while he thought about this. Sometimes thirty seconds can be a very long time. "Does Maslow know he has a sister?" he asked finally.

"Of course not."

Jason scratched his head, astounded. Jerome Atkins was one of those perfectly ordinary-looking men who had a secret family. His son had a sister he didn't know about. "Do Grace and Dylan know about your wife and son?"

"Of course. Grace knew from the beginning that I was married with children. She was the one who wanted a relationship. I had nothing to do with it. It was her idea to have a baby."

Jason quickly did the math. If Maslow was thirty-one and his twin sister died when she was eleven, then Dylan was conceived twenty-*one* years ago, when Chloe was very ill and about nine months before she died. Twenty-one years ago when the family was in crisis, Jerome was having an affair. Twenty years ago his legitimate daughter died and his illegitimate daughter was born. To Jason, the juxtaposition of those two major events sounded more like calculation than coincidence. Jerome Atkins had a lot to do with the relationship. And the catastrophe to his wife was much greater than the loss of a child. She had lost her husband at the same time. Not only that, Maslow had to have been profoundly influenced. Well before he lost his sister he lost his father, too.

"I didn't abandon them, if that's what you're thinking," Jerome

said. "I've always spent time with the Rodriguezes. Grace is a wonderful woman. Dylan is a lovely girl." He gave his nose another little wipe.
In body language, that meant he didn't believe what he was saying.
The Rodriguezes. He called his second family the Rodriguezes, as if
they belonged in another category, another world.

The clocks in the office ticked on like little time bombs, and Jason's
heart beat along with them. All of a sudden everything was speeding
up. April would want to talk to the Rodriguezes, and so did he. He
watched Jerome Atkins's face as the man recovered his poise.

"I don't believe either of them had anything to do with Maslow's
disappearance. I told you, Grace is a fine woman. She never thinks of
herself."

"What are you suggesting?"

"Absolutely nothing. I just wanted you as his supervisor to know the
facts of his life, even if he himself did not."

With his confession off his chest, Jerome Atkins reiterated his position on his relationship with Grace Rodriguez. He wanted confidentiality concerning it. Then, white-faced, he gave Jason his second
family's address in Long Island City and the phone number. After he
left, Jason went over their conversation in his mind. Once again he felt
sad and frightened for Maslow. It seemed clear to him that Jerome
Atkins's motivation in paying the visit was not so much to help his son,
but to start the spin for his wife and the rest of the world if he was unlucky. If his son was dead and the truth about his second family came
out.

FORTY-TWO

PEACHY KNEW SHE WASN'T THROUGH with her first find. She yanked on the leash, insisting that they continue working. John gave her another biscuit and let her go. Mike tagged along behind and was with them as they circled back and she suddenly stopped a second time, barking happily at something that looked like a small cigar. John praised her lavishly as Mike squatted down to examine what turned out to be a human finger.

"Anything?" April ran toward them.

"Yeah." Mike looked at it carefully. Even without touching or moving the finger, it was clear this was not the digit of a man who wrote prescriptions. He was sickened by the crude way the finger had been hacked off and hoped they wouldn't find the rest of the body scattered all over in such small pieces.

"Oh no! Oh God, no," April cried when Mike's unstated wish was granted a few minutes later, and Peachy found Pee Wee James in the bushes only a few feet away.

She stayed with the body, waiting for the Crime Scene unit. But Mike elected to continue tracking with the dog. That is, he followed along behind the dog and trainer as fast as he could in cowboy boots with heels and no traction. An eerie feeling of unreality had settled over him concerning the whole case. The death of Pee Wee James particularly shook him. April had been almost distraught last night, wanting to go out and search for him. It had been his call to shut down for the night. Now he felt responsible for the man's death.

He didn't like to think that April was never wrong. But the truth was her instincts were flawless. He'd been wrong to let Carla stay in his place Monday night. He'd been wrong not to go looking for Pee Wee last night. He'd been wrong not to alert the CP Precinct about the dog trainer, and last, he'd been wrong about the dog. He was having a very bad day.

The Doberman saved them from the humiliation of some innocent civilian's discovering Pee Wee's body. Whether or not there was a connection between Maslow's disappearance and Pee Wee's fatal crack on the head was still a mystery. But why the killer chopped off his finger was a question for the headshrinkers. They definitely had a loon on the loose.

In any case, Mike felt a powerful surge of pride in April's judgment as a detective and half wanted to jog back to tell her that as far as he was concerned, she could be the primary in the case no matter how Iriarte or anybody else felt about it.

It was not yet ten o'clock when dozens of detectives, uniforms, and two EMS units arrived to deal with what had been variously reported as one to three homicides in the park. Peachy was still at it, and Mike had hopes that she would "find" Maslow, too. He was scrambling down a hill after the dog as Peachy dragged her trainer along a footpath, then plunged into the bushes, came out, galloped parallel to the paved walk, then finally stopped abruptly, shivering all over. She pointed her long snout at a bench and yelped crazily. Mike picked up his pace and trotted up just in time to see Zumech give her a biscuit that was big enough to choke a horse.

The dog was yelping at a powerful odor that was like a dead mouse rotting behind a wall, maybe a little stronger. Mike's first thought was how it didn't fit with the bucolic park scene. It didn't fit at all.

Central Park had a wide variety of aromas. On a summer morning, tree and flower aromas mingled with essence of hot dog, falafel, and pretzel. Mike could smell them now. The zoo on the East Side and the rowboat lake closer to the West Side added their own extracts to the potpourri. In the fall and winter there was the enticing smell of roasting chestnuts. In the late autumn and early spring, musty odors of wet earth and decaying leaves predominated. Garbage emanated from wastebaskets more powerfully when it was warm and not at all when it was cold. And other forms of human effluvia were from time to time clearly discernible—urine, vomit. But the stench of old corpse was one smell visitors didn't come upon in Central Park.

"Don't touch anything," Mike cried as he made a quick assessment of the site. On the bench was a Styrofoam coffee cup that might have fingerprints or better yet saliva that contained DNA of their killer. On the grass beside the bench was an empty, crumpled-up potato chip bag. Ditto with fingerprints there. The shocking item that didn't belong was the tip of a man's shoe. Peachy was yapping up a storm, but Mike was still puzzled by the odor. The dog's first "find" also had smelled like this, but he doubted that here lay the body that yielded it.

He took a few seconds to form an impression of the site. He didn't see things with the precision of a criminologist, but he was methodical and had an eye and nose for detail. While he couldn't name the bushes behind the bench, he could see they'd been trampled and that branches had been broken off, not cut with a knife. The shoe that poked out from under the bench was a brown, loafer-like slip-on. He sucked the end of his mustache. Maslow Atkins had been out for a jog. He'd been wearing sneakers. This shoe was not likely to have been his.

Suddenly the dog threw herself on the ground and lay there with an air of dejection. Zumech gave her a last pat and straightened up. "I hate this part," he muttered. "So does Peachy. Look at her; she gets depressed when they're dead."

Mike didn't remind Zumech that the dog had known that someone was dead before she ever got out of the car. She had no idea she'd been brought here to Central Park to find a living person. The dead smell had gotten her right away. He wondered if the dog knew the difference between the smell of a dead man and a dead something else. He wondered if the dog was smart enough to "find" things in their order of importance. It occurred to him that the tissue samples were a hoax of some kind.

The two men each took a side of the park bench and moved in for a closer look. There was not much to see. Set back from the path, a large branching oak tree had some kind of overgrown bush on either side. Once they got behind the bench it was clear that the two shrubs had been disturbed quite a bit. Several branches that had connected the two bushes had been broken off to create enough space for a nest of leaves. It was a small space, not nearly big enough for a body. The reek that had driven Peachy nuts might have been hidden under the leaves at some point, but now it could be seen clearly. The fist-sized chunk of "soft" tissue looked as if it had been dragged out and chewed on by a small animal.

"Don't touch," Mike warned again.

Zumech stood back, frowning. "This is weird," he said uneasily.

"Very weird," Mike agreed.

"Looks to me like someone's hunting."

"How do you mean?"

Zumech lifted the Yankees cap off his head and scratched at his crew cut. "I haven't seen the use of body parts to attract prey in a long time. The *Montaignards* used them in Vietnam to train the dogs to smell out the VC. You weren't in 'Nam, were you?"

Mike shook his head. He was only a boy in the sixties and seventies.

"I was. But before that I used to do a lot of hunting upstate. The first lesson I learned from my uncles was if you'd killed the doe and wanted to catch the buck, you cut out the uterus and laced the area with her scent. The buck would come running."

"Hardly sounds fair," Mike muttered.

"All's fair in love and war. This guy I used to know hunted humans that way in 'Nam."

Mike pulled out his radio and tried not to react irritably to John's acing him with his war stories.

"There was this guy they called Tunnel Rat. The Cong lived in this seventy-five-mile maze of what were called the Cu Chi tunnels, you know. To hunt them, Rat would slither down two-foot-by-two-foot holes on his stomach all alone except for his army dog, called Rocket."

"That's interesting. Does it have anything to do with our case here?"

"Oh yeah, it pertains."

"Give me a minute to call this in." Mike lifted his police radio and called in Peachy's fourth "find." It sounded just as weird to him as the others. In fact, this whole thing was looking more and more like a nut job. Zumech looked pretty strange himself, crouching on all fours with his face close to the ground.

"You were telling me about deer uterus," Mike reminded him. "Did they cut up women out there in 'Nam?"

Zumech finished his examination and jumped to his feet. "People, yeah, not just women. I'd heard of lacing scent to attract animals for hunting, even done it myself. But the *Montaignards*, where this guy Rat learned his stuff, they used the scent of people. Trained their dogs with human body parts. The way it worked was the U.S. Army would compensate them for all the K.I.A.V.C. they killed. To prove the kill and confirm the body count, they removed the ears of the dead."

"Oh yeah, how did our guys know whose ears they were?"

"Just a story I heard from a guy I used to know." Zumech hunkered down again.

"How does it compute here?"

He shrugged and changed the subject. "When I got back in '69, the Department was hiring without background checks, giving special consideration to veterans, you know; especially those with combat experience. You weren't around in the late sixties, but it was riot time here."

"Yeah, I know all about that." Mike didn't want to hang around for the lecture.

"They had a special unit manned by former marines and paratroopers. Those were the guys they wanted on patrol in the street. Tactical Patrol Force, it was called. Sounds good, huh?

"This guy, Tunnel Rat, was in that. He was there for the riots in Harlem, the riots at Columbia, too. After that, he was assigned to training the Department's bomb-detecting dogs. Until '86 he trained dogs and responded to suspected explosive devices. He worked over at Rodman's Neck."

"Uh-huh." Mike nodded. Most everybody trained at the firearms ranges and tactical house there. So what? The sun was on its ascent, getting hotter by the minute. They were waiting around for the forensic unit.

John glanced at his watch. "In '86, the Department decided to obtain additional dogs and it was the Rat's job to train the cops and their trackers. They're especially effective in missing or abducted children's cases."

Mike glanced at his watch, too. The history lesson was informative, but where was it leading? Zumech didn't seem to mind his impatience.

"As you know, Rodman's Neck is one bridge away from City Island. During his years in the Bomb Squad unit, the Rat used to go over there for lunch. And he made friends with a deputy warden of corrections. Know what this guy's job was?"

"Ah, this is where the body parts come in, right?"

"Smart."

"I'm a detective," Mike murmured.

"So, Warden Kelly supervised the fifty-man prison inmate crew that buried the City's unknown dead. The site was Hart Island, a ten-minute ferry ride. Every day, fifty to a hundred bodies lay there in the sun, in the cold, in the rain, whatever. The unclaimed bodies were put in flimsy wooden boxes. If the bulldozer that buried them broke down, sometimes they sat there for several days oozing fluids. Pretty putrid. The sweet smell of death was perfect for training the dogs. The Rat went over there once a week. And you know, sometimes those inmates were clumsy and accidently knocked over a few of those boxes and the stuff just oozed right out."

"Uh-huh." Mike was getting the picture. Was this glob on the grass in front of them a cop story, or what?

"You know, after the Rat started training the dogs out on Hart Island, many a promotion was lost. A funny thing happened when he hunted with the dogs, often a body would turn up in an area that was supposed to have previously been searched."

"Oh yeah?" Now Mike was interested. It just happened that yesterday this area had been previously searched.

"Uh-huh. The brass at One PP always applauded Rat's work big time, but never knew why he did such a good job." John put his Yankee hat back on. "He used to collect the stuff in jars."

"Jesus, you still do that?" Mike said with a smile because Zumech was clearly the Rat of his story.

"Nah, we don't need to do that anymore. These days you can get any scent you want mail order. Verisimilitude doesn't matter one whit to the dogs."

From a distance came the sound of a chopper. The whole West Side of the park was being treated like a huge crime scene. Someone must have thought it was a good idea to bring in a bird. For sure all the activity wasn't because of the homicide of a homeless man. EMS and

Crime Scene units were appearing on the scene in minutes. Brass from downtown and numerous precincts uptown were beginning their ritual drop-ins. Interest in the operation was spreading like marijuana under grow lights.

When Mike left with Zumech, the separate areas of Peachy's "finds" were being roped off with yellow tape and a criminologist was drawing a map of their locations. No expense was being spared. Because of a number of high-profile police brutality cases in the last year, the department was having major trouble with its image. Morale on the street was low and the PC was on the line. Not only that, it was an election year. The mayor wanted to be governor. It looked like any possibility of killings in Central Park was a first-rate opportunity for a publicity blitz.

Zumech snorted, "Jesus, a bird." Then he dropped his zinger. "My guess is someone from 'Nam is involved in this."

"Yeah, you're right, the victim."

"No kidding!" Zumech looked surprised. "How do you know that?"

"I knew him." Mike's hair blew all over the place as the bird hovered over them, then moved off to a safe distance and slowly descended to the grass.

FORTY-THREE

"OKAY. GO AHEAD, do it." Brandy lay back on the sofa in her father's apartment. It was midmorning. She was pissed at her mother and certainly hadn't gone to school as she'd promised. Nor had David. Neither of them had even considered it. They'd planned to smoke her dad's pot and enjoy the show.

"Just like that? Don't you want to see them bring him out?" David was shocked by her changing the subject so quickly. He was excited about the killing. He wanted to talk about it and think about it for a while. He hadn't expected such a high feeling and didn't want to lose it.

The heehawing of the ambulance was getting louder. Soon the news of a dead man in Central Park would be everywhere, and the TV vans with the dishes on top would be back on Central Park West. The TV crews would be out again, and there would be plenty to watch. In a few hours they'd be able to see it all over again on the news. He'd thought the whole purpose was to see it on the news, tape it all, and watch it again and again for the power it gave them over the whole city.

"They found him," Brandy said with a little shrug, as if it didn't matter to her now. "We can take a break for a while."

She wiggled her little bottom and smiled her cute little smile, neither of which had David ever been able to resist. "Too bad you don't have your laptop. We could look at those cute pictures again," she said.

"You really liked that, didn't you?" he said without enthusiasm. He wanted more appreciation for ridding the earth of a piece of scum. The drunken bum had attacked her last night. He'd saved her life. He was a *hero*. She should be more interested in that than porno.

"What's the matter? I thought you wanted to fuck," she said.

"Sure I do." David frowned. The truth was he wasn't sure he actually *did* want to right now. This lack of interest made him wonder if he was gay. He felt a little funny to say the least. Maybe something was wrong with his meds. Maybe the Ritalin was making him gay. Or it could be he just wasn't in the mood. He was still rattled by his mother and father yelling at each other about him again. So early in the morning and so loud they woke him up. He hated that.

He also hated being in Brandy's father's place. He didn't want to get caught there with his pants down. Who knew if the maid came on Thursdays or not. Brandy had lied about that kind of thing before. Once she'd said the maid didn't come until noon and the maid showed up at ten-thirty. David didn't entirely trust her. And then there was the sex thing. Each time he thought the tests were over, she came up with something new for him to do to prove he really loved her. And now he'd really done something important, and she didn't seem to care.

"What's the matter, David?"

"You know, you'd be history right now without me. Did you see me take that guy down? I was amazing. How about that ride, too? I bet you never thought I'd remember the way."

"Daaavid, come over here."

"Aren't I a great driver? I've got the whole city freaking. I make people disappear. Two people, for Christ's sake! And I take down the enemy. I'm the king. Say it."

He was sitting in an armchair by the sofa and felt like a king. "I'm the master," he announced.

"Daaavid. It was *my* idea."

"You can't make people disappear. Only I can do that. Admit it." He laughed, thinking of the disappeared and dead. He'd set out to do one, but he'd gotten three people in just two days. This was way more sophisticated than shooting someone from a window. This was exerting his power over the whole city. And his parents were stupid. They were completely unstable . . .

"Come on, David, let's do it."

He didn't look at her, didn't want a repeat of yesterday. The truth was he didn't think he could do it. When he saw people having sex on the internet or the pay-per-view videos his parents didn't know he watched, it looked like going into butter. That's how he thought of it. He thought sex was kind of like coming to a gate, the gate opening, and his going through it. But every time he tried with Brandy there was, like, this wall down there. A brick wall. They'd be fooling around, and he'd kind of try to get into her and it was like hitting a brick wall. And then she'd change her mind. He was feeling good. He wasn't in the mood to hit a brick wall right now.

Weeks ago, after camp was over and they were bored waiting for school to start, Brandy had come up with this idea about killing some-one. They'd been high, and they wondered if they could kill someone and get away with it. He'd thought about it in the same kind of way he thought about parachuting from an airplane and skiing down a moun-tain where no one had ever been before. He'd heard of people getting to a ski slope like that. Really cool. He'd asked Dr. Clog a whole bunch of questions about killing. Had he been in the army? Had he ever killed anyone? What did it feel like to kill someone? If you killed someone in war, were you sorry afterward? He needed some information on the subject.

Every question he asked, the psychiatrist answered, "You must have a reason for asking me this."

"Just wondering," David had told him. "You know."

"Why don't you tell me your thoughts about school. This is a very important year for you. You're a junior now. How is that studying for the SATs going? Aren't you preparing for a pretest next week? You want to do well, don't you?"

Clog proved once again he was a fool with no real interest in David at all. The man was just an employee of his parents with a job to tor-ture him just like they did. Four hour pretest! That's all he could talk about. It was a fucking disaster. The SATs weren't until October. Why did they have to bug him about this in August?

Brandy hiked up her sweater so he could see her stomach and breasts. "Come *on*, David."

At the sight of her tits David felt some stirring down below. What the hell. He pulled himself out of the chair and moved over to the sofa. The sound of the sirens were going as Brandy made room for him, unzipped his pants. He was reliving his moments of strength. How they'd beaten the old bum and thrown leaves on his body. Only a few hours later Zumech's red Jeep turned up, and Peachy howled like crazy. It was all happening just like they imagined it. They'd orchestrated the whole thing, and Brandy was finally, actually, really turned on.

She freed his cock from his underpants and played with it, clicking her tongue pierce as she squeezed and rubbed it. He went to another place in his head, an amusement park where there were all these colors and rides. His brain was whirling as she pulled down her own jeans. When he tried to get in, there was that wall again. He was in an amusement park, lights flashing bells ringing on her body that was so soft and curvy, and still he couldn't get through that wall. Then, suddenly Brandy changed course and put his thing in her mouth for a second, just a second, and he felt the steel knob that was her tongue pierce. After that she put it down there where the wall was. This time she guided him inside her. She bucked with her hips a few times—and it was unbelievable.

Just unbelievable. David found paradise at last. God finally smiled on him and he felt bliss. In the middle of his bliss, his cell phone rang. He knew by the way it rang and then rang again that the caller was his mother, but he was too busy thanking God to answer it.

FORTY-FOUR

T EN PEOPLE including Janice Owen's boss and her boss's boss were in a meeting in the conference room when her secretary, Denise, came in and handed her a note about David. Janice had been paying strict attention to the proceedings. She knew what everyone in the room was wearing. She knew from the expressions on their faces all their feelings about the contents of the ten-page memo they were discussing. She knew the substance of the memo's communication. She had not, however, listened to a single thing anyone had *said* since they'd all gotten their little coffees and nondairy creamers and sweeteners and sat down to strategize.

Janice couldn't concentrate because she was thinking about her bed, a king so wide it enabled her husband night after night, month after month, never actually to touch her no matter what his position or how much he tossed around. If he didn't snore like a pig, she wouldn't know he was there at all. No good-night kisses, no messing around in the kitchen. Nothing. Janice was on a rampage, her every feeling offended by Bill's humming in the shower as he fondled his very *large* erection while he no doubt fantasized doing it with the ugly bitch Peggy, who was now giving him expensive ties with lovebirds on them.

Janice was furious at herself for having been so nice, so accepting of his long work hours, his exhaustion, and his worry over his work, which he had the bad taste to keep reminding her brought in the *bacon*. Peggy was twenty-eight, blond, thin as a rake, and a conniving bitch who wanted a husband even if she had to resort to stealing one. Janice felt like a jerk for not taking this Peggy thing seriously a lot sooner. Murder was too good for the girl. The bitch deserved a lingering painful death. How could this be accomplished, she wondered. Shooting her would be too easy. Poison? Disfiguring disease? Cancer?

Janice's thoughts turned to money. Bill made three quarters of a million a year, plus a big bonus. Janice made a hundred and fifty thousand. She could not live as well if he divorced her. She could not manage their son's behavior on her own—but maybe she could. Maybe divorce would be better for them all. She could take Bill for everything he had. New York State was great for women. She could get a lawyer to calculate the value of Bill's partnership in his firm over a lifetime and demand half. It happened all the time. Bill would either have to pay her big-time alimony every *month* or give her many millions of dollars up *front*. Either way, she would keep the apartment *and* get child support for David—who needed tutors and doctors and college money and heaven knew what else. Bill wouldn't have much left for any kind of life with Peggy. Ha!

But who would *she* go out with? What kind of life would *she* have with a troublesome teenager and no husband? Janice took the note from Denise and read it. Her bad day suddenly got worse.

David's school is on the phone, was what the note said.

"I'll take it." Janice folded the piece of paper and was out of her chair without a beat. What was it, ten in the morning? She checked her watch. Uh-uh, not even. It was nine-forty-eight, way too early for something like a broken bone in sports. Second period was Contemporary American History. No, David hadn't gotten hurt in some accident. The school hadn't burned down. She knew what this was about.

She changed gears in an instant. See what a wonderful mother she was. She was at work in an important meeting, she had a life of her own; she was good at her job. Did she hesitate when the boy's school was on the line? Here they were in the middle of a merger, she had important things to do. She could not afford to jeopardize her career, but, as always, her son came first. That was more than Bill could say. The school never called *him*.

Janice sailed down the hall to her office and took the call on her own line. "Yes, Janice Owen," she said sweetly.

"Oh hi, Mrs. Owen. This is Margery Redich at Prep. I'm just calling about David. He didn't come in yesterday or this morning. I didn't get a call back from you yesterday when David didn't come in, either." Her perky voice suddenly took on a slight accusatory tone.

The rage caught Janice right in the throat. Both days she'd driven David to school herself. They'd had nice conversations. *This* morning she'd left him right in front of the door. Her chest constricted with the betrayal of both the men in her life. After the way she'd stuck her neck out for David, she should bust him now, let him get expelled. He should be *punished* for this. But it never occurred to her to let such a thing happen.

"Oh, I'm so *sorry*," she gushed. "I know I should have called. We're in the middle of a merger here, and I'm a little distracted. David is really sick. He has the flu. Must be a stomach virus or something. He'll be in tomorrow for sure. He's at the doctor now."

"Okay, just checking. Have a good day, Mrs. Owen."

"Thank you *so much* for calling. My mistake for not letting you know sooner."

Janice hung up and dialed her husband.

"Mr. Owen's office, may I help you?" The precise voice of Bill's male secretary came on the line.

"You certainly may, Greg. Is he there?"

"Oh, Mrs. Owen. He's on the phone right now. Shall I have him call you when he gets off?"

"No, I need to talk to my husband *now*. It's an emergency," she said coldly.

"He's on long distance."

"It's still an emergency, Greg."

"Okay, I'll try."

Janice looked at her watch. She'd been gone a minute and a half. They wouldn't miss her for another two. Bill came on the line a full minute later.

"What is it, Janice?"

"David is playing hooky again. Fat lot of good you did in your little talk with him this morning."

"Is this what you're calling me for?"

"The school just called. This is serious."

"I thought you took him there yourself. It's not my fault if he doesn't stay."

"Whose fault do you think it is, *mine?*" Janice was appalled at this outrageous suggestion.

"I certainly can't be responsible if you get him all upset in the car." Bill's tone was not nice at all.

"I don't get him upset," Janice protested.

"Look, I have to go to court in five minutes."

"Bill, I want you to come home early tonight. We'll have dinner together and talk. This is very serious. They're going to kick him out if he doesn't knuckle under."

"It's not knuckle *under*. It's settle down."

"*Whatever!* Bill! We have to do *something*."

"Fine. Just get him on the phone and tell him to go to school now."

"Ah, I can't."

"Why not, Janice?" Bill was impatient now.

"I told the school he had the flu."

"Well, tell David to have a miraculous recovery."

"Okay, I'll tell him," she said meekly. "Are you coming home tonight?"

"Of course I'm coming home. Where else would I go?" He hung up without saying good-bye.

FORTY-FIVE

AT TWELVE-THIRTY Igor Stanislovski, one of the criminologists from
CSU, was just finishing his last sketch of the crime scene. The remains of Pee Wee James were bagged and ready to start their journey
across town to the Medical Examiner's office for autopsy. More than
two dozen uniforms from three precincts were keeping away the curious as April consulted with Charles Ding, a new investigator in the
Medical Examiner's office.

Charles was a hail-fellow-well-met type with a wandering eye and
distracting tic that got worse when he was nervous. He must have been
pretty nervous right then because the whole time his head was bent to
examine Pee Wee, his right eye winked steadily at April, giving him the
appearance of a lecherous schoolboy. In fact, he was a serious guy.

"Typical drunk. Lots of scars, sores. Eczema on his hands and arms.
Poor circulation in his legs. Look at those ankles. I wouldn't be surprised if he had gangrene in that foot. We'll know later, not that it matters. I'm not removing his shoes now. Bottom line, I'd say someone hit
him on the side of the head, then attempted to bury him. Maybe he
was interrupted. Looks like a pretty disorganized killer," Charles said.

"Probably the half-assed work of another drunk. He certainly appears to have died right here." Igor threw his own two cents in. "You
notice there's not much disturbance in the ground. Who knows, maybe
it was an accident."

Igor had some kind of Balkan accent, and a limp that was the result of a hollow-point bullet he'd taken in the calf several years back while attempting to stop a bank robbery one day when he went to deposit his paycheck. By now he'd finished bagging the potato chip bag, the Styrofoam cup, the shoe, three buttons, part of a sock, a crushed Coke can, an Alcoholics Anonymous key chain with its "God-grant-me-the-wisdom" credo deeply encrusted with dirt, and several gallons of earth, grass, and leaf samples. The ground had been tromped by the hordes. There were no clear shoe imprints from which to make plaster casts.

Igor was five-four, had the bluest eyes and the biggest head April had ever seen. These days he was wearing his thick blond hair in a ponytail. Of all the Crime Scene people, April thought Igor was the best. She respected his opinions, but he didn't know anything about Maslow's mystery patient. Pee Wee's murder could also be the work of a small female who couldn't possibly bury a body.

Ding's eye wandered over and winked at Igor. "We'll know more when we open him up." He removed his rubber gloves, bagged them, replaced them with a fresh pair, then trotted off to examine the soft tissue samples Peachy had found. "Bye now," were his parting words.

Igor frowned and circled the air with his finger. April shook her head at him. *Don't make fun.*

"Good to meet you, Charlie. Thanks," April called after him.

"*De nada*," the Chinese replied.

Spanish! April snorted and turned to Igor. Pee Wee was dead and it was all her fault. A Chinese saying fit his life well: "Loss upon loss until at last comes rest."

Last night she'd trusted Mike and followed the credo "By letting go, it all gets done." Her reward was Pee Wee's eternal rest. Now she felt beaten by the mischief of unknown devils.

"I help out, don't I?" Pee Wee had said only yesterday.

Not enough, Pee Wee, not enough.

"Make your eyes bright enough from evil to lead you away" was another saying among the thousands April had learned. None of them fit in America 2000. In the thousand department the worst was "A thousand years is not enough to honor a parent."

Actually, April thought thirty years of parent honoring was an awful lot. Trying to brighten her eyes from the evil of Pee Wee's death, she turned to Igor with her ten thousand most pressing questions. Her cell phone rang and "Private" popped up on the screen.

"Sergeant Woo," she said.

"Yes, hello, April, it's Jason. Is this a better time? I really have to talk to you."

"Talk away, I have one minute."

"Have you found Maslow?"

"No, but we found someone else."

"Really, who?"

"Yes. It's getting spooky out here, Jason. We've got a head case for sure. Can we meet?"

"Someone's dead?"

"Yes, a homeless man."

"Oh, this is not my department."

"Well, that's not the weird thing, Jason. I need your help here. This isn't pick-and-choose time. You brought this situation to me."

"Did I?"

"Yes, you did."

Jason groaned. "You cops, always playing with the truth. I asked you about one of my students, only that. What's the weird thing, April?"

"We have some finds of soft tissue."

"You got me on that, April. Soft tissue from what?"

"Maybe human, maybe not. Our tracker found it buried, you know, near the body, but in different sites. The tissue didn't come from the homicide victim so it could be a whole other thing. What do you make of it?"

Jason groaned again. "April, I'm a psychoanalyst. I work with the living. And among the living. Look, it's weirder than you think."

It was her turn to be surprised. "Really, how's that?"

"I'd like you to treat this as confidential for the moment if you can. But, I just had a little visit from Maslow's father. He has another family. Maslow has a sister he doesn't know about."

"He has a sister?" April was excited.

"Yeah, twenty years old."

"Who's the mother? Where does she live?"

"She's a woman Maslow's father works with, an employee of his. Mother and daughter live in Long Island City. Where the hell is that?"

"In Queens. Jesus!" April was unnerved by the sight of Woody Baum, careening across the grass toward her in Iriarte's Lumina. He was driving the car like an off-road SUV with the lieutenant in the passenger seat and Lieutenant Margaret Mary Joyce, commander of the Detective Squad of the Two-O and April's former boss, in the backseat next to Captain Higgins, the CO of the precinct. From the other direction came the Jeep of Captain Reginald. Shit, what was this, turf war?

"What?" Jason asked.

"Look, Jason, something's come up. I have to go—"

"Wait, I have an address for you," Jason cried.

April turned the page of her notebook. "Okay, sure. Give me the address. I'll go see the sister, where does she live?"

Jason gave her the Long Island City address. She wrote it down quickly, then shoved her notebook into her purse, her eyes nervously on the Lumina that seemed to have her targeted for a hit. She stood there trying to be cool, and Woody stopped just short of crashing into her.

Then, still dressed for summer in a butter yellow suit, mango shirt, mint green tie, and straw hat, Lieutenant Iriarte jumped out of the car and slammed the door. "Woo, what the mother-fucking *hell* do you think you're doing?" he screamed.

The sudden loss of face like the bang of a popped balloon in front of her former bosses made April's head swim. Neither Captain Higgins, who didn't like girl cops, nor Lieutenant Joyce, who didn't like *her*, had ever spoken to her quite like that.

Joyce, a big swearer herself, looked pretty surprised by the attack. She got out of the car moving one plump leg at a time, a frown gathering on her pugnacious face. Higgins was out of the car. Baum jumped out. Captain Reginald, CO of the Central Park Precinct, was out of his Jeep, running toward them, too. April prayed for bloody turf war.

"Good morning, sir. Lieutenant Joyce, congratulations on your promotion. Good morning, Captain Higgins, Captain Reginald." April gave them all a second, covered all the bases except for Baum, who had seemed a little too happy with the opportunity to run her down.

"Yeah, and congratulations on yours. I always knew you'd make good." Lieutenant Joyce glanced at Iriarte and gave April a real smile. "And congratulations on your upcoming nuptials, too," she added.

"My nuptials?" April blushed some more.

"Yeah, I heard you and Mike are getting married. I like it when my best people get together. *Mazeltov.*" This was for all the captains' benefit. A few courtesies before the ax fell.

Higgins guffawed at the Yiddish.

"We're just friends, Lieutenant—" April said. She was freaked by all the brass and saw her career careening toward a desk job in Housing for sure.

"Enough of the chitchat," Iriarte interrupted her peevishly. "I've had complaints about you, Woo." He eyed Captain Reginald.

Thousands of years of prescribed correct Chinese behavior for people of lower rank, including and especially females, had coded April's genes to make her bow to the ground, to smack her forehead on the earth, and beg for forgiveness for her lack of wisdom and any involuntary foolishness that she might wrongfully have committed. Correct Chinese behavior warned that the tongue was dangerous to the throat. In other words, shut up.

Being in a new country and new century altogether, however, a reasonable modification of forehead knocking might be to wither to half-self, cast her eyes down, and attempt to disappear. This self-effacement tactic to appease an irritated boss, though, was at odds with her more recent training from Lieutenant Joyce and Mike Sanchez, who were big stand-up-for-yourself people. For a second she was *almost* conflicted about which way to go.

"I'm with Lieutenant Sanchez," she said officiously. "He's working Special Case on the Atkins case. Last night he requested a second dog tracker, I suggested John Zumech. I worked with Zumech when I was in the Two-O. Do you know him, sir?" she asked Iriarte.

"He's worked in here before." Captain Reginald affirmed Zumech's credibility, then waited for the shit to hit.

"What does Zumech have to do with it?" With the comment from the CP CO, Iriarte's mood darkened further. His tongue worked its way around his mouth unhappily.

"It was his dog that found Pee Wee James." April glanced at Lieutenant Joyce. She nodded. *Way to go, April.*

"Is that the victim?" Baum blurted out.

April nodded at Captain Reginald. Now was not the time to mend fences with him. She turned to Iriarte again. "What happened, sir? I had the vic in an interview room yesterday morning. When I returned last night at 2100, I found out he'd been released at noon. Now he's dead. Unfortunate." Now she was stepping way out of line.

Iriarte didn't like it one bit. His tongue punched out the side of his cheek. Clearly whatever report he'd received on the homicide hadn't revealed the victim's identity. He didn't like hearing it from April.

"It's James?" he said unhappily.

"Yes, sir," she told him. Pee Wee was zipped up in the bag. The finger was packaged separately.

Iriarte watched the removal of the remains with the distress of someone about to lose a promotion.

"Hey, this was your investigation, April. As far as I'm concerned, you can take the homicide," Joyce said with a smile. "You'll solve it one, two, three, right, Captain?"

"Yeah, good plan," Higgins agreed. He didn't want the case in the Two-O. They hadn't caught it in the first place. Why take on a big problem?

The Central Park Precinct wasn't set up for homicide investigations. That meant that the closest precinct was Midtown North, just what Iriarte didn't want. No one wanted Special Case in it, either. Made them all look bad.

"April was the best detective I ever had, right, Captain?" Joyce said.

"No question," Higgins agreed.

Now April could see why the three of them had come together. They all wanted April to take the heat for the homicide. The dog barked, easing the tension. Looked like the search was over. Mike strolled toward them with Zumech. Peachy was at his side, heeling nicely. The two men were in serious conversation. No sign of Maslow.

"Fine, April is the primary. She set up the search, she gets the homicide." Iriarte gave her an evil smile.

"Thank you, sir, I need Woody here for a few hours, mind if I take him?" The little bastard.

As far as Iriarte was concerned the conversation was at an end. The homicide fuckup was on April's plate; that was all that mattered to him. He'd lose her when it was over.

"Yeah, he'll take us back and then you're welcome to him. He's a terrible driver."

FORTY-SIX

AROUND NOON Jerry Atkins appeared in Grace's doorway for a minute. He wiggled his finger at her, then walked away. Grace glanced at Craig. He was eating a *calzone* at his desk and drinking one of those huge containers of Coke, careful not to drip on his work. He didn't notice her leave.

Grace and Jerry had a method for meeting during the day. He would go downstairs to the newspaper stand in the building, and she would meet him there. He always said if anyone saw them together it would look like a coincidence. She thought it was pretty silly, so what if people saw them together? They'd worked in the same office for almost twenty-three years, longer than anyone else.

In the beginning of the relationship he used to call her into his office several times a day. They spent hours discussing all her problems, her life plan and options, and of course his distress about his empty marriage. She'd sit on his sofa, and they'd talk as if there was nothing else in the world to do. He was a wealthy man. He took her out to lunch and to dinner and promised to help her in her career. No one had ever paid that much attention to her in her entire life. At twenty-one she'd enjoyed his pleasure in her prettiness and never for a moment thought forty-four was old. Now, because he was paranoid about the telephone, he would E-mail her to meet him at the newspaper stand, and the only time she saw him socially was at the firm Christmas party.

She got downstairs first and was busy reading tabloid scandals in the private lives of the rich and famous, and predictions of the end of the world before 2002, when Jerry turned up. He motioned toward the door, and they went outside. It was a gorgeous day, but neither was in the mood to notice. Jerry turned south on Third Avenue. It was lunch hour and the sidewalk was jammed.

"Any word from Dylan?" he asked.

"No. Have you spoken to the police?"

"Yes, I had a telephone call from the Mayor. I also had a call from the Police Commissioner's office, too. Everybody's working on this."

"The Police Commissioner called you?"

"His office called." Jerry spoke with obvious pride. "A deputy commissioner assured me they were doing everything they could to find my son. He sounded like a very nice man. I also spoke to some detectives. They didn't seem very competent. I hate to break this to you, but there's been a murder in the park. Not Maslow. I was right that this has nothing to do with Dylan."

"A murder?" Grace was horrified. "Who was murdered?"

"Just a homeless man. A mental patient."

"Did you tell them about Dylan?"

"No, I didn't, Grace. I didn't think that would help the situation. It would only confuse things."

He didn't tell the police his daughter was missing? Grace was overwhelmed by anger. They walked downtown, moving with the crowd. She hadn't eaten anything for nearly two days. Somehow, she wished that Jerry would ease her suffering and offer to take her to lunch so she could talk about the daughter she'd loved and nurtured for so many years, pour her heart out, and receive some comfort that she was not alone in caring about what happened to her.

"I went to see Maslow's supervisor, Dr. Frank," he went on.

"Oh?" What good would that do?

"I told him about Dylan."

"Was he surprised?" she asked. What about me, Grace thought. "What did you say about me?"

Jerry shook his head. "He asked some questions about her life, our life together. I told him the information was confidential. We don't want the police to know about this."

"Why not?"

"My hope is that he will try to contact Dylan himself."

"I told you Dylan is not at home."

"I know, but don't upset yourself, Grace. She always comes home. She has nowhere else to go."

Grace felt her frustration spiral. Sometimes she wanted to kill Jerry. So many things about him were infuriating. He collected their receipts, even from the drugstore and Starbucks. He knew every purchase. That irked her and Dylan so much. He went over their credit card expenses as if he were the one who was responsible for them. But the truth was he didn't pay his own share of their life together. She even paid his cleaning bills, and she was *poor*. She had nothing of her own. He'd always insisted on being the head of her family without taking any of the responsibility a husband would take. Now the Mayor of New York City was in touch with him about Maslow, and no one cared at all about her. For the first time she knew how his wife must feel.

"Who is this person who's supposed to get in touch with Dylan?" she asked.

"I told you. He's a psychiatrist. He'll talk to her, find out what's going on with her. If she knows something about Maslow's disappearance, I know he'll tell us."

"I thought you were so against psychiatrists."

"But you were so worried, my sweetheart, my darling." He stopped and gave her a tender look. "I did it for you. You said you wanted all the children safe. Well, I have the appropriate people working on it. Whatever you want I do for you." He took her hand and squeezed it.

She knew how his mind worked. As far as he was concerned, the situation with her was now under control.

"Now be patient. I think we'll have this taken care of soon and then we'll get back to normal," he told her.

She gave him a look. Get back to normal? They'd never get back to normal. They'd never been normal.

"Don't look at me like that. When everything settles down, I'll marry you and adopt Dylan, I promise." He brought her hand to his lips and kissed her fingers in the middle of a whirling crowd.

Grace couldn't bring herself to say she'd heard all this before. After the kiss to her fingertips, Jerry left her without offering lunch, and she went back upstairs to her office. In the kitchen she poured herself some very old coffee and tossed in two packets of hazelnut nondairy creamer. Lunch. She took the cup and returned to her cubicle. Craig wasn't there. But she knew his habits. He'd gone off to sneak a few cigarettes and have a piece of cheesecake. In the quiet moment she called the police and asked for the detectives handling the Maslow Atkins case. The man on the phone asked her name. She told him who she was. She was put on hold for a long time. Finally the man came back on the line, gave her a name, and told her where to go. The address was across town on West Fifty-fourth Street. She took a taxi.

FORTY-SEVEN

A S THE BLACK OF NIGHT gave way to gray, Maslow knew he was not in a tomb limited to the size of his own body. Beyond his feet was an open space large enough for at least four people to move around. That was comforting. He was stuck in the back of a cave and needed to get to the front, the mouth, the opening. Out. And he had to get out soon. He had more than himself to think of now; he had to get Allegra out.

Hours after the attack her cries still tormented him. He replayed the horrific moments over and over and tried to calculate from her screams what had happened and how badly hurt she might be. Had she been stabbed by the knife the girl had waved at him? Was she slowly bleeding to death? Who were that boy and girl? What did they think they were doing and why? Were they stoned on something? Would they return? How soon? Never? The questions kept coming. And the big one—what could he do to get help?

Through the long night hours Maslow heard Allegra moaning, struggling to breathe, and he talked to her, kept talking. He had no idea what he was saying. All he knew was that the girl was injured, and she was crying. He wanted her to get up, move closer, and help him get out of there. Then he wanted her to talk to him, but he knew from the sounds she made that she was gagged—she couldn't talk. Then all he wanted was for her to stop crying. And now she had stopped. For an hour or more, there had been no sound from her but the ragged pull of her breath. He could hear the rats scuffling around her.

"Allegra, hang in there, kid," he told her.

Then through a solid wall of pain in his back, Maslow heard the whine of chopper blades and the wailing ambulance sirens. He heard a helicopter come, and he heard it go. It seemed to happen in only seconds. Too fast it was gone. His voice was hoarse from calling. Somewhere outside there was activity. Someone was getting help. But no help came to them.

"Allegra! Hey, Allegra."

No sound now.

A new panic seized him, not that he would die, but that she was dying. She was being eaten by rats as he lay there, doing nothing. They went for the soft tissue, for the eyes first. He was terrified, kept talking to her and calling for help. And when she stopped whimpering, he began clawing at the crumbling ceiling over his head, no longer afraid of the dirt falling into his face. He braced his hands against the earth above and dragged himself forward with his heels and bottom. He was not paralyzed, not helpless. He had only inches, hardly enough room to raise his knees and force his burning calf muscles to grab hold. He forced himself to move.

Again came the memory of childhood when he'd hid under the bed with the springs in his face, how he'd crawled in and out. That had been a safe place. This one could be a grave for two. His arms and shoulders were stronger now, his feet full of the bee stings of reviving life. By centimeters he snaked himself across the sharp rocks of the cave floor, tearing skin off his back and legs and bringing down sand and gravel on his face.

Agonizingly, he shoved himself along, a few inches at a time. Searing pain nagged at the muscles in his buttocks. He kept going. Two more feet, and the solid rock was much higher above his hands. A sudden shifting of a rock over his head made him scramble. He rolled over and inched backward on his hands and knees. He was in open space when a rock gave way and fell on the place where his head and shoulders had been only moments ago. The shelf had collapsed like a sand castle on the beach. The cave was narrower now, the air was foul with thick clouds of sand. His heart raced as he tried to catch his breath. Two rats scuttled over his bleeding hands. He smacked them away and sat up. Ahead of him he could see Allegra's motionless body.

Maslow reached his arms over his head and stretched his back, then he flexed his knees and feet. He was dizzy and disoriented. A lump on the side of his head felt as big as a tennis ball. A gash in his forehead hurt like hell. His stomach growled, but he felt no obvious break in his legs.

"Shhh. It's okay. It's okay," he mumbled. He had no idea he was making the sounds or to whom he was talking. His back still hurt, but his legs were moving. He was muttering, moving along the cave floor, feeling the rough stones with his hands. In the dim light he could see the form of Allegra. A lump, not a very big one. It looked as if her head was half buried in sand. Beyond that, bars and dim light.

"Allegra." He crawled toward her.

His knee snagged a jagged rock. He collapsed forward. His hand slipped into a puddle of stagnant water. Furious movement from the water. A ball-sized slimy something jumped out and hit him in the face with a splat.

"Frog," he told himself.

He covered the last feet and crouched over Allegra's body. She lay half on her side. Her hands were tied behind her back. The side of her face was covered with blood. Her eyes were closed, but her skin was warm. Maslow found the carotid pulse in her neck. One of her own socks was stuffed in her mouth. He pulled the sock out. She was groaning when he tried to untie her hands. Then he saw that her foot was caught under the gate.

He reached under her head and shoulders to get her face out of the dirt, and was shocked when her hair fell off in his hand.

FORTY-EIGHT

MIKE HAD WORKED THE SPECIAL CASE UNIT out of Midtown North
before. On the last case he'd used the tiny office located outside
the detective squad rooms. He didn't want to go there now. April had
not yet returned from the park so he decided to use the desk she shared
with the other supervisor of the squad, Sergeant Teeter. Today was
Teeter's day for the desk, but Teeter was out in the field. The department was going nuts on the homicide.

Mike was aware of the meeting of commanders in the park, but it
had nothing to do with him. He got his assignments from downtown,
and precinct politics didn't affect him one way or the other.

His job was to find Maslow Atkins. When he arrived at Midtown
North at half past one, Lieutenant Iriarte was downtown at a press conference, and the squad was packed with detectives from several units,
working the time lines to trace Pee Wee's last hours and the people
who had been in contact with him.

The roundup of street people had already begun. In the holding cell
four bedraggled males were cursing and spitting, muttering to themselves, protesting their innocence of whatever crime had come to the
attention of the police. They didn't know that they were a gathering of
Pee Wee James's known associates and that the police were looking for
his killer. Several were too drunk to process anything. Mike made a
quick survey of them. He didn't know any.

Several detectives were smoking. Toxic fumes filled the room. Mike hadn't had a cigarette in nearly two years. Sometimes the smell of smoke bothered him, but he longed for a cigarette now. He couldn't help feeling Pee Wee's life had ended because of his need to show April who was boss. He felt bad about that. She'd stayed behind with the criminologists. It made him think he was in trouble with her again.

Because he had neglected the situation with Pee Wee James last night, he went to interview the last detective to see him alive. He found Detective George Maas typing at the computer on his desk, a number of people crowded around him. George was short and wiry, had kinky hair and a big nose with an ugly red spot developing into a pimple on the tip of it. The man looked unhappy. His mustard yellow tie had a massive coffee stain streaking the front. Under his arms and all around his shoulder holster, he was sweating profusely into his khaki shirt. He appeared to be thinking hard and ignoring the talk around him. Mike had never heard April mention his name. Either the man was new or a nonentity.

"Hey, George, I'm Lieutenant Mike Sanchez, Special Case Squad." He held out his hand to be friendly. The crowd made room.

George examined the hand to see if a demotion was lurking there. "IAB?" he asked suspiciously.

Mike shook his head. He had nothing to do with Internal Affairs. "Special Case," he repeated.

"Everything I know is going in here." He tapped his fingers on the computer board. "It wasn't my call to release the guy."

"What happened?" Mike asked, taking a seat on the corner of the desk and edging out the listeners.

"The lieutenant told me to interview James, then to report what he said. I did. After that, he told me to give him a fiver and let him go." Maas shrugged. "That's what I did."

"Is that usual?"

"What, sir?"

"The fiver."

"Not exactly usual. We do it sometimes." He didn't look happy with this.

"Why this time?"

Maas shrugged. "No idea. I just do what I'm told."

"Did you drive him anywhere?"

"Are you kidding?"

"So you gave him a fiver but didn't drive him anywhere."

"That's right."

"So what did you and James talk about?"

"The guy was a hard-core wino. We've had him in here before. A big troublemaker. Whenever he could stand up, he was fighting."

"What about yesterday?"

"Yesterday he couldn't stand up. He had the DTs. He was shaking all over, thought the sky was raining with insects." George shrugged again. "He couldn't tell a tree from an elephant."

"What did he tell you about the incident on Tuesday night?"

"By the time I saw him, he'd forgotten all about it. All he told me was there was some kind of fairy godmother who was going to give him a twenty every day for the rest of his life. That's about it. At the time he was in here we had a situation with some South American tourists . . ."

"Oh yeah, what was that about?"

"They were upset a homeless person was sharing the planet with them." Maas smiled.

"What was their complaint?"

"Oh, I'm not sure what they came in about. I didn't handle the complaint. But the lieutenant didn't like it when Sergeant Woo brought the wino in. When she left, the lieutenant told me to get rid of him. So I gave him the five dollars and told him to get going." George seemed pretty stressed. He lit up an unfiltered Camel.

Mike inhaled the secondary smoke, not liking Maas one bit. "Turns out that wasn't such a good move," he murmured.

"The homicide could be a coincidence. Nobody believed a word he said." Maas went back to his typing.

"Time will tell." Mike got off the desk. The crowd in the squad rooms was thinning now. People were going out into the field.

He returned to April's office and sat down at her desk. Her office had remarkably little of her in it. Not a single thing of a personal nature was on her desk. Only a little plaque with her name on it indicated she even sat there. A tissue box was the extent of niceties. Mike swiveled back and forth in her chair. Last night on the news a Department spokesman had quoted the highly favorable park safety figures. Today, dozens of detectives were heading out to the homeless shelters, train stations, and public parks looking for people who had known and fought with James, and the knife that cut off his finger.

A lot of people were asking questions. Mike wanted to talk with the two kids who had spoken to April about Zumech and his dog. Something wasn't right there. Zumech was convinced of a Vietnam angle. He wasn't so sure. He dialed April's number. When she answered, she told him there was a break in the Atkins case.

"Maslow's father has a girlfriend," she said through static.

"No kidding," Mike said.

"And Maslow has a twenty-year-old sister."

"How'd that come out?"

"Maslow's father told Jason Frank. He'd wanted to keep it confidential."

"How does the sister fit in?"

"This may sound a little far out, *chico*, but my guess is the girl is his mystery patient."

"The one you saw last night?"

"Yes. Where are you?"

"Sitting at your desk. Look, I'm sorry about last night. The whole thing. You made the right call on Pee Wee. I blocked you. My mistake."

"Yeah," April said.

The deadpan Chinese used to be impossible for him to read. Now it was way too easy. Chinese silences were full of meaning.

"You have an address on the sister?" he asked.

"I do."

"Have you located her?" he asked.

"Not yet."

"You coming in?" he said finally.

"Uh-huh."

That was the best he could get out of her. "Fine, I'll be waiting. We'll find him," he assured her. About Maslow.

"Do you have a plan?"

"Yeah, I have a plan. Go back to square one."

"Better hurry up," April murmured. "The clock is ticking."

FORTY-NINE

G RACE RODRIGUEZ WAS SHOCKED when she entered the Midtown
North Precinct and connected with New York City law enforcement for the first time in her life. The building was old and bare of any
comforts whatsoever. Hard surfaces everywhere were covered with
decades' accumulation of black grime from city streets. She noticed the
signs warning of pickpockets in several languages, police equipment
she couldn't identify. The officers looked large and rough in their blue
uniforms. The faces of the most wanted criminals posted on the walls
looked no more frightening to her than the officers with the weapons
hanging from their belts. Not even the sight of several Latinos com-
forted her. None of them smiled at her. Inside the precinct everybody
was either busy or trying to look busy, and the people at the front desk
were sharp-voiced and impatient, like the waiters in coffee shops.

When she went to the desk and asked for the person in charge of
the Maslow Atkins case, she was told to sit down and wait. She sat on
a hard chair and watched uniforms walk back and forth. Both the men
and the women had a special police walk that frightened her. None of
them looked at her or asked her if she needed help. She felt unimpor-
tant and invisible. This frightened her, too.

Throughout her adult life, Grace had always identified with poor
people who couldn't speak English well, didn't have jobs and nice
homes, and couldn't properly care for their kids when they were sick or
in trouble. And she'd seen the movies where the police were corrupted

and mean. But now she saw that being in a police station was like entering poverty itself. When she went to the bathroom, she was shocked. It was worse than any hospital, post office, train station, court building she'd ever seen. She couldn't imagine why any of the people she saw here would want to work in such a place or how they might be able to find her daughter.

After an hour, she was so agitated she went to the desk a second time and asked who was in charge of the case. She wanted a name. No one seemed to know who was in charge. After a few minutes of calling on the phone, a mean-looking Hispanic woman sitting at a lower desk said, "Sergeant Woo."

"Sergeant Woo?" Grace swallowed the bad taste in her mouth. She wasn't sure what kind of name that was. "Could I see him?" She was becoming indignant at the way she was being treated. So many people walking in and out. No one paying attention. "I have to leave soon."

"She's out in the field," came the cold answer.

"Can I talk to someone else?" she said. "I need to talk to someone now."

"No one is available."

Grace felt tears sting behind her eyes. All she wanted to do was find her daughter. "This is important! When is she coming back?"

"We'll let you know."

Grace returned to her chair and wondered if she should call Jerry. He lived on Park Avenue and was an important man. No one would dare to treat him like this. But calling Jerry was out of the question. He didn't want anyone to know he had a daughter. He was the one who'd put them in this position in the first place, the strange limbo of being alone and possessed. Jerry didn't approve of her taking any independent actions when it came to their daughter. At the same time, he wasn't there to take care of things himself.

Secretly, Grace had always believed his story that he was a good man caught in a bad situation, that he wanted to do the right thing for her and Dylan, but didn't want to hurt his wife and son. She'd thought that his loyalty to the two of them demonstrated his sensitivity, not his selfishness. She'd always wished that his wife, who was mean and ugly and old and would certainly take half his fortune should they divorce, would just die to spare them the agony.

So many times when she'd been hurt or angry with Jerry for one slight or another, she'd tried so hard not to feel that she was, in the end, alone. Now she knew that she and Dylan were indeed alone.

She was thinking that she had come to the wrong place with her story when a beautiful Chinese woman, exquisitely dressed in a rust-colored suit and purple blouse, came in the precinct door.

The officer at the desk shouted at her, "Sergeant, someone's looking for you."

The woman stopped at the desk to talk to him, and he pointed at Grace. Immediately she came over.

"I'm Sergeant Woo. How can I help you?" She had a low voice with a slight New York accent.

Grace was shocked. This Chinese woman was in charge of Maslow's case? Jerry had told her the Mayor himself was involved. The police department was doing everything possible to find him. Jerry would not be happy to think this woman was the best they could do. Grace herself was not very optimistic about a Chinese woman detective.

"Ah, I wanted to talk to someone about Maslow Atkins."

"Good. Thank you for coming. Have you been waiting long?" the woman asked politely.

Grace had gotten to her feet. Now she looked down at her hands. Yes, she had been waiting long. She had some information, but now she wasn't sure she wanted to give it. The detective's face was polite but unreadable. Grace didn't feel comfortable talking to her.

"They didn't know who was in charge," she said after a slight hesitation.

"I'm sorry, it's very chaotic around here today. I guess no one sent you upstairs to the detective unit."

"No."

"Well, come upstairs now. We'll find a quiet place to talk. It's only on the second floor, do you mind taking the stairs?"

"No. That's all right." Grace followed the Chinese woman cop without a Chinese accent. She didn't know what she was going to tell her.

Upstairs, behind the door that was marked "Detective Unit," they walked into a room full of smoke. A lot of people in plain clothes were in there, walking around smoking and sitting at the desks, talking on the phones. The sergeant ignored them. She stopped outside a tiny office with a glass window in the door. Inside a man with a big mustache was sitting at a desk with a plaque that read "Sergeant April Woo" on it. Grace realized that the detective's name was April. She felt sick and wished she hadn't come.

"Would you wait here for a moment?" The sergeant went into her office. Her back was to the window. Grace couldn't see her or hear what she said. The man came out. The woman sat down at her desk.

"You may go inside now," the man told her. He, too, spoke in a polite manner.

Grace could tell he was Latino. She gave him a grateful smile and went into the office.

"Sit down," Sergeant Woo said.

Grace sat down. The man with the mustache came in and sat down in the chair beside her. He had a nice smile and was wearing a very strong aftershave that was sweet and spicy and familiar to her.

"Lieutenant Sanchez is in the Special Case Squad. He's in charge here," Woo said.

Grace stared at the two of them. She realized the cops she was dealing with were Spanish and Chinese. She wondered if this was not a very important case, after all. No one here seemed to know what was going on or who was in charge. Where were the Americans?

"I'm Grace Rodriguez," she said softly. "Thank you for seeing me."

"Thank you for coming in," said the lieutenant called Sanchez.

Grace sniffed, trying to hold on to her composure. Cops were tough, she knew. And her child was illegitimate, named after a seventies folk singer. Her Dylan turned out to be as strange as the singer was, a weird duck, delicate as glass—and missing since yesterday. Grace felt ashamed about having to describe her difficult child like an item for the lost and found. The two cops waited.

"Maslow Atkins is my boss's son," she said, flushing deeply.

The two exchanged glances. "Take your time."

"I don't know whether you have spoken with Mr. Atkins. I asked him to tell you about us, but—" Grace sniffed. "Well, he's a very private person."

The Spanish lieutenant nodded. He seemed like a nice man. Grace chewed on her lip. She hadn't wanted it to come out this way. She hadn't wanted to harm her daughter. She'd wanted her and Jerry's story to end well. She'd always expected it would. Now her hopes were down the toilet. She could never trust him, never be with him again. She cared only for her daughter. Saving Dylan. The two cops waited. She took a deep breath.

"Jerome Atkins and I have a daughter. Our daughter, Dylan, is twenty and missing since yesterday." There, she said it.

Her eyes overflowed and tears coursed down her face. She couldn't help it. The Chinese detective passed over the tissue box. Grace took one and pressed it to her face.

"I'm sorry. I haven't been able to tell anyone about this. It's been hard. No one knows about my life. I'm sorry."

"No problem. We cry all the time, don't we, Lieutenant?" Woo said.

The lieutenant nodded. "Your daughter, Dylan, does she know her half-brother, Maslow."

Grace shook her head. "Jerry didn't want Maslow to know about us. So, I didn't think so. But Dylan found out about her half brother years ago. She's always been passionately interested in knowing him. Her father was dead against it."

"And when did Dylan contact him?" this from the Chinese.

"Ahh, well, she might have been following him. I don't think they knew each other. Dylan promised her father that she wouldn't contact him. But she was angry at him and . . . you know kids. They don't always keep their promises." Grace dabbed at her eyes.

"Angry at . . . Maslow?"

"No, her father."

The two detectives exchanged glances again. Grace was afraid she'd said something she shouldn't have.

"Maybe I'm wrong. I'm just—I'm very upset. I don't know where she is, and he's missing, too. It's all so horrible. Both of them missing. It's—"

"Miss Rodriguez, did you know your daughter is seeing a psychiatrist?"

Grace was shocked. "Dylan? No. She would never—what makes you think that?"

"Do you have a photo of her?" Sanchez asked.

"Um, not with me. I can get one." Grace put the tissue to her nose. A psychiatrist? Where was this leading? Had Dylan gone crazy? Was she in a hospital?

Sergeant Woo pulled a thick stack of photos out of her purse and shuffled through them. Finally she found the one she was looking for. "Is this Dylan?"

Grace took the picture and stared at it. Her daughter's thin face stared out at her from a frame of long black hair.

"Where did you get this?" Grace was astounded.

"It was taken yesterday afternoon at Maslow Atkins's office."

"No!" Grace couldn't believe it.

"Maslow is a psychiatrist. Dylan was in treatment with him. She called herself Allegra Caldera. When we spoke with her, she was waiting for her five P.M. appointment."

Grace closed her eyes. A little tear squeezed out. She never would have imagined that her daughter could devise such a scheme. Amazing. Dylan had outwitted her father and found her own way to get to know her brother. Grace dabbed at her wet eyes. She couldn't help feeling a little surge of pride at her daughter's ingenuity. Waiting for her appointment! So there had been a man in her life. A brother. A giggle erupted from her throat like a bubble in a fish tank. Dylan had a touch of her father's deviousness. "Where is she?" she asked.

"Maslow and Dylan had a fight on Tuesday afternoon, and Dylan may be the last person who saw him before he disappeared," Woo was saying.

"What?" The fabric of Grace's suit was soaked under the arms.

"She was seen with him just before he went into the park."

Grace was confused. "But you said you saw her yesterday in his office. Did she know why you were there? Did you know who she was?"

"Yes, she knew we were looking for Maslow. No, she didn't tell us she was his sister. She was pretending to be someone else. She didn't appear to know he was missing."

"Well, how did your conversation end? Where did she go? You don't suspect her of anything . . . ?" The question hung in the air.

The Chinese woman spoke softly. "I told her I wanted to talk with her again. She said that was fine with her, gave me a fake telephone number, and took off." Sergeant Woo looked as disturbed by the whole thing as Grace was.

The lieutenant got up quickly and left the two women alone together. The Chinese detective kept her for a long time asking her many questions about Dylan's life and her activities in the last few months, but although Grace talked a great deal, she didn't seem to know her daughter very well.

FIFTY

A T HALF PAST ONE David and Brandy were back on the East Side having cheeseburgers in the Plaza Diner. Brandy had finished hers and
was chewing on one of her waffle fries when her cell phone rang. She
pulled it out of her knapsack and watched her mother's home number
pop up.

"Hey, Mom, what's up?" she answered, feeling pretty good about
herself and her day.

"Oh, God, Brandy! I'm so glad you're alive," Cheryl cried.

"Of course, I'm alive. What's the matter? You sound weird."

"Jesus H. Christ. I just got a call from a detective. That's what's the
matter. Do I need this right now? Do I?"

"Is Dad spying on you again, Mom? I thought that was all over."

"It's not that kind of detective. It's a police detective, and it's not
about *me*, Brandy. It's about *you*."

"Me? Wow."

"Where were you last night? I want to know what the fuck you've
been up to, you little bitch."

Brandy took a French fry and doused it in catsup. "Mom, you know
it hurts my feelings when you talk to me that way."

"Brandy, you get me all upset. I swear to God you're a menace. I
hate to think about it. Where the hell are you?"

"I'm in the locker room at school. I'm getting ready for gym. And you should speak a little softer. Everybody can hear you, Mom. Do you want them to think you're crazy?"

"Listen to me. I'm going to speak as loud as I fucking please, you hear me? What are you trying to do, ruin my life?"

"I don't know what you're talking about. I was at home with you. You had your plastic surgery, remember? You were feeling like shit. I was keeping you company."

"You were not keeping me company. I have no memory of that."

"Well, you remember your surgery, don't you?" Brandy had another French fry and offered one to David. He looked worried so she gave him a little squeeze under the table.

Cheryl shut up for a moment. "Look, Brandy, that is a little secret between you and me. You don't have to tell the entire world about my personal business."

"Fine, I won't mention it. But I was home with you. I can't help it if you were taking painkillers and didn't know what's going on."

"Brandy, I'm only going to ask you this once because I need to feel we have an open and honest relationship. Did you do something that requires the attention of the New York City Police Department? Tell me the truth, because your Dad is going to—"

"Uh-uh, no way."

"Fine. Good. That's all I have to hear. I will believe that." Pause. "Then how come this Lieutenant Sanchez had your name and telephone number and is coming over to talk to you?"

"I'm going to get my name in the newspaper. I may get a medal."

"You, Brandy Fabman, are going to get a medal? Excuse me, but I must have missed something."

"I told you yesterday this guy was missing in the park. And I—"

"What were you doing in the park? I thought you were with your father."

"That was Tuesday."

"What was yesterday?"

"Yesterday was Wednesday. I walked home through the park."

"The way home from school does not go through the park. And I told you—"

"Jesus. It was daylight. The park is *fine* in the daytime. Don't you want to hear my story?"

"Okay, tell me the story."

"I was walking through the park and there was this dog. It was a tracking dog, but not as great a dog as Peachy. Remember Peachy?"

Big sigh. "Yes, Brandy. I remember Peachy. He found you covered with cow manure in Montauk."

"Yes, yes." Brandy bounced in her chair. "In a nursery greenhouse. Anyway, it was so cool. These cops were asking everybody questions, you know, looking for this guy. And because of the tracking dog there, I told them all about John. I told them John's dog was much smarter than their dog. And you know what? You won't believe this, Mom. This Chinese cop, she *knew John*. She actually knew him. So, like, we have this great conversation, and I go, 'Call John and have him look for the guy.'

"And you know *what*? She did call John. Today Peachy was out there and he *found* the guy. Isn't that just amazing? I solved the case. I'm a celebrity. Maybe I should be a cop, Mom. She had this big gun. She told me I could shoot it and everything."

Another big sigh. "Brandy, why didn't you tell me all this yesterday?"

"I didn't know they'd find him."

"About the dog and the cops and all that. You didn't mention any of it. In fact, I don't remember seeing you last night. We didn't have dinner together, did we?"

"You're not going crazy like Dad said, are you, Mom?" Brandy took another French fry, dipped it in catsup, stuck out her tongue at David, showing off her tongue pierce that just drove him nuts.

"I'm not crazy," Cheryl screamed. "He just says that to get back at me."

"For what, Mom?"

"Don't change the subject. Where the hell were you last night? That's the question."

"Don't you remember? You were in this horrible mood because Aston didn't call you after your surgery. Do you think Aston won't marry you when he sees your fat lip?"

"Brandy, I don't want you talking about that."

"Okay, Mom. But you were in a stinking mood. You didn't want to order in or anything."

"Brandy, I've had a hard week. I hope you're not lying to me about this."

"How could I be lying?"

"I don't know, sweetheart." A third big sigh. "I'm just trying to heal, you know, from a truly abusive relationship. And I can't imagine your getting mixed up with police or awful people in the park. You know what I mean? People get killed in there, and I don't want you to get killed. I want you to be a healthy girl."

"I am a healthy girl. I'm going to gym, aren't I?"

"Look, this cop is coming at quarter to three on the dot. He was going to pick you up at school, but I talked him out of it. I swear to God if I didn't feel so fucking terrible I'd come and get you right now."

"Thanks Mom, I love you."

"And don't call your father about this. It's none of his business."

Brandy hung up, laughing. "She is such a flake. I swear to God."

David finished the waffle fries and ordered a brownie hot fudge sundae. "I don't feel so hot."

"Did you take your Ritalin? You know how that tears your stomach up."

"I feel funny."

"You always feel funny."

"Maybe I should call my mother."

"Yeah, go ahead."

David reached for his phone but it rang before he could dial her number.

"Mom!"

"David, I've just been pulled out of the third meeting today because of you. Why didn't you go to school this morning? Why humiliate me like this?"

"I'm really sorry. I just felt so sick. I couldn't hold my head up."

Her tone changed immediately. "What's the matter?"

"My stomach hurts. I don't know. My head hurts. I just can't concentrate when it hurts this much. I didn't want to bother you with it."

"The school called."

"I'm really sorry. I didn't want to bother you."

"You're supposed to go to the nurse when you feel bad. That's what the nurse is for."

"I know. I didn't want to make a big deal of it."

"Well, David. I hope you learned your lesson. I don't want a repeat of last year. You have to stay in communication. I thought we had an understanding about that."

"We do."

"Well, I called you about a dozen times and you didn't pick up."

"I was sleeping."

"And that wasn't the only call I got."

"I bet I can guess. Was it a cop?"

"Yes! How did you know?"

"I talked to a cop yesterday. They were taking everybody's name and number. It's no big deal."

"He's coming over to the house. I'll be there in a half an hour. I'm leaving early. I'm going to call your father, too. If the police get there before I do, I don't want you to say *anything* until I get there."

"What did he tell you?"

"He wanted to know where you were last night."

David licked his lips. "I was at home."

"I know, sweetheart. I'll see you in a few minutes."

David raised his hand for the bill. "I gotta go. He's coming to my house first."

FIFTY-ONE

MIKE STOOD WAITING outside the red-painted door of the Owens' Park Avenue apartment for a full ten minutes. He kept checking his watch and thinking of Grace Rodriguez begging them to find Dylan but not to tell anyone that she was Maslow's half-sister. First go-round with these kids was his. He was meeting April afterward. She was still trying to get the story on Dylan Rodriguez from her mother.

Finally Mrs. Owen opened the door. "Oh, I didn't hear the bell," she said, admitting him with a little flurry but no apology.

Janice Owen was a tall, big-framed, pale-faced woman in an expensive-looking gray suit and red blouse. Her fingernails were a matching fire engine red and her fine straight hair of many golden hues was more than just air or blow-dried. She wore a gold necklace of large chain links with a silver dollar–sized antique coin in the middle. A matching bracelet peeked out of one suit sleeve and a gold Rolex out of the other. Her wedding ring was a plain gold band, and her blue eyes made it clear that she was not happy to see him.

"Yes, come in. I'm Janice Owen, David's mother. I'm sorry the place is such a *mess*. The maid didn't come in today. I just got back from the office. I'm Vice *President* at York Bank," she said as if she were the only one.

"It's crazy right now. We're going through a *merger, another* one. You know how that is, officer—?"

"Lieutenant Sanchez," Mike told her. She didn't offer her hand so he didn't offer his. As for mergers, his own little company of forty thousand had merged Transit, Traffic, and Housing police not too long ago. It had caused a major shakeup among the bosses so he did know how it was. He noticed that the apartment was immaculate even without benefit of maid.

She went on, "David's father, my husband, is a corporate partner at Debevoise *Plompton*. That's the Wall Street law firm. What can we do for you?" She was very self-assured.

The foyer, painted as red as the front door and its owner's nails, was as large as Mike's living room. The four doors leading off it were all closed. Like a tugboat leading a garbage scow, Mrs. Owen brought Mike into a wood-paneled library with a huge TV, surround sound in its bookcases, a burgundy leather sofa, two black-and-white-and-red tweed armchairs, a large coffee table covered with ostrich eggs and balls made of woven twigs that had a strong pine smell. A bar in the corner featured many wine bottles, crystal glasses in various shapes, and colored liquors in fancy decanters. It was a grand place, a fantasy place. April would like it because red was a lucky color. But it was not Mike's kind of thing at all.

Janice watched his face for a reaction.

"Beautiful room," he said dutifully.

"Thank you. Please sit down." Mrs. Owen took a chair and crossed her legs.

Since the chair opposite her was about three blocks away, Mike sat on the sofa. "As I told you on the phone, Mrs. Owen, I'm here to talk with your son, David."

"Well, let's get this over with as quickly as possible. He's under a lot of stress. He's a junior in high school, and I don't want to upset him. You know how important *junior* year is for college. He has his heart set on Amherst, his father's *Alma Mater*, and that's about *the* hardest school to get into." She seemed to take it for granted that Mike would be interested in this.

"I will try not to upset him. Where is he?"

"Oh, we're always in touch. I know where he is every moment. I called him on his cell phone. He's on his way home from the *doctor*." Janice Owen was a woman who had cultivated the appearance of composure and ease. She gave Mike a comfortable smile that showed just how uncomfortable she was. "He should be here any second."

"What's wrong with him?"

"Oh, he's had the *flu* for the last few days, nothing serious." Janice tapped her fingers on her knees. "It's terrible to start the school year *sick*. It puts them at *such* a disadvantage, and he has to struggle as it is. *Documented* learning disability." She shook her head. "We've never been visited by the *police*. David is a good boy. We've never had any trouble with him at all." She finally ventured to ask the question on her mind. "What is this about?"

"Does David miss school a lot?" Mike kept on the flu story.

"Oh no, no. He doesn't miss school at all. He's a very *serious* boy. No, this week he's been *terribly* sick. He couldn't get out of bed for days. Even last weekend he was *extremely* droopy. Sometimes it happens at the beginning of the year. You know how it is, hundreds of kids, all those germs getting passed around. Would you like something to drink? I have something soft if you'd like. How about a *cookie*?"

"No thanks."

Mrs. Owen glanced at her Rolex. "What do you want to talk to David about?"

"His name came up. We're just checking on a few things."

"Do they always send lieutenants to question schoolboys?" She gave him an ingratiating smile.

"Oh sure. It's no big deal." Mike pulled on his mustache in a self-deprecating way, then took out his notebook. He started jotting down his impressions. This irritated Mrs. Owen enormously.

"Is there anything I can tell you?" she asked coldly. "I'd love to clear this up for you. I know my son very well."

"Not really, not at this time."

The front door opened and closed. "Oh, there he is, thank God!" She quit the chair in a single motion and hurried into the hall, closing the door after her.

Mike heard her voice, and the muffled sound of a boy's reply, but none of the words that passed between them. The two of them came into the library together, Janice Owen clutching her son's arm. The boy was big, very big, rumpled but well dressed. He had a sullen expression, but no worse than most of the kids his age, and he was doing just fine on his own. He didn't need his mother to prop him up.

Mike got to his feet.

"I'm sorry to keep you waiting, sir," David said politely. He glanced quickly at his mother, then back at Mike. He tried, but was not able to repossess his arm.

"This is Lieutenant Sanchez," she told him, holding on for dear life.

"You're not the guy we talked to yesterday," David remarked suspiciously.

"No, I'm not," Mike said.

"What's going on?"

Mike smiled at him and spoke in his nice-guy voice. "That's what I'm here to ask you. Your mother tells me you've missed a couple of days of school."

David hung his head. "Yes. I'm sorry. I should have gone to the nurse."

"Why don't you tell me about it," Mike suggested and sat down again.

David stood where he was and spoke mostly to his supreme authority, his mom. "I just went to a friend's house," he told her. "No big deal." He didn't seem a bit afraid of Mike.

"Would you rather talk about this at the station?" Mike asked.

"No, no!" Janice said. "That won't be necessary. He'll come clean," she said, now joking a little. "Go ahead, David, tell the officer everything and get it over with."

David stood in front of Mike as if he were on the carpet and Mike were the headmaster of his school. He lowered his chin to his chest and mumbled, "I didn't feel well. I cut school. I hung out with a friend. "I'm sorry, Mom. I know I should have told you."

"The friend's name?" Mike asked.

"Brandy Fabman."

"Jesus," Janice exploded. "That girl!"

Mike turned to her. "I'd love that glass of water you offered."

She blushed as she caught herself opening her big mouth with an editorial comment. There was no water source in the room. She couldn't send her son or her secretary from the office, or her maid, to the kitchen to get water. She had to leave the room and wait on a cop herself.

David acknowledged Mike with a respectful smile for pulling off the maneuver.

"And what did you and Brandy do?" Mike asked when she was gone.

"Today? We went out for breakfast. We walked on Madison Avenue. We went to her place. We watched videos." He blushed and scratched his head. "That's about it."

Mike picked up the blush and knew what they'd been doing. "How about yesterday?"

"Pretty much the same thing. We go to the Plaza Diner on Madison. They'll tell you we were there. It was, like, a one-time thing. Brandy was upset. Her mom had this surgery and wanted her to stay home. I was just keeping her company. I hate school."

"Oh, *David.*" Mrs. Owen came back into the room with a glass of water in her hand, shaking her head angrily. "How could you say such a thing? You love school. Without school, you'll never get ahead in life." She handed the glass of water to Mike. "Here you go."

"Thanks." Mike felt kind of sorry for the kid. Maybe he didn't want to get ahead in life. "Tell me about the dogs," he said.

"What dogs?" Now Janice Owen was really taken aback.

Forty-five minutes later, with a clear picture of David's situation at home, Mike was in the elevator on his way up to Brandy Fabman's apartment. What he'd seen was a kid involved with a girl. He was playing hooky and felt bad about lying to his mother, but didn't seem to have anything else on his conscience. A lot of kids were like that. David had a lovely home, prominent family, concerned mother. Not an uncommon picture for this, or any other part of town. The father was on his way home but didn't make it before Mike left. Mike did not think it was the right moment to bring up the pot-smoking issue. He wanted to get David alone in the station house feeling safe before he really questioned him about his comings and goings in Central Park—with the tape recorder going and another detective at his side. Maybe a woman. He had no particular female in mind, of course. They'd make a video of his statement. He'd been in the park. He wasn't clean, and none of it was part of the fiction he told his mom.

He also thought that the story about John and the dog sounded pretty odd, but kids loved animals. Mike had always wanted a dog himself. He didn't get the feeling the boy was involved in the Maslow case. David had never even heard of Maslow, had no connection to him, or motive for hurting him. But Mike was a detective and would not rule anything out. What he thought he saw was a kid seeking attention to please a girl. But there was a lot more going on than he was willing to tell in front of his mother.

At the Fabman home, Brandy opened the door before he rang the bell. She was a small girl, all excited by the visit. She was wearing jeans and a sweatshirt. She looked like any kid still in the baby fat stage.

"Hi, I'm Brandy," she said. "Were you the cop terrorizing David?"

Mike nodded. "He's a lot shorter now. I'm Lieutenant Sanchez."

"You're cute," Brandy said.

Under his mustache, Mike smiled. Then her mother wiped it off his face. Cheryl Fabman appeared and immediately took center stage. A real stunner, Brandy's mother had the looks that Janice Owen could only dream about. Slender body in a green cashmere T-shirt and matching green silk toreador pants. High heels made her legs look two miles long. She, too, had red nails and heavy gold jewelry. Maybe the nails and jewelry were symptoms of a disease called the Park Avenue Syndrome.

"Hi, I'm Cheryl, Brandy's mom. Please speak freely," she instructed him, as if she were the one doing the interview. Then she grabbed his hand and held on to it for a while.

Brandy smiled at him and showed off her tongue pierce. Cheryl turned her head, caught sight of it, and almost fell down in a dead faint. Apparently she hadn't known it was there.

FIFTY-TWO

AFTER THE POLICEMAN LEFT, Janice was too keyed up to return to work. She wanted some answers and once again she was enraged at her absent husband. She and David had been visited by the *police*. It was outrageous. Poor David was being harassed for cutting school. She did not think the police were the appropriate ones to bother her about it. This was a family matter. She talked to herself, because Bill wasn't there to consult. She was upset because the lieutenant who had come to talk to them had no education himself; he probably hadn't been to college and didn't know what David's stresses and issues were all about. The man was clearly in awe of their lovely home and envious of their situation, and he wanted to humiliate them by interrogating their child.

After the lieutenant left, David gave her no comfort *at all*. After everything she'd done for him that day, he just grunted and retreated to his room the way he always did. That left her with nothing to do but pace back and forth in front of his door, sniffing at the air flow. If the true purpose of the cop's visit had something to do with David's taking drugs, she was going to be *really* angry. She *Would Not* tolerate drugs in her home. This was definitely Bill's fault.

As she paced, Janice relived the Sunday evening several years ago when David had come home from an afternoon play date with some friends so drunk he could hardly stand up. They had gone out to an Italian restaurant for dinner despite his obvious inebriation. When David's head literally fell into his plate of spaghetti, Bill thought it was a riot. To divert them from *any* possibility of a substantive discussion about alcohol, he regaled them with stories of his own drunken days at Amherst and all the fun it had been back in the good old seventies.

"Good thing you didn't order a tomato-based sauce," he quipped, proud that his son was being initiated into manhood.

"Wait a minute. It's not the same," Janice had protested. But when she pointed out that Bill had been in college when he'd started drinking and David was only in the eighth grade—and also that it was a far more dangerous world these days—Bill had aligned himself with David in pooh-poohing her and causing her to react with more heat than she meant to. Because of Bill's lack of parenting skills all of this had happened.

Finally she knocked on his door. "David, I want to talk to you."

No answer.

She knocked again. "I'm sleeping," came the answer.

"At this hour?"

"I'm tired."

"*David!* You have a psychiatrist's appointment in half an hour. You've got to get going."

"I don't," came the sleepy reply.

"Yes, you do. Open this door right now," she bellowed.

"I don't feel well, I'm going to cancel."

"You *can't* cancel. He'll charge me anyway."

David opened the door and showed his tired face. "He won't charge you if I'm sick, will he?"

"Of course he will, he doesn't know you're not faking." Janice softened at the sight of him. Her baby.

"But what if I'm really sick?" he asked, quite reasonably, she thought.

"Well, frankly, David, he doesn't give a damn. He wants to be paid anyway. And today, you've been a bad boy. You have plenty to talk about."

"Nooooo, Mom, please. I feel like shit."

"Well, you are shit, David. I'm very angry at you for all this and so his your father."

"Is Dad here?"

"He's on his way. He was tied up in traffic."

"*He'd* say I can cancel."

"He would not. These are expensive fees, and we're paying them to make you well, so put your shoes on and get out of here." She gave him a not unfriendly swat on the bottom.

"Don't do that, Mom," he protested.

"Come on, you know your mommy loves you. Just get going and learn something useful. Then you can pass it on to me. Ha ha. I need to know what's going on with you."

"Jesus Christ," he muttered.

"And none of that language," she barked.

When he was out of the house, she breathed a sigh of relief. She hadn't wanted to show too much interest before but now she went into his room and sniffed around some more. She didn't have a clue what drugs she was searching for or what they looked like. But she had at least an hour and a half to check things out. She knew marijuana looked like oregano, and pills were pills. How hard could it be? And the paraphernalia they used for drugs was pretty self-explanatory, too. If she found it, he was never going out again.

She searched his closet, his knapsack, his bed, none of it smelled good. The sheets and pillowcase on his bed smelled horrible. The kid had to bathe more often. Use deodorant, something. She picked up rank underwear. She tried to think of everything, even went through the plastic containers the CDs came in. Nothing.

When she got to the computer, she paused. It occurred to her that David's secrets might somehow be in there. She booted the thing up and looked into the document file. There was nothing but school stuff in there. She knew he went into the internet at night. Sometimes when she woke up in the middle of the night, her phone light showed his line in use. When she pushed the intercom to find out whom he was talking with, there was only music playing softly. His download files were listed in My Docs. "David's Friends" consisted of E-mails back and forth, mostly jokes. She checked the file "Teen" and found some interesting titles. "Mommy 1" was the one she opened first.

"Jesus Christ!" Her mouth fell open when she saw what Mommy was doing with a boy about David's age. "Jesus Christ. He's a pervert."

She didn't know whom to call first. The psychiatrist who was treating David, or her husband, Bill. She opened "Mommy and Daddy" and couldn't believe her eyes. This was worse than drugs, worse than bad grades, worse than ADD. Her son was a *pervert* of the worst kind. She called her husband. Bill's secretary answered.

"I need to talk to my husband."

"Bill's gone for the day."

"Where did he go?"

"He didn't say."

"When did he leave?"

"Oh, an hour ago, maybe longer."

Janice swore and tried his cell phone, but Bill must have turned it off. Like his son, he broke the connection whenever he didn't want her to reach him. She hated to break down and have a drink to calm her nerves, so she got more and more disturbed about the whole family situation as she waited for them to come home.

FIFTY-THREE

M IKE WAS BACK AT MIDTOWN NORTH at half past four. He was ru-
minating about Brandy Fabman's acting out with the tongue
pierce, the tight sweaters, the beer drinking/pot smoking in Central
Park, and, of course, the playing hooky, all to compete with her sexy divorcée mother. The boy was obviously smitten by her. Their stories
were the same. They claimed that what they'd been attracted to—the
sole reason they'd been targeted by police on the scene—was their interest in dog tracking. They'd been drawn to the scene by the appearance of Slocum's dog, Freda. April said there was something odd about
them. There was certainly something upsetting about them. But did
they know anything about Maslow Atkins? Had they known Pee Wee
James? He wasn't sure yet.

When he returned to the station, the detective rooms were still
mobbed. April was in her office with Assistant DA Leonore Jacobi. The
two were in deep conversation when he came in and occupied the
empty chair. The DA was a small thin woman with a face that was all
jutting bones and nervousness who liked to grab people by the hand
and hold on, peering deeply into their eyes. She did that to Mike as
soon as he plopped down beside her.

"Hey, Mike, nice to see you. You look like a different guy," she said,
locking him in one of her famous visual embraces. "Nice shirt. Well,
this case *definitely* needs your touch," she joked.

Even though their moment together had been short-lived and long ago, she was giving him the treatment just for the fun of it, and he liked her the better for it. April was inscrutable.

"Same here, Leo. Haven't seen you around in a while. You look great, nice haircut, nice suit." He smiled at her cap of short curly black hair and the newest look in fall suits, winter white in a heavy fabric that was definitely rushing the season. Her nails were still bitten to the quick, her cuticles were bloody, and she'd eaten off all her cinnamon-stick lipstick. Only the dark lip liner remained. Same old Leonore.

"It's too heavy. I'm sweating like a pig," she said, writhing on the chair a little for him.

Mike blew air through his nose, laughing. "Well, better to sweat like one than look like one. Speaking of pigs, *querida*, you still with that deadbeat boyfriend of yours?"

Leonore glowed with the attention. "Yeah, Sam's still defending the bad guys. We try not to talk about it over dinner. He thinks he'll flip me one day." She smiled at Mike, radiant. "You've been reading about those death row cases in Illinois?"

"Uh-uh. Tell me about it."

"This is no joke. They've started testing the DNA of convicted rape/murders on death row. Turns out more than one in ten is innocent in Illinois. They had to stop executing there. I wouldn't want to get arrested in a state like Texas. Makes you wonder, don't it?" Another big smile at Mike.

"Hey, the meter's running," April murmured.

Leonore turned to her. Smooth. "Thank God we know what we're doing here in New York. Maybe some day we'll have an accredited lab. What do you have, Mike?"

"Not a lot. Two kids who like dogs and play hooky. What do you have, April?"

April made a face and glanced at her pages of notes. "I've got a mess. A real weird puzzle. I talked to Grace Rodriguez for almost two hours. She works for Atkins's father and has been his girlfriend for twenty-three years. Same old same old. She loved the guy, thought he would leave the wife he hates and marry her. She's a very attractive woman, didn't you think, Mike?" she glanced at him.

"Not my type. I never liked blonds."

April smiled. "I'm not touching that. So two decades pass, and no wedding bells. That would be enough to make any mother crazy."

"Eh, lot of people don't get married anymore. Who needs it?" Leonore cracked.

"Some of us are still traditional, Leo," Mike replied, looking at April and liking her smile.

Leonore snickered. "God, if *you're* talking this way, the world must be coming to an end."

April was smooth, too. She went right on. "Well, apparently being illegitimate bothered Dylan pretty bad. Grace said she's been worried about her daughter's mental health for some time. Atkins hates psychiatrists and didn't want her to go to anyone. Grace was torn between the two of them, wanted to be a good mother, wanted to protect her boyfriend. I felt sorry for her."

Mike shifted in his chair. He still didn't understand how this all fit together. If Dylan was the center of the case, where did Brandy and David fit in?

"What?" April responded to the unasked question.

"Nothing. Go on with your story."

"Dylan applied to the analytic institute where Maslow was a candidate, gave a false name and identity, and for about four months her own brother was her analyst. A first. Relatives aren't supposed to treat each other, you know. According to Jason Frank, who's Maslow's supervisor on the case, Maslow was anxious about it from day one. Something must have tipped him off on Tuesday. That night he wanted to see Jason, but he disappeared." April sat back. "She could be some kind of psycho."

Leonore chewed on her fingers. Mike reached into his pocket for a breath mint. "Miss lunch again?"

"Thanks." She took one and handed the tin across the desk to April.

"Is it lunchtime already?" April looked surprised.

"It's dinnertime," Leonore said. "Do we have a hypothesis?"

April sighed. Mike knew she was thinking that twenty-four hours ago Pee Wee James had been alive. And Pee Wee had known something. And it was his fault for not listening to her. He shook his head. *Burro.*

April chewed on a mint. "When I talked to Dylan yesterday, she maintained her identity as his patient, Allegra Caldera. Maybe she took off. Maybe she's a killer."

Woody knocked on the door. "Coffee, two lights, Sweet 'n Low, one tea?"

"Thanks, Woody," April said.

"Hey, Mike," Woody greeted him.

"Pull up a pew," Mike said. There was no chair, but then he didn't like Woody much.

"Yeah, sure. Where are we?" He leaned against the wall, sipping his light coffee as April dipped a Lipton's tea bag into her Styrofoam cup of hot water.

"Pathological sibling rivalry. Maybe Dylan killed her brother to be her dad's only child and heir," Mike said.

"Nice," Woody said. "But I don't think so. That girl was a doll, don't you think?" He held up a flier with her picture on it. *Have you seen this girl?* And the number to call. The phones were ringing off the hook. The manpower to answer them was a major problem. Culling through each tip took forever.

April gave Woody some credit. "Good touch, the camera, Woody. And you noticed how freaky she got when you took her picture?"

Woody gazed at the photo. "It's quite a story," he murmured.

"Look, I've got to get going." Leonore slapped her hands on her knees and stood. "I'll talk to my boss about this. Whatever it is—kidnapping, murder. Get a warrant to search the girl's place. Maybe something there can shed light on all this." She gave April a conspiratorial smile. "What about you, Mike?"

"Well, April's friend John Zumech thinks this is a Vietnam thing."

"No kidding, why?"

"They trained the dog trackers there with human body parts so they could find the Vietcong hiding in the tunnels."

Leonore threw up her hands. Where was this going?

"The vic was a Vietnam vet," April said.

"I don't know anything about any tunnels in Vietnam. Are you suggesting we have tunnels in Central Park?" Leonore asked impatiently.

"He's referring to the soft tissue finds," April translated.

Mike nodded. "Zumech's theory is the tissue was a plant, you know, maybe as a hoax or a message of some kind about Vietnam."

"What kind of message, and why does it have to be something to do with Vietnam? Why not something else?" Leonore gathered up her stuff. She didn't like this angle.

"Like what?"

"Like a medical student hoax?" April threw in. "Maslow is a doctor. Maybe he was treating a doctor nut. Are there other possibilities?"

"I'm just quoting John. He's convinced this tissue thing has something to do with Vietnam. Pee Wee was a vet."

"I'm not following you on this one," Leonore said.

"The tissue samples turned up the day after Slocum's search with his dog," Mike went on.

"You're suggesting that someone saw the rescue dog on the news, then came out and planted the tissue samples later? Why?" April demanded.

"It wasn't my hypothesis. It was John's," Mike replied.

"What about the killing of Pee Wee? Who would kill him?" Leonore drew blood on a cuticle, checked her watch. She wasn't interested in this. Too far-fetched.

"Maybe Pee Wee really did see Maslow out there. Maybe someone didn't want him sobering up enough to tell what happened," April said.

"I don't see what this has to do with the tissue finds. It wouldn't have taken a dog to find them. Look, I've got to run."

"Maybe they were planted to cover Maslow's scent. Yesterday we were searching for Maslow. Maybe we would have found him today. We didn't even have time to get Peachy on the trail. The dog was distracted from the word go." April looked unhappy. "Mike, how did your interview go with those two kids? Did you meet their parents?"

Mike paused. "The boy, David Owen, looks like something of a nerd. His mother is a big shot at the bank where she works. Public relations, and *Dios*, did she work a public relations number for the kid. I get the feeling he's a major disappointment. Right in front of me she says he has ADD. I didn't see any signs of hyperactivity. He didn't act aggressive or even angry. He was very polite to me. But what do I know? I'm a cop." Mike shrugged modestly.

Leonore was interested. "Medication?" she asked.

"Maybe, for ADD. I'd call the kid a loser. But we'll have to dig a little more. A few weeks ago we had a case of a kid freaking out in school, burning people with cigarettes. He put out someone's eye. When we asked why he did it, he said it seemed like a good idea at the time. He didn't even know the kid he injured."

Leonore shook her head. "I'll never have children. So, where was David Owen last night?"

"At home in his bed. His mother said he had the flu. He's missed school for two days because of it."

"Not true," April cut in quickly. "She's either lying or doesn't know what she's talking about. Yesterday afternoon he was out in the park with his knapsack looking pretty healthy to me." She sipped her tea and grimaced at the taste. "What kind of mother?"

"She seemed very concerned. Kept saying, 'I love this boy.' She was out at a party last night. The father was at work."

"So no one was home to confirm he was there." Leonore perked up. "What about the girl?"

Mike pulled on his mustache. "The girl is a whole other thing."

"I'll say," Woody remarked.

"Her mother's a recent divorcée, recently restructured. She wanted to give me a private viewing of her new butt."

April made a face. "Where was her daughter last night?"

"She said she was at home and Brandy was with her the whole evening." Mike smiled.

"Well, if this is all we've got, you two have a lot of work to do. You have my number. Let me know when you have an autopsy report." Leonore pecked Mike on the cheek before heading out the door.

"Good working with you again," he murmured.

"Yeah, sure. Bye, April, take care." With that she marched out.

April turned to Baum. "Woody, we need a search warrant for Dylan Rodriguez's apartment. Get on it," April ordered.

"Can I finish my coffee?" he asked.

"At your desk."

He pushed himself off the wall, went out, and closed the door.

"What's that all about?" Mike said.

"He almost ran me down this morning. So, you slept with her, too." April clicked her tongue.

Mike looked shocked. "Naw."

"Looked to me like the two of you have something going."

"She's got a serious boyfriend. They've been together for years. What's the matter with you?"

"Doesn't matter, I can tell."

"Naw. She's nice, though, isn't she?"

"Who dumped who?"

"The whole thing, *nada*. Two ships passing in the night."

"My mother warned me about the perfume. I absolutely despise womanizers."

"Maybe a long time ago, but that's all over. If a man has a perfect woman, why keep looking?"

She tilted her head to one side, like a bird, considering. He smiled. One good thing about April was she could move on. She moved on now. "This is some kind of bizarre kid thing, isn't it?" she murmured.

"Looks like."

"What's your take?" She swiveled in her chair.

"We need to bring them in and talk to them together. There's something here. I know it."

"It's the dog, isn't it?" she said. "We keep getting back to that."

"Yeah, it's the dog thing. No doubt about it."

FIFTY-FOUR

A FEW MINUTES LATER April called the ME's office to find out if the autopsy on Pee Wee was done yet. As she hung on the phone in her office, she thought about Grace Rodriguez in the dark about the activities of her own child, about Mike and how much she loved him. She thought about Skinny Dragon's wanting the best for her like any mother, and like many mothers, not getting it quite right. Skinny had spent many hours educating her about all the Pernicious Influences in the bodily landscape that led to trouble with men. Skinny had learned these things from the Chinese "fake" doctors she consulted frequently in Chinatown.

Chinese medicine was complicated. It dictated that the precipitating factors in illness could be external, as in the case of attacking diseases, or they could be internal, arising from one of the seven emotions. Running from woman to woman was one of those disharmonies that was caused by emotion rather than germs. Mike told her she was the perfect woman. If he believed it, then happiness must be the cause of his problem.

According to Skinny Dragon, excess joy scatters the *Shen Qi*—heart energy. Skinny warned that men get reckless when feeling too good. The heart gets muddled and uncontrolled and can't be contained. Skinny herself worked on the principle that being mean to her husband and daughter was good for them. Happy, soft-hearted people were notorious for wasting their money and bodily *Qi* outside the house. The Dragon was dead set against that. April tapped her fingers impatiently, waiting for the ME.

After a long time, Dr. Gloss came on the line.

"This is Dr. Gloss."

"Sergeant Woo, Midtown North."

"Oh, hi there, April, interesting case."

"Tell me."

"I haven't got anything down on paper yet, but this guy James was a walking disaster."

April had known Pee Wee for a year or two and wasn't surprised. "What killed him?"

"Oh, he had lung cancer and cirrhosis of the liver, and a number of other things that must have made his life pretty uncomfortable, including gangrene in his left foot. Let's put it this way, the man didn't exactly have a bright future. But I'll give it to you in a nutshell. He has a number of bumps on his head, recent cuts and bruises on his face. Looks like he was beaten repeatedly with a branch. Tree bark and leaf particles in his wounds. Big hematomas on his chest. Looks like he'd been stomped and kicked in the side, too. A real brutal thing. He was lying down during the attack. There were no defense wounds on his hands . . . scalp lacerations on his forehead. The important head injury, however, was on the right side of his head. It put quite a dent in his squash and caused a subdural hematoma. Blood clot on the brain to you. Here's the interesting part. When the skull is cracked like an egg and begins to bleed inside, there's no place for the blood to go except down to the brain stem, and when it does that, the brain gets choked. Death comes fast. But this was a focal injury, in one spot, and it caused slow bleeding in his brain that occurred over a period of many hours. If he had been a healthy person in a car wreck, and been taken to a hospital promptly, we could have saved him." Gloss paused.

Pee Wee had left the precinct at noon. When April last saw him, he'd just peed in his pants. He'd been drunk but had no head injury. "What are you suggesting?" she asked.

"Well, depressed in the hair and scalp were fragments of cement and brick. You know what these homeless guys die of most frequently?" the ME asked.

"Exposure."

"Exposure is not a cause of death, April. No, a lot of these guys die because they drink too much or take an overdose and fall down."

"Dr. Gloss, the man was badly beaten and someone cut off his finger. You're not going to tell me he died falling down."

"Well, the cause of death is a subdural hematoma, but his skull depression was probably caused by a sidewalk."

"You're telling me he fell down?" April was incredulous.

"Or he was pushed down. Anyway, he got up and maybe walked around for a while."

"With his brain bleeding? Is that possible?" April asked.

"It's possible."

"Then later somebody beat him with a tree branch. Was he alive when his finger was cut off?" April said.

"Yes, but probably unconscious, one hopes so."

"Can you give me a time frame?"

"I'd say he died between eight to twelve hours ago. Some time between midnight and three."

April thought about it. The sidewalk did it some time after noon. What did Pee Wee do after he left the precinct? When did he enter the park? He met someone there and was attacked, and sometime between midnight and three, he died. Ducci, the dust and fiber man, had his clothes and the bagged items they'd found in the area. The park bench had been dusted for fingerprints. If they were lucky something would come up.

The DA wasn't going to like it, but her boss would. There wouldn't be too much paperwork, and no one was going to blame the death on what might or might not have happened in the station house. No one beat him with a sidewalk there. No fodder for Internal Affairs in this.

Gloss was still talking. "Another interesting thing. There were some small black flecks on the dead man's clothes. At first we thought it was car paint, but there were several little chips and one bigger one, and they were brittle but nowhere near as hard as the spray paint used on cars. Our guess is nail polish. Ducci will know."

"Black nail polish? So there was a woman involved," April said.

"That's right. My guess is that maybe he attacked her."

"With a dent in his squash?"

"Head trauma victims can get pretty aggressive sometimes. As I said, they don't collapse right away."

"So you think he got into an argument with a woman. She fought him off, chipped her nail polish, and hacked off his finger while he lay dying. I've heard of revenge, but this seems a little extreme. The amputation was pretty messy. What did she use, anyway? The nail clipper?"

"A knife. Obviously not a very big one, maybe a boning knife."

"How about a razor?" April asked. Dylan used razor blades for her tummy cuts. But she wasn't wearing nail polish yesterday when April saw her.

"Uh-uh. Not sturdy enough. Maybe a pocketknife. Or a small Swiss Army knife. Would have been a struggle though, if he were awake."

"Maybe that's how the nail polish got chipped."

"Did I say he was lying down?"

"Yes, you mentioned it. Okay, I guess I'm getting a picture. It was a savage attack and he was already pretty out of it," April said at last.

"Do you have anyone in mind for the assault?"

"Nothing solid yet. Thanks," April said.

"We'll have a full report in a few days," Gloss told her.

Few weeks would probably be more like it, April thought. Poor Pee Wee. She sat brooding at her desk. Now she knew some of the physical evidence they were looking for—the knife that had cut off Pee Wee's finger, black nail polish. Diaries, letters, anything to indicate state of mind. The problem was they had been looking in the wrong places. She peered out the window of her office at the swarm of detectives in the squad room. She knew Brandy Fabman had been one of Pee Wee's attackers. Now she was worried about Maslow, really worried.

She dialed John Zumech to give him the news.

He answered on the first ring.

"Hey, John," April said.

"April, I was just going to call you. What happened to you this morning?" he demanded.

"I had to follow up a lead. Sorry, I didn't mean to run off. Anyway, we have a preliminary death report on James. Gloss says he fell, and the sidewalk hit his head. But he bled for hours and had plenty of time to get into a fight and have his finger cut off before he died."

"Sounds complicated."

"Yes, and I'm bothered by how it all fits together. I'm thinking maybe Pee Wee knew where Maslow is. When I was questioning him, he kept telling me about someone who was taking care of him, paying him off. Maybe he hid Maslow somewhere, then moved him later. Anyway I think he's still in the park." The pressure to get going was killing her, but she didn't want to start with the bad news.

"How can I help?" John asked.

"How well do you know Central Park? Maybe we missed something. What about tunnels or hiding places we don't know about? There must be maps or something that would show everything over and under the ground. Surveys, whatever."

"I don't know anything about maps and plans. Parks Department would have that." Zumech was sounding very cold.

"It was just a thought. It popped into my head." April wondered what was up with him. "You know, I can't help thinking, if Maslow isn't on top of the ground, he may be under the ground. We know Peachy can find a buried man. She's done it before. What do you say we try again?"

"Well, she could if there's a breathing hole for his scent to escape," Zumech said slowly.

"But even if Maslow's scent is gone from, say, the street, I could still show you where Slocum's dog was working and where she got stuck. We could take it from there," April suggested.

"Fine, I'll do it. Do you have a clean scent item?"

"I can get you one."

"You get it, I'll be there in an hour."

"John, I really appreciate this, but I think I'm hearing something in your voice." Now she could tell him the bad news.

"I was going to call you about those soft tissue finds we had this morning. I knew there was something weird about them."

"For sure," April murmured. She could feel him squirm on the phone.

"Well, I think I know where they came from."

"Where did they come from, John?"

"When my wife got home from work a few minutes ago, she thanked me for cleaning up the garage. And the thing is, April, I didn't. I planned to, but I never got around to it. You know how it is."

April chewed on that for a moment. "You had body parts in your garage, John?" she said finally.

"Yeah, for training the dogs. I don't use it anymore. I can get the scent mail order—anything I want, fear, death. Fear is good when you're tracking escaped prisoners. I forgot about it. But my wife was always complaining about the smell. It was gone this morning. April, I'm reeling over this. I can't believe it."

"We'll have to dust your place for prints, John. I hope your wife didn't clean up."

"Well, let's just say I have a good guess who did it. I'm not happy about it, in fact I'm pretty sick. It isn't going to look good for me."

"Your little friends Brandy and David. They may have killed Pee Wee."

"Oh God, that's bad. You pick them up. I'm on my way."

April hung up. John had kept human tissue in his garage. Nobody here was looking good. She decided she'd call Jason and tell him first. David Owen had a shrink. That meant there had to be something major wrong with him, right? Now they had three kids in trouble. Only Dylan had a motive for hurting Maslow. But to April's eye, that sad sack of a girl wasn't looking like much of a suspect now.

FIFTY-FIVE

MASLOW STRIPPED OFF HIS T-SHIRT and gently put it under Allegra's head. He probed her skull with his fingers. Some lumps and bumps. No tears in her scalp or face that he could feel. Without a wig, her head was much smaller than he'd thought, and her own hair was very short, like a pixie's. This surprised him. He couldn't imagine why she'd worn a wig or what she looked like without it, but none of that mattered. Keeping her alive was his concern right now. Her pulse was strong. She moaned as he struggled with the laces tied around her swollen wrists.

"How are you doing?" he asked.

"Ahhh."

"Sorry, can't help it." He picked at the knots, ignoring her groans, and finally worked the last one loose.

"Oww. That kills," she sobbed, sucking in her breath as her arms were freed.

"Hang in there. Good girl."

"I'm dying," she whimpered. "I don't care."

"Uh-uh. Don't die. I can't lose you now." He chafed her hands, then gently rubbed her wrists to get the circulation going. She made crying noises.

"Don't."

"You're doing okay," he assured her.

"Oww."

"How's that, better?" He rubbed life back into her arms and hands.

"It kills. My leg!"

"We'll get it out. You'll be fine," he assured her.

But in the dimming light, she didn't look so fine. Her body was curled in an awkward position and her nose was badly smashed to one side. She yelped when he touched the leg caught under the gate.

"Owww."

Hunger gnawed at Maslow, but he was moving now, his body beginning to obey his commands. He felt nauseated and needed water, but knew that Allegra needed it more. She was dehydrated, and he was afraid she was going to go into shock. He was shivering pretty badly himself and had to get them out of there.

Beyond the bushes, the light was fading. He feared their captors got active at night. He didn't want to be there when they came back. He crouched in front of the mouth of the cave. It wasn't very big and now he saw how they were trapped inside. The gate blocking the entrance was about thirty-six inches wide and had bars at four-inch intervals. The smell of rust was strong in the damp air. The gate was clearly very old.

He called, then listened. Nothing. Called again. Then he felt the bars one by one. The sharp, scaling metal cut his fingers. The bottom and sides were still sturdy, but the vertical bars were thinner and he could feel that many of them had rusted nearly all the way through. The gate itself was no higher than three feet, but there were only a few inches of space above it, not enough to climb over it. Inside the cave, sand was still falling from above. More of the ceiling might collapse at any time. Maslow was worried about the circulation in Allegra's ankle. Soon she would lose her foot. He tested the gate. If he could lift it a few inches, he could ease the weight on her ankle. He could move her foot out.

"Oww," she screamed.

"If you can bear just a little more, I think I can get your foot out."

"Stop!"

"Just a little more."

Her voice croaked. "No. I have to tell you something."

"Sure, as soon as we're out."

"No! Now!"

"In five minutes, I'll have you out of here. I promise."

Her voice was angry and tearful. "I'm going to die in here, and you won't listen."

He kept working.

"You never *listen!*"

"Allegra—"

"I'm not Allegra. I'm Dylan. I'm your sister."

Silence. Maslow was trying to lift the gate and save the girl's foot. He didn't want to argue. "You're my sister." Whatever. She was very good at stories.

"Owww. Stop! Your father is my father." She took a few gulping breaths of air. "I wanted to meet you. That's all. It was like a hunger I can't even explain."

Stunned, Maslow sat back on his heels. Pain blasted through the muscles and torn skin of his calves.

"What?" He stared at her dirty, battered face, nausea sucking at his gut.

"Jerome Atkins is my daddy."

Maslow's brain swirled back four months. In her written biography, she'd described a father unwell and crippled who'd needed help going to the bathroom. In great detail, she described the outhouse behind the modest house where they'd lived and how her father had abused her there from the time she was five or six.

"He didn't want you to know."

Maslow shook his head as if he had water in his ear. "How do *you* know?" he asked softly.

"I saw a newspaper article about him when I was ten. Some award he got. It mentioned your mother and you. I was—it was horrible. After that, there hasn't been a day of my life that I didn't think about you." Allegra was having trouble breathing.

"Shh. You don't have to—"

"I want to tell you. I wasn't supposed to know you. Daddy was with you on holidays. He was with me and my mom the day before or the day after. Sometimes you went away on vacation, and we'd wait for him to come home. We were shadows. I felt like a shadow person." She panted. "I was always a shadow person."

Maslow felt the nausea rise and water fill his mouth. He could hear the rats scuffling nearby, waiting for another chance at them. He didn't want to wretch.

"I kept trying to tell you the truth about Daddy, but you wouldn't listen."

Maslow closed his eyes. No more confessions. He had to get them out of there. He didn't want her to use up her energy and die, didn't want to throw up and be useless because of what she was telling him.

"That day I called you—well, I'd called you before. At first I just called to hear your voice."

"How did you get my phone number?" he asked.

"I got it from information."

Of course. He was a doctor, anyone could find him.

"I listened to your voice on tape. And one day, you answered."

Maslow remembered it well.

"You thought I wanted to be your *patient*. And then before I could say anything, you were giving me times that you were available."

"Jesus." Maslow was rubbing her hands furiously. Small hands, like his.

"Owww."

Bites. She had rat bites on her hands. Maybe one on her cheek, too. Her nose was a mess, she was going to lose her foot soon; and she wouldn't stop talking.

"I'd wanted to meet you for so long, and there you were inviting me to come and see you. Just like that. It was like God coming down from heaven and making my dream come true. You didn't ask who I was or what I wanted. You just gave me a time and told me where to go. And when I met you, you looked like Daddy, like me, but you didn't see it. You asked me what my name was. I don't know, I just said the first thing that came to mind."

"We have to get going." It was too terrible. Maslow didn't want to hear any more.

"And then we made another appointment for a few days later. I was so excited. I had planned to tell you that first day. But you were so nice to me. You asked me all kinds of questions. How could I tell you I was just a nobody, with a nothing story. Nobody ever hit me or hurt me in any way. I wasn't starving. I went to school. It wasn't like I was *deprived* at all. What could my complaint be? Last year I took a course on domestic abuse, so I made up a story like that. I wanted to tell you the whole truth, everything. But I liked being with you. I liked the interest you took in me. It was your idea that you analyze me. I never would have thought of it."

"Oh God!" He was such a jerk. Maslow could see just how it happened. His nausea overwhelmed him. The subway rumbled and a clump of dirt fell from the ceiling behind them. What if she was right and they were going to die in there? He turned away and gagged. A little sour acid came out of him, nothing more. His head spun, and she was still talking.

"I knew, as a patient, I could see you five days a week, every week. But if I told you I'm your sister, who knew what you would do. I felt really bad. On Tuesday I was going to tell you no matter what, but you brushed me off."

"I have to lift this gate, Allegra," he said. "So we can get out of here."

"My name is Dylan Rodriguez and I don't care that I'm dying."

"Oh God." That was what Chloe had said.

Dylan stopped talking. She'd told him what she wanted him to know and now she was finished. The gate was wedged in such a way that he couldn't get it up. Frustration at so many ruined lives made him howl like a dog at the rats in the corner, the shadows in the night.

FIFTY-SIX

CHERYL WAS FUSSING AROUND in her new kitchen with the music on and the door half closed. She didn't have any particular intention of cooking anything, but she wanted to make things nice. Her decorator had considered his job done when the appliances were in and the wallpaper was up, so it was up to her to arrange the small appliances and even the utensils. Because of her surgery last week and a number of other things on her mind, Cheryl hadn't gotten to it until now. At the moment, she was trying to decide which was better next to the sink, the Cuisinart or the coffeemaker. Or maybe the toaster oven.

The plain truth was she'd had it with recovery. She wanted to go out and do something, but two things prevented her from taking off. The day was pretty much over in Manhattan, and she didn't think it was such a good idea to go out with things so unsettled with Brandy. Therefore, she was stuck in the house with nothing to do.

She needed the comfort of a man and called Aston at his office.

"Mr. Gluckselig's office."

"Is Aston there?" Cheryl asked.

"Who may I say is calling," his bitch of a secretary asked.

"Cheryl Fabman."

"Oh, Miss Fabman, he's out of the office on vacation this week."

Cheryl was shocked. He hadn't told her he was going anywhere. "Where?" she demanded.

"I'm not at liberty to say." The sweet tone was pure gloat.

Cheryl hated her, and hated Aston, too. She was terribly upset. It was Thursday. That meant she had a whole weekend to wonder what it meant. She chewed on her new lips, worrying as she moved things around on the countertops. She had no idea what the whole thing with Brandy was all about, didn't want to think about it, but brooded about it anyway.

Maybe she was upset about the divorce. People said divorce was bad for kids. Well, it was bad for her, too. She didn't have as much money as before. Her lifestyle had shrunk to nothing. And she couldn't just pick up and go to Jamaica like Aston could. Maybe the toaster oven was better next to the refrigerator. Cheryl checked her watch. Brandy had been in her room ever since the detective left. Cute guy. He didn't seem put off by Brandy in her motor-mouth mode. And her wacko story seemed to sit okay with him. He didn't know Brandy like she did.

Sometimes the kid didn't say anything for days, and then suddenly she was talking a mile a minute and wouldn't shut up. Jesus Christ, why couldn't Brandy be more like her? Cheryl considered going in and talking to her again. But what was the point? The little bitch was sulking now. It occurred to Cheryl that she was not able to handle her daughter, and that was very unsettling, too. She wasn't having a good day.

She chewed on her new lips, which felt weird but looked great. She looked so great she wanted to cry. In her brand-new kitchen a shooting pain in her side made Cheryl double over and almost fall to the floor. She knew the stabbing pain meant she missed Seymour and the life they used to have together. He happened to be a big slob and snored like a horse, but she'd known him for twenty years. And even if she did aim for a richer man to marry next, it wasn't so easy to land one. Seymour had done everything she ever asked of him, except forgive her for one *tiny* slip. It seemed unfair.

And worse, he was recovering from it, had a new girlfriend who Brandy said was really nice when they went out to dinner together. Prettier and nicer than her, and much younger, the little bitch had been thoughtful enough to report. Cheryl felt the tears coming. Jesus Christ, how could that child of hers cause her so much pain. One child was all she'd wanted. Why did it have to be such a difficult one?

She sighed deeply a few times, sat down at the counter on one of the stools her decorator had bought. She'd specified only two stools because she'd hoped Aston would marry her before the year was out and they would move to a bigger place. She was feeling awfully low. What if she had to stay in a six-room apartment forever? She wondered if Brandy was part of the problem of landing Aston. What if he didn't marry her because Brandy was such a brat? What if Brandy went to college and left her alone? Cheryl poured herself a glass of wine and thought about Seymour with a younger woman enjoying what should be hers. She thought of him, worry-free and happy without her and Brandy.

Why should he be free of responsibility at a time like this, she asked herself. Shouldn't they be in conference on this, consulting on how to handle their mutual daughter? Shouldn't they present a unified front to her? Shouldn't they be thinking about the importance of family and pulling together in a time of crisis? Shouldn't they be talking about getting back together again before it was too late?

She thought about all this and poured herself another glass of wine. Seymour didn't have a God damn thing to say about anything. In their marriage he'd given new meaning to the term silent partner, but maybe he'd changed. She checked her watch, then picked up the phone and dialed his office number. He was still there at seven-thirty.

"See?"

"Who's this?" he said gruffly.

"It's Cheryl. Please don't hang up. If you don't want to talk to me, just listen."

Silence on the other end.

"How are you?" she chirped.

"I'm fine, Cheryl, but I'm very busy. What do you want?"

"I've been thinking about you, honey, just wondering how you are. You know."

"I'm fine, Cheryl. Is that it?"

"No, I wondered if you ever feel, you know, sad about the family?"

Silence on the other end. Cheryl didn't let the silence unnerve her. She knew Seymour very well. He hadn't a clue whether he felt sad or not. He was like a tank on a battlefield. Whatever was going on around him, all he did was keep moving forward. Now she let the idea of sadness sink in a little.

"How do you find Brandy?"

His voice took on an edge. "What do you mean by that?"

"Well, you're seeing her regularly. She's pretty happy about that. How do you find her?"

"What are you talking about, Cheryl?"

"Your visits with Brandy," Cheryl said impatiently. "You took her to dinner at the Posthouse just two days ago. She had a steak. How did she seem to you?"

"Cheryl, I don't know what you're talking about. I haven't had dinner with Brandy in three weeks. She doesn't want to see me."

Cheryl was stunned. "You're kidding?"

"Why would I lie about something like that?"

"Um." Cheryl was at a loss for words.

"Did Brandy tell you she's been with me?" Seymour asked.

"Yes, she did."

"A lot?"

"Yes, she's been with you a lot."

"What about Tuesday night?"

"Yes, Seymour, she was with you Tuesday night. You went to the Posthouse. Is it coming back now?"

"No, she was not."

"And you know what, a police detective came to see us tonight. Brandy has been cutting school."

A very long silence. "Well, you know, she comes over to my place when I'm at work sometimes. I know she's done it at least once. The maid told me. What do the police want with her?"

So that's where Brandy went. She hung out at her dad's. Cheryl made an exasperated noise.

"She said she was interested in the tracking dog searching for that man who disappeared in the park. Apparently, she got to talking to some cops about it and they wrote down her name."

"Didn't I see something on the news about it?"

"I don't know, See. What's going on with her?"

"How would I know? She won't see me, Cheryl."

"This is very disturbing. Maybe we should meet and talk about it," Cheryl said brightly.

"I don't want to meet, Cheryl."

"Seymour, your daughter is in trouble." It was only reasonable. She'd wear something serious-looking; nothing provocative. He'd see how great she looked. And she'd be sweet, she'd be forgiving. She'd appeal to his sense of family, responsibility.

Seymour raised his voice on the phone. "And why is she in trouble, Cheryl? Why doesn't her mother know where she is most of the time?"

"Just wait one little second. Don't blame me for Brandy's problems. You're the one who dragged the family through the mud with that horrible lawsuit." Cheryl felt the rage rising again.

Seymour clicked his tongue. "This is ridiculous. Put her on the line."

"But I'm not finished."

"Put her on the line, Cheryl."

"Maybe we should do family therapy." Conciliatory again.

"Maybe we should have when I suggested it three years ago."

"You didn't," Cheryl protested.

Seymour sighed on the other end of the line. Cheryl hated that sigh. "Forget it, I'll call her myself."

He hung up. A few seconds later the phone rang and Brandy's line lit up. It rang four times then stopped. The eight-thousand-dollar phone system had caller ID. Seymour's name popped up on the screen. Brandy could not fail to know who was on the line. Curious, Cheryl got up and went to Brandy's door and opened it. The phone was ringing, but Brandy wasn't there to answer it.

FIFTY-SEVEN

Brandy and David met in front of Bloomingdale's. On Thursdays the store was open until nine. Brandy wanted to have a makeover for the TV shows she was going to be on, but David was already waiting for her when she got off the bus on Lexington. She'd taken a bus because all she had was four dollars and an ATM card for an account that had no money in it. Her father was always at least two weeks late with the alimony checks just to make her mother angry, and her mother was a big spender. She always needed it bad. Right now Cheryl and she were penniless. It was no problem to live off the credit cards, but Cheryl had taken away Brandy's cards to punish her for lying, and Brandy hadn't had a chance to steal them back yet.

David crossed the street to meet her. She gave him a peck on the cheek the way Cheryl did with her boyfriend, Aston, and was disappointed that he didn't look happier to see her.

"What's the matter?" she asked, hoping he didn't think she was a dork for using public transportation.

"This sketchy-looking detective with cowboy boots asked my mom all kinds of questions about me. She's freaking out. She hates cops." He looked angry about it.

Brandy laughed. "He talked to my mom, too. She thought he was cool and asked him if he was single. Totally inappropriate as usual." Still laughing, Brandy grabbed his arm and steered him across the street. "Isn't this cool?"

"Tcheesh. Where are we going?"

"Bloomingdale's."

"Oh, no," he cried. "I can't stand that place."

"We can get something to eat in the restaurant there."

Brandy was excited. She went through Bloomingdale's revolving door, and glanced at the stairs leading down to the Lexington Avenue subway. Suddenly she got the idea that they could go downtown to the Village, hang out there. They could go to Queens or Brooklyn or the Bronx, or New Jersey. They could get on an Amtrak and take a train to Florida. She'd always wanted to do that. They could go on a killing spree across America like the ones in the movies. That would be better than being on TV. Mostly she wanted him to buy her a present to prove he loved her.

David hung back. "Look, I can't stay. My mom will kill me if she finds out I didn't go to my shrink."

"What does he do, call your mommy when you don't show up?" she teased. Inside the store, she stopped by the purses to study a Prada bag. She glanced at David to see if he'd buy it for her.

"Nah, he doesn't call. He doesn't give a shit." David wasn't thinking about the Prada bag. He was twitching all over, worried about his mother's mood. He didn't want to get yelled at.

The saleslady moved closer. "Can I help you?"

"I hate this place. Let's get out of here," he said.

"Okay, whatever." Disgusted, Brandy got on the escalator and they traveled up to the main floor. She got off and dawdled as much as she could in the vast cosmetic section, then the men's store. Finally, he dragged her out on Third Avenue. Sam Goody was across the street. Brandy thought he might buy her a few discs, but David couldn't handle the music store for more than thirty seconds, either. He wasn't in a buying mood.

"Come on, let's go," he said angrily. "I hate shopping."

"Buy me something," she urged.

"Why?"

"Because I want some new discs. You're my boyfriend. You're supposed to get me stuff."

"Fine, I'll get you a pizza. Then I have to go home."

"I don't see why." Sulky, Brandy followed him out.

David raised his hand and punched her lightly in the arm. "Better watch out. Like *The Talented Mr. Ripley*, I can make anybody disappear."

"Yeah, right." She punched him back, not happy without the present.

"Two for dinner?" Inside California Pizza Kitchen, a girl who looked like she ate all the leftovers came over with two menus. She led the way up the stairs to the second floor, where David pointed at a corner table in the back.

They ordered.

"What did you do with the finger?" David asked.

"Oh, I forgot it."

"What do you mean you forgot it? I thought you were taking it with you for a souvenir."

"I was, but I dropped it."

"Now you tell me. I wanted that, you nut."

"You're the nut. You go to a psychiatrist."

"Yeah, but I don't need it. Half the time I don't even go. I'm really bummed about the finger."

Brandy leaned over the table and lowered her voice. "Okay, tell me."

He looked at his watch. "Tell you what?"

"How you killed him? Tell me everything."

"I punched him, then I kicked him. Then I strangled him," David said simply.

Brandy bounced in her chair. "It sounds cool. You're cool."

David turned around. Four tables were occupied but nowhere near them. "You know we could get fingers from the other two."

"This is true. We could, and we should. You fucked me over on the cave-dwellers."

"You're crazy. I didn't fuck you over."

"Yes, you did. You got spooked before the others were done. How am I supposed to trust you if you get scared so easily?"

He smacked the table. "Jesus, you know what happened. We had to go."

"All right, fine. We finish up tonight. You can get their fingers. Whatever." Brandy sulked. She'd done it with him, and he hadn't bought her a bag or a disc or anything. He was fucking her over. Killing one guy was not good enough. How was she going to go on TV as the girlfriend of a serial killer now? "I'll never trust you again," she muttered. He snorted in reply.

The waiter came with the pizza.

"Hurry up. I have to go home now, or I'll get in trouble," he said.

Boys! She shook her head. "You can't do this to me. You made a promise."

"So what?"

She put a slice of pizza on his plate and took one for herself. "If they find him, and he isn't dead, he'll tell. You don't want your mom to find out, do you?"

David shook his head. "You're a real pain in the ass. I said I'd finish it up tonight."

She looked at him with those big eyes. "I'll come with you," she said. She ate the first piece quickly and took two more.

"Yeah, thanks." He glanced at his watch again.

She stared at the pizza on his plate. "Aren't you going to finish this?"

He shook his head again. "I have to get home," he said softly.

"Why go home? Why not go from here." She took the last two slices of the pizza with a little smile. "If the cops come back, you won't get a chance to get out later."

"Okay, you're right. Let's do it now." He raised his hand for the bill.

FIFTY-EIGHT

MIKE WAS IN THE MIDDLE of a clot of smoking men in the squad room. April went out and caught his eye. She didn't say anything, just returned to her office. Seconds later he joined here there, smelling like a smoker.

"New?"

"I just talked to the ME. Pee Wee died of a head injury."

"No surprise there." Mike sank into a chair.

"Yes. Surprise. Dr. Gloss thinks Pee Wee may have fallen, or been hit on the head earlier in the day, then wandered around for hours. He says the attack in the park isn't what killed him. The earlier head injury was the cause of death."

"Wow." Mike inhaled, exhaled, sucked on his mustache. "Where does that get us?"

April gave him a grim little smile. "Quite a ways. We have some evidence on Brandy and David."

"Those kids? Ah Jesus. What does he have?"

"Nail polish for starters. Black nail polish chips on Pee Wee's body. Brandy was wearing a color like that yesterday when I talked to her in the park. Dr. Gloss told me Pee Wee's finger was cut off when he was still alive. That's something."

"And she was cool as a cucumber an hour ago."

"There's more. Hey, stop him for me, will you?" Behind Mike, April saw that Baum was getting ready to go downtown with his warrant request to search Dylan Rodriguez's apartment. The man was so slow filling in a form, this time he'd gotten lucky. He wasn't going to have to hang around the courts waiting forever for a judge to give his autograph. They had new suspects now and new apartments to search.

Mike followed her eye and called out the office door. "Hey, Woody."

He trotted into the office looking pleased not to be banished anymore. "What's up?"

April liked having the floor. "Woody, you're off the hook on Dylan's warrant request. And hold on for this one. Brandy and David were Pee Wee's attackers."

"They were?" Woody was surprised.

"Yeah. That puts them in the park last night. When I spoke to John, I thought I'd feel him out about trying another search for Maslow." April swiveled back and forth in her chair. "You know, Mike, that whole story you told me about tunnels in Vietnam made me think, I don't know, maybe Maslow is there, under the ground somewhere."

Mike nodded. "I thought of that. Drainpipe or something."

"And Peachy never had a chance to search because she got distracted by dead smells, and then we got distracted by Pee Wee's homicide. We never looked for Maslow, either over or underground. So I thought we might take Peachy out and try now. Those kids must have gone out to Zumech's place last night and stolen his body parts to throw Peachy off track."

The two men stared at her. Mike chewed on the ends of his mustache. Woody made faces. "Body parts?"

April checked her watch. "I've got people out watching the buildings where they live. But we should get going. John is on his way into the city with the dog. But who knows, maybe we won't need her. We'll bring Brandy and David into the station. If they're involved in the Maslow disappearance, we'll know soon. I also have a BOLO out on Dylan Rodriquez."

"Body parts, *querida?*"

April gave him her deadpan look. "John Zumech kept body parts in his garage for training the dogs. Brandy and David knew all about it."

"Okay, I gathered this morning that John had some personal concern about this. And then David told me all about his father's Mercedes. I didn't put the two together."

"This gives me the creeps." April swiveled angrily. She knew what Mike was thinking. She'd talked to the girl and boy yesterday, let them go. He'd questioned them again today and hadn't been alerted to the danger. Both of them had missed the signals. She was not able to comfort herself with the fact that it happened all the time. It wasn't unusual to come back and question a suspect many times before getting the real story. It wasn't always so easy to nail someone. But in this case, Pee Wee might not have died. And somewhere Maslow might still be out there.

Mike gave Woody the Owens' number to check the garage. "Find out if David took the car out last night, will you?"

It was time to move. April touched his arm. "Did you ask David's and Brandy's mothers if there were any firearms in their homes?"

"Yes, April. I did. Neither family has an interest in guns. In fact, David said he's terrified of them."

"Well, Brandy is interested."

"Her mother said they both hated guns. Put on your vest anyway," he ordered.

"Okay, I'll borrow one for you."

"I don't need one," he protested."

"Rules is rules. I'll borrow one for you. You'll wear it."

He smiled. "It's nice to be together."

"Yeah, sure. How much backup are you thinking?"

"They're just kids, Mike said. "Little crazy rabbits. We'll keep this thing low-key. The fewer people the better. What do you say?"

April nodded. They could call in for backup if things got hairy. Good thing Iriarte had gone home. One fewer person to worry about.

At eight-forty-five an astonished Janice Owen opened her front door to April, wearing navy slacks, and a jacket with "POLICE" in big yellow letters across the back.

"Mrs. Owen, I'm Sergeant Woo," April told her.

A tall man with blond hair, wearing a well-cut dark suit, appeared in the doorway beside Janice Owen. "What's this all about?" he asked, looking very surprised.

"Mr. Owen, I'm Sergeant Woo." April introduced herself again. "This is Detective Baum." Woody was standing behind her. He inclined his head but didn't say anything. He, too, was wearing a police jacket. The couple was horrified by them.

"Yes, yes. Hello. What's going on? Where's David?" He looked panicky.

"Do you mind if we come in?" April said gently.

There was a pause in which nobody moved. The couple locked eyes.

"No, of course not." Mr. Owen was the first to back away from the door. His wife was frozen. He took her arm and moved her back. "Come in. What's the problem?"

"Thank you." April entered and looked around the large foyer. It was every bit as grand as Mike had described it, but she was no longer intimidated by the trappings of wealth. She felt fortified by the jacket that broadcast her business. On Park Avenue no one was going to shoot her for wearing it. She was in a hurry to talk to the boy. Woody followed her inside. Two uniforms waited out in the elevator foyer. The Owens were in shock.

"We need to talk to your son, David," April told them.

"He isn't here. You'll have to come back." Mrs. Owen kept a wary eye on Woody, standing at ease, one hand holding the fingers of the other in front of his partially zipped jacket, as if she thought he might open fire at any moment with the pistol she knew was concealed in there.

"Where is he?" April was surprised. John had told her the boy was grounded.

Mrs. Owen raked a hand through her blond hair, talking quickly. "He's on his way home from a doctor's appointment. He called to say he's stuck in traffic."

"When was that?" April asked, pretty sure he was in the apartment.

"An hour ago. What is this all about?" Mrs. Owen was trying to stay cool. The hand raised to her throat was trembling.

They stood in the grand foyer, the two cops and the parents of the missing suspect. For April, having to telling someone a precious loved one was dead or injured was the worst thing in the world. Telling a parent that a loved child had hurt or killed someone else was almost as bad. These parents had no idea what was coming. Mr. Owen put his hand on his wife's shoulder. April could see him signal her to shut up.

"He took your car out last night," she said, starting with an easy one.

"Is there a problem with that? Borrowing the family car is not against the law. All kids do it." He looked at his wife. The kid took the car out. He hadn't known that.

April gave him a neutral face. "He's doesn't have a driver's license."

"So what?" The lawyer began to bluster like the wind kicking up in a storm.

Then the wife joined in. "A detective was here this afternoon, and we've had three other calls from the police this evening. Why are you harassing our son? He hasn't done anything."

April nodded at Woody. He escalated quickly.

"We're investigating a homicide, ma'am," he said.

"A homicide?" Mrs. Owen was astounded. "What could David know about a *homicide*?" She grabbed her husband's arm. "Tom!"

"What homicide, where—?" he responded to her alarm.

"We're not at liberty to talk about it at this time," Woody said, looking at his boss.

"Look, I can't let you talk to him until I know what this is all about. You can make an appointment and can talk to him with a lawyer present." Mr. Owen moved to open the door. The kid wasn't there. He wanted them to go. But it didn't work like that. He was just another parent who didn't know what was going on with his child and couldn't do anything to help him.

April felt a little sorry for them. "In ordinary circumstances that would be fine. But that won't be possible tonight. One man is dead, another is missing. David may be the only one who can help us find him."

"Oh God." His mother swooned.

"I'd like to see his room."

Janice Owen made a small cry, as if her whole world were coming to an end.

"I need to consult a lawyer about that," Mr. Owen said.

"For Christ's sake, you are a lawyer, Tom."

"Not a criminal lawyer, Janice."

"I'm not going to take anything at this time. But we have to secure the room," April interjected.

The two began to argue between themselves. Now was the time for blaming. Later would come the time for defending. April knew the whole story before they did. Her only interest was locating and talking to the boy. She found his room. He wasn't in it. It had a strong and not appealing boy smell that almost made her change her mind about taking something. But she did take something. She bagged the pillowcase on his unmade bed. Then she called in Officer Hays, who'd been waiting outside the apartment. He taped up the door of David's room with police tape and stayed behind to make sure no one went in and touched anything before they got a search warrant. April and Woody were out of there.

A few blocks uptown when Mike and several officers searched the apartment for Brandy, the completely hysterical Cheryl Fabman carried on a tirade against her missing daughter and the entire world. Neither mother could raise their child on the cell phones they'd purchased to keep in constant touch.

FIFTY-NINE

WHEN APRIL AND WOODY ENTERED the park at Seventy-seventh Street, John Zumech's red Cherokee and Mike's red Camaro were already parked side by side on the grass. The two men were talking quietly, waiting for them. Peachy sat in the passenger seat of the Jeep with her muzzle resting on the partly opened window. There was no repeat of the morning's frenzy in the dog now. But four people were off their radar screens, and the officers were pumping adrenaline.

Woody stopped the car next to the other two and killed the engine. They had BOLOS (be on the lookout) for Brandy, David, Dylan, and Maslow. Nothing yet.

April took a deep breath, made a quick prayer, and got out. This was where Maslow had disappeared and she and Woody had started on this case forty-eight hours ago. The temperature had dropped twenty degrees to the low sixties, and the humidity was high. Conditions were almost the same as then. She felt a little chilled in the evening air and was glad she'd changed into the long pants and sneakers in her locker.

Tonight a deepening cloud cover obscured the sky and threatened more rain. The park lights were on, glowing eerily in another steamy Indian summer evening.

John raised his hand, and the two men approached. "Have you got your maps, April?" Now he was wearing the Search and Rescue orange jumpsuit with bulging pockets. A water bottle hung on his belt. He had raccoon eyes and his jaw was clenched, emphasizing the scar beside his mouth. He held the flat leash in his hand.

"How are you doing, John?" April greeted him.

"Pissed. I've been thinking about what happened last night. Peachy and I must have been out running when David came. She would never have let anyone near the house. Not even someone she knows." He shook his head angrily. "This is hard to believe. I don't know what happened to them. They were solid kids."

"They're dopers, and they're out here somewhere," April said grimly.

"The bastards made a fool of me for trusting them. They violated everything sacred about this profession—and when it gets out I had those jars in my garage—shit, the press is going to go nuts."

Not to mention the people a little closer to him, like his employer, the PD, and maybe the health department. April glanced at Mike. He tapped his watch.

"Are we waiting for anyone?" she asked.

"Everyone at CP knows we're here. About a dozen officers are en route," Mike said.

"Woody checked out the Owens' garage. The Mercedes is there now, but David took it last night. The garage attendant doesn't punch the time cards for cars with regular spaces, but he was certain David returned the car before they closed their gate at midnight. After that, the customers have to ring for entry."

Woody with the sensitive nose put his two cents in. "The garage guy told me the car stank so bad when it came in, he had to spray it with air freshener before he would get in."

Zumech swore. "I'll kill the little snot."

In the Jeep, Peachy whined. The trainer changed his tone to warm honey. "Good girl. You good, good girl. You ready to get started, sweetheart? That's great. Just a minute and we're going to work." He signaled the dog, and Peachy became silent.

John was over the top. His jaw was working so hard April could hear his mandibles pop.

"John, are you okay?"

"Let's get going. I want to nail him."

"Do you think Peachy can find him?" April asked.

"My guess is that David has been out here a lot. He knows the park well, and murderers do often return to the scene of the crime. We know he was here yesterday afternoon. We know he was here last night when he attacked your victim. If he's here now, Peachy can find him."

"What about the Fabman apartment?" April asked.

"I called Fabman at home. He told me he's been in frequent touch with his ex-wife. Neither of them knows where their daughter is," Mike said.

A little whine from Peachy. These humans were sure taking their time.

"Hey, Peachy, Peachy, Peachy. We're coming, sweetheart."

"I have a present for you." April jerked her head at the car. Woody retrieved the scent bag and held it up.

"That's David?" Now John was really excited. "I have one, too, but mine is real old." He produced an old Pathmark shopping bag, tied at the top and sealed with masking tape.

April handed John the scent bag with the pillowcase from David's unmade bed. Triumphantly, John took it to the Jeep.

"Look, follow me at a distance, will you? You still stink." He directed this over his shoulder at Mike. "And by the way, this is going to be a wild ride. David's been all over the place in the last two days. If he's been where Maslow is and we're real lucky, Peachy could lead us there. But she may just pick up David's scent and take us a bunch of other places. Don't panic if she takes us all the way back to his apartment on the East Side. Peachy is a genius, but doesn't know from time frames. All she knows is where the scent particles pooled."

John stopped by the car and gestured for the three cops to step back while he opened the car door, snapped on Peachy's leash, and talked to the dog. He gave her a biscuit, crooned softly to her in tones women dream of hearing from their lovers. Then he opened the scent bag for Peachy to smell. The dog took her time with the bag, licked at the pillowcase as if it were food, tried to jump in.

April, Mike, and Woody stood off to one side. A few people watched them from a distance. They were used to being stared at.

"Go find," John said finally.

Peachy lifted her head to air scent, forgot the earlier command for silence, gave a little yip of joy, and took off, dragging her master and the three police officers after her.

SIXTY

DAVID AND BRANDY WALKED west on Sixtieth. David was trying to think things out. A detective had been to his house. By now his dad would know that. His mother and father never agreed about anything, but they would agree about this. If they found out he'd skipped his shrink, they'd punish him big time. If they found out about the car, they'd freak out completely. He didn't want to get in trouble, but he didn't care anymore. By now he and Brandy had long ago missed the six o'clock news on TV. He needed a drink or a joint, something to chill so he wouldn't worry so much. They hit Park Avenue. David's stomach stabbed him with killing force. His ulcer was killing him. He could almost feel it begin to seep blood. The pressure to do something really bad on his own was tremendous. Something without Brandy nagging at him and getting in the way. He felt like killing the girl in the cave his own way. That should be his job alone. He could do it the way he wanted. Then he could tell Brandy about it later. That was the best way. Two of them together never got the job done right. She'd forgotten the finger. That was pretty irresponsible. He wouldn't have done that.

They stopped on the corner. Brandy looked up. The wind was kicking up, and the sky had completely clouded over. He used that as an excuse.

"It's going to rain, maybe you better go home," he said.

"I don't want to. I want to stay with you." She took his arm.

He pulled away from her. "Look, Brandy, it would be better if I handled this myself." He started walking faster. He'd made up his mind.

Brandy followed him a few steps. "David, don't you love me?"

"Sure, I love you."

"If you love me, why didn't you buy me a gift?"

"What are you talking about?" He wasn't in the mood for this.

"You didn't buy me a gift. You're supposed to do that," she complained.

"Jesus, Brandy, I've got stuff to do. How about I bring you a gift? A human sacrifice. Would that do it?"

"Maybe. But I want a Prada bag, too."

He snorted. Prada bag. "Go home, Brandy."

She skipped to catch up. "Maybe I don't want to."

"It's not yours to choose. I'm the boss here. That's the way it has to be."

"Who says so?" Defiantly, she put her hand on his arm.

He took her fingers and bent them back until she squealed. "Ow, that hurts. Let go."

"Who's the master?"

"You are, now let go."

He let go and backed away.

"You hurt me," she said with tears in her eyes.

"I did not. You forced me to do it. Now go home and behave yourself."

She rubbed her wrist. "Will you meet me later?"

"Yeah, sure." He was thinking about the girl in the cave and what he could do to her.

"Call me on my cell?"

"Sure."

"Will you buy me a Prada bag?"

"Whatever. You're my girlfriend, aren't you?"

"Yeah, I need taxi money."

He gave her a twenty and hailed a cab going north on Park.

"You love me, don't you?" she said as she got in.

"I said you're my girlfriend." He slammed the car door and walked west. He hit Madison, then Fifth. He was wearing his Nike Airs and felt good to be alone. He crossed Fifth Avenue and saw the horse and buggies lined up across from the Plaza Hotel, where his parents used to take him for lunch at the Palm Court on Sundays when he was a little boy. He paused for a moment to take two Maalox. He saw two cops standing around outside the hotel. They didn't look his way. He crossed Fifth Avenue and entered the park on Fifty-ninth Street. He started walking northwest with his hands in his pockets, glad Brandy was gone. The evening was cool and damp, and for a few precious moments he was free of everyone.

As he stumped along, it occurred to him that he could double back and come out at Sixty-fifth Street, or Seventy-second, then walk home and the game would be over. But the unfinished business gnawed at him. He wanted to get on top of that girl and squeeze the life out of her with his bare hands. He kept to the same course toward Sheep Meadow and the West Side. When he was deeper in the park, he started jogging. He never saw any cops in police jackets or Zumech in his orange SAR suit. He was coming from the opposite direction and missed their operation a mile away.

He slowed his pace when he reached the lake. At nine-thirty people were still walking on the paths. He crossed the little bridge over the reeds where there used to be water and dove into the brush on the Central Park West Side. The path ended at the bridge, and the wild foliage and the grass took over. He plunged through the grass and found the gravel of the old lake bed. Here the grass was at its end-of-the-year highest, way over his head. Just as he hit the lake bed, it started to rain.

SIXTY-ONE

MASLOW WAS DRIPPING with sweat. He had been working for hours without a break, hoping to dig and pry his way out before all the light was gone and he could see no more. A rock on the outside wedged the heavy gate in place. When he could not open it from the inside, he tried to lift it high enough to move Dylan's foot from under it. But there was not enough room above. He could lift the bottom only a little before the top edge struck against the roof.

Dylan screamed each time the gate shifted a little, but he gained a few precious inches by stuffing his running shoes into the gap. In the hours after that, he dug frantically around and under her pinned limb, using both hands and the sharp edge of a rock to create a depression, a trench deep enough to ease the pressure of the gate on what he could now tell was a jagged piece of bone. Dylan's body was flung at such an awkward angle that her own weight, slight as it was, worked against them. The leg continued to swell, filling all the space he created.

The extraordinary closeness of the situation created an even greater anxiety in Maslow. In his world, he was forbidden to talk to a patient outside office hours much less sit with her in a coffee shop. Touching even her hand would be the greatest violation of all. Now he was taking her pulse and manipulating her limbs and talking to her with love and the intent to convey it. He was caught in an upside-down world where the lines between evil and good could no longer be drawn. A child was his enemy. A former patient was his sister, never to be a patient again. The sand was shifting, and he had no certain place.

As night fell, the only hope of saving Dylan was for Maslow to get help. He switched tactics and began grinding away at a spoke of the once-stout barrier. He could not squeeze out with only one spoke missing, but with two gone he thought he might have a chance. He started with the weakest one, so badly rusted it chipped and splintered into spiny fragments in his fingers. He sawed at it with a rock and his bare hands, oblivious to the cuts the stone and rust made on his palms.

Dylan had a high fever and was hallucinating now. The things she mumbled made no sense, just like Maslow's whole life and what he'd thought was his history. Nothing made sense anymore. Outside all he could hear was the bark of a city dog and the steady rumble of the subway. Inside his head was a throbbing that wouldn't ease. His back and legs trembled with his efforts to break the spoke free. He was frantic. Beside him, a second sister was dying. This one was even more precious because she came as an unexpected gift when he'd thought he was all alone. Even worse than that, she was dying for the sole reason that she had wanted to be with him. No one else had ever cared for him that much.

"You're doing well," he told her. "Very well. Just a little while more. Hang in there with me."

"No, no. The elephant is broken," she muttered.

"I fix elephants," he told her.

For Maslow, nothing had ever mattered to him but being a doctor. He'd worked all his life for the two magic letters after his name and the meaning they gave his existence. There was no reason in what was happening to them. She was going to die right in front of him, and there was nothing he could do to keep her alive.

It was pitch-black now. He stopped his sawing to scream again for help, but before the yell was out of his mouth, a crack of thunder struck so loud he thought it was an exploding bomb.

"Mommy," Dylan whimpered. He reached over and took her hand for a moment.

Then he returned to the spoke, jerking it with all his weight. This time it cracked at the top. Another clap of thunder split the sky. Maslow pried the spoke toward him with bleeding fingers. It hardly budged. He picked up the rock and used it as a wrench, braced his bare feet against the base of the gate and worked the rock toward him.

The spoke broke free in his hand and he fell back, panting. Just then the clouds let go, and rain hurled down out of the sky. A flash of lightning reached into the dark. Maslow stretched his hand through the space. His arm and one shoulder fit through, but his chest stuck. He could feel drops of rain wash his hand.

"Stay with me. I'll have you out soon," he murmured to Dylan. One more spoke and they would taste freedom. He would have them out before their captor returned. He was sure of it.

SIXTY-TWO

PEACHY SURPRISED APRIL by traveling five blocks south. She crossed Strawberry Fields, sniffing the hard-packed end-of-summer grass in a state of deep concentration, oblivious to her trainer grasping the end of her leather leash and the detectives following fifty yards behind. Strawberry Fields was separated from Sheep Meadow by the Seventy-second Street transverse. Just before she came to the crosstown road, lightly trafficked at this hour, she suddenly swerved east toward the lake. There, she traveled around the bottom finger, the southernmost tip of the lake north to Wagner Cove, stopping once to raise her head and sniff the air.

Trotting along behind them, April felt a little light-headed in the cool evening air. She knew that whenever John went on a search and rescue with the dog, he always took several thick meat sandwiches and Snickers bars with him for energy. The dog didn't need more than a few handfuls of dry dog food, a cup and a half of water a day. And, of course, his treats for incentive. People running four, five, ten miles in a few hours, however, needed much more than that.

In the station house April had thought of the flashlights, the vests, radios, telephones, Velcro restraints, plastic cuffs, but she'd never considered the need for food at all. It was a common failing of hers. She didn't like eating the pizza and sweet, high-fat foods the other detectives and officers were always eating on the job. No matter what the conditions, she always relied on her body to sustain her until there was time to locate food worthy of her palate. It wasn't always a wise policy. Last night around one A.M. she'd eaten very well. This morning and to-day, she'd had practically nothing. Around one, someone had handed her a donut, the official food of the Department. Then she'd drunk strong tea without milk and sucked an Altoid late in the afternoon. Now it was after nine. Her mouth felt furry and her stomach cried for food, but she wasn't thinking of food. She was thinking of Maslow Atkins, the missing man.

She started off at a brisk pace, power walking, and pumped for the hunt. John's SAR suit and Peachy's orange necklace radiated a ghostly glow in the darker patches of park between lampposts. With a storm coming and almost no one around, the park felt huge. Eight hundred and forty-three acres. Mike paced along beside her. Neither had anything to say, but the energy between them was electric. They had their rhythm now. Hunting together, they could walk all night if they had to. April could hear Woody a few paces back, unused to using his feet, breathing hard through his mouth.

Suddenly Peachy stopped. John stopped, and they stopped. The beautiful terrace of Bethesda Fountain was to their right. The east bank of the lake was to their left. The dog lifted her large head, sniffing the air as if lost. Her body was tense, uncertain. John opened the scent bag and let her bury her head in the pillowcase. When she was finished rooting around in it, she dropped her head and charged up Cherry Hill to Bow Bridge.

They were now mid park at Seventy-second Street. Above them was thirty miles of woodland Ramble, Belvedere Castle, and two more bridges. To the east was Center Drive and Literary Walk. If they stayed in the mid section of the park, between the east and west sides, and traveled south, they would skirt Wollman skating rink. But Peachy headed north across the Bow Bridge into the Ramble. She followed the path as it veered up the slope. Immediately between the path and un-dulating rock was a stand of trees. Lampost #7413. April's heartbeat accelerated. Six months ago just north of the castle, a mentally ill homeless woman had been found strangled to death. She didn't want to discover Maslow had suffered a similar fate.

After ten more minutes Peachy faltered, lost again. She stopped, turned around three times, sniffing the air. Then, keeping the lake on her left, she found lamppost #7523, another block north. There, a large tree with a double trunk that split off again to form a third trunk held her interest for a while. She stuck her head close to the deeply grooved bark. The tree bordered the water and was surrounded by hard-packed ground. April wanted to approach, but Zumech waved her back.

"How are you doing, *querida*?" Mike spoke suddenly.

"Okay. I'm thinking we should have more people out here."

"How about we give the dog a few more minutes?"

The wind had picked up, agitating the leaves all around them and shaking April's hope. They had no real hint of where Brandy and David had gone. They could be anywhere. The dog looked confused, and now April doubted their brilliant idea of coming here. Peachy had brought them many blocks east of the place where they'd found Pee Wee this morning. It now seemed that working the tracker at night with a storm kicking up and David's scent as their guide—when they were really searching for Maslow—might be the stupidest idea she ever had. She didn't want to say that to Mike, however. They stood in the dark while the weather deteriorated around them and the dog sniffed the tree.

After what seemed like an eternity, Peachy lost interest in the tree and plunged south again. She retraced her own steps to Bow Bridge, crossed it, and this time took the east path toward Bethesda Terrace. It was better lighted here. April moved her feet, worrying about the time and thinking in her heart they'd made a big mistake. The wind was blowing like crazy, whipping branches around. The park was empty, and now April could see the presence of CP officers, safe and dry in their vehicles. On the park roads and off the roads, unmarked units had begun to cruise, on the lookout for Brandy and David. But the Ramble was deep and thirty miles long; people hid in the foliage there all the time. They'd have to get out of their units if they wanted to help. April put the thought out of her mind.

Ahead of them Peachy was traveling dead east now. She crossed the Bethesda terrace, jogged around the fountain, and ran up the stairs to the Seventy-second Street crosstown drive. They had done a thirty-five-minute detour. Now she was hurrying toward Fifth Avenue and the East Side. This was way out of the way, far from where the cars were parked and where April and Woody had responded to the 911 call two nights ago. If Peachy had the scent, it now looked as if David might be headed home. He lived on Sixty-fifth Street and Park Avenue. Brandy lived on Seventy-fifth and Park Avenue. Maybe the two kids had come out, then gone home again when the weather worsened.

April checked her watch. They'd been out over an hour. It felt like four hours. She was sweating now, was tired and beginning to despair. Suddenly Peachy veered south once again, toward Fifty-ninth Street. She picked up her pace and ran down the Mall toward Literary Walk, then took the Center Drive south. In twelve minutes at a dead run, they neared Fifty-ninth Street and April could hear the comfortable clack of horseshoes on the pavement as a line of buggies headed home before the storm. She stopped for a moment to catch her breath. It looked as though they'd lost him.

SIXTY-THREE

WHEN THE RAIN BROKE FREE of the clouds and sleeted down on him, David had a feeling of intense exhilaration, like being at camp all over again. At camp in the Berkshires, the weather was often hot and humid. The rain would threaten scheduled activities for hours or days, then suddenly make a grand entrance with thunder and lightning during intercamp sports competitions, canoeing. In the middle of hikes, on camping trips. The rain showed up like a good friend at a boring party, disrupting the carefully planned schedules, making people run in all directions, and providing exquisite relief in the chaos it brought.

Rain on his face, on his sweatshirt, soaking his shoes had never bothered David. It meant freedom, the end of responsibility. In the rain, no game could ever be lost, no bad feelings were ever aroused, no restraint was there to hamper and frustrate him. Rain scattered everything. Now, as always, the boom of the thunder cleared the park. And the light, sound, and water show had a special message for him. The rain had come to protect him and assure him that he was right to send Brandy home. He was right to do things his own way. He was wet through, and he was given the signal—not to go home, get dry, and forget about everything bad he could do; but rather to move forward, secure in the safety of his privacy.

He knew just what he was going to do. He planned the event as a special souvenir for himself that he could savor all the rest of his life. He would lift the gate free. He would go into the cave. The shrink would be there, still alive, but helpless. He would set up his flashlight in the cave so there would be just enough light to see what was going on. He would pretend the helpless man was his own shrink. Then he would lie on top of that girl. He and Brandy had seen her on Central Park West a couple of times before. Brandy dismissed her as an ugly girl, but she always said that about everybody. Really the girl was very pretty, tiny and thin. Last night, he'd enjoyed hurting her, and making her beg for mercy.

The problem then was it had all happened too fast. Brandy got too crazy when she was high. She made a mess of everything. You had to do this kind of thing slowly, deliberately, not in a panic. From now on he would do things right. He would set it up carefully, and the shrink would be there as his witness. This time he wouldn't have to be in a hurry, for no one could frighten or stop him from doing whatever he wanted. He could take his time and enjoy squeezing the breath out of her. And he would savor knowing that someone was watching as he did it.

As he hiked purposefully in the rain, he remembered that squashing was a recognized method of killing. In American History, he'd read about the witches of Salem. They used to kill them by drowning, but also by piling stones and rocks on them until they couldn't lift their chests to fill their lungs with air and were crushed to death in their own graves. A good way to get rid of anyone. He particularly liked the idea of crushing a very pretty girl to death with the weight of his own body. After the girl was dead, he would suffocate the shrink. That would be no effort at all. The man was small and practically dead already.

David had thought to bring along a really good knife. It was much better than Brandy's. It had a serrated edge for cleaning fish cartilage and could cut through anything. He liked the idea of his competence in this area. He had thought out many aspects of this mission, and it turned out that he was smart and knew what he was doing. When he was finished, he would end up with two fingers, and Brandy, who was way too impulsive, would have none.

Thunder struck as he pushed through the bushes. Then lightning.

In the lightning he saw two rats huddled together outside the gate. He cursed and threw a rock at them. They ran away. He directed his flashlight where the rat had been and saw the foot sticking out. His heart sank. What fun would it be if the girl was already dead. He approached the gate swearing softly.

SIXTY-FOUR

BITCH. Damn bitch."

Maslow heard the voice. Then the crunch on gravel. A crack of thunder ruptured the sky. The noise covered his soft signal to Dylan. "Shhh." As if she could hear him and respond. There was nothing from her. A flashlight raked the area.

"Damn!" The voice was full of anger. Frightening.

Quickly, Maslow moved to the back of the cave before the light could catch him. His breathing sounded loud and ragged in his ears, but the boy didn't hear it.

"What the fuck!" He was talking to himself as he shone the strong beam on Dylan. She was out of it, didn't move. The light traveled along the ground.

A sudden flash of lightning illuminated him, just for a second, from behind. Maslow was horrified by the sight of the boy, dripping wet and at the peak of his health. The monster who had captured and beaten and terrorized him and Dylan looked huge, like an athlete, a football player or mountain climber. Even in the best condition, Maslow would not have been able to take him on. Now he was weak and dehydrated. His legs were shaky at best and his head ached from the blows he'd received. There was no way he could fight him now.

The light froze on the gate bottom. The boy's attention was drawn to Maslow's sneakers stuffed under the gate and the gap where a spoke had been.

"What the fuck!" he said again. He shone the light into the cave looking for Maslow and didn't locate him at first.

Maslow had thrown himself down in the corner, trying to look as if he had given up and died hours ago. The boy kept the light on him, shifting it back and forth from the shoeless feet to his hands buried in dirt, to his head. Maslow saw the light move and kept still. He had a wild hope that the boy would think Dylan was dead and he was dead, and that he would just go away.

But the boy was angered by what he saw and squatted down to assess the situation. He saw the sneakers and the digging that Maslow had done in his attempt to free Dylan's leg. Then he shone the light on Dylan more carefully this time and saw that her hands were no longer bound.

He swore again.

Maslow held his breath as the boy poked Dylan's foot. She groaned. That galvanized him. The rock was still wedged against the gate. Now he picked it up and moved it. Then he wrenched the gate away. Dylan was not so out of it that she didn't feel the metal tearing her flesh. She screamed.

Maslow screamed, too, but the boy didn't hear him. Thunder was booming in the sky, and he had something else on his mind. He entered the cave, bending low to get inside. He shone the light on Maslow. Maslow held his breath and didn't move as the boy half-walked, half-crawled closer to get a better take on him. He poked Maslow with his foot, curiously, as if he were some thing, not a person. When Maslow didn't move, he kicked him in the ankle, then in the side. The breath was knocked out of him, and still he didn't move.

Maslow hurt in new places now, and he was enraged by the arrogance of the boy. The kid didn't see them as alive, as people. He didn't give a shit what he was doing to them. The arrogance and the raw sadism was more than Maslow could bear. If he had been strong enough to kill, he would kill now. But he was afraid to move, afraid of what the boy would do to him next.

Satisfied that he was no threat, the boy turned around and concentrated on Dylan. She was weeping feverishly, talking gibberish a few feet away. The boy was interested in her.

"Turn over," he said.

She didn't acknowledge him. This annoyed him. "I want you to turn over." She didn't comply, so he rolled her over himself.

Maslow thought he would lose his mind as he saw the boy talking to her, moving her arms and her legs to suit him.

"No, no." She muttered something inaudible.

The boy paid no attention to her. "Put your arms around me and hug me," he said.

He got down on his knees. He didn't like her position and moved her body around some more. Maslow couldn't figure out what he was doing.

"Hug me."

The boy lay down beside Dylan and started pulling at her clothes.

Maslow's heart pounded. No. No! He was choking on his indignation, his rage. The boy was pure evil. Never had he seen such evil. He could not lie there and watch when the boy pulled up Dylan's skirt and rolled on top of her. Maslow rose up out of the ground and struck out like a pit bull attacking a lion.

SIXTY-FIVE

THE ORANGE GLOW of Zumech's SAR jumpsuit was way ahead of April as Peachy reversed direction again, and turned northwest back toward the lake. The air was heavy and the grass was wet. The temperature had dropped a few more degrees and the mist had turned into a fine drizzle. April was in pretty good shape, but hadn't hunted at night for a long time. Ten years ago this would have been nothing. Her first job had been in Bed Stuy, where she'd been on the streets day and night for eighteen difficult months in a really rough neighborhood where she'd felt small and defenseless, but had never bothered much about her physical comfort in the heat, wet, or paralyzing cold.

Now she was no longer used to running at night with her gun at her waist and her extra equipment slamming against her side with every step. She perspired in the vest and waterproof windbreaker, hampered by her own precautions. This night maneuver was coming to nothing, and she was sorry that she'd worn the vest. It was one of the new ones, cost nearly four hundred dollars, and fit her small frame nicely. It was supposed to breathe and be cooler than the older models but still be strong enough to stop any bullet out on the street. The first two claims were proving false. She hoped she'd never be a test for the third.

She was winded and discouraged as the dog changed direction yet again and the weather worsened. Mike was ahead of her, and it annoyed her that he was moving faster now than she was. Woody straggled along at her side. She felt horrible. She'd made another tactical error, trying this search at night. They were idiots, out in a storm with all four people they were looking for way off their radar screen, somewhere in the wind.

Trotting northwest after the dog, she was furious at herself. Suddenly Woody's light went off beside her. The fog closed in to a tighter circle. Lightning hit, cracking the sky. A boom of thunder followed.

"Shit." Woody stumbled and swore as the sky opened up and the rain hit with full fury, almost knocking them over with its force.

Monsoon time in Manhattan; it always happened in summer and early fall. Dry in her jacket, April's head and feet were drenched in seconds. Their search party was over. The park was empty, the sky as dark as deepest night. The dog was moving west.

Ahead, Mike stopped to zip his jacket. Then he moved on, his flashlight pointed down at the path. April kept a slower but steady pace, her eye on Peachy's orange necklace and John's jumpsuit just visible and still moving west, now at a run. April checked her watch. They'd been out an hour and forty-five minutes.

The dog and trainer raced on in the rain. And April ran after them, panting and exhausted. She was certain that the dog was heading back to the haven of the red Jeep Cherokee. They were rained out. No dog could smell through a hurricane. She was deeply disappointed at their failure, and she was also ashamed because she, too, yearned for rest and warmth and praise from her boyfriend. Peachy would get her treats whether she'd lost the scent or not. But April had messed up, she'd lost all three of her suspects and was in big trouble. Big.

In six minutes, they were back almost to where they'd started. But Peachy did not stop at the cars. April saw Peachy's orange necklace as she skirted the water's edge on the east side of the lake, traveling north along the patch of water until it became shallows and finally grass. Water poured down on their heads, muting John's excited cry of victory as Peachy hurled herself into the grass and disappeared.

SIXTY-SIX

IN A CRACK OF THUNDER, Maslow grabbed the boy by the back of his jacket and jerked him off Dylan. Unlike the boy and Dylan, he made no sound. All his effort went into the attack, and the boy was caught by surprise.

"Hey!" The boy pushed the sobbing girl from him like a rag doll that had gotten in his way. He tried to get up. As he unfolded his body, his forehead smacked a rock jutting from the ceiling.

"Shit." He swore and held his head. His foot knocked the flashlight over, dousing the meager light.

Dark took over the cave again but for the lightning outside, flashing like a strobe in a downtown club. Inside, it smelled of rain, sweat, blood, and fear. Maslow went for the boy's knees. Cursing some more, the boy fell hard, and the two grappled on the sharp, stony cave floor, struggling for advantage. Maslow tried to kick his opponent in the balls but couldn't get to him. So he pummeled with his fists as hard as he could from above, landing his blows on the boy's head and neck.

"Cut that out!" The boy's cry was high-pitched and carping. He was actually complaining.

Maslow tried to pin him, but the younger man outweighed him by at least fifty pounds. He flipped Maslow off him, and with one cuff, exploded Maslow's head with a thousand excruciating pin lights of pain. Maslow lay where he had fallen, stunned and immobilized.

Muttering angrily, the boy searched for the light, found it, and righted it so he could see again. Then he returned to the girl and his task of torturing her as if nothing had happened. First he didn't like the way she was lying and moved her around.

She was awake now, crying and begging him to stop. Then suddenly she became quiet. Her body twitched. Maslow could see convulsions in the light. The boy was pleased by these movements.

"Hug me," he said again.

Her head went back and forth.

He lowered his body on her, holding her down.

"No!" The cry was sharp.

He raised himself up a little, excited. "Put your arms around me. Come on."

She couldn't. He let himself fall down on her, crushing her. She bucked against him.

"This is a good feeling. Isn't this good?" he said.

After a few minutes, the pain eased a little in Maslow's head, and he started thinking again. He was a doctor, and a doctor's mind was a repository of secret knowledge. He clicked through it as if his brain were a computer. What part of the body could he attack with little effort? A hat pin behind the ear would kill him in a few seconds. In the Bellevue ER, he'd seen a rich eighty-two-year-old woman killed that way by her greedy son. But Maslow didn't have a hat pin, let alone a knife or a gun.

Maslow groaned involuntarily. David looked his way.

"Isn't this good?" he said. Below him, he was pulling up Dylan's short shirt.

Maslow's hand scrabbled around in the dirt, searching for the imaginary hat pin. He stopped when it connected with a metal object, the broken spoke he'd dropped when the boy appeared. He grasped the precious rusted iron in his hand and pulled himself up. The boy was now lost in himself and Dylan's agony.

Maslow crawled toward him. Using the spoke like a sword, he took wobbly aim, pointing straight at the carotid sinus. He swiped at the nape of the neck, striking the sharp edge into the soft skin so hard it sheared through the artery that fed the boy's brain. The boy howled with pain and grabbed his neck as the hot blood spouted out.

"Are you crazy?" he screamed. He was off Dylan again. In an angry frenzy at the attack, and apparently unaware of how badly he was hurt, the boy grabbed the weapon from Maslow's hand and lunged at him. In a second Maslow was covered with blood.

SIXTY-SEVEN

A PRIL HEARD THE SCREAMS ahead and knew where Mike was headed. He reached the little bridge over the lake bed where water was no more, reaching it just as Peachy's barking rose to a delirious pitch. In a burst of energy she didn't know she had, she followed Mike across the bridge. Woody unholstered his gun.

"Put that away," she barked. There was too much confusion in the sounds she heard, and she was terrified that Woody might get too excited and shoot in error, hitting Mike or John, the victim, or even herself.

Rain slated down on her face and neck, blinding her. She lost Mike and couldn't see what was going on ahead. She stepped off the bridge and the muddy path gave way. She tumbled down the bank, twisting her ankle as she landed hard on the stony riverbed.

"You okay?" Woody got to her and felt for her arm, his gun still in his hand.

"Yeah, fine. Help me up," she said impatiently. Woody yanked her to her feet before she had a chance to say, *gently*. His gun was pointed at her knee. "Holster your gun!" she commanded angrily. She couldn't get more specific than that. The man was a menace, but he holstered the gun.

Through a dense thicket they heard chaotic screams and shouts. Peachy was yelping like crazy, a hero in her finest hour. Mike was trying to take command. She heard it before she saw it.

"Help! Help us, please!"

"Police. Drop that. Put your hands up."

"Put your hands up. Oh my God!"

"Good girl, Peachy. Good girl."

Then a miracle occurred. The rain ended as suddenly as it had begun, clearing the air almost instantly. April ignored the shooting pain in her foot as she pushed through the dripping bushes. Quickly Mike had holstered his own gun. Now his flashlight illuminated a scene none of them would ever forget. Three people in a cave so small no one else could get in. And blood was everywhere.

Most prominent in the scene was the dog barking triumphantly, for she'd found what she'd been looking for and won the prize. The long-sought smell of David's sweat was now combined with his blood, and the delighted dog was hanging on him, trying to kiss him and lick his seeping wound.

April was on her radio calling for backup and three EMS vehicles. Staying calm and speaking as tersely as she could, she described the critical nature of the situation and gave their location before she went in to help. She had no clear idea of the extent of the carnage. In all the mud and gore, she could not at first tell what had happened in there. When she signed off, hung the radio on her belt, and moved closer, she had a view into unfathomable horror.

The face of the missing jogger was unrecognizable, filthy and awash with blood. It poured out of a gash in his forehead and from his nose. A girl April couldn't immediately identify lay on the ground with her skirt pulled up around her hips. Her face, too, was bloody and her features indiscernible. Her nose looked broken and ragged bone could be seen sticking out of her ankle. Was this Brandy? Dylan Rodriguez? She couldn't tell.

And last, the boy, David, was bent over, holding his neck with one hand. The other brandished what looked like a bloody poker. Blood gushed out of his neck, and he was the one who was screaming.

Peachy had him pinned against some structure that looked like a gate. She had no idea of restraining him. She was greeting him, slobbering on him, and humping him with all the joy of a long-lost friend while David shrieked his head off, "I'm hurt, I'm hurt. He stabbed me." He sounded like a lost little boy.

John took command of the dog, thanked her lavishly, and moved her out of the way. Then he heeled Peachy and took off for the cars to set up his flares and continue talking on the radio through Central to lead the medical teams in to the closest access.

"April, we need your help in here," Mike said.

April responded quickly. Now was the dilemma of which injured person to attend to first—the perpetrator or the victims. Once long ago, when April was a rookie, she and her partner were the first on the scene of a jewelry store robbery gone bad. The perp had shot the owner in the neck. Her partner ran after the perp and April crouched on the floor with a hand clamped over the victim's wound, talking to him for five interminable minutes until EMS arrived.

Together April and Mike moved David out of the cave, lay him down. Mike put his jacket under the boy's head and clamped his wound. April went in for the girl. She, too, took off her jacket. Underneath was a cardigan and a shirt. She ripped them both off to cover the sobbing girl. April was stripped down to her bra and talking softly to soothe the girl, when she realized it was Dylan. She took Dylan's hand and squeezed it.

"It's April Woo. Hold on there, you're going to be okay. I'm with you, just hold on." April kept talking. "Your mom's waiting for you. Just a few more minutes. Dylan, can you hear me? We're going to get you out of here."

"Don't move her, don't move her," Maslow cried.

"I'm not moving her. How are you doing?" April held Dylan's hand but turned her attention on him.

"Don't worry about me. I'm fine." The voice sounded strong.

"Good, take my jacket. I've got her." April handed him her jacket. "Woody, take Dr. Atkins out. Hurry."

For once Woody had his brains screwed in. Despite Maslow's protests, he half-carried him out of the cave.

Turned out, the three officers and the dog tracker worked perfectly together, so well, in fact, that before EMS arrived, Woody had covered his boss with his own shirt and given his jacket to Dylan. They were all on a high, having done what they set out to do, and saved three lives in the process.

Back on Park Avenue, Brandy Fabman missed the storm. Long be-

fore ten, she'd slipped back into her building unnoticed by the two officers on a three-minute coffee break from watching her building. She
was at home in bed, dreaming of the money she would make when her
story was sold to the movies and of the skimpy dress she would wear on
her TV appearances.

At two in the morning, when David Owen and Dylan Rodriguez
were both in operating rooms having emergency surgery, Cheryl Fabman got her wish to be reunited with her ex-husband. She and Seymour stayed all night together in a police station where they waited for
a lawyer to come and deal with the kidnap, assault, and attempted
murder charges against their daughter.

EPILOGUE

JEROME ATKINS AND HIS WIFE, Adina, received the news early Friday morning at their Park Avenue apartment that their son, Maslow, had been rescued from the small cave in Central Park where he had been held captive since Tuesday evening by two Park Avenue teenagers who attended fancy private schools. The couple hurried to the hospital for a reunion with him. Several hours later, they appeared holding hands at a scheduled press conference. Also present at the news conference held at Roosevelt–St. Luke's Hospital on Columbus Avenue were Lieutenant Arturo Iriarte, Sergeant April Woo, Lieutenant Mike Sanchez, and Dr. Jason Frank, described (to his chagrin) as a close friend of the Atkins family.

During the conference, held in time for the local five o'clock news, a hospital public relations spokesman reported that Dr. Atkins had been heroic in his efforts to save his half-sister. Dylan Rodriguez had been captured and severely beaten while searching for Maslow after earlier police attempts to find him in the park had failed. She was in stable condition after surgery. No mention was made of the awkward circumstance that Dylan had been Maslow's patient.

Smiling broadly in an elegant silver suit, Lieutenant Iriarte stepped forward into the flashes of many cameras and video cams. Looking every inch the boss of bosses, he described in great detail the planning and execution of the rescue. After seven minutes of air time (later cut to thirty seconds), almost as an afterthought, he introduced two officers who had implemented the operation. The two officers, though clean and wearing the clothes from their lockers, looked appropriately grubby and modest. They in turn gave credit for the remarkable rescue during one of the worst thunderstorms in New York history—which caused flooding and power outages that were still creating problems throughout the city—to NYPD dog tracker John Zumech and his Doberman pinscher, Peachy, who had kept going despite impossibly difficult weather conditions.

The two officers, Woo and Sanchez, were recognizable to that certain segment of New York City residents who followed the Metro section of the *Times*, the running sagas of the *Post*, and the front-page stories of *The Daily News*.

After them Jerome Atkins, looking very happy at the bank of microphones outside the hospital, said that he and his wife had never given up hope that their son was alive and were deeply relieved and grateful for his return. Questioned about his twenty-year-old daughter, Dylan, and long-term relationship with coworker Grace Rodriguez, Atkins said there was nothing to the rumor. With his wife by his side, he explained that Grace Rodriguez and he had had a short relationship many years ago and had since remained friends for the sake of their child. He further added that Adina, his wife and best friend of thirty-eight years, knew all about his youthful indiscretion and had forgiven him years ago.

Dr. Maslow Atkins's hospital physician then reported that although Dr. Atkins was not able to appear live on camera, he had a statement to make. He was grateful to the New York City Police officers who had saved him and his sister and that he was happy to be alive.

Clips appeared on all the local network and cable TV programs and on the national morning news. In the following days, media attention would focus heavily on the lives of Brandy Fabman and David Owen and the debate over the punishment children should receive for their violent acts. But that was the news circus.

For April and Mike, the time of action was over. Now would come the long days of getting the facts and answers, tying up the loose ends, working with the DA's office, doing the paperwork. And who knew, perhaps even an IAB investigation of their own part in the case. In any event, they knew that when the red lights went off the video cameras, the department lights would come up hard on them.

They'd been up for over thirty-six hours when Jason stopped on his way out to say good-bye.

"Thanks," he said to them. "I owe you everything."

"True," April replied deadpan. "Name your next child after Mike."

Jason froze. His face did a wild dance of surprise and horror as he did a quick calculation. "Are we pregnant?" he asked. Had Emma told April something about them before he knew it himself?

Always the detective, April reached a conclusion and smiled. People with babies still did it. She glanced at Mike. Enjoying Jason's discomfort, too, Mike let a little grin peek out from under his mustache. They caught each other's eyes.

Jason got the joke. "Very funny. Don't change the subject. I really appreciate the way you handled Dylan and kept her part out of the story. She's going to need even more help now." He shook his head. "This is a therapeutic nightmare. A nightmare."

Then his mood lightened. He smiled and shook Mike's hand. "To look on the bright side, it could have been much worse, very much worse. Gotta go. Believe it or not, I have a patient in ten minutes." He waved and took off, looking pretty good for someone who was in a lot of trouble at his own shop.

Mike put his arm around April and gave her a squeeze. "I love you." He tickled her ear with his mustache. "Home, *querida*?"

April had washed her hands and face but otherwise didn't look or smell very good. Her lovely suit and blouse of yesterday were not that clean either, after the long day she'd put in. She raised a hand to her hair, flat as a pancake and definitely in need of a stylist.

Five is a very important number to the Chinese. Five flavors, five elements, five humors. Five times Skinny Dragon called on April's cell phone to yell at her about it. Skinny had seen an earlier news clip of April and Mike on the way to the hospital in Mike's Camaro. The Dragon said all her friends had seen April with blood on her face sitting next to the man Skinny Dragon had already told them was history. Why show up on TV looking so bad? Why cause poor old mother to lose face. Why so thin? Sai's friends had said April look too thin.

And by the way, if worm daughter and Spanish ghost planned to get married, she would hang herself in shame was her final jab.

April was actually pleased with the fourth call. The suicide threat meant the Dragon was in the final stages of resistance. In the fifth call came the bribe. Skinny told April to come home right away. She would make dinner herself. Very good dinner. But April wouldn't go anywhere near it.

The only hunger she was aware of at the moment was for Mike and a quiet place to be alone. Frankly, she didn't think it would be so terrible to sit across the breakfast table from him and hear him try to get out of whatever happened or didn't happen with Carla for the rest of his life. She could bone up on the Chinese cure for excessive heat. Maybe it was something really nasty.

"Home," she agreed.